AF272952

The Wolf Tale

A.N. Lexén

The Wolf Tale

Part 1

The Wolf Cross

© A.N. Lexén 2024

Publisher: BoD – Books on Demand, Stockholm, Sweden

Printer: BoD – Books on Demand, Norderstedt, Germany

ISBN: 978-9-1809-7553-7

Table of Contents

For the reader   11

The Author's Words   13

Prologue   15

1. A Terrifying Nightmare   17

2. Hugo's Secret   27

3. The Poltergeist   36

4. The Two Wolves   47

5. Escape to The North   58

6. A Missing Brother   68

7. The Man and The Hawk   78

8. A Family Secret   90

9. The City in The Sky   99

10. The Dream Walker   107

11. Demon Worshipers   116

12. Nari's Portrait   125

13. Children of The Gods   133

14. The Military Force   143

15. The Moon God   153

16. The Wolf Cross   162

17. Legion   172

18. A Family Reunion   181

19. The Fire Wolves   190

20. The Fylgja   200

21. A Special Book   209

22. Santa's Sledge   218

23. The Monster in The Tarn   227

24. A creature of darkness   238

25. Jack's Origin   248

26. The Traitor   257

27. Váli's Confession   266

28. Gargoyles   277

29. Di Inferi   287

30. Trollhammer Mountain   297

31. Silver   306

32. Fáfnir's Prisoner   316

33. The Magic Fire   324

34. The Half-brother   333

35. Twin Swords   342

36. Thrúd   352

37. The Battle   358

38. The Night of The Werewolves   369

39. Showdown   379

40. The Last Stand   389

41. The Grave of Eva   398

42. The Gate   409

Epilogue   422

HÄRJEDALEN

THE FLATRUET MOUNTAIN RANGE

FLATRUET

RU FOREST

GRAVE OF EVA

⊙ MESSLINGEN

⊙ FUNÄSDALEN

• THE EGGSHELL TARN

FOREST OF THE HARE

⊙ TÄNNÄS

⊙ HEDE

TROLLHAMMER MOUNTAIN

OLD MILL FOREST

TROLL FOREST

SUN MOUNTAIN RANGE

FOREST OF THE SUN

LAKE OF SVEG

⊙ SVEG

WOLF DEN

HÄRJEDALEN

BURN FOREST

DALARNA

TANDSJÖBORG ⊙

SOUTH TO DALARNA

For the reader:

The places in Sweden described in the book are real, sometimes combined with mythological legends and local stories.

For more in-depth information about the gods, goddesses, and beings described in the book, the information is collected in Norse mythology, Sami mythology, Finnish mythology, Russian mythology, Baltic mythology, Slavic mythology, Greek mythology, Roman mythology, Jewish/Christian mythology, and in older fairy tales and folktales. This also applies to the magical objects found in the story.

There are hidden secrets and hidden connections to older tales in the book for those who want to search, because that's always the case – the search is part of the adventure!

A.N. Lexén

The Author's Words

This world is dying, I feel it in the wind and in the ground – yes, even in my soul! What I am about to tell you is our common story, the story of where we came from and where we are going.

When I look up at the night sky, I find it hard to believe that the universe is threatened – not by anything that we can see or detect, but by a darkness that is imprisoned. A darkness that once almost devoured the galaxies. Through the efforts of the elves, eight magical rings were forged from the golden dust of the World Spirit, shielding the darkness from the worlds.

In order to prevent the rings from being misused, and accidentally unleashing the darkness, they were distributed among the families of the gods to guard until the end of time. Three were given to the Aesir gods, who, like warriors, had led the fight against darkness and were hailed as heroes. One was given to the children of Kronos, the giants who were the first to walk in our world. One was given to the fairies, the guardians of magic from Avalon. One was given to Mimer, the guardian of the world spirit. And one was given to humans, who were created in the image of the gods to guard Middle Earth – the gathering place for the remaining worlds of the universe. The eighth ring was then sealed in the bowels of the underworld.

But the peace did not last long, as another weapon was forged in secret. In Álfheimr, Wayland, the master smith of the elves, was consumed by jealousy and rage. He, who had forged the rings, considered himself entitled to be the guardian of them, and when he was not entrusted to any of them, his soul was darkened. Blinded by his hatred of the gods, Wayland forged, with the help of darkness, Gambantein, the dark sword of vengeance, to free the darkness and once again plunge the worlds into its abyss.

It was not long before the darkness began to seep out into the universe again, and the people turned on each other. The giants, who had previously fought against the darkness, were ensnared by Wayland's promises of power and fought against the gods. Even the elves, the wise gods who watched over the gift of life, began to fight among themselves.

Then, when the humans, whose hearts were most easily deceived, betrayed their creators and began to summon demons to the worlds with the dark magic of Wayland, a dark time began for the people of Middle Earth that came to be known as the "Dark Age", when darkness reached the very heart of Middle Earth and all hope seemed lost.

Then Mimer and his sons intervened by defeating Wayland. He and his two brothers were banished to a distant place, and the smith's sword was hidden deep in the roots of the World Tree. The Fates, servants of the World Tree, succeeded in clearing Middle earth of the impending darkness, although some of the darkness had taken root in the hearts of the humans and could not be removed – if so, the humans would be wiped out.

Now, when the old god repeats this to me, and asks me to tell you, know that the wars, diseases, and catastrophes that have plagued humanity in the last century are a sign that the veil of darkness is once again thinning out. There is not much time left, the visions I have been having are dark and scary. It is time for me to tell you about those in whose hands our fate lies, and about their struggle that will determine the future of all of us. Through my visions, I have seen them, and by the gods' intervention, I am allowed to follow their adventure and tell it to you.

A.N. Lexén

Prologue

The woman darted through the forest, with the wind whipping around her. Her hurried footsteps splashed through the darkness, her arms cradling a precious child. Despite the cover of night, she knew she was not safe. She could feel the child's breath against her skin as she hurdled over logs and dodged through the trees. Her heart pounded in her chest as she ran blindly, unsure of where to go or how to protect the child.

As she emerged into a clearing, the sound of destruction echoed through the forest. She knew her pursuer was close behind, and desperation filled her every step. Just as she thought she could run no further, an arm reached out from between the trees, and yanked her into the shadows. Before she could scream, the stranger clamped a hand over her mouth and pulled her and the child to the ground.

Her heart raced as she heard the sound of her pursuer's footsteps drawing closer. But then, in the distance, the sky exploded in black flames. The woman's fear turned to confusion as she watched her pursuer step out of the trees, bathed in a dark fire.

With bated breath and trembling limbs, the woman waited anxiously as her pursuer rushed away from the spot where she and her rescuer lay pressed against the ground. The grip around her mouth relaxed, and she abruptly pulled away from the person holding her. As she recognised the man rising from the ground, she looked puzzled.

"What are you doing here?" she asked.

The man, with long golden-brown hair, smiled at her and put one hand on her shoulder.

"Saving you, it seems," he answered.

The woman embraced him. He held her for a long time before she finally let go and looked around nervously.

"What if he comes back? Where will I go?" she whispered, wiping the tears from her face.

The man pulled something out of his bag, and the woman gasped in amazement as she examined the stringed instrument.

"Is that what I think it is?" she asked.

He nodded with a smile.

"We have found a safe place for you, the old man is waiting for us," he answered.

With newfound hope, the woman cradled the child in one arm and laid the other arm around the man's waist.

As the man plucked the strings of the instrument, a gust of wind suddenly swept them up into the sky. The woman looked down in awe as the world below grew smaller and smaller, until she and the man vanished with a flash.

Unbeknownst to them, the dark fire had erupted on the very spot were they had stood just moments before. And as they soared away, they never noticed the furious figure with jet-black hair that fell to his knees and let out a roar of anger into the night.

1. A Terrifying Nightmare

Darkness and fog enveloped him from all sides as he slowly fell.

"Where am I…?"

Wille barely felt how he was falling through the fog. Instead, it felt as if he was slowly sinking deep down.

"Strange…"

He tried to reach out his hand, and slowly touched the dark fog that surrounded him.

"Is this…real…?"

His mind struggled to comprehend the situation, but the more he tried to focus, the more exhausted he felt. His eyes grew heavy, and just as he was about to succumb to sleep, a sudden flash of light jolted him awake.

He found himself standing on the dirt road in front of his house, the familiar red building with the dense forest looming behind it.

As he approached the front door, he noticed someone standing on the steps facing away from him. The sunlight made it difficult for him to make out the person's identity.

As the person turned towards him, the sky above began to darken ominously. A wave of darkness swept over the house and the figure on the stairs, leaving Wille gasping for breath.

The person reached out his hand, and suddenly it struck Wille who it was.

Oscar and Wille had been inseparable since their days in primary school. Oscar had an insatiable thirst for adventures, and he always managed to convince Wille to join him on his escapades.

Wille tried to scream as Oscar stood there with his hand outstretched towards him, while darkness literally crashed over the house like a wave and reached him to his knees, but he couldn't make a sound. Instead, he started running towards Oscar, stretching out his hand as he approached his friend, who stood motionless as the darkness undulated around them.

Wille was only a few meters away from Oscar when he fell down in confusion. The darkness was like a lake around them, and he reached up to his calves. He struggled, but the darkness pulled him down and held him in an iron grip. Wille stretched his hand up as far as he could towards Oscar, who was leaning over him, and took a deep breath as he was pulled down into the pitch-black darkness.

Oscar's silhouette flickered above him before it disappeared, and was replaced by darkness. Wille tried to move upwards, but something pulled him downwards with such force that he finally couldn't resist anymore. The glow of countless stars lit up like a rain dance in front of his eyes as he slowly fell through a shimmer of blue-violet light.

"SPLASH!"

Wille fell through what he perceived as yet another surface of water, sinking faster and faster, before he eventually felt solid ground beneath his feet.

The dizziness and nausea overwhelmed him, causing him to collapse on his knees for a moment. He got up slowly and looked around in confusion at what felt like the bottom of the sea. Everything around him was black, he could only sense the movements around him and tried to take a step forward.

A flash of light spread around his feet and swept away the darkness as if it were leaves.

Light and darkness swirled around him, and he found himself standing on a stone floor surrounded by a dim light.

He looked around and found that the stone floor stretched a good ten metres in each direction. Wille had never seen anything like it, it looked like someone had laid stones by hand and formed a perfect symmetry in the floor. He looked back and was surprised to see that the floor looked just as wide in that direction. He couldn't see any walls, but the stone floor seemed to continue through the swirling light that surrounded him.

"So much to do, and so little time…"

Wille jumped and spun around when the muffled voice was heard behind him. A silhouette appeared a few meters from where he stood. The figure wore a long, dark cloak, whose headgear effectively hid his face.

"Who are you?" Wille asked nervously.

The stranger did not answer, but began to move towards him and stopped barely a meter in front of him. An eerie fog spread around them, and Wille trembled nervously as he stared at the stranger hiding under his hood. The chilly fog rose up like a mist between them, and he sensed that the stranger was smiling ominously.

The stranger slowly raised a hand and pointed towards him. Wille reflexively took a step backwards, and an eerie, cutting, laugh was heard from the stranger.

"Are you afraid?" a hollow voice asked.

Wille tried to shake his head, but his courage failed him. Something made his stomach clench, and he wanted to run away, but his legs did not obey him.

"I'd be more concerned about what was behind you if I were you," said the stranger, who, with a cutting laugh, lowered his arm and took a couple of steps backwards.

Wille felt himself grow cold inside, he felt he was being watched. Slowly, as if in a trance, he turned around and felt like he wanted to scream, but his voice stalled.

Behind him was himself, or at least something that resembled him. An eerie silhouette appeared like a dark reflection just a few centimetres in front of Wille. The shock of having someone so close behind him turned to horror as Wille realised that something was terribly wrong.

The silhouette smiled an eerie smile that exposed pointed teeth. Wille allowed his gaze to wander from the terrifying teeth, past the nose, and to its eyes. He felt his knees go weak because, where the eyes should have been, he stared instead into narrow gaps of darkness. The figure had no eyes but black, empty eye sockets.

Wille felt how his feet began to move away from the creature, he ran to the left as he felt it brush past him. A bang was heard as the creature hit the ground right where he had just been standing, while the stranger's voice was heard behind him.

"Give up, boy, you can't outrun it," laughed the stranger, whose voice echoed softly in the void.

Wille ran through the chilly fog, which now lay like a thick mist around him. He stumbled and landed on the ground with a dull thud.

Just as he turned his head, he saw the creature flying towards him through the thick fog, its mouth open and its fangs exposed. Wille instinctively put his arms out in front of him and felt a sharp pain that bore into his arms.

The last thing he experienced before his consciousness faded was the stranger's eerie laughter from within the fog.

෪

"Wille, wake up!"

Wille slowly opened his eyes and blinked in surprise. He found himself in his bed, in his own room. The darkness was gone, as were the stranger and the terrifying creature. He noticed how he was standing up in bed and had almost stumbled over the edge. At the foot of the bed stood his two-year younger brother Hugo, staring at him in horror.

"You screamed so loudly that it echoed throughout the house," Hugo said, startled.

Wille looked around in surprise. He still didn't know if he was awake for real this time. But he did not have to think about it for very long before the door to his bedroom was thrown open, and their mother rushed into the room with a panicked look on her face. Her blue shirt dress fluttered wildly as she stopped and looked at them.

"What's going on?! Why did you scream?"

Wille met his mother's gaze.

"I had an unpleasant dream," he managed to answer.

His mother put her arm on his forehead.

"You're freezing!" she exclaimed in a surprised voice.

Wille felt weak in the knees, and his head felt like it was going to be split in half. He felt ashamed, he was sixteen years old and hadn't had nightmares for years. He used to tease with his brother, who still slept with stuffed animals at night, but now he had woken both his mother and his brother in the middle of the night.

"There's an hour left before you should have gotten up," said their mother, as she glanced at the clock above the door. "There's no point that you go back to bed, we'll go downstairs and heat up some apple lemonade, and you can tell me what this was all about. Put your clothes on before you go downstairs."

Wille suddenly realised his predicament when he stood up in bed in just his underpants and immediately jumped down from the edge of the bed and grabbed his trousers. He met his brother's gaze, who looked at him with both concern and amusement.

Hugo picked up a pillow and threw it at Wille, which resulted in a pillow fight followed by a wrestling match, which Wille won as usual. Hugo gasped for breath between laughs as he lay on his stomach in bed, begging for mercy.

Wille sighed to himself and let go of Hugo, who immediately went into his room to get his clothes. He never learns, Wille thought as he tightened the belt around his waist. He had trained in martial arts for several years and was significantly stronger and more agile than Hugo, who was slightly taller than him but weaker. Nevertheless, he liked their wrestling matches, it was a sibling thing.

Wille walked out of the room and jumped up when the door to his bedroom unexpectedly slammed shut behind him.

"How are you?" Hugo asked when they met at the landing. "Do you need help down?"

Wille met his grey eyes in surprise. Normally, they would push each other and try to see who could get down the stairs first. But from Hugo's look, it seemed that he had decided to take it easy this morning.

"I'll be fine," Wille answered, and he shivered when Hugo reached out his arm to support him.

From the hallway at the bottom of the stairs, they could hear their mother standing in the kitchen, heating apple lemonade. Wille felt a little more comfortable when they went through the kitchen and sat down on the couch in the living room. As long as he could remember, they had always been given apple lemonade when they were sick or otherwise not feeling well, and strangely enough, the lemonade always seemed to give them their energy back.

Sitting down on the sofa, a mug was placed on the table in front of him, and Wille stared at the steaming lemonade.

Hugo sat next to him on the chaise longue with a cup of his own, and their mother sank into the armchair opposite.

"Wille, tell me what happened," she said in a calm voice.

Wille took a sip from his cup and felt the warmth from the apple lemonade spread through his body. His trembling ceased immediately, and he felt more relaxed. It was magical how the lemonade could warm up the entire body so quickly.

He took a few more sips and slowly began to tell us what he remembered from the horrible dream. As he talked, Wille noticed his mother becoming more concerned, while Hugo seemed confused. When he finally told them about the stranger and the terrifying figure, their mother stood up.

"This stranger, did he say anything to you?" she asked.

"He asked me if I was afraid, and said I couldn't run away from it," Wille replied. "But it was just a dream, right?"

His mother didn't answer, but she walked quickly through the living room and pulled one of the drawers out of the big chest of drawers that held the TV.

She picked up something small that she was holding tightly in her hand and turned towards them.

"When you come home from school, we have to talk, there is something..." she interrupted herself and lowered her voice in a trembling tone, "that I have to tell you."

Wille and Hugo looked at each other in surprise, and then just as uncomprehendingly at their mother.

"Hold out your hand, Wille," she said in a firm voice.

Wille did as she said, whereupon she gently placed the contents in his hand and closed his fingers around it. She squeezed his hand for a long moment before she let go. He carefully opened his hand and stared in amazement at the wrapped cloth in his hand.

Hugo gently leaned over him to get a better look as Wille unfolded the cloth.

Wrapped in the thin layer of cloth was a strange necklace. It resembled a cross, but it was completely unlike any other cross Wille had seen before. It had carved edges at the bottom three points and a deeply embossed cross in the centre. But it was the topmost tip that caught his attention. Instead of having edges like the other three ends, it looked like some kind of upturned animal head. It had finely carved ears, a snout, and clearly marked eyes.

Through the mouth of the head ran the actual chain, which was to be worn around the neck. Both the chain and the cross were made of dark metal and felt heavy in the palm of the hand. Wille could feel a strange energy coming from the necklace, almost as if it tried to communicate with him.

He looked at Hugo, who looked engrossed in the necklace, and turned to their mother, who had tearful eyes.

"It's called a 'wolf cross'," she said as she wiped away her tears. "I want you to wear it from now on, not take it off."

"Mom, what is this about?" Wille asked in disbelief, but his mother just shook her head.

"We'll talk tonight, you have to go to school," she replied, and began to remove the empty cups from the table.

Wille cast a glance at the clock above the stove and realised that she was right. They had been talking for an hour and a half. The school started in an hour, and they hadn't even had time for breakfast yet.

At that moment, his stomach started rumbling. Hugo came and put down a plate of eggs and a sandwich on the table.

Wille stared up in astonishment, he had been so engrossed in the necklace that he did not notice that Hugo got up from the couch.

They ate quickly in silence, then hurriedly put on their coats and were just about to go out when their mother grabbed Wille and spun him towards her before fastening the necklace around his neck and snapping the lock.

"Never take it off," she repeated, before giving them both a hug and pushing them out through the door, which creaked shut with a thud after them.

Both boys looked at each other in surprise before starting to walk along the road. They walked in silence for a while.

Their house was behind a grove of trees, barely thirty minutes' walk from the school. The house was secluded, and the nearest neighbour house was some distance away.

They had walked this way many times and were used to walking, even in the dark. Still, the road felt longer than usual when they crossed the railroad, and thoughts ran through Wille's head.

Hugo broke the silence by starting to sing, which was not unusual. Hugo had a clear and fine voice, and Wille liked to listen when he sang, even though he would never admit it.

"Oh, come on," Hugo said, laughing when he saw Wille's face. "It's probably just some protection against bad luck."

They began climbing the steep ridge that overlooked the school. Even though Horndal was a small village, it was still big enough to have a secondary school.

Wille felt the snow crunch beneath his boots. He thought of all the times as he and Hugo had rolled down the ridge and returned home with deep scratches on their arms and legs. He brought his hand to the necklace and felt its weight.

He couldn't let go of the thoughts that had come after that morning, but decided to leave them until they got home.

Wille looked at his brother with a smile before bending down and picking up some of the cuddly snow, which he quickly formed into a ball and threw towards Hugo.

Hugo, who was walking two steps ahead of him, did not notice the hard snow that came hurtling towards him, before it hit the back of his head with a smack.

The wet snow ran down Hugo's dark blond hair and into his neck. Howling with laughter, Wille ran as fast as he could down the slope of the ridge towards the primary school buildings below, while the snowballs whizzed past his head and Hugo's clear singing voice changed into angry swearing.

While he heard Hugo's clattering steps behind him, Wille zigzagged across the football field, before he arrived at the secondary school building, where he pulled open the door.

Wille quickly dove as a snowball flew over his head. He then quickly closed the door and held on for a moment before letting go of the handle, and then ran upstairs while hearing the teachers shouting for Hugo, who had run in with his arms full of snow.

Wille could hear running steps behind him and thought that it was Hugo following him up the stairs, but when he looked back, he saw no one there.

Puzzled, he looked around. This was not the first time he had heard strange footsteps, or, for that matter, had doors slamming shut behind him, in the last few weeks. He shook his head and took off his outerwear before entering the classroom.

Wille did not see the blue, flaming eye staring down at him from the ceiling. It flickered and disappeared without a sound, leaving the corridor in an eerie silence.

❧

Ida looked after her sons as they disappeared behind the bend in the road. With increasing anxiety, she went to the bedroom to find a pen and paper and sat down at her desk.

She began to write, and when finished, she took the little note and walked over to the window.

She put her fingers in her mouth and whistled a clear, ringing melody.

A silver-winged hawk landed on the window sill, and she lashed the note to its leg before it flew away again and disappeared above the trees.

Ida stared longingly in the direction where the hawk had disappeared, before she took a deep sigh and returned to the kitchen.

"And so it begins," she muttered to herself as she took out a key and unlocked a door in the pantry, where she picked out several golden apples.

2. Hugo's Secret

Wille felt his nervousness rising – he didn't know the answers, and time was running out.

"Five minutes left!"

The voice echoed through the room, but Wille could barely hear as he struggled to concentrate. Sweat ran down his forehead as he looked one more time at the blank answer field in front of him. He looked around the room, and several of his peers also seemed to be struggling. One was lying down with his head on the countertop, looking like he was crying.

"Three minutes left!"

Amanda Svedin, a rotund woman in her fifties, let her sharp gaze roam across the classroom. She was their teacher, and at the start of the lesson, she had hand out the thick booklet that made up the national test in grade nine.

Wille took a deep breath and began to write without really knowing what he was answering. Mathematics had never been his strong point, and he suspected that he had not answered many of the questions in the booklet correctly.

He looked up at Lovisa, who was sitting diagonally in front of him. For a moment, he just wanted to sit down next to her, stroke her golden-brown hair, and hold her.

"Last minute!"

Wille, who had lost track of time while daydreaming, flinched and scribbled down a few last numbers as Amanda got up and stood in the centre of the room.

"Drop the pens!"

Wille sank into the chair, feeling completely exhausted. He looked towards Oscar, who gave him a thumbs up. When it came to math, Oscar was light years away from him because, while Wille was struggling to get through the numbers, Oscar always made it look easy.

"Wille!"

He was pulled out of his thoughts and looked at Amanda Svedin's outstretched hand.

"Wille, I asked for the booklet," she said irritably.

Wille picked up the booklet and felt how it was quickly snatched from his hand. He saw his teacher quickly collect the rest of the booklets and go back to her table.

"Before we finish, I have something to tell you," she said brusquely, waiting for silence.

"We have a new student in the class," Amanda continued. "And I want you to be on your best behaviour."

As soon as she said that, the door to the classroom opened, and a boy Wille had never seen before walked in. He was slim and looked like he had an uncertain expression on his face, as he let his gaze wander across the room.

Wille thought the guy looked nervous as he stood in the doorway, and didn't seem to know if he should go in.

"This is Liam Rottespieg," Amanda said. "He just moved here, and will be attending his last term with us."

Liam walked slowly to the centre of the room.

"Hi," he said gently, raising his hand in greeting.

The rest of the class looked at him in surprise.

"Liam, you can sit next to Wille for now, and we'll go through your school results later," Amanda said before turning to the board to start the next review.

The slim, dark-haired guy pulled out the chair next to him and sat down without saying a word. Wille felt a strange tingling in his spine but tried not to show it. He noticed that he was fingering his necklace, and he looked at Lovisa again. If only she knew how he felt for her, he thought longingly as he let his thoughts wander. It felt as if he was floating on clouds, and he didn't notice when the rest of his class left the room.

It wasn't until Amanda was standing right next to him and, in a stern voice, called for Wille's attention that he realised, in confusion, that he was the only student left in the classroom. He excused himself and hurried out of the classroom, before directing his steps towards the dining room, where lunch would soon be served.

On the way down to the ground floor, Liam was waiting for him on the stairs. Wille felt insecure as he approached.

Liam smiled gently at him as he came closer.

"Hi," Liam said uncertainly, as he looked up at Wille as he passed the bench where Liam was sitting. "Wille, was it?"

Wille nodded and greeted him back. "And your name is Liam," he noted as he continued to walk down the stone steps. "Where are you from?"

"Germany," Liam replied with a smile, passing a couple of eighth graders who were heading the other way. "So, does anything fun happen at this school?"

Wille stopped and started telling them about the place where they used to hang out in the evenings and about their martial arts club, where they used to meet a few times a week, which Liam seemed to find interesting.

Wille was about to ask if he wanted to come along and try it when he was interrupted by a noise in the corridor below.

"YOU, GAY BOY!"

The words cut through the corridor and immediately attracted several glances from other students.

Wille took a few quick steps down the last set of stairs and stopped when he reached the corridor below.

At the far end of the corridor, he saw Hugo standing with his back against a cupboard, and in front of him were two eighth grade boys standing with their arms leaning against the lockers, effectively blocking Hugo's opportunities to get out of there.

Wille started walking with quick steps towards where his brother was while one of the boys punched Hugo in the stomach, causing him to collapse on the floor.

"What's wrong?" one of the guys asked, looking down at Hugo, who was on his knees and holding his stomach.

"Maybe you want a different kind of pain?" the guy continued sarcastically before bending down, grabbing Hugo's legs, and starting to drag him across the floor.

Wille felt the anger boiling inside him. He was almost there when Oscar appeared from the other direction, grabbed the one guy's arm, and pulled it so hard behind his back that the guy howled in pain.

Just as the other boy turned to help his friend, Wille threw himself on top of him.

There was a lot of commotion as both boys rolled around on the hard floor and flailed their arms, but Wille, who practiced judo, quickly gained a grip around his opponent's neck and held his prey in a firm grip with his face pressed against the floor.

Meanwhile, the other guy had broken free, and swung a punch at Oscar's head, which he barely managed to avoid by dodging.

As the guy threw another punch, a hand grabbed his arm and swung him hard to the floor, whereupon Liam straddled the guy.

Oscar came over to Wille, who got up and let him take over his grip around the other guy's neck, whereupon Wille ran to his brother who tried to get up against the cabinets.

By then, the corridor was in chaos as other students flocked around the combatants. Several teachers were trying to get students out of there and get an overview of what was going on.

It wasn't until Amanda Svedin and another teacher pushed through the wall of people that the rest of the students started to move out of the building and towards the canteen.

Amanda stood over the boys with her arms crossed and a scowl on her face, while the other teacher helped Wille raise Hugo from the floor. She let her gaze wander from Oscar, who held one of the boys in an iron grip around his neck with his face to the floor, to Liam, who stood with his knee pressed into the lumbar spine of the other guy, and finally to Wille, who was holding his brother under his arms.

"Oscar and Liam, let them go," she said in a harsh tone.

Oscar gently loosened his grip on the guy's neck, and Liam removed his knee from the other guy.

The two boys got up coughing and tried to run away, but were stopped by the other teacher, who roughly grabbed their arms and held them down.

"No one is going anywhere until we sort this out," Amanda said sharply, whereupon the second teacher began dragging the protesting boys towards the teachers' workroom, which by now was empty because most of the teachers were busy chasing away students to the canteen.

Oscar and Wille took hold of each side of Hugo and followed Liam and Amanda.

The interrogation that followed lasted almost an hour, and the whole story was revealed. The boys who had been harassing Hugo were suspended from school for three days and sent home under loud protests with home-work.

Hugo was examined by the school nurse, who concluded that he had not suffered any major injuries, apart from a minor concussion from hitting his head on the cupboard.

She firmly pushed him down on the bed with the admonition that he should lie there for at least fifteen minutes until she had ensured that his pupils responded properly to movement and light.

Wille, Oscar, and Liam sat down on a sofa in the headmaster's office, with Amanda Svedin opposite them. She looked grim, and crossed her arms over her beige cardigan.

"First of all," she began. "I don't ever want to see such judo moves used at the school. At least you had the good sense not to press around the guy's neck, but I hope you realize he could have suffocated."

"Secondly, the next time something happens, you are to come and get me – is that understood?!" she asked sharply.

All three boys nodded slowly.

"Good," said Amanda. "I know things speed up fast sometimes, but at least one of you could have picked me up."

"Thirdly, you will be given a warning and a letter with you explaining the seriousness of the situation, and I expect to get the letters back signed by your parents tomorrow."

Amanda looked at her watch and stood up.

"You've missed lunch," she said with a deep sigh. "But I have called and asked the kitchen staff to set aside some food for you. I want you to eat and then return to your classes. And no sulking, understand?"

All three nodded again and stood up.

"Wille, can you stay for just a little while?" Amanda asked when they were on their way to the door.

Wille turned around and saw from his teacher's gaze that there was no idea to disagree. He sat down on the sofa again as the door behind them closed.

"Wille, did you know that your brother was exposed by this?" Amanda asked. "They found out this about him and have been on him every day for the last two weeks."

Wille felt confused and shook his head.

"No, I didn't know that he was gay...I mean, that he likes guys," he replied, looking ashamed. "When I heard what the other guys were saying, I didn't think they meant anything by it. Do you mean that he is..."

Wille couldn't get the words out, he still felt confused from the morning and now this. Hugo, his brother who he spent time with every day and whom he felt he could talk to about everything, had kept this secret from him. The thoughts ran through his head, wondering how he had missed this.

Amanda looked at him thoughtfully, as if wondering how much she should tell him.

"Two weeks ago," she finally said, "it came out that Hugo liked a boy in his class who apparently didn't have the same feelings for him. I noticed after a while that Hugo was being ostracized in class, and when I talked to him, the story came out, so I talked with his teacher."

Amanda let that sink in for a moment before continuing.

"Because things were not improved by the teacher addressing it, I had a talk with the class on Friday. After that, things got better. There became a different climate, and I think Hugo and this guy are friends today. Unfortunately, there were some guys in the parallel class who also found out about this, and did not take it as well as Hugo's class did."

Amanda hastily looked at her watch again.

"Hugo is still with the school nurse, if it's not too serious, you can take him to the canteen," she said. "I'll talk to his teacher again, and if the kitchen staff asks, then tell them that it was me who decided that Hugo could eat now. I'm sure you have some things you want to talk about."

Wille got up uncertainly, and started walking towards the door. He did not recognise himself in reality anymore. His brother, whom he loved very much, had kept this secret from him. He decided to get Hugo, and headed for the school nurse's office.

ℰℛ

"Thanks for the help over there," said Oscar, as he and Liam walked into the dining room building. "Where did you learn to swing people like that?"

"Curious?" Liam asked with a sly smile, and quickly ushered Oscar into the old theatre under the dining room. "I can show you some moves."

"Can't you show it tonight at the club?" Oscar asked, puzzled. "We were going to the dining room."

Liam didn't say anything, but closed the door behind them and turned around to face him. Oscar felt like he wanted to scream, but the words got stuck in his throat as he stared into Liam's blazing blue eyes.

ℰℛ

"Are you okay?" Wille asked, as they stepped out of the school nurse's office. "She told you to take it easy."

Hugo looked shamefully at his brother, and nodded. He felt how all the eyes in the corridor were directed at him.

The horrible feeling in his stomach had gotten better, but Hugo could hear the whispers from other students as they stepped out into the winter cold.

"Do you hate me?" he asked.

Hugo felt the tears start to run down his cheeks and noticed that Wille put his hand on his shoulder.

"Damn it, Hugo, you're my brother, and I love you just the way you are. I was just surprised, you've never told me about this before", Wille said while he put his arms around Hugo and hugged him.

"Come on, we need to eat", Wille continued and started to pull him towards the dining room building.

They didn't see Oscar or Liam anywhere when they entered the dining room door, and Hugo wondered if they had already eaten. They sat down at one of the tables, and the staff came out with two plates of spaghetti and meat sauce.

"So, who's the new guy?" Hugo asked.

Wille told him that Liam had come into the class after their national exams, and that he had made him a table neighbour. They had not had time to talk much with each other, but Wille thought he seemed nice.

"I want to thank him," said Hugo. "For the help before."

"But when did you start liking guys?" Wille asked and took a sip of water from his glass.

Hugo shrugged his shoulders and said, somewhat ashamed, that he had started looking at a guy in the class called Max. However, Max had given him away, laughed at him, and then told the rest of the class. After that, no one wanted to hang out with him. Not even the friends he used to hang out with wanted to know about him.

Their teacher had asked Amanda Svedin to come to the classroom and hold a conversation with the whole class.

After that the atmosphere had improved, and even though Max didn't share Hugo's feelings they became friends.

Wille was just about to say something when he got a message on the phone.

Hugo saw how Wille's face froze as he took up the phone.

"What is it?" Hugo asked, and got a nasty feeling when Wille handed over his cell phone to him.

He took the phone and saw that it was a picture message from Oscar. He almost choked when he saw the picture.

The picture showed Oscar lying lifeless in a pool of blood on the floor of the theatre. The text message below read: "Would you like to come and play theatre with us? /Liam".

They stared at each other for what seemed like an eternity before they quickly rose from the table and rushed out of the dining room.

The old theatre was downstairs in the same building as the dining room. It hadn't been used properly for many years, but the occasional local theatre group used to have performances there sometimes.

The stairs leading up to the dining room were almost empty, and only a few students on their way out of the library looked on in amazement as they flew out of the dining room and down the steps.

When they reached the entrance to the theatre, they stopped, and looked at each other, confused.

There was a dark shadow over the solid door, and they stared at it for a moment, bewitched, before yanking the door open.

As they passed the strange glow, Hugo felt a wave of fear wash over him. He looked at Wille as they stumbled into the dimly lit theatre, who, judging by the look on his face, felt the same way.

In the middle of the stage floor, a body lay motionless in a pool of blood. Liam stood leaning over the body with a crooked, unnatural smile that revealed a row of fangs.

The door suddenly slammed shut behind them, and Hugo whirled around as the lock clicked.

3. The Poltergeist

Wille took a few steps forward before stopping and staring at Liam's face. From one eye, there was a sharp red glow, and from the other eye, a dark blue flame flared up.

Hugo was gasping for breath behind him, but Wille hardly noticed as he stood rigid with horror, being reminded of the dream he had that night.

"Liam, what…" Wille began to ask, but was immediately interrupted by a hollow voice, emanating from Liam.

"I was expecting you to come alone," growled Liam, his eyes lighting up the room.

He then turned to Hugo.

"I should have neutralized you myself instead of relying on those idiots," he lamented.

"What do you mean?" Hugo asked. "Who are you?"

Liam let out a roaring laugh.

"Who do you think gave them the idea to harass you? I've been following you for two weeks, just waiting to make my move. You should have been passed out on that bedside table until this was over," he hissed.

Suddenly, Wille's attention was drawn to a movement in the corner of the stage. To his surprise he saw Lovisa tied to a chair with a rag in her mouth, looking terrified.

Wille was still confused, and unsure if he had actually woken up that morning. Everything seemed surreal, and nothing felt right. He glanced at Lovisa, who was struggling against the ropes that bound her. How was it possible that no one in the school had noticed the commotion, and where was the janitor when they needed him.

"Yeah, Lovisa heard about the commotion in the hallway and went looking for her brother," Liam said, his satisfaction evident. "So, I took the liberty of reuniting them."

Wille couldn't believe that Liam really orchestrated all of this. Just as he was about to speak, Liam cut him off.

"There's no point in calling for help," he said. "We're in a separate sphere now, and no one can hear us from outside. As for the caretaker, well, let's just say he's no longer with us."

Wille noticed how Hugo had started to move sideways during the conversation so that he stood next to Liam, who turned his head unnaturally and smiled ominously.

"Do you really think you have any chance against me?" he asked. "You couldn't even defend yourself in the hallway."

Hugo stared into those glowing eyes and looked suddenly unsure, but he had just given Wille the opening he needed – and Wille flew at Liam from the front while Hugo threw himself over him from the side.

Lovisa began to jerk violently, as Liam's smile suddenly became even wider when his mouth opened once again and emitting a piercing scream that tore through their ears.

The boys were hurled across the stage floor by the sheer force of the sound waves, and Wille landed painfully on a row of benches below. He tried to cover his ears, but the scream was too powerful. A trickle of blood ran between his fingers as he tried to block out the sound.

The lights in the ceiling shattered, and the rows of benches were sent flying against the walls.

Just as suddenly, Liam stopped his scream.

"That hurt, didn't it?" he sneered with a sarcastic voice.

Wille strained to hear anything over the ringing in his ears, while Hugo trembled against a wall next to the stage drapery. Liam raised his hand, summoning a lightning ball. As he waved his hand, the curtain wrapped itself tightly around Hugo, leaving him helpless.

"It's time to end this," Liam continued.

As Liam raised his hand with the lightning ball, it seemed as he was about to attack. But he lowered his hand again.

"This doesn't have to end like this. You have something I want," he said, pointing towards Wille, who was surprised and pulled out his necklace from under his shirt.

The necklace felt heavy in his hand, and his fingers tingled strangely.

"Right," Liam said coldly. "I noticed when you arrived at school that you had it on you, which makes things easier because I don't have to take it from your disgusting mother."

Wille stared at Liam, who raised his hand with the lightning at Hugo.

"Give me the necklace, and I'll let your brother and your friends live," Liam continued coldly.

He took a few steps towards Hugo who was huddled against the wall, seemingly terrified.

Wille took off his necklace. He weighed it in his hand, and felt a strange energy from the strange cross. He walked onto the stage, and continued towards Liam with the necklace stretched out in front of him.

Liam now stood with the ball lightning ball extended just a few inches from Hugo's face, and the other hand outstretched towards Wille as if to receive the necklace.

Wille went into a trance, and was now so close to Liam's hand with the necklace that he felt the coldness radiating from Liam. Their eyes met and he sensed that he would not survive, that neither of them would.

Just then, the door was violently kicked in, and Wille's mother stormed into the room. Her expression was one he had never seen before – a fiery rage surrounded her, and her long silver hair whipped around her face. A powerful aura of purple energy enveloped her, and Wille watched a hawk swoop down from the rafters and attack Liam.

Liam let out a deafening roar as the bird attacked, which causing him to lose control of the lightning ball he was holding. It hurtled towards Wille, who realised he had no chance of dodging it. Bracing himself, he squeezed his eyes shut, preparing for the pain that would soon hit him.

Then his mother was standing in front of him, with the purple aura billowing around her like a web. She held her hands out in front of her and parried the lightning, which flew back towards Liam – who was still waving his arms to ward off the hawk that was attacking his face.

It wasn't until the hawk flew away that Liam noticed the lightning ball that was rapidly moving towards him. He put his hands up, as if to protect himself, but didn't seem to be in time before the lightning hit him with full force.

Liam's scream cut through the room, as his body seemed to absorb the lightning and made him look electric.

A violent shaking of the floor caused a pole hanging above the stage loosened from its fastenings. Wille threw himself forward, and pushed his mother away just as the heavy structure crashed into the stage floor.

Liam clawed with his hands in front of him, before collapsing to the floor and disappeared in a cloud of smoke.

When Wille looked over to where Liam had been just a few seconds earlier, only a large pile of ashes was left.

While his mother untied Lovisa's rope, Wille ran over to Hugo who had collapsed on the floor.

After checking that his brother was okay, he then ran over to the body that was lay in the pool of blood.

Pulling down the hood of Oscar's hoodie, he breathed a sigh of relief when he felt the faint pulse of his friend.

However, there was another body lying nearby, and it was the source of the blood. Wille's heart sank when he recognised the janitor's face, who they had often played pranks on before. The old man's eyes were now lifeless, and he had no pulse.

Lovisa and Hugo helped to lift up Oscar, who was unconscious, and they had difficulty keeping him upright.

Wille looked over his shoulder at his mother, who was leaning over them. Her face was still furious, but she didn't look as hardened anymore.

"We have to leave, now!" she said firmly, and turned to Lovisa. "You and your brother can come with us."

"But what's going on? Who was that?" Lovisa stammered, pointing to the pile of ashes. "And Oscar, will he be okay?"

Ida gave her a hug. Wille saw how Lovisa was trembling, but he couldn't tell if it was due to shock or fear.

Finally, Ida let go and said in a low voice, "Your brother will be fine, but we can't stay here. The barrier that surrounded the room has almost disappeared, someone could come in at any time and see all this. You will have to come home with us, and then we will talk about what has happened and what is going to happen."

Wille was puzzled.

"What do you mean 'will happen'?" he asked. "Who, I mean, what was he?"

"We'll talk at home," his mother replied firmly. "They'll find him soon, and we don't want to be here," she continued, pointing to the dead man, before hastily pushing them towards the doorway.

Wille cautiously peered out into the corridor, and saw that several teachers were entering through the front door. He quickly pulled his head away and announced the others.

His mother glanced around, and stopped at the stage door on the other side of the room.

"Quick, this way," she said.

They helped carry Oscar through the door, and just as Wille was about to close the door behind him he heard Amanda Svedin stormed into the room together with what seemed to be half of the teaching staff.

"What is the noise here...", Amanda began, stopped at the sight of the dead man and brought her hands to her mouth.

She looked over to the stage door, as Wille disappeared outside.

❧

They continued over the ridge, and through the forest, until they reached the house. There Ida stopped, and motioned for them to wait while she carefully sneaked up to the house. After a while she waved to them from the door.

Hugo and Wille carried Oscar inside and laid him on the sofa, while Lovisa sat down and began running her fingers through her brother's blond hair.

Wille moved one of the armchairs, and sat down next to Lovisa. She put her head against his shoulder, and started crying again. He hugged her, but he felt just as shocked himself and couldn't say anything.

Meanwhile, Ida busied herself with preparing apple lemonade. Hugo arranged cups for everyone, and soon they were all huddled together with warm mugs in their hands.

Hugo was the first to speak up.

"Mom, what's really going on?" he asked.

His mother took a deep sigh, and looked at all of them.

"You've seen things that you weren't ready for, especially you and your brother," she answered, looking at Lovisa.

At that moment, Oscar started to move. He opened his eyes, looked around in surprise, and then slowly got up.

"What happened?" he asked. "Where is Liam?"

Lovisa wrapped her arms around him and couldn't hold back the tears, which flowed uncontrollably down her cheeks. Oscar looked surprised, but hugged her with a smile.

They sat for a long time, before Wille pushed a cup of apple lemonade towards Oscar.

"Here," he said urgently, pointing to the cup. "Drink that, and you'll soon feel better."

Oscar looked suspiciously at the steaming mug, and then took a careful sip of the hot drink.

Wille and Hugo then told in brief what had happened just an hour earlier.

In the middle of the story, Lovisa's cell phone started ringing. A quick look at the display showed that it was their father. She looked up at Ida, who nodded approval.

"Hi dad", Lovisa replied.

A gesture from Wille made her turn on the speaker.

"Lovisa, where are you? What's going on? I got a call from the school saying that you have disappeared, and that one of the staff has been killed," said the desperate voice, and Wille realised that their father must have wondered where they were when they didn't come home after school.

"I'm okay, Dad," she managed to say, attempting to keep her voice steady. "I'm at Wille's place, and Oscar's here too. Hugo got beaten up at school, and we didn't want him to go home alone."

Her father let out a sigh of relief from the phone.

"But wouldn't it have been enough if Wille had gone home with him?" asked her father in exasperation.

Lovisa's eyes darted around the room in panic, unsure of how to respond. Just then Ida stepped in, took the phone from Lovisa and walked away.

Wille turned to Oscar, who still looked confused and overwhelmed, and continued recounting what had happened. When he finished, there was a long pause with no one saying anything. Oscar still looked as if he was processing all the information, and didn't seem fully convinced.

Ida came back to the living room and sat down in the armchair with a sigh.

"Turn on the TV," she said softly.

Wille sensed what she wanted to show, and switched on the news.

A picture of their school showed up, and a reporter explained that there had been an attack; that one of the staff had been killed, and that five students had disappeared. The reporter interrupted himself, and received a message.

"We have just received confirmation that four of the five students previously suspected to have disappeared in the attack have been found safe and sound. They left the school on their own accord and made their way home earlier in the day after a fight in which several students were involved. The police are continuing the search for the fifth student. It is too early to say if it is a kidnapping, but it is clear that this will take time to investigate. All students were sent home after the dramatic events, in which some kinds of explosives were detonated in a room under the dining hall, where the deceased employee was later found by his colleagues. A perpetrator was seen escaping through a side door, but has so far not been identified or apprehended. The school will be closed for a week ahead for a technical examination of the premises."

Wille turned off the TV and looked at his mother, who was slumped in the armchair. She motioned for him to sit down again before continuing to talk.

"Your father was very worried when you didn't come home like you used to, and didn't hear from you. In addition, the school had contacted him and told him that you had absconded before the attack. As you know your father is out of town and won't be home until later tonight, so we agreed that it would be best for you to stay with us until tomorrow."

Both Oscar and Lovisa nodded slowly in response. Wille guessed that they were still both confused and shocked by the events that had unfolded. He himself did not know what to think, and still expected to wake up in bed at any moment.

"What attacked you," Ida continued, "could be described as a demon, a poltergeist to be exact."

Everyone stared at her in amazement.

"A demon," said Wille uncertainly. "I know what we saw was strange but…"

"Those eyes," Lovisa interrupted stiffly. "The flaming eyes, they were unnatural."

"Demons take pleasure in spreading fear, they feel nothing but hatred and malice towards others. They do not hesitate to inflict pain, and some of them can drain the life force out of their prey if given the chance," Ida explained.

Wille stared in shock at his mother and glanced at Hugo, who seemed frightened.

"But even if I were to accept that that was a demon, why did it attack us?" he asked. "And why did it say that it had been watching us for two weeks?"

His mom shrugged and looked over to the front door.

"Did you say two weeks?" she asked hastily.

Wille nodded, and she leaned forward in the armchair.

"It wasn't after you," she replied, looking at him. "You were just a means to an end."

Everybody looked at him, and Wille felt more shocked by that message than the knowledge that demons exist.

"Me? What did it want from me?" he asked, trembling with his voice.

His mother let out a heavy sigh, and looked at him with sadness in her eyes.

"It didn't want you in the first place, but the necklace you're wearing," she answered. "You, on the other hand..."

She paused, then continued.

"It probably would have killed you as soon as you gave it the necklace," she concluded, and let it sink in for a moment.

"But why?" asked Wille in amazement.

His mother looked at them inquiringly.

"Because you, me and Hugo come from the family of the gods," she replied.

As if to show that she wasn't joking, the purple aura she had during the battle began to shine around her again, before she got up and walked over to Oscar and Lovisa who hastily backed away.

Ida took no notice of it, but bent down over Oscar and put her hand against his head.

Oscar began to look more relaxed, and Wille saw how his pale face began to gain colour again.

Lovisa looked questioningly at her brother, who smiled.

"Thank you," he said, gently before turning to his sister. "It's all right, I'm fine now."

Oscar started drinking his cup with the apple lemonade.

Lovisa, who hadn't touched her cup, looked suspicious but started to drink too. It wasn't long before she had the same calmness about her as Oscar. Wille recognised the effect of their mother's lemonade, it cured strangely enough most things and even traumatizing experiences it seemed.

Wille's attention turned to Hugo, who appeared to be lost in his thoughts and sipping his lemonade in silence. Their mother gestured for Hugo to come with her, and they walked towards her bedroom. Wille observed them from afar as they sat on the bed and talked for a while. Suddenly Hugo broke down in tears, and their mother comforted him.

"Wille, did you know about this?" Oscar asked in surprise. "I knew you were special, but a god…"

Wille met his gaze, and shook his head.

"It's not like I knew," he said plaintively.

"It's okay, I don't look at you differently because of it," Oscar continued, laughing. "But please warn me before you start doing any magic, okay?"

All three laughed, and the mood lightened up when Ida and Hugo came out of the bedroom.

"So, what happens now?" Wille wondered, as his mother sat back down in the armchair.

"We evacuate the house tomorrow, a friend will help us," she replied sadly. "We are not safe here anymore, we have to expect to be attacked again. And you two…"

Ida turned to Oscar and Lovisa.

"You two will forget all this. You will forget about the demon, what I have told you tonight, and you will forget that you know Wille and Hugo."

There was complete silence, and Wille couldn't believe it. Not only were they leaving their home, his friends would forget him, and he would never see them again.

"No, no, I won't agree to that," said Lovisa, who looked completely devastated. "I will never forget you!"

Oscar also looked despairing and began to protest, but interrupted himself quickly when he saw Ida's stern look.

Lovisa started crying again, and Wille held her head to his chest to calm her down.

"Wille, I understand how you feel, but they can't come with us where we're going. It's not allowed," she said sternly. "Besides, what will their father say if we take them? And if they still know about us when we leave, there's a good chance that they will be attacked for the sake of it."

Wille realised that his mother was right, but that didn't make him any less saddened by it. He looked at Lovisa, and got a painful pang in his stomach. Oscar looked at him sympathetically and lowered his eyes to his sister.

Ida began to make up the sofa, and set out another cup of lemonade for Oscar. Lovisa was allowed to sleep in Wille's room, with a sharp reminder not to stay awake too long.

Wille stroked her cheek. A tear fell on his hand, but he didn't care. He knew he wanted to tell her, but he didn't know how to say it.

"Lovisa," he began gently, "I..."

Before he could finish, she shushed him by placing a finger over his lips.

"I already know," she said with a smile.

Wille felt a warm sensation in his chest, realizing that Oscar must have told her. Wille kept no secrets from him, and, as expected, Oscar never kept secrets from his sister.

"Wille", she then said. "I want to be with you, that's why...I mean, this whole day has been so strange and now we're never going to see each other again from tomorrow?"

Wille nodded because he understood exactly how she felt. The pain in his stomach still felt strong the more he thought about having to be separated from them tomorrow.

Lovisa curled up into a ball, and fell asleep with her head buried in his chest. Wille lay awake for a long time, he didn't want it to end. The last thing he thought about before he fell asleep was the wonderful feeling of having her close to him, and then closed his eyes.

4. The Two Wolves

The scream that woke Wille that night was piercing. He looked around, and discovered that Lovisa was gone.

Another heartbreaking scream was heard from downstairs. He got out of bed, and grabbed his clothes.

Hugo's door was open, but his brother was not in his room. Wille flew down the stairs, and stopped at the foot of the stairs where he tried to take in what he saw.

Oscar and Lovisa stood on the sofa, and pressed themselves against the wall. Below them something dark was floating around on the floor, and a slimy tentacle was trying to grab their legs.

Wille looked around, and noticed more dark puddles in the living room and in the kitchen that seemed to be alive.

When the dark outlines on the floor discovered Wille they moved towards him from all directions, as he tried to get to the couch to help his friends.

The scream echoed through the house again, and Wille realised that the screams were coming from his mother's bedroom. He changed direction, and rushed towards the door on the other side of the kitchen which he threw wide open.

In one corner of the room stood Hugo, held by a pillar that reminded him of the oily darkness of the kitchen and living room. It had wrapped itself around his waist, and held him firmly in its grip, while it slowly made its way up his neck.

But it wasn't the scariest thing in the room. Their mother was lying on the floor below the tattered bed, staring up in horror at the large figure towering over her and growling.

Wille realised with horror that it was an enormous pitch-black wolf leaning over his mother, exposing its enormous fangs. He stood as if petrified, while Hugo struggling to free himself from the slimy pillar that held him.

"Wille, do something!" shouted Hugo as he ripped one arm free from the oily mess.

Wille flinched out of his trance, and took a step into the room as the big wolf turned its head towards him. He stared in horror into the red, glowing, eyes that bore into him.

"Well, well," the wolf said in a raspy, dark voice. "The prodigal son joins us."

The shock of having a talking wolf in the bedroom was immediately replaced by fear. Wille started walking backwards as the large wolf began to move towards him.

The wolf was enormous and Wille, who was one hundred and seventy centimetres tall, had the same eye height as it.

For a moment he wondered how it had entered the house, but then he saw to his horror that half the wall on the other side of the room had been torn away and large drifts of snow were drifting into the room.

"You look different from what I imagined," said the wolf, grimacing badly.

"Different?" Wille asked, trying to keep his voice steady. "Who are you and what do you want?"

The wolf let out a roaring laugh and turned his head back to their mother, who was still lying on the floor.

"You haven't told him much, have you?" the wolf asked, and smiled mockingly.

"You're a valuable pawn in the war to come," the wolf continued, as it turned its head towards Wille again. "Unfortunately for you, you are also a pawn that my mistress does not want on the board when the war begins."

Wille hastily looked over to Hugo, who had the goo over his face and was began to have difficulty breathing. He quickly made up his mind and made a run for his brother, but the big wolf was too fast and threw himself on top of him.

Wille landed on his back with the wolf's jaws over him. He pushed hard on the wolf's chest, and flailed with his feet, while the big wolf's jaws approached his face. He put one hand on the wolf's nose and tried desperately to push the huge jaws away. The stench of dead and rotting carcasses made him gag with nausea.

As the wolf's jaws were about to close around Wille's head, something suddenly happened – the wolf was pulled away from him.

Wille stood up and watched in amazement as the wolf was pulled out through the same opening it had come in through, and thought he saw another wolf pulling the beast's tail.

Their mother got to her feet and rushed over to Hugo, who was hardly visible through the oily rag.

"Wille, the necklace!" she shouted to him.

Wille reached into his pocket for the cross and threw it to her. She caught it and pushed the necklace into the dark shadow that was holding his brother imprisoned. A sizzling sound was heard from the darkness when it dissolved.

Hugo fell forward into his mother's arms. Wille ran up to them and squatted next to his dazed brother.

"Wille, I must go out and see who is helping us," said his mother, and looked towards the opening in the wall. "Help the others and get out of here!"

Before Wille could protest, she had disappeared through the opening and out into the snow. He put Hugo on the floor, and hurried back to the living room. The dark shadow now covered most of the living room floor, and had managed to get hold of Oscar's legs. The darkness began to creep from his leg toward his waist, and Lovisa found herself in an intense tug of war to prevent Oscar from being pulled down completely in the dark goo.

While Wille tried to avoid the oily mess, he watched with horror how Lovisa lost her grip on Oscar's hand.

Oscar tried to stand up, but was pulled down on the floor while the darkness devoured him.

Lovisa cried out, and tried to pick him up again.

"Lovisa, no!" Wille cried in despair.

She stood up and looked towards him. Wille held the necklace in front of him and carefully threaded his way through the black that enveloped his legs. The closer he got to the couch, the more intensely he felt himself being pulled down towards the dark shadow, but when it came too close to his necklace, the same thing happened as inside the bedroom and the darkness dissolved.

Wille had reached the sofa when the darkness tried to get hold of his arms, and force him down to the floor.

"Lovisa," Wille said, reaching out his hand to her.

She didn't take her eyes off her brother and moaned.

"Lovisa, I can't save both of you, you must let him go or all three of us will die," Wille said with effort, while the darkness gripped his waist.

Lovisa looked at him, then at Oscar, and nodded before she took a firm grip on Wille's outstretched hand, climbed over him and up onto the window ledge.

Over at the entrance to the bedroom, Hugo had woken up and was ready to receive her.

Lovisa looked down at the darkness between her and Hugo's outstretched arms, and threw herself forward.

The darkness stretched up like a pillar and tried to catch her. It just missed, and she landed so hard in Hugo's arms that they fell backwards.

The darkness climbed up Wille's chest. He tried to use the necklace and dissolve the darkness, all the while struggling to move towards the safety on the other side of the room. The darkness pulled at him like snares, and he didn't know if he would make it. Then he felt something pecking his shoulder.

Hugo and Lovisa had untied a curtain rod, and held it out in front of Wille who immediately grabbed it. The intense tug of war that followed was like nothing else. The darkness tightened around Wille's neck and waist like whips. He put the necklace to his throat, and heard the gurgling sound of the resolution, before he literally flew towards Hugo and Lovisa when the darkness released its grip, and he fell over them on the floor with a thud.

The darkness moved quickly towards them, and Wille got to his feet. Hugo helped Lovisa to get up, and all three of them fled out of the living room and into the bedroom.

Lovisa was crying, but there was no time for Wille to try to comfort her as they had to get out of the house.

They climbed out through the hole in the wall, and Wille put his hand up to stop the others as he watched for the wolf.

A movement some distance away caught his attention. By a tree at the edge of the forest, something was moving. He signalled to the others to be still before he crept forward.

At the foot of the tree, the figure of a wolf appeared, but it was not the same wolf that had been in the bedroom earlier. Even though this wolf also dark fur, it was much smaller in size than the giant wolf he had seen earlier.

Wille slowly crept forward, and the wolf tentatively turned its head. Wille followed the trail of blood in the snow and saw that it was injured in one leg. The wolf looked at him for a moment before it started talking.

"He's chasing her in the forest, I couldn't stop him," the wolf whispered weakly.

Wille looked into the dark forest, got up and started running. He heard both the wolf and Hugo calling after him, but he just kept running. The forest closed in around him and Wille had to stop to see where he was. He had run so far into the forest that it was no longer possible to orientate himself.

After his eyes became accustomed to the darkness, Wille could make out trees lying torn down all around him. He knelt down by the nearest tree, and breathed heavily when he saw the deep claw marks in the tree's bark.

He noticed blood trails in the snow that led deeper into the forest, and decided to follow them. The longer he followed them the bigger the blood stains on the ground, but they were still nothing compared to the giant paw prints that stood out next to the blood trails.

Finally, he stopped and froze when, with his head bowed, he noticed that the blood trail had turned into a large puddle on the ground in front of him, and in the middle of the pool of blood his mother lay motionless.

Wille threw himself forward towards the lifeless body, went down on his knees and turned her face.

A faint, almost indistinct breath told Wille that she was alive – for the moment anyway.

"Wille," his mother coughed, as blood came out of her mouth. "You have to get out of here, he can't take you."

"Shh, no one is going to take me, or you," he said, as tears began to run down his cheek. "You're going to be fine, I'll take you back and boil apple lemonade and it will be fine!"

Wille felt that he could not keep the tears away as he bent down towards his mother's face.

She looked up at him, smiling.

"My beautiful boy, I should have told you everything a long time ago. There is much you still don't know," she said, coughing up blood as she talked. "Now you must be strong, take care of Hugo and your friends!"

Wille couldn't think about Oscar right now, who had been snatched from him just a moment earlier, it was too much.

"Go north," his mother said in a serious tone. "There will be helpers who will find you, but until then you must be careful, don't let the darkness take you."

"Mom, you can't die, you can't!" Wille exclaimed, crying and feeling her cold hand caressing his cheek.

"I love you, but I have to go now," she said, and Wille saw how her gaze faded before it slowly disappeared.

She collapsed in his arms, and Wille let out a painful cry before burying his face in her arms.

A cracking sound was heard behind him, and Wille's tearful face spun around. The big wolf stood a dozen meters away, watching the scene with its red eyes fixed on the woman on the ground.

"How touching," the wolf said in his drawl. "But don't be sad, you will join each other again soon."

Wille felt his anger overcome his fear. He stood up and let out a furious howl before he began to run towards the big wolf, who laugh loudly with delight.

Before Wille could reach him, the smaller wolf jumped out of the forest and stood between them with his back turned to Wille. The smaller wolf looked over his shoulder at Wille, who had stopped but was still shaking with rage.

"I'm sorry I couldn't protect your mother. But I can't let you throw yourself to your death, you are too important for that," said the smaller wolf in a sharp voice.

Wille felt the anger throughout his body. How could this wolf, whoever he was, be so brazen as to stand in his way.

A scream behind him made Wille jerk and turn around.

Hugo and Lovisa had come out through the forest, and he saw how Hugo collapsed on the ground while Lovisa put her arms around him comfortingly.

"The best part," said the big wolf, laughing out loud with excitement. "The sorrow and helplessness of the prey!"

The smaller wolf still had his eyes fixed on Wille.

"Get out of here, I'll find you later," said the wolf, before turning its gaze back to the black beast.

The giant wolf threw himself at the smaller wolf, and the two of them tumbled around in the snow as they pulled and tore at each other.

Wille tore his eyes away from the battle, and ran to his despairing brother.

He brusquely pulled Hugo to his feet and half shouted at him that they had to get out of there.

Hugo stared back tearfully before he nodded and began trudging away from the glade.

All three ran through the forest, and back to the house.

Before they reached the house Wille put his hand up again, as a sign that they should stop.

"We can't go back there," he said firmly. "That shadow, or whatever it is, might still be in there. Besides, the wolf will come back here."

"We can go to my house," said Lovisa, her voice still shaking. "Maybe Dad can help us."

Wille and Hugo nodded in agreement, after which all three of them started running again.

Lovisa and Oscar lived less than a kilometre away, but it felt much further when they ran along the highway.

When they came within sight of the rest of the village, they suddenly stopped. The streetlights were out and not a single light was visible in any of the houses, even though it was almost morning.

They made their way through the desolate back roads and finally arrived at the right house.

Lovisa felt in her jacket pocket, and pulled out her house key. With a trembling hand she unlocked the door.

"Daddy," Lovisa called out as loud as she could.

After a while, quick steps were heard somewhere further inside the house and a large man with a short light brown beard appeared in the hallway.

Wille had been there many times, and immediately recognised Lovisa and Oscar's father Tommy.

"LOVISA!"

Tommy ran up to her and wrapped his arms around his daughter, who was crying openly.

"What has happened?"

He looked at the boys and recoiled in horror at the sight of the blood on their clothes. Quickly, he reached the door, and looked around outside before hastily closing it.

"Where's Oscar?" he asked, sweeping his gaze over the three of them.

Lovisa was crying furiously, and Hugo started to say something but was interrupted by Wille.

"He is dead, and so is our mother," Wille replied quietly, before he sank down on the floor and felt the tears start to run down his cheeks.

Tommy looked as if he had been punched in the face. He turned pale, and looked from one to the other.

"What do you mean by that?" Tommy asked sharply, with horror in his voice as he sank to his knees.

As best they could, they recounted the events that had taken place in the last day. Wille was expecting some kind of reaction from Tommy, but he just sat on the floor and leaned his head with his thick, brown hair against his palms.

When they told him about the two wolves, Tommy suddenly twitched and got up again.

"Of course you've made up this story, you're in shock after the attack at the school and now you've been attacked by wolves," he said, and walked hastily towards the kitchen.

"No, it's not like that", Wille tried to say, but it was useless because Tommy was already in the kitchen.

They heard Tommy unlocking something, and when he came back, he had a rifle with him.

"Dad, please don't go there," Lovisa said, grabbing his arm. "I don't want to lose you too."

But Tommy removed her hand, and waved away her objections.

"Make sure the boys take a shower and put on clean clothes," he said sternly. "They can borrow clothes from Oscar, just make sure you wash their wounds first."

"There's been a power cut for a while, but the electricity seems to be back now." Tommy continued. "Don't worry, I'll get Oscar and their mom. And if there are any wolves there, they won't live much longer."

Tommy went out of the house despite Lovisa's protests. They heard him start the car and drive off. All three of them looked at each other with concern and wondered what would happen next.

❧

The car turned into the yard of the boys' house. It was dark in the house, and Tommy thought that it must be because of the recent power cut. He got out of the car, and took the safety off the rifle, before sneaking around the house and getting a shock when he saw the hole in the bedroom wall. Inside, the bed was smashed and stuff was scattered all over the room. Cautiously, he crept through the bedroom and into the living room, with the rifle pointed straight ahead and his finger on the trigger. Not a sound was heard in the house and there was no sign of either Ida or Oscar. He went upstairs but it was just as empty.

A creaking sound from outside made Tommy look out a window. Out of the forest came a gigantic wolf, the biggest he had ever seen. It was pitch black and walked across the farm in the direction of the village.

Tommy froze when he saw the blood dripping around the beast's mouth, which disappeared out of sight.

Tommy made his way out the same way he had come in, and went a little way into the woods in the direction from which the beast had come. What he found inside in the glade made him freeze with fear. He quickly turned around and ran back to the car again. There was a roar from the engine as the truck drove back towards the village.

໑

When all three had showered and changed clothes, they gathered downstairs in the living room.

Hugo had a scratch on one shin, but otherwise they were fine. They sat there for a long time without saying anything.

"Wille, what happens now?" Hugo asked after a while.

Wille wished he had a good answer to that question, but he didn't. He felt empty inside, and still struggled not to start crying when he thought about their mother. He just shook his head at Hugo, who he realised must be struggling with the same grief.

Suddenly, a scratching sound was heard from the front door. All three of them froze and looked towards the hallway.

Wille cautiously crept forward, and peered out a window. He pulled back his head, and looked thoughtful, before he went out into the hall, opened the door, and stood sideways against the wall while the dark-furred, smaller, wolf limped into the house.

The wolf continued limping into the living room before collapsing on the floor. Wille locked the door and walked back into the living room, just as Hugo and Lovisa walked up to the wolf. Hugo bent down towards it, but Wille went forward and tried to stop him.

"It's all right," said Hugo calmly. "He's on our side."

"How can you be so sure?" Wille asked worriedly.

Hugo looked up at him in surprise.

"He saved our lives today. First, he dragged that monster out of the bedroom, then he tried to defend mom while we were busy in the living room," Hugo replied. "He was wounded by the other wolf, so I gave him some lemonade that I found in the bedroom. That's how he got the energy to chase after you."

5. Escape to The North

He felt a pang of guilt in his stomach. They had the wolf to thank for so much, and Wille had immediately become suspicious of it.

He bent down to examine the wolf's wound. It did not look deep, and he assumed that it was just exhausted.

A rattling sound was heard as a key turned the lock on the front door. Tommy rushed into the hallway and slammed the door behind him, before entering the living room with a pale face. When he saw the wolf lying on the floor, he immediately pointed the muzzle of the rifle at it, but Wille stood in the way, with his arms outstretched.

"Move, Wille," Tommy said in an unusually harsh tone. "That thing is dangerous!"

Lovisa stood by Wille, and Tommy looked astonished.

"What are you doing?" he exclaimed. "GET OUT OF THE WAY!"

"Dad," said Lovisa firmly. "This wolf saved our lives. If it were not for it, the big wolf would have killed us earlier."

Tommy looked unsure, but finally lowered the rifle and sank down on a chair.

"I saw everything," he said. "The hole in the wall, the chaos inside, and your mom out in the woods."

It felt as if Wille's stomach knotted itself up in pain when he started thinking about the incident in the forest glade. Lovisa went up to her father and took the rifle from him, secured it, and put it on the kitchen table before asking the question that scared them the most.

"Did you see Oscar?" she asked, with tears in her eyes.

Her father shook his head in disbelief.

"No, and no dark mess in the kitchen either. But I saw the giant wolf. It was huge, unnatural…", he stopped abruptly.

"Garmr," a voice was heard behind them.

All three spun around and stared at the wolf, which was lying with its head in Hugo's arms.

"He is called Garmr, the beast from hell," said the wolf.

"It talks," Tommy stammered out, but the others took no notice. Too many strange things had happened in the last twenty-four hours for them to react to it.

"Why is he after us?" asked Wille, looking at the wolf. "And what was that dark thing that took Oscar?"

The wolf looked at him in disbelief and sank down with his head in Hugo's lap again.

"I don't have time to explain," it replied. "We have to go."

"We're not going anywhere until you explain what all this is about," said Tommy, sounding angry. "Gods and hellish wolves – I demand an explanation! I have lost my son…"

"Garmr will come looking for us," the wolf interrupted in a hushed voice. "He won't stop until we are all dead, and I don't have the strength to protect you."

Wille looked thoughtfully at Tommy, and told him what their mother had said about going north.

Tommy looked completely confused, but quickly got up from his chair and turned to Lovisa.

"Take the boys upstairs and start packing clothes while I stay down here to pack food and medicines, we leave in half an hour," he told her briefly.

Hugo glanced over his shoulder as they reached the stairs.

Tommy scrutinised his gaze and then said in a calm voice: "Don't worry, I won't hurt the wolf."

Wille and Hugo sadly went through Oscar's closet. It felt wrong to have to wear their dead friend's clothes. When they had finished and filled two backpacks, they met up with Lovisa at the stairs. They didn't say anything, but they didn't need to because they all missed Oscar. He was the one who would have led them through the adventure.

When they came downstairs, Tommy had prepared several bags and coolers. He had changed into camouflage coloured hunting clothes, and his hunting guns were packed in a bag, and he had even managed to patch up the wolf that was waiting for them down there.

Wille saw to his surprise that although the wolf was not as gigantic as the black beast, its ears reached up to his nose. A shiver went through Wille's body, and he looked uncertainly at the wolf, which he guessed was a height from paw to head of about one hundred and fifty centimetres.

"If that monster is a hell wolf, that means you're from…", Wille interrupted himself thoughtfully when the wolf stared at him with his amber eyes.

The wolf shook his head in response.

"My name is Váli," he replied. "I come from the home of the gods just like you."

Wille bowed his head and examined the deep, amber eyes. He sensed no malice from the wolf, but sensed a great sadness in his face.

Hugo and Lovisa both smiled wanly at the wolf.

"So, are you like magic or something?" Lovisa asked. "I mean, because you can talk."

Váli looked up at her and chuckled.

"Well, I guess you could say I'm magical. But I'm not really a wolf, even though it looks that way," he replied.

"What do you mean you're not a wolf?" Hugo asked.

Just as Váli was about to answer, the front door opened, and Tommy came into the hallway.

"We're leaving now," he said briefly.

They took their backpacks and went out of the house. When Wille came out into the yard he saw that Tommy's car was still in the garage. Confused, he turned to Lovisa who smiled, and pointed to a large black off-road vehicle.

"That's Dad's hunting car," said Lovisa. "He rebuilt it with insulation, it will be perfect for us."

Wille knew that Tommy hunted, but had never seen the car he used for hunting before.

They loaded the backpacks into the cargo area, and Wille wondered how Váli would fit in the car. Hugo opened the door to the back seat and peered in.

"Since you and that wolf seem to be getting along well, I thought that he can lie in the middle and have his head in your lap," Tommy said to Hugo when he came up to them. "It will be a bit crowded, but it's possible. Lovisa, you sit on the other side, and you, Wille, sit in front with me."

"Is everyone ready? Let's go," said Tommy, without waiting for an answer.

Wille helped Váli into the car. When everyone had settled down and put on their seat belts, Tommy turned to Wille.

"Your mom said we were going north, but did she say exactly where we were going?" Tommy wondered.

Wille shook his head, and Tommy looked at the wolf in the back seat.

"Do you know where we are going, wolf?" he asked.

Váli seemed to want to comment on the fact that Tommy had called him a wolf in such a derogatory way, but apparently changed his mind.

Instead, he said: "Go northwest, there is a mountain range there that you call 'Flatruet'."

"That far up? Well, we have relatives along the way who will be glad to see us," Tommy said, and started the car.

He hit the gas and started to drive out onto the highway.

Wille saw how their home village disappeared and was replaced by dense forest.

"And now that we're off, are you, wolf, going to entertain us by telling us what's really going on," Tommy said.

Váli sighed and laid his head on Hugo's knee.

"Wille, how much did your mother tell you?" he asked, directing his eyes to the front seat.

Wille explained the events again, and Váli listened attentively. The sun had already risen and they had crossed the county border when he finished the story. Váli gave another sigh, and waited a while before saying anything.

"Yes, as your mother said, you have god-blood in your veins," said Váli, looking up at Hugo, who gently ran his hand through the dark fur.

"But what does that mean?" Tommy asked irritably. "What do you mean 'god-blood'? Aren't they human? Can they die?"

It was clear that Tommy's patience was running out.

"And what happened to my son?" he asked, as they turned off the main road.

"I can only tell you what I know," Váli replied, pretending not to notice Tommy's irritation. "There are several worlds around your world, and a long time ago the people of the worlds lived together. Your world served as a hub for these worlds, and the gods created you to nurture it."

Váli paused before continuing.

"But a darkness spread through creation, infected the worlds, and brought with it deformed creatures. The war that ensued cost enormous lives before they managed to shut out the darkness. But the darkness had infected your hearts, where it grew and fed on your souls. The gods could not remove it, so instead they used magic to weaken the darkness and strengthen your resilience. Then they cut off the worlds from each other, and retreated so as not to risk feeding the darkness," he concluded.

There was a moment of silence in the car, they had arrived at a new town, and as they turned a roundabout, Tommy looked nervously at the car's odometer, which was looked worryingly low.

Wille felt how hungry he was and was grateful when they turned off at a manned station for supplies.

When the car was back on the road, and everyone was enjoying sausages and bread, Tommy turned off at a small forest road, which became increasingly dense.

"We might as well try to make it on the smaller roads so we attract less attention," he said between bites. "There is a village a couple of miles down this road, we'll stop there and camp for the night and plan the rest of the journey in peace."

"Go on with your story, wolf," said Tommy in a somewhat calmer tone, and cast a glance at Váli, who was devouring one of the sausages that Hugo gave him.

"After a while, you forgot about the other worlds and the gods that once created you. But the darkness in your hearts is slowly growing stronger, and throughout history, it has led to wars and conflicts. The gods have tried to guide you, even if they have not been physically present," Váli said, licking his lips. "But some time ago, the barrier that held the darkness in place began to thin, and darkness once again began to spread from world to world."

"But what does all this have to do with us?" Hugo asked, looking at the dark-furred wolf in his lap. "We haven't even known who we are."

Váli looked up at him with a sad expression, but before he could answer, the car suddenly lurched so hard that Tommy turned the steering wheel in a panic. Then the car lurched again, and Wille looked out in horror at the beast outside.

The red eyes that met Wille's gaze were unmistakable – Garmr ran alongside the car, and tried to push them into the ditch.

Tommy swore loudly, and increased the speed.

Wille looked out again, the road was narrow and he could see that the wolf was having trouble keeping a steady pace when it running alongside them.

Another push caused the car to lurch so sharply that Tommy almost lost control of the car.

Lovisa screamed and pointed in front of them. Wille turned his head and saw that someone was standing further ahead on the road.

Tommy slammed on the brakes, and everyone was automatically thrown forward.

Wille closed his eyes, and prepared for a crash. But it never came. When Wille looked up, he saw instead that they were travelling through the same dark veil that he had seen at the school earlier. Then the veil was gone and they were back on the road.

Tommy stopped the car with a loud scream from the brakes, after which both he and Wille got out of the car.

The road behind them was just as clear as it had been a minute before, and no dark veil was visible. The mysterious figure was gone, and Garmr was nowhere to be seen either.

Tommy walked around and inspected the car, which seemed to have received only some damage to the sheet metal. Then he took a deep breath and sank to his knees behind the car. Wille came up to him and sat down.

Tommy looked up pleadingly with his grey eyes.

"I don't know if I can do this, Wille," he said quietly. "It's too much to take in! Gods, demons, hellhounds…up until this morning, I was living in a normal world with Oscar and Lovisa. And look at me now, I have lost Oscar, and I don't know if I can protect Lovisa. And you and Hugo…"

His voice broke and he leaned his head against the car. Wille didn't know what to say, his world had also been torn apart so he knew exactly how Tommy felt. The longing for his mother was still like a knot in his stomach, and he felt the tears coming.

Without a word, he grabbed Tommy's arm, and helped him get back on his feet. Their eyes met in agreement, and Tommy nodded slowly before returning to the driver's seat. They drove along the road without saying more.

The atmosphere was tense in the car when they arrived at the village Tommy had been talked about, 'Korså Bruk'.

They passed a river, and what looked like the remains of an old smithy. In the small village, Wille could see old timber farms that resembled their own house.

Wille looked at Hugo, and from the look he received back he realised that his brother was thinking the same thing. They missed their home, the safe place where they had grown up, and where their mother had watched over them.

A man ran out into the road, and waved for them to stop.

Tommy left the car, and went out to talk to the man. Wille couldn't hear what they were saying, but he could tell from the body language that it was an intense discussion. After a while, Tommy came back to the car.

"The villagers let us stay one night in the village, no more," he said, looking worried. "Apparently there's been a lot of strange things happening here the last few nights, strangers wandering around. They just don't trust us."

Wille was wondering where they would spend the night when they came to a lake, where Tommy stopped and turned off the engine.

Wille jumped out of the car and stretched. He heard how Hugo and Lovisa helped Váli out of the car.

Váli looked dazed after the violent journey. Wille saw how the wolf shook itself before it started walking around the car towards him. Váli stopped in front of him, sat down, and looked him in the eyes.

"I never thanked you," the wolf said after a while. "For not leaving me back there."

"You saved us, we can't just leave you behind," Wille said in surprise, crouching towards the wolf. "We're the ones who should be thanking you!"

He looked deeply into the wolf's eyes. Hugo and Lovisa came around the car and joined them.

"You said before that you're not really a wolf, what did you mean by that?" Wille asked, without breaking eye contact with the wolf.

Váli lowered his head and looked at the ground.

"I'm a god, just like you," he replied without looking up. "I was turned into a wolf."

"Transformed," Hugo said in surprise. "Why?"

"By my father," replied Váli, looking quickly at Hugo.

Wille thought he saw tears in the wolf's eyes.

"But why would your father turn you into a wolf?" Lovisa asked dismayed.

"My father is evil," replied Váli, scratching the ground. "He is so evil that the other gods chained him inside a crevice where snakes bite him night and day."

"But if he transformed you into a wolf, why didn't the other gods just turn you back again?" Wille asked, looking puzzled by what Váli had just said.

Váli seemed to hesitate with the answer, and began to shake violently, whereupon Hugo gently ran a hand along the wolf's fur as if to calm him down.

"I did something unforgivable," Váli finally said. "So instead of turning me back, they banished me to your world, doomed to wander forever as a wolf."

Wille listened in amazement to what he heard. Váli was still shaking, and Hugo gently stroked his fur.

"What did you do?" Wille asked as calmly as he could. "What was it that was so terrible that you deserved this?"

Váli looked up at him, and now Wille could see clearly that he had tears running down his face.

"I...I...", Váli tried, and took a deep breath.

"I killed my brother," he finally managed to say.

Wille, Hugo, and Lovisa looked at each other in a hurry, while Váli stood up, and fled into the forest.

"Váli, wait!" shouted Hugo, but the wolf was already engulfed in the night's darkness.

❧

Váli walked into the forest, and lay down on the ground. Memories of his brother cut into his chest like knives.

"I miss you, Nari," he whispered, and closed his eyes.

A tear made its way down his cheek, as memories of his brother smiling at him changed to the memory of his dead body lying torn apart on the ground.

❧

After Váli left them at the car, Tommy had started unloading the trunk. He had found a good campsite by the lake. Now he breathed life into a campfire, while Wille and Lovisa pitched the tents.

Hugo stood on a jetty, and looked out over the open water. The sun was about to set, and gave off a reddish glow that spread over the lake. Hugo thought about Váli, and how despondent the wolf had looked before he had left them. He was both shocked and worried at the same time.

Hugo felt a strange feeling in his stomach that he had never felt before.

Why did he felt such anxiety about Váli's disappearance, they had just met him and barely knew who he was, let alone whether he was trustworthy.

To his surprise, Hugo felt a tear run down his cheek. Stunned, he wiped it away with his sweater, and tore his eyes away from the dark forest where Váli had disappeared.

6. A Missing Brother

Oscar felt Lovisa's grip loosen before he was pulled down to the floor and into the cold darkness that waited there.

He tried to get up and desperately reached up his hands towards Lovisa, but was mercilessly pulled down to the floor again.

His vision began to blur, and he felt himself losing consciousness as darkness crept up on his face. The last thing he heard before everything went black was Lovisa and Wille screaming his name.

Then nothing. He fell into what felt like a void, while shadows danced before his eyes, and then he hit the ground with a hard thud.

Oscar got up slowly and rubbed his legs, which were sore from the hard landing. He looked around in the darkened room. When his eyes adjusted, he could make out the dark, bare walls that surrounded him.

"Hello," he called out eagerly. "Lovisa? Wille?"

There was no reply, and Oscar began to feel his way around the room. The walls were reminiscent of damp cave walls, and he could feel pointed shapes that unevenly emerged as he ran his hand over the wet wall.

A sound up ahead made Oscar stop and press himself against the wall, as someone was walking towards him.

A figure appeared to his right, and Oscar felt his chest go cold. The figure had a long, billowing cap that fluttered like torn rags. The figure's head was concealed by a hood, and Oscar could feel his body freeze as he tried to see the hidden face. He could feel all the joy draining out of him and being replaced by horror and dread.

"So, you ended up here," the figure said in a chilling voice, motioning for him to follow.

Oscar stood rigid with horror and could not move.

The terrifying figure seemed to be floating towards him, and a three-clawed hand grasped Oscar's arm.

The horrible face that met Oscar's gaze sent a cold chill through his body.

Where there should have been eyes, two red dots shone from under the darkness of the hood.

The icy claws gripped his arm so tightly that Oscar screamed in pain, whereupon the figure turned around and began dragging Oscar further into the eerie cave.

Oscar could see stone figures emerging out of the crevices, representing people who seemed to be writhing in unnatural positions. Some seemed to be scratching their faces, others had their arms outstretched as if looking for something to grab onto.

It began to get lighter the further into the cave they got, and Oscar put his hand in front of his eyes as they entered a large hall lit by countless torches.

In front of him, Oscar could see several figures sitting on seats carved out of massive stone blocks in a large ring.

The three-fingered figure threw Oscar onto the hard stone floor in the centre of the ring, and sat down on an empty seat.

Oscar knelt down and stared up at the figures around him. They all wore similar hoods to those worn by the eerie figure, except that theirs did not look torn. They had their hoods up, effectively hiding their faces, and he counted the figures to seven in total.

One of the figures stood up and slowly pulled the hood down, revealing its face. Oscar widened his eyes and stared in amazement at the woman who appeared in front of him. Half of her face was the most beautiful he had ever seen, while the other half looked like a rotting corpse.

The woman walked forward and stopped in front of him.

"Who are you?" Oscar managed to stutter out, looking up at the woman without being able to decide whether she was the most beautiful or the most disgusting creature he had ever seen.

The woman smiled slyly at him and turned around.

"That boy will do," she said, and went back to her seat.

Good enough for what, Oscar wondered in confusion. None of the other figures moved, but sat with their eyes fixed on him.

"Bring him in," the woman commanded, in a tone that drilled into Oscar's head.

Steps were heard behind him, and he turned around.

Two creatures with white skin and empty eye sockets were coming towards them, dragging a figure that looked half-beaten to death, and Oscar gasped for breath.

The figure they were dragging was none other than Liam, the demon who had almost killed him earlier.

They stopped a few steps away from Oscar and waited. Liam looked up, and Oscar saw that he was bruised.

"Your Highness," Liam blurted out. "I have not…"

The woman picked up a black stick that was standing next to her, and struck the end of it so hard on the floor that the sound echoed in the hall.

Liam fell silent, looking terrified.

"You failed," the woman hissed, and the eye on her beautiful side flared into purple flames.

"You know what the punishment is for those who fail me," she said, and Liam fell to his knees and asked for a second chance.

Oscar could see something moving behind the stones further into the hall.

"I beg you, give me another chance!" Liam pleaded, now crawling on all fours, and pulled on the hoods of the other figures, who did not move a finger to help him.

Suddenly, two large wolves appeared from behind the boulders and entered the circle. Although the wolves were not as enormous as the black wolf that Oscar had seen at Wille's house, they were much larger than normal wolves.

Oscar crouched on the floor, as the two wolves approached. He could see that one wolf had a blood-red coat, while the coat of the other wolf had a darker blue colour. However, they didn't take any notice of him. Instead, they began circling around Liam, who was crawling on the stone floor, desperately begging for another chance.

The woman raised her staff, and pointed it at Liam, and the wolves pounced over him. There was a shriek, as one wolf grabbed him by the throat, and the other wolf tore off his arm. Oscar turned away, but he could still hear the wolves tearing Liam apart.

"So, boy, you must be confused," the woman said in a soft, venomous voice.

Oscar looked up at her in horror, and noticed that the purple flames in her eye disappeared as she spoke.

"The darkness that took you filled your heart, and would have swallowed you up, but your heart was too strong, so you ended up here instead."

"Where am I?" Oscar asked nervously.

The woman smiled at him again with that eerie smile. "This is a place between the world of the living and the dead, where souls cross over to the other side. A world where souls are tormented and demons are born," she replied.

The two demons, who had dragged Liam in, grabbed him by the arms on either side of Oscar.

"And since you ended up here," the woman continued, "you're going to replace the demon you took from us."

Oscar flinched desperately as the two demons began to drag him away. He saw the remains of Liam's torn-up body on the floor and began to scream in despair.

"You won't struggle much longer," he heard the woman saying before the demons dragged him out of the room.

❧

"I miss him," Lovisa said, wiping her eyes as she threaded the tent peg through the loops.

Wille looked at her with a pitying look.

"I know," he said. "So do I."

The fire crackled briskly, and Tommy unfolded a scaffold over the fire.

Then he took out a hook and hung a large pot over the fire before starting to open the cans.

Hugo came walking along with a couple of large water cans, which he placed on a bench next to the tents.

Tommy looked at them for a moment.

"I know you've been through a lot the last few days," he said. "But as long as we stick together, we'll be fine."

He didn't look convincing, but Wille nodded.

"I'm worried about Váli," Hugo said, looking at the forest behind them. "It's getting dark, and he hasn't come back yet."

"Don't worry about him," Tommy said, and followed Hugo's gaze in the direction where Váli had disappeared earlier. "He's a wolf after all, and wolves have good night vision. I have a feeling that he's not far away."

Hugo nodded, and Wille put a hand on his shoulder. The pot began to simmer, and Tommy gave them each a bowl which he filled with a generous ladle of the hot slurry.

Wille looked down into the bowl. It looked like carrots and brussels sprouts, as well as other unidentified things that he could not decide what it was. He took a bite, and felt the pungent flavour embrace his tongue. He swallowed hard, and Tommy laughed at his disappointed look.

"Well, it's not home cooking," Tommy said, laughing. "But it's healthy, so eat it while it's hot."

They ate in continuing silence, and Tommy lit a hurricane lantern next to the fire. He took out a map, and placed it on the bench in front of them. The youngsters leaned forward to see better in the dim light of the lantern.

"We're here," Tommy said, making a circle on the map.

He pulled the pencil aside and circled a town that didn't seem far from where they were.

Wille studied the map for a moment, then quickly looked up at Tommy, who continued to draw with his pencil.

"We take the forest roads from here and will come out just north of the next town tomorrow, where we'll stop for supplies and water," said Tommy authoritatively.

"Then we'll take the back roads to the north," he continued, pointing his pencil at some roads that ran alongside the main road.

"We will stop here to spend the night, and our goal is to get here," Tommy concluded, and made a circle around a small village at the top of the map.

"But we were going to Flatruet?" Wille asked in surprise.

"We are going to continue there," replied Tommy. "But Lovisa and I have relatives in that village, it will be a good place to stop before we continue."

Wille turned to Lovisa, who nodded in agreement.

When they had finished eating, Lovisa grabbed Wille's arm and pulled him from the camp. Hugo looked up and smiled to himself as he returned to the dishes.

When the dishes were done, Hugo carefully slipped away and placed a bowl of leftovers on the ground for Váli before going to his tent, starting to unfold his sleeping bag.

∽

Lovisa dragged Wille a good distance from the tent site. Not until they had reached a headland with old, dilapidated fishing sheds next to a quiet bay did she stop, looking at him with sparkling eyes.

Wille began to get nervous, and felt himself sweating. Without warning, Lovisa embraced him with a kiss. He felt the warmth in his face, put his own arms around her shoulders, and closed his eyes.

They let go of each other, and Wille nervously met her gaze. Those sparkling, clear eyes said everything he wanted them to say. He had been waiting for this, and now they stood all alone as the last rays of sunlight set over the forest.

A rustling sound nearby interrupted them, and they looked around quickly.

The rustling continued, and Wille stood in front of Lovisa and tried to see something in the darkness.

"Váli," Wille called out nervously. "Is that you?"

☙

Tommy rushed out of the tent when he heard his daughter's screams coming from somewhere in the forest. He stared desperately into the darkness, without being able to locate where the sound was coming from.

Hugo crawled out of the tent when the scream was heard.

"Stay in the tent", Tommy said, and threw his arm out to him before rushing into the forest.

Hugo suddenly realised that he was alone in the camp. He peered anxiously into the forest and thought he saw several shadowy creatures roaming around.

He caught sight of a wolf slowly walking towards him from the road, and stopped some distance from the tent.

Hugo froze as it was not Váli he saw in front of him.

Several wolves appeared from the forest, and the first wolf began to growl at him. It walked sideways towards the tent, where Hugo slowly retreated further in and curled up in the sleeping bag. He could hear several other wolves roaming around outside the tent.

Suddenly, a wolf head appeared inside the tent opening. It growled, and clearly bared its teeth at him.

Hugo pressed himself against the back of the tent, terrified, and felt himself beginning to panic.

Suddenly, there was a commotion outside the tent, and the wolf head disappeared again.

Hugo could hear what sounded like a battle outside, and wolves were yelping furiously. He didn't dare move, but lay still in his sleeping bag until the sounds stopped.

"You can come out now," a familiar voice called.

Hugo crawled out, and he found himself standing behind Váli. Five wolves sat in a ring around them, and another wolf sniffed Váli gently before yelping. Váli responded with a bark, and turned to face Hugo.

"They won't hurt you," he said calmly when he saw Hugo's nervous look. "They thought you were demons."

Hugo wrapped his arms around his neck. Váli looked surprised, but then laughed at the unexpected hug.

"I haven't been this popular in a long time," he said happily.

Footsteps were heard as Tommy came back from the forest. His face was ashen, and Hugo realised that something had happened. In his arms, he carried Wille, who had blood running down his forehead.

When Tommy saw the other wolves, he stopped and looked uncertain. However, upon spotting Váli and Hugo in front of the tents, he continued to walk past the wolves.

Hugo ran forward, picked up his injured brother, and gently laid him on the ground. Wille looked at him with a weak gaze that radiated fear and anxiety.

"Two demons took Lovisa," Wille said softly. "They dragged her off into the forest, and I couldn't stop them. They threw me into a tree like I was a rag."

Hugo looked up in horror at Váli, who nodded.

"The other wolves that live here in the forest have been smelling the demons and trying to chase them away from here. However, they have proven to be incredibly fast and have managed to stay in the area," Váli said, examining Wille.

"You have a concussion and need to rest," said Váli, turning to the other wolves.

Wille stubbornly tried to get up but immediately fell down again, and Hugo caught him.

Váli growled warningly at Wille.

"I said you need to rest, so lie down. Me and the other wolves will take care of this," the wolf said, lifting his head. "You, Hugo, can stay and look after him."

A clicking sound was heard as Tommy came back from the car and unloaded the rifle. Hugo saw that the man's previously shocked face now glowed with rage. The wolves took a step backwards and yelped anxiously, but a loud bark from Váli made them calm down.

"The other wolves run ahead of us and start tracking them. I will go with you, and as soon as they find the demons, they will try to drive them towards you so you can shoot them. It will be like the hunting techniques that you humans use," Váli said, and Tommy nodded briefly.

Váli let out a sharp bark, and the wolves rushed into the forest with Tommy close behind them.

Hugo gently pulled Wille into the tent, and tucked him into the sleeping bag, before going to fetch his own sleeping bag from the tent next door. He crawled anxiously down next to his brother, and fell asleep. He had not been asleep very long when he was awakened by a strange light outside the tent. He tried to push Wille, who was snoring without waking up.

Hugo crawled out of his sleeping bag, carefully opened the canvas, and went outside. Inside the forest, he saw a young girl who was on her way away from the camp. A strange white light illuminated the road where she had passed earlier.

Lovisa, Hugo thought, as he made his way out of the tent before following the mysterious girl. He tried to call out to her, but got no answer.

When they reached the old fishing sheds, the light from the girl flickered, and she disappeared.

The headland immediately went pitch black around him, and Hugo could no longer orient himself.

There was a creak on the footbridge that led out to the headland, and Hugo turned around, still without being able to see anything.

He turned around again, just in time to see the outline of the demon that was hurling itself toward him.

☙

Wille couldn't believe his eyes, he was actually flying. Cautiously, he tried to stretch his arms and discovered that he had wings. Strangely enough, he felt no fear. He was enveloped by a conscious calmness, and looked down into the deep forest, where he heard the wolves eagerly searching for the demons.

His winged body turned, and he flew back towards the camp again. Wille dove closer to the treetops, and was horrified to see one of the demons drag his unconscious brother towards the houses in the small village. He tried to dive down towards them, but the trees were in the way, so he flew back to the tent and dove through the opening, where he saw his own body lying and snoring loudly.

7. The Man and The Hawk

He jumped up in confusion, before spotting the hawk sitting next to him. Wille was surprised when he recognised the beautiful silver wings. It was the same hawk that had helped them during the attack at the school.

Suddenly, he remembered Hugo and Lovisa. He stood up quickly, feeling how he wobbled, realizing his head had not recovered from the blow earlier.

On trembling legs, Wille got out of the tent and started walking towards the village. He noticed that the storm lantern was still lit but didn't bother to extinguish it.

"So, you're awake now," came a voice from behind him.

Wille turned around and got into a fighting position.

A man sat on a stump and observed him. The hawk flew out of the tent, and landed on the man's shoulder.

Wille examined the man from head to toe. The man looked older than Tommy, and had a billowing cap that swept around in the gentle breeze that came from the lake.

Under the green coat, Wille could see a coarse white sweater and a pair of dark wool pants. The boots that the man wore seemed to be made of coarse leather, but what puzzled Wille the most was the man's face. Even though the man looked old, he seemed to have a smooth facial feature that suited the long silver beard.

"Who are you?" Wille asked uncertainly without lowering the position he was standing in.

The man smiled kindly, stood up, and walked towards him. Wille automatically took a step backwards to brace himself against the ground in case needed.

The man laughed, and Wille did not perceive any malice in him but was still on his guard.

"I am a friend," the man replied.

Wille felt himself sweating nervously, as the stranger reached out, and put his hand on Wille's forehead. Suddenly, he felt the headache diminish and disappear.

"I'm not as good at it as your mother was, but I think this will do," said the stranger, and took a step backwards.

Wille felt his hand on his forehead, amazed.

"Did you know my mother?" Wille asked uncertainly, and the stranger nodded in response.

"She was loved by all who belong to our family," the man replied, and lowered his gaze. "Her death will be mourned by many when the news arrives."

Wille felt a pang of sadness building up in his stomach.

"That wasn't a bad spirit walk you did, by the way," the stranger continued, smiling at Wille, who shrugged.

"Spirit walking?" Wille asked, and the stranger smiled.

"You let your spirit wander over to my hawk," the man replied, and looked over to the bird sitting on the stump.

"Have you never done that before?" the man asked curiously, whereupon Wille shook his head.

"Interesting," the man continued, running his fingers through his beard. "You are still a diamond in the rough."

Wille suddenly remembered why he was in such a hurry.

"My brother and my friend," he said, looking at the man pleadingly. "They were taken by demons. Can you help us?"

The man nodded in response.

"I saw your brother following the skogsrå just as I came here," he said. "I'm afraid I was too late to stop him."

"The skogsrå, what is that?" Wille asked in surprise.

"The skogsrå is a forest spirit who enjoys luring people into the forest, and getting them lost. Usually she lures men away, charm them with her appearance, and then leaves them helpless in the forest," the man replied, looking at the hawk who sat down on his shoulder.

"Are there such creatures?" Wille asked sceptically.

He wondered whether the old man was making fun of him, but the man looked serious as he continued talking.

"You have seen demons and wolves that talk, and you have been told that you are a god. Yet you doubt that there are other strange beings?" the man asked rhetorically.

"Of course I've heard about forest creatures," Wille replied, puzzled. "But I thought they were just fairy tales."

"Assume that all the supernatural creatures you've heard about exist," said the man, looking slightly amused at Wille's puzzled expression.

"Okay," Wille finally said. "But even if I accept that there are such beings, it's incomprehensible how it managed to lure Hugo away, he doesn't like girls. Besides, I saw one of the demons drag him away when I was in the hawk."

"My guess is that the demon forced the skogsrå to try to lure your brother away," said the man grimly.

"And that the skogsrå took the form of a young girl to mimic your friend, whom the demons had already taken."

"But why?" asked Wille, growing impatient.

The old man turned his attention to the village.

"I am afraid that someone is trying to trick you by capturing your friends," he replied seriously, as he started to walk towards the road.

The man motioned for him to follow, and Wille ran to catch up with him. When they had passed the car and reached the first house, Wille stopped abruptly and gasped for breath.

Even though it was dark, Wille could make out the outline of the dark, oily, shadow that he had seen at home. It covered most of the roads through the village, sending people running in all directions.

"I have to help them," said the man in a serious tone, pointing to the water wheels at the entrance to the village. "The demons took your friends in there, but be careful. There are stronger forces than the demons at work in there. I will come as soon as I can and help you. Whatever you do over there, don't take off your necklace."

The man hurried off to help the villagers, and Wille looked at the built-up roof of the water wheels before he began to move. He wished Tommy and Váli were with him, but they were in the forest, and would not get there in time.

He made his way to the entrance to the village and ran to avoid the darkness that appeared randomly on the ground before he stopped in front of the water wheels.

Although the wheels were only enclosed by a roof of poles, it was eerily dark and quiet there. He wished he had taken the storm lantern with him.

A murmuring sound could be heard further down the aisle, and he saw that Lovisa and Hugo were suspended by a chain over one of the wooden wheels. They were securely fastened, and each had a rag stuffed in their mouths.

Wille rushed towards them, just as one of the demons slipped out of the shadow, and blocked his way. He stopped, and looked at the chalk-white face covered in scars, and the coal-black eyes that were fixed straight at him.

Suddenly, the second demon appeared so close to him that Wille fell to the ground, and slithered away from it.

Lovisa tried to say something through the rag in her mouth, and Hugo stared terrified at him.

When he had slithered a bit away, Wille bumped into something strange. He felt it with his hand, and a cold chill ran through his body when he realised that it was a foot and a leg he had slithered into.

As if in a trance, Wille tilted his head back and saw the face of a tall man with flowing black hair, who was leaning over him with a wicked grin on his face.

Wille rolled to the side, then knelt with his gaze fixed on the dark-haired man, who laughed and locked eyes with him.

The man was tall and rather thin, with a pale face whose hue was emphasized by the black hair that hung down to his shoulders. The man wore a dark tunic, with a long cape sweeping along the dusty floor.

"So, you finally found your way here," the man said, with a chuckle. "It wasn't easy to get you here alone!"

Wille swept his eyes across the room to assess the situation. His brother and his girlfriend were each hanging from a chain further away, bound and unable to move, and below them were the two demons. In front of him stood the man, who radiated such evil that Wille hardly dared to look at him. This did not look good, he had limited options, and did not dare to make any hasty movements.

"Your friends are safe for now," said the man, whose dark eyes glittered.

"Whether they will make it out of here, however, is entirely up to you", the man continued, crossing his arms.

"What do you mean by that?" Wille asked without breaking eye contact with the man.

The man's eyes narrowed, and he seemed to try to drill into Wille's head.

Then the man made a quick gesture with one hand, and one of the demons quickly walked towards Lovisa.

Lovisa screamed from behind the fabric, as the demon put his hand on her shoulder, and a black light began to flow from the demon.

"Stop," Wille shouted, and ran towards the demon.

The other demon blocked his path, and Wille turned around to face the sneering man who waved his hand in a sign to the demon, who left Lovisa hanging unconscious.

"You love her," said the man, grinning with a self-satisfied smile. "Good, that will make this even more interesting. These demons are devourers of souls, feeding on sucking the life force from their victims."

Wille turned around again, and stared in horror as the other demon walked up to Hugo and prepared to subject him to the same treatment that Lovisa had just received.

"You disgusting monster!" Wille exclaimed in despair.

The man laughed aloud, and his eyes narrowed.

"Is that what you say to the one who saved you from that big wolf?" he asked, smiling slyly.

"Was that you?" Wille exclaimed in surprise. "Why?"

The man smiled, and paused his answer for a moment.

"I don't want my son to be food for that beast," the man replied, looking at him confidently.

It became completely silent, and Wille felt like he was about to sink through the floor. He had never seen his father, and his mother had never talked about him. Every time he had tried to bring up the subject, she had only told him to wait until he was older, and now this evil man was standing here claiming to be his father.

"It came as a shock, I see, but it doesn't surprise me that your mother never mentioned who got her pregnant," the man said, wrapping his fingers around his pointed chin.

"But it doesn't matter now," he continued. "Tonight, you get to choose who means the most to you, your brother or your beloved girlfriend. You can only save one of them, and if you don't choose one, you will lose them both."

Wille turned around, and watched in horror as the demons placed their claw-like hands on Hugo and Lovisa.

Hugo screamed, as the black light drained his life energy.

Wille stood paralyzed, as he couldn't choose between his brother and the person he loved.

He met his brother's agonizing eyes, and they stared at each other. Tears flowed down Hugo's cheeks, and Wille realised that he didn't have much time.

"Take me instead," he said in a defiant voice. "You can have me, and this necklace, if you let them go."

Wille held out the necklace to the man, who was now examining him with a more curious look.

"I haven't seen that cross in a while," the man said sternly.

The man didn't lift a finger to stop the demons' attack, and Wille could hear Hugo's sobs behind him.

He narrowed his eyes at the man, who looked relentless.

"Take me instead, I say!"

Now Wille had a desperate rage in his voice, and did not let go of the man with his eyes.

"A brave gesture," the man said, as he struck out with both hands, and waved at the demons to stop.

The sobs subsided behind Wille's back, and he exhaled slowly as his idea seemed to have worked!

The man seemed to think for a moment. His eyes shone with an unpleasant black light.

"Well, I'll give you a chance. Surrender yourself and that necklace, and I'll let your friends go. If you try anything, I'll let the demons have their fill," the man said, and a black beam burst from his eyes.

Wille felt as if he were in a trance, as the beam that intertwined their eyes drew him closer to the man. It was pointless to resist, he thought, because then the demons would devour his friends.

Wille was only a few steps away from the man when a gunshot echoed, and one of the demons fell forward.

At the same time, Váli and the other wolves threw themselves over the other demon.

At that moment, a great sword fell across the black beam, and the spell was broken. Wille staggered backwards, and stared at the old man, who stood before him with a sword in both hands that seemed to glitter.

The black-haired man hissed something inaudible and raised his hand, whereupon a black ball of fire flew at the old man, who sent the fire in the other direction with his sword.

A bang was heard as the dark fire struck the large iron bracket of the wooden wheel, and a large hole appeared behind the smoke.

"You shouldn't have interfered," hissed the black-haired man, glaring angrily at the old man who stood before him with the shining sword.

The old man looked furious and took a step towards the black-haired man, who raised his hand again.

Several black fireballs flew through the room, and Wille had to throw himself down in order to avoid being hit.

Meanwhile, Tommy used the rifle as a bat, and fought against the wounded demon, who got up again after the shot, while the wolves struggled against the other demon, who was roaring angrily, and grabbed the neck of one of the wolves.

A swishing sound was heard as the demon threw the wolf against an iron fence, whereupon it landed at Wille's feet and twitched a few times, before it became lifeless.

Wille looked up at Lovisa and Hugo, who were hanging above him, and began to climb the nearest wooden wheel.

The ropes around Hugo were firmly tightened, and Wille realised that it would take time to get him down.

A new black sphere passed over Wille's head, and missed him by just a few centimetres.

After what seemed like an eternity, he untied the last knot and Hugo fell to the ground, where he curled up. Wille turned to Lovisa, and started to untie her rope, when one of the demons appeared in front of him.

The horrible eyes were fixed on him as the demon's hand grasped around Wille's neck. Then Tommy was there, driving a large knife through the soul eater's throat. There was a hissing sound as the demon landed on the ground next to Hugo and began to dissolve.

Wille watched as it writhed in agony, before it melted together and left a pile of ashes.

Tommy climbed up next to Wille and began to cut the ropes from which Lovisa was hanging.

Meanwhile, Hugo got the rag out of his mouth, grabbed the knife that was on the floor, and rushed off to help Váli, who was now left alone against the other demon.

The other wolves were lying injured on the floor, and faint sounds were telling Wille that they would not be getting up again for a while.

The hissing sound was heard again when Hugo tackled the soul eater, and with Váli's help, he dropped it to the floor, whereupon Hugo drove the knife into the demon's neck.

Tommy got Lovisa down. She was still unconscious, and Tommy nodded to Wille, who was relieved.

Wille then turned towards the fighting men again and saw that the black-haired man stood surrounded by black flames, which had appeared between the two men.

"Enjoy the victory, boy," said the black-haired man. "I'll be back, he can't protect you forever!"

The man was consumed by the flames and disappeared.

The old man turned to the others. He examined Lovisa carefully where she lay in Tommy's arms.

"She will recover," the old man said, meeting Tommy's gaze. "She's just unconscious."

Tommy nodded at the man and managed to get out a mumbled thank you.

Then the old man walked around among the wolves. Wille could hear the man singing something in a low tone. The wounds that the wolves had received in the battle were healed, and all the wolves stood up on unsteady legs.

Váli walked forward, and seemed to communicate with the wolf who seemed to be the leader. Then they lowered their heads to each other in what looked like a polite gesture, whereupon the wolves turned began to run away.

Váli turned towards Wille and Tommy.

"They thanked us for our help with the demons," Váli said calmly. "Now they can roam freely without worry."

Hugo walked up to Váli and started patting him. Váli looked at him and licked his face. Everyone laughed as Hugo pulled his arm across his face, with an annoyed mumble about how rude it was.

Just then, several of the villagers joined in, staring in horror at the burnt iron brackets, and several of them put their hands over their mouths when they saw Váli.

An older man walked up to Tommy with a serious expression on his face.

"We're grateful that you saved us," the man said, looking nervously at Váli.

"We don't understand exactly what happened last night, and we won't talk to any outsiders about it, because who would believe us?" the man continued, not taking his eyes off Váli. "However, we would like you to leave, as we don't want any more trouble here."

"We understand that," said Tommy. "We'll leave as soon as we've packed our things."

The man nodded, and the villagers began to leave. Some walked nervously around Váli, seeming afraid of him.

Váli remained on the ground until the last villager had left. Then he stood up, and began to trudge away, closely followed by Hugo and Tommy, who carried Lovisa.

Wille waited, and looked at the old man.

"I know what you want to ask," said the old man, with a mixture of sadness and compassion in his voice.

Wille nodded, and waited for an explanation.

"But you're not ready for that," the man said firmly, and put up his hand when Wille started to protest. "When the trip is over, I'll tell you everything, but you must be patient."

He left Wille with the questions hanging over him.

&

It had started to get light when they arrived at the tents again. Tommy decided that they would tear down the tents at once and that the young people could sleep in the car if they needed to.

While Wille and Hugo demolished the tents, Tommy stood and talked to the old man. He pointed to the map, and the old man nodded in agreement. Lovisa, who had recovered, loaded the food and water containers into the car.

The old man walked up to the tents, where Hugo and Wille had just gotten a tent into one of the bags.

"You have a long road ahead of you, but I'm sure you'll make it," the old man said, smiling. "I'll come after you later, I have some things to take care of first."

"How will you catch up with us?" Hugo asked, puzzled.

The old man laughed at the question, as he pulled out an object from inside his clothes, and gave it to Hugo.

"It's an ocarina," the man said as he watched Hugo study the object. "I want you to take care of it for me until I see you next time. And don't worry about how I get around, I'll find you when the time comes."

The man disappeared into the forest. Wille and Hugo looked at each other, before moving on to the next tent.

After a while, Váli came out of the forest in the same direction the old man had disappeared earlier, amused by the boys' astonished faces.

༄

There was a rattling sound as the woman opened the door, and the boy looked horrified at her disfigured face.

"What do you want from me?" he exclaimed, with horror in his voice, as the woman walked calmly into the room.

The boy scrambled across the floor, as far as the chain around his foot would allow, and the woman stopped a meter away from him. She took the glass bottle out of her pocket, and placed it on the floor.

"Your friends are becoming a problem," she said, and took off the cap of the bottle. "It's time for you to go back to them, because that's what you want, isn't it?"

There was a hissing sound from the glass bottle, and the boy watched in horror as the oily darkness crept up.

His screams echoed in the hallway, as the woman pulled the door closed and opened another door in the hallway.

In the centre of the room, a demon sat in a tailor's pose on the bare stone floor in a meditative state.

"So, you came," the demon said without looking up. "I was wondering just when you would ask me for a favour."

"Don't forget who you serve," the woman said, with a steely tone in her voice. "You will do as I command, when I command, and in the way I command – is that understood?"

"Who is the lucky one this time?" the demon asked.

She answered, causing the demon's eyes to flare up in purple flames. It closed its claw-like hands and began to chant aloud. A circle of symbols began to glow on the floor around them, and an image of the boy and his companions appeared. The woman smiled as she watched the odd group of people pack their tents and get into the car.

8. A Family Secret

Lovisa winced as the car sped along the bumpy road. She ran her fingers through the fluffy wolf tail and looked around the car.

Hugo was sleeping with his head leaning against the window. Váli had his head in his lap and seemed to be sleeping deeply. She looked at them for a moment and smiled. Hugo had both arms around Váli's head and almost seemed to embrace him, a sight Lovisa found cute.

She glanced up at the driver's seat and met her father's gaze in the rearview mirror. A snore from the passenger seat told her that Wille was also fast asleep.

"Where are we?" Lovisa asked sleepily, trying to locate herself from behind the window.

The dense forest enveloped them on all sides and the sun peeked through the tree branches. They couldn't have been driving for long, she surmised, looking up at the sky.

"We've crossed the border into Dalarna," Tommy replied, and turned left at a four-way intersection. "We have an hour's drive to the next town, I think you'll recognise it there."

Wille turned with a quick movement and Tommy looked at him with concern. Lovisa felt worried when she saw Wille wriggling back and forth where he was sitting.

She thought about everything that had happened in the last few days and felt that she was still struggling to take it all in. Then she remembered the big wolf and shuddered at the thought of its disgusting jaws. She couldn't get her red eyes out of her mind and nervously peered into the trees, expecting to see the giant beast come rushing out of the forest and try to overturn the car again.

"Lovisa," Tommy said seriously. "I don't know what will happen, and I don't know what we will see on this trip. But I promise that nothing bad will happen to you. I couldn't protect Oscar, but I will be there for you no matter what."

Lovisa met her father's gaze in the rearview mirror again and saw a tear slowly run down his cheek.

Just then Wille woke up, and looked around. Lovisa reached and put her hand on his shoulder. He turned around and smiled at her, before taking her hand in his own and squeezing it.

The car left the forest road, and got onto the asphalt again. After another intersection, they drove past a larger town called Falun, and several other villages, and Lovisa started to recognise herself when Tommy, after a while, turned off the road to a small village called Bjursås.

They drove up a mountain and eventually arrived at an inn. Tommy turned off the engine.

"Let's go inside and eat," he said, drawing his fingers on his chin. "I'm afraid you'll have to wait in the car, Váli. The windows in the back are tinted, so no one can see in, but try to keep your head down anyway."

Váli nodded and looked pleadingly at Hugo.

"I'll bring you something," said Hugo, who immediately understood the meaning of Váli's look and ruffled his fur.

When the car was locked and the party found a table in the inn, Lovisa felt herself relaxing. They had been attacked so often in the last few days, that she had found it difficult to settle down, but now it seemed like they would finally get some much-needed peace for a while.

Observing her father, Lovisa couldn't help but wonder where he got his strength from. Even after everything they had been through, he remained calm and collected.

"Dad, won't people wonder where we have gone?" she asked anxiously.

The boys, who had been engaged in a private discussion, fell silent and waited intently for Tommy's response.

"The school is to be closed for a week, during which time no one will miss you there," Tommy replied, looking thoughtful. "I have called my boss and requested a leave of absence from work. Even if someone were to miss us, we'll be long gone before they realize we're gone."

Lovisa looked relieved at her father's explanation, while a waiter came and started serving them.

Wille and Hugo threw themselves at the pork fillets.

Lovisa watched them as she ate. She had not thought about it before, but the boys were clearly not used to eating out in the forest. She herself had followed her father and brother into the forest for as long as she could remember.

They used to fish, and in the summers, they often slept under the open sky. The food that her father cooked in the pot was something that they had grown accustomed to and she hardly noticed the taste anymore.

She looked around the large room. A fireplace crackled next to the tables, and gave the room a cozy atmosphere. Through the windows, it was a nice view from the mountain, and she dreamed herself away among the clouds.

"Are you full?" Tommy asked after a while, as he chewed the last piece of his salmon fillet.

Hugo slurped up the last soda and nodded in satisfaction. Wille sank down on the chair and stifled a belch, which Lovisa interpreted as a clear sign.

When everyone was full and satisfied, Hugo insisted on having a grilled pork fillet for Váli, which Tommy grumbled and bought, before they left the inn.

"Now I think you should continue your story, Váli," said Tommy, looking in the rearview mirror as the car rolled down the hill. "Since we were interrupted yesterday."

Váli, munching on the pork fillet Hugo held out to him, swallowed a bite and then looked up at Tommy in surprise when he was addressed by name.

"Yes, where were we?" he said in a tense voice. "Oh yes, I had told you about the darkness, about the worlds, and about the veil that is getting thinner. And you wondered what it had to do with you."

Váli took a bite before continuing.

"In the first war against the darkness, the elders didn't know what it was or where it came from, let alone how to get rid of it. They told one of our best blacksmiths to forge a weapon so strong that it would eradicate the darkness and restore freedom to creation. The smith forged a sword from the brightest stardust, the oldest bark from the world tree, the purest water from the primeval spring, the noblest metals, and the wisest sight. But he needed one more ingredient."

Váli noticed that he had everyone's full attention.

He took the last piece of pork tenderloin from Hugo's hand and chewed it up.

"In order to work properly, the sword needed to be blessed by the World Tree, so the blacksmith went deep down to its roots to get a piece of the tree's soul as a final ingredient," Váli said. "Nobody knows what happened down there, but when he came back, he wasn't the same anymore."

Hugo handed over the water bottle and Váli drank gratefully until the bottle was almost empty. Tommy turned off the highway and drove onto another dirt road. As a result, the last few sips of water ended up on Hugo's trouser leg instead of in Váli's mouth, and Hugo swore.

"The sword that the smith forged, he filled with dark magic and so much evil that the elders had to intervene. The destruction wrought by the sword was immense during the battle, but they managed to disarm him and imprison him and his two brothers on an island," Váli continued.

"Then something horrible happened. Your mother, and two other goddesses, were kidnapped and taken to the island where the blacksmiths were being held. The roles were suddenly reversed, as the blacksmiths held the three goddess' captives on the island. During her captivity, your mother gave birth to a child," Váli said quietly.

Wille looked nauseated, and looked back at Hugo, who seemed to have frozen with his hand over Váli's coat.

"Anyway," the wolf continued. "The other gods saved your mother, and in the battle, two of the blacksmiths escaped. To protect her and her newborn child, she was therefore hidden in the human world."

"Wait a minute," said Wille. "You talk as if it were one child, but we are two, how does that make sense?"

Váli twisted uncomfortably, and Hugo patted him.

"It's because you're half-brothers, you have the same mother but not the same father," he replied.

There was silence in the car, and Wille gasped for breath. The shocking news completely depressed the mood. Lovisa stared dumbly at the front seat, and Tommy remained silent.

It wasn't until several minutes later, when the car went down with one tire in a hole, that Hugo broke the silence.

"So, who are our dads?" Hugo asked gently.

"Your father is one of our most esteemed gods," Váli replied, looking at Hugo's expectant gaze.

"You like to sing, don't you?" the wolf asked rhetorically. "I have heard you, and you have as beautiful a voice as your father. His name is Bragi, and his singing voice can mesmerize just about anyone. For some time, he lived with your mother, and they had a child, you, Hugo."

Váli cast a quick glance at Hugo before continuing.

"But as you grew older, the elders thought it best if your father left, so as not to attract attention. Until you grew up, and could come back to us, we had to keep some distance."

"And you, Wille," Váli said, turning his head. "I am sure that by now you have begun to realize who your father is, you met him last night."

The look on Wille's face reviled that he wasn't going to like what he was about to hear, and Váli hesitated for a moment.

"His name is Wayland," Váli said in a low voice. "He was the gods' own master smith, and could make the most beautiful of jewellery, and the strongest of weapons. He could forge magical items that no one else could even dream of. Until that night, when everything changed."

Váli tilted his head again and looked sad.

"Like I said, no one knows what happened, but somehow it seemed like he lost his soul to the darkness that night. When he was then imprisoned, his brothers demanded to go with him. The three of them later managed to trick another god to bring your mother and the two other goddesses, to the island. Your mother was forced to give birth and would have died there on the island if it were not for the other gods."

The car lurched to a stop, and Tommy turned and stared at Váli. Lovisa met his shocked gaze, and she felt uneasy.

"We're here," Tommy said briefly, staring intently at Váli. "I think that was a little too much information."

"But what I would like to know before we get out of the car, is who the old man who helped us last night?" he continued in a questioning tone.

"He is one of the elders I told you about earlier. He took care of me when the others expelled me from our common home, and without him I would never have made it here," Váli replied, smiling.

"One of the elders," Wille said, wondering. "Why did they turn you into a wolf, and then help you?"

Váli shook his head.

"He is one of the three brothers who created your world and one of the heads of the god families. He should have been the leader of the elves, the younger of the godkind, but instead he chose to leave, wandering among the humans. Your mother and he were good friends, they stayed in touch even after she went into hiding," Váli replied.

"Elves," Tommy said, frowning. "I thought that was a myth that was told to children, and made into fantasy movies?" he said questioningly, looking at Váli, who laughed at the underlying question.

"You humans have forgotten everything we taught you. You are so pre-occupied by your technology that you no longer care about what's around you," Váli replied with amusement. "And when you try to remember us, you manage to make elves with pointed ears, and dwarves as warriors."

"Can we meet elves and dwarves?" Hugo asked, his face lighting up.

Váli looked at him with amusement.

"Believe me, you don't want to meet dwarves," he replied, narrowing his eyes at Hugo. "They are greedy, and hate both gods and men. They stay down in their caves deep underground, where they dig out metals and other things that they sell to us gods. They almost never show themselves above ground."

Váli paused again and looked at them.

"But you might meet some elves, if you're lucky," he said as he stood up, and looked at Tommy. "We made it to the next stop, didn't we?"

Tommy nodded in confirmation.

"Good," Váli said. "If you don't want to have an accident in here, I suggest that we leave the car."

He made a face, as if to show that he needed to get out, whereupon they all opened the doors and started to get out.

⁊

Amanda Svedin paced back and forth in the office, struggling to process everything.

Yesterday she had gone to the home of Lovisa and Oscar to check out on them, but only found an empty and desolate house. She had tried knocking, but no one had answered.

When she then went to Wille and Hugo's home, she had felt a growing anxiety in her stomach.

As she parked the car, her instincts had told her that something was terribly wrong.

She had walked around the house and been shocked by the large hole. Judging by the amount of snow, it must have formed after the snowstorm the day before.

She had searched the house, but found no trace of the boys or their mother.

It was only when she came back out through the hole that she noticed the tracks in the snow. She had felt a shiver when she saw the size of the giant prints. The tracks had led into the forest, and after some hesitation, she had followed them.

The terrifying sight that had met her in there – she still couldn't get it out of her mind.

There was a knock on the door, and two policemen entered with grim faces. One of them closed the door and stood at the side of the room, while the other one sat down on the chair opposite the desk.

"Well?" Amanda asked excitedly, sitting down in her office chair. "Where are the children?"

"We have been to both houses, and they are sealed off pending a forensic investigation," said the policeman in the chair. "The body you found in the woods looks like it was attacked by a very large animal, you didn't happen to see or hear anything out there, did you?" he asked, scrutinizing her as she shook her head.

"We don't know where the children are," the other officer replied. "But there are indications that all the children were in the other house on the night in question."

"After what you told us about the fight and after what happened at the school earlier that day, we believe that...", the first officer began, but stopped when he met his colleague's gaze.

"We believe that the father of the other children came to pick them up, and that he then accidentally shot the mother when he went to shoot that animal. After that, we believe that he panicked about what he had done and kidnapped the children", the second police officer continued.

"Kidnapped?! Tommy would never kidnap the children!" Amanda exclaimed sceptically. "He was like an extra father to Hugo and Wille."

"That's not all," said the standing police officer. "We believe that he is also behind the murder at the school."

Amanda's mind raced, and she was completely confused.

"And the children?" she asked in a trembling voice. "Do you really not know where they are?"

The policeman got up from his chair.

"We think we know where they are going," he said, moving towards the door. "Don't worry, we'll find them."

One policeman left the room, and Amanda sank back into her chair again. The other officer stopped in the doorway and turned to face her.

"Have you told anyone else about this?" he asked, leaning against the door frame.

She looked up at him and shook her head again.

"Good," he said. "Keep this to yourself for now. We'll be in touch so you can come in and give us more information."

Amanda stared wide-eyed at the officer as he closed the door to her office. She never got to see his eyes, which blazed with a fire as black as the night's darkness. Nor did she hear him hiss at the other officer to deal with the witness and her family.

9. The City in The Sky

The cold water washing over Hugo felt good after he dipped his head under the surface. Tommy sat on the rocky shore and prepared the fire.

Their camp was next to a large stream that ran down the mountainside. They had pitched their tents at a windbreak next to a wooden bridge that crossed the rapids, before Hugo had thrown off his clothes and waded out into the thundering water with Váli, while Wille and Lovisa had walked away a bit to be alone for a while.

Despite the fact that it was the end of March and still winter, Hugo thought it felt wonderful to be able to throw himself into the water and, for a moment, forget everything that happened over the last few days.

When he came up out of the water again, Váli appeared next to him, and with a yelp, the wolf splashed him with a cascade of water. Hugo retaliated by leaning over Váli's back and wrestling him into the water.

"Guys, the food is ready," Tommy called out after a while.

Váli and Hugo raced out of the water, but the wolf was too quick, and waited smilingly on Hugo at the fire.

"I'll get the others," said Tommy, and walked away.

Hugo stood by the fire to warm himself, while he quickly put his clothes back on. Váli picked up a bowl with his mouth and walked over to him.

Hugo laughed when the wolf sat down in front of him, with the bowl dangling from his mouth, and tilted his head. Hugo took the bowl, scooped up a portion from the pot, and set it down for Váli, who threw himself over the bowl and devoured the contents before picking up the bowl again.

Hugo, who couldn't help but laugh, poured another portion for the hungry wolf.

ᴄ᷃ᴐ

Her lips felt soft when they met his own, and her wet golden-brown hair spread in the water around them. They smiled at each other and he wrapped his arms around her.

Two days ago, Wille thought he would never see her again. Now that they were together, it meant everything to him, and he never wanted to be separated from her. His body tingled as they held each other in the cold water.

"Lovisa," a voice suddenly came from the forest, and they quickly let go of each other.

"It's Dad, he can't find us like this," whispered Lovisa in a panic, and started to get out of the water.

They got up on the wet rocks and just had time to wrap the towels around them when Tommy came out of the forest. He looked from one to the other and then threw another towel to Lovisa, which she wrapped her hair in.

"Lovisa, you can go to the camp and start eating, I need to talk to Wille a bit," said Tommy. "We'll be there soon!"

Lovisa put on her clothes and Wille smiled nervously.

When she had gone a bit further down the path, Tommy turned to Wille, and tightened his eyes.

Unable to meet his stern gaze, Wille lowered his face to the ground, and felt a hand on his shoulder. Tommy's eyes had softened, and he smiled at Wille.

"I know you like each other, it shows even if you don't think so. But I want you to take it easy, okay?"

Wille nodded gently, and Tommy sat down on a stump with a deep sigh before continuing.

"I don't know what awaits us on this journey or even if we'll arrive safely. If anything should happen to me, I want you to promise that you will take care of Lovisa and protect her. Can you promise me that?"

"Of course," said Wille, surprised by the sudden request. "But we will all manage, won't we?"

Tommy looked at him for a long time and nodded with a smile, before getting up and putting his arm over Wille's shoulder.

"Come on, the food is getting cold!"

☙

They ate the stew with a good appetite as the sun went down and night settled over their camp.

"Váli," said Wille, taking the last bite of his stew. "Can you tell us more about the demons?"

Váli looked up from his bowl and licked his lips. He had swallowed his seventh bowl of food, and seemed full.

"The first thing you need to know is that there are different kinds of demons with different powers," Váli replied, drinking voraciously from the bowl of water set down in front of him.

"But what are they? And where do they come from?" Lovisa asked, and looked up from her bowl.

Váli finished drinking from the bowl before answering.

"You have seen the darkness, haven't you?" Váli asked.

Everyone nodded and waited patiently for the continuation.

"What the darkness does when it makes contact with a person is that it devours the person's soul, and then breaks down the body," Váli continued, meeting Lovisa's gaze.

"So, they die?" Hugo asked, picking up the bowls.

"Worse," Váli replied, sitting down in front of the fire. "When the darkness feeds the last bit of the person's soul, the person ceases to exist. The person is destroyed, because there is no soul left to cross over to the other side."

Lovisa started crying and put her head in Wille's arms.

Tommy looked as if he had been punched in the stomach, and sank down with his forehead in his palms.

"But," Váli continued, looking at them sympathetically. "If the person's heart is strong, the person can survive the attack. That's what the gods made sure of when they established the barriers around our worlds."

"So, Oscar could be alive?" Lovisa asked, wiping the tears from her face.

"If he made it, he has passed on to the other side," Váli replied, and walked up to her. "That's one of the questions we can find the answer to when we get to where we're going."

"But this still doesn't explain the demons," said Wille, who had gone pale in the face.

Váli turned to him, and his eyes darkened.

"Like I said, what I've told you is what happens when the darkness breaks a human. But with a god, it is different, our souls are born from the World Tree itself and cannot be destroyed. When darkness consumes gods, their souls are darkened, and they turn into what you call demons," he continued, looking up at the starry night sky.

"Everything you see, the entire cosmos, is part of the World Tree. And like a tree, it once flourished beautifully, with an infinite number of worlds branching out through different galaxies. Now, there are only a few worlds left, and many of them are ruled by evil that want nothing more than to let the darkness wipe out the last of what remains."

Váli looked at their fascinated faces.

"Maybe we should try to go to bed early tonight," he said. "I think we should leave early tomorrow."

∞

They helped with the dishes and hung the wet towels to dry over the glowing bed.

Wille and Lovisa crawled into their sleeping bags and closed their tent.

Tommy was already snoring loudly from the tent next door, and Hugo crawled into their own tent when Váli stopped him.

"Come, there are some things I want to show you before we go to bed," he said, and pulled Hugo by the sleeve of his sweater as they walked away from the camp.

He followed the wolf over the bridge and into the forest. They followed the struggling rapids up the steep slope.

The forest thickened around them, and Hugo had trouble seeing where he was going. Several times, he lost his footing as the rocks rolled away under his feet. Finally, he bent down at the edge of the cliff to catch his breath.

Váli, who was waiting for him in the dark, yelped so loudly that Hugo jumped.

"Are you always so easily frightened?" Váli asked with amusement.

Hugo threw himself over the wolf and wrestled him to the ground. They rolled around on the rocky surface, and Váli playfully nibbled his arm, before they sat down on the edge of the rock shelf.

"Nice moon tonight," Váli said, looking at the night sky.

Suddenly Váli began to howl, and Hugo shrugged in surprise when he saw that the wolf began to glow in a silvery white light. The light spread in circles around them, and Váli looked luminous. After a while, he stopped howling and turned to Hugo, who was sitting with a stunned look.

"Váli, what's going on?" Hugo asked, eyeing the wolf from the head down to the paws, which were still glowing.

Váli smiled at him, and his eyes looked peaceful.

"The moon," he replied calmly, turning his face to the moon again. "The Moon God gives me power."

"How does that work?" asked Hugo, looking at the moon.

"The Moon God is my grandfather," Váli replied, as the silver-white light began to shine around him again. "He watches over me and gives me magic."

"What kind of magic?" Hugo asked, puzzled.

"Do you have the ocarina with you?" Váli asked back.

Hugo reached inside his jacket, took out the strange object given to him by the old man, and studied the small holes on the silver instrument.

"You can play with me when I howl," Váli said confidently. "Then you can feel the magic around us."

"But how?" Hugo asked, examining the object. "I don't know how to do it."

"Put it to your lips and hold your fingers next to the holes. Then you close your eyes and disconnect from everything around you," Váli replied, and began to howl again.

Hugo put the instrument against his lips, closed his eyes, and cleared his thoughts as best he could.

At first, nothing happened, then he noticed how his fingers started to move. Hugo was frightened, but let his fingers continue to move over the holes of the ocarina.

The melody that came out of the instrument was enchanting and blended with Váli's howling into something wonderful that warmed Hugo's chest. He opened his eyes and was shocked by what he saw.

The sky was bathed in the light of an aurora borealis, that stretched from one edge of the sky to the other.

In the aurora, Hugo thought he could see the outline of a city, with high towers and sparkling spires. But that was not all Hugo saw, as he continued playing the ocarina.

The forest seemed to be teeming with life, he saw small dots of light that illuminated the forest, almost as bright as the starry sky.

What a magical sight, Hugo thought as his finger movements began to slow down, and Váli stopped howling.

"What happened, Váli?" Hugo asked. "And what are all those little lights in the forest?"

"Congratulations," said Váli, smiling at him. "You have just learned to open the gate to Asgard, our home."

"Asgard," Hugo said, sounding astonished.

"You mean that?" he asked, pointing up to the outline of the northern lights, which were fading.

Váli nodded and sat down, facing Hugo.

"But how do we get there?" Hugo asked, taking his eyes off the illuminated night sky.

"What you have done is open a window to the world of the gods," Váli replied, without taking his eyes off Hugo.

"But we cannot pass over there from here. To do so, we must be in a place where the earth's magnetic field is thinner, and the nearest place is the mountain where we are going."

Hugo turned his gaze to the northern lights again. The outline of the city was now barely visible, and he could no longer see the golden spires he had seen before.

Váli nudged Hugo's hand, still holding the ocarina.

"That is a magical instrument, made by one of our smiths. With it, you can channel your own magic," Váli continued, without taking his eyes off the instrument.

Hugo looked at the instrument.

"What can I do with it?" he asked.

"You can do a lot of things, but you have to discover them yourself," said Váli, and turned his gaze to the moon. "Until you learn how to use it properly, you can take help from the moon every night. It will guide you as it did tonight, you felt your fingers move, I guess?"

Hugo let his gaze wander down to the forest. The lights were still visible in the darkness but were starting to fade.

Váli followed his wondering gaze.

"Fairies," he said quietly. "They are the guardians of the forest. By opening your magical abilities, you see things that I see, like fairies. They are shy, and almost never show themselves openly, but through magic, we can see them and interact with them."

Váli signalled that it was time to return to camp.

The way down was considerably more difficult than the way up, and Hugo had a hard time keeping from slipping down the slope.

When they finally arrived at the camp, Tommy's loud snoring could still be heard.

Váli crawled into the tent and curled up at the opening. Hugo began to unroll the sleeping bag, and was struck by a thought.

"Váli," Hugo said, noticing how the wolf lifted his head slightly. "How old are you really?"

The wolf seemed surprised by the question.

"That depends on how you look at it," he replied. "We gods do not age the same way as humans, we can stop our ageing and, to some extent, rejuvenate ourselves. You could say that I am seventeen years old, how old are you yourself?"

"I'll be fifteen in a few days," Hugo replied, and crawled into the sleeping bag.

He found it hard to fall asleep without his stuffed animal that he had left at home, and looked hesitantly at the big wolf for a while, before he moved the sleeping bag closer to Váli, who was watching him without saying anything.

"Váli," said Hugo, and received a vague murmur in reply. "Will you come with us to Asgard?"

A sad sigh was heard from Váli, who was trying to sleep.

"I hope so, I really hope so," he replied, and sighed. "Try to get some sleep, we have a long day ahead of us tomorrow, and you need to be rested."

Hugo closed his eyes and fell asleep to Váli's rustling breath. He had not slept long before he woke up with a jolt and realised that Váli was gone.

10. The Dream Walker

Someone put a hand on his shoulder, and he turned his head, only to be met with a friendly face.

Hugo widened his eyes in surprise, and the stranger put his finger in front of his mouth.

"Who are you?" Hugo asked, looking shocked at the dark-haired guy lying next to him.

"Relax," said the stranger, brushing his hand across Hugo's cheek. "It's me, Váli."

"Váli?!" Hugo exclaimed, feeling puzzled. "But how is that possible?"

Váli put his hand around Hugo's head and gave him a kiss. Hugo had never felt anything like this before, his body tingled as their lips met.

The dark-haired guy let go of him and stood up.

Hugo couldn't take his eyes off the guy, standing in front of him with no clothes on, and reached out his hand.

"Come, I want to show you something," he said, pulling Hugo to his feet.

Hugo stood up and embarrassedly noticed that he had no clothes on either.

The dark-haired guy laughed when he saw Hugo's embarrassed expression.

"Don't worry, it's just a dream," he said with a smile.

Hugo hesitated but eventually followed him out of the tent, where an undulating purple shimmer lit up the night.

"This is your dream, and I am your guest," said Váli, waving his hand in the air.

The surroundings changed, and Hugo saw that they were by a thundering waterfall, rushing down the mountain.

Váli took his hands and embraced him with another kiss, before picking Hugo up and carrying him in his arms towards what appeared to be a narrow footbridge built over the roaring rapids.

"Váli, how can you be in my dream?" Hugo asked as they moved towards the bridge.

∽

"Wake up, Wille!"

The words sounded far away when Wille opened his eyes and saw the wolf standing with his face close to his own.

He automatically flinched, but calmed down.

"Váli, what are you doing in our tent?" Wille asked sleepily and stood up in his sleeping bag.

"There is no time to explain, wake up Lovisa and get dressed – quickly!" Váli replied and left the tent.

He shook Lovisa awake, and they quickly dressed and went out. It was still dark outside, but Wille could see that the hawk had returned and was sitting on a stump.

Tommy came out of his tent and unloaded his rifle.

"Váli, what's going on?" Wille asked, looking around in confusion for demons.

"Hugo is sleepwalking," the wolf replied. "I woke up and noticed that he wasn't in the tent, so I started tracking him. Then the hawk appeared and told me that Hugo was moving north and that he seemed to have a strange shimmer floating around him."

"Does the hawk know where he is going?" Tommy asked, hanging his rifle over his shoulder.

The hawk, sitting on a rock, made some screeching noises.

"It says that he seems to be heading for a bigger river further up the mountain," replied Váli after a while.

"The hell's waterfall!" Tommy exclaimed, with panic in his voice.

"Hurry up, it will be quicker if we take the car there," he said, and began running towards the car, with the others close behind him.

∽

They stood on the bridge and held each other. Hugo met the gaze of the bare-chested guy, while the water roared below and the purple light surrounded them.

Hugo felt his body tingle, and he let go of Váli.

"What is it?" the guy asked. "Are you still bothered by the fact that we have no clothes on?"

Hugo nodded in embarrassment.

"I thought you liked it," the guy continued, smiling. "Although you might prefer to see what I really look like?"

The dark-haired guy's eyes changed, and he grabbed Hugo's neck with one hand.

Hugo opened his eyes in horror as the young guy in front of him began to grow taller, and transformed into a middle-aged man with a long, black cowl.

The hand that wrapped around his neck grew larger, and large claws grew out where the nails should have been. The man's hair turned from black to grey, and the amber eyes turned into purple flames.

Hugo struggled desperately for air as the man tightened his grip around his neck. It began to rain as the purple glow was replaced by a whipping storm.

"I hope you had a nice dream," the man said sarcastically, baring his fangs, before lifting Hugo over the metal railing that held up the bridge.

"Did you know that if you die in your dream, you die in reality", the man continued, and smiled ominously.

Hugo stared down at the thundering water beneath him, and the rocks that stood out where the water levelled out.

Then he stared again into the demon's purple-flaming eyes while he vainly grasped for something to hold on to.

❧

The car stopped, and they all jumped out. They called out for Hugo as they followed Tommy towards the roaring water.

Wille ran alongside Váli, and stopped when they came out of the forest at the cliff that led down the rushing water.

On a footbridge that led over the rapids, Hugo stood and hung over the metal bar that held up the bridge.

Tommy rushed forward and grabbed Hugo, carrying him back to the edge of the cliff, where the others were waiting.

"Hugo!" shouted Wille, trying in vain to shake his brother to life without result.

Tommy checked the boy's pulse and nodded towards Wille, who again shook his brother.

"It's no use," Váli said, looking at Hugo lying on the ground, seemingly lifeless. "Someone has his consciousness in their grasp, and he won't be able to wake up on his own."

"But what should we do then?" exclaimed Wille, looking in despair at the wolf leaning over Hugo.

"Only you can save him," replied Váli sharply.

"Me?!" Wille exclaimed in amazement. "How?"

"You must spirit walk," replied Váli urgently. "You must get into his dream and awaken him from within."

"But I've only done it once," said Wille uncertainly. "And then it was unconsciously, I don't know how to do it."

"You have to touch him and focus your energy. The easiest way is to lie down next to him. But hurry, we don't have much time," said Váli, and sat down.

Wille felt unsure and looked at Lovisa before he leaned against Hugo's back while closing his eyes, while focusing his consciousness on Hugo. After a while, he felt his consciousness numb, and he became unaware of his surroundings.

భా

Hugo struggled where he hung in the demon's grip, but it was useless.

He looked down again at the thundering water and felt the anxiety creeping up on him.

The demon grinned and loosened its grip slightly, so that Hugo's neck sank down into the demon's grip.

"This is the best moment, when the fear and anxiety shine in the prey's eyes," said the demon with a sneer.

Then voices were heard calling Hugo's name. The demon looked troubled for a moment, but then laughed.

"They can't help you," he said, looking amused at his victim. "I control the dream, I control what happens."

And the demon let go of his neck.

Hugo waved his arms in panic, and someone grabbed him.

On the bridge, standing over the edge with his arm in a tight grip, stood Wille, struggling to pull him up.

The demon looked shocked at first but laughed before giving Wille a hard kick in the side, sent him flying and lost his grip on Hugo.

Hugo got hold of the metal bar that made up the railing of the bridge, and tried to get up, but he did not get a good grip in the whipping rain and became hanging with one hand grasping the bar.

"I must congratulate you," said the demon in a hissing voice, at the same time that he started walking towards Wille, who was lying in the grass. "No one has ever been able to get into my victims dreams before."

"Who are you?" Wille asked, trying to stand up.

The demon stopped and looked at him with amusement.

"But how rude of me, I did not know that you usually ask demons for their names," said the man in an ironic voice.

"The name is Incubus, and I must assume that you are Wille," he replied, and turned to Hugo again, who tried in vain to pull himself up onto the bridge.

Wille got up on wobbly legs, and Hugo noted that the demon was now between them.

"I have to say that when she asked me to seduce and kill a male victim,

I never thought it would work, but your brother was more gullible and compliant than I could have hoped for," said Incubus, smirking at Hugo.

"I've never seduced male victims before, my sister usually takes care of that. But I guess sometime must be the first," he continued, and took a tight grip on Hugo's arm.

Hugo screamed in pain, while Wille rushed forward and threw himself over the demonic man.

The demon let go of Hugo's arm and tried to grab Wille, while they fell backwards and landed on the hard wooden bridge, where they rolled around in a violent struggle.

But the demon was strong, and he grabbed Wille's throat.

"It's useless," said Incubus, lifting Wille up in a chokehold. "I control the dream and decide your fate."

Hugo watched in horror as the demon held his brother out over the thundering rapids, just as the man had done to him.

"Hugo!" Wille called out to him. "Whatever he says, it's your dream. You can control it, you can help us!"

The demon's grip on Wille's neck tightened, and Hugo heard how he was suffocating. He closed his eyes and tried to calm down, while at the same time trying to separate Wille from the demon in his mind.

A flash of light appeared in front of his field of vision, and when Hugo opened his eyes again, Wille was standing at the edge of the cliff, while the demon was still standing on the bridge and looked confused.

Hugo closed his eyes again and appeared next to Wille, who flinched in surprise.

"I see you've learned to manipulate the dream," said Incubus, staring angrily at them. "It won't help, I'm too strong to be defeated by two kids."

Hugo shuddered as he looked into the demon's blazing eyes. He tried to hold back Wille, who rushed forward and threw himself down on the bridge while giving the demon a kick in the waist, so that he fell backwards.

The demon, who had tried to counter the attack with his claws, staggered down on his back before flickering and appearing behind Wille. The demon grabbed Wille's arm while wrapping his arm around his neck in another chokehold.

"I told you it wouldn't help you," Incubus hissed, and ran his claws over Wille's cheek. "I still control the content of the dream, you won't get out of here alive."

The demon suddenly lurched forward and released his grip as Hugo swung a tree branch at him.

Wille took the chance and tackled the demon so hard in the side with his elbow that the demon lost its footing, and fell over the edge of the rickety bridge.

There was a roar as the demon plunged into the rushing water and disappeared out of sight.

Wille sank to his knees beside Hugo, seemingly exhausted. Their eyes met, and they smiled at each other while the lashing rain subsided and the forest faded away.

❧

Hugo woke up with a jolt and met Váli's worried gaze.

Behind them, Lovisa was helping Wille get to his feet, and Hugo saw that his brother seemed dizzy.

Wille gave Lovisa a hug, before he turned around and took off his jacket, which he handed to Hugo, who felt how he was freezing where he stood in just underwear.

"You're freezing!" Tommy exclaimed as he helped Hugo put on the jacket. "Don't worry, we'll sort it out when we get back to camp."

"It's okay," said Wille as he walked up to Hugo, who was curled up in the jacket, and was bleeding from both his legs and feet.

When they got to the car, Wille let him sit in the front seat so he could be left alone during the drive.

The car slowly rolled away as Tommy drove as carefully as he could along the bumpy road.

Lovisa lay down in Wille's arms with her arm around him.

Before Hugo fell asleep, he saw her father smiling at them.

❧

"So, he failed," said Oscar, looking at the unconscious demon lying in front of him.

The woman with the disfigured face standing next to him raised her staff, and Incubus was enveloped in purple flames and disappeared.

"What a waste of time," the boy continued.

The woman smiled with her beautiful face.

"But you won't fail," she said, as they walked out into the corridor where Garmr was waiting for them.

"I want you two to cooperate," she said in a gentle tone.

Oscar looked at the giant black beast with distaste.

"You want me to cooperate with him?" he asked, pointing to the black wolf.

The woman raised her staff, and the boy quickly complied.

"You will cooperate, and you will get more help," the woman replied sharply, and raised her staff, whereupon the wolves with their blood-red and dark blue fur appeared.

Garmr yelped in confusion at the two newcomers, who sat down on either side of the great beast.

"And what do we do if *he* shows up again?" asked the giant wolf in his dark voice.

"You know what to do," the woman replied coldly, looking at Garmr with her empty eye.

"I don't want to see any more failures," she continued, waving her staff in front of them. "And as for that man, I will deal with him."

With those words, she turned and started walking down the dark corridor. As she left the wolves and the young boy behind her, her eye flared up again in purple flames that lit up the darkness.

"Are you sure this is a good idea?" a voice was heard from behind her.

The woman paused in her steps. A figure in the same dark cloak she was wearing herself appeared in the darkness.

"Hades," she said in her slurred voice.

The figure took off his hood and stood in front of her.

"What do you really think that boy can do?" the man asked with his arms crossed.

The woman raised her staff, walked around the man, and continued down the corridor.

"Do you really think you can control him, Hela? Do you think you can do whatever you want without asking us?"

The man's aura transformed into turquoise flames that lit up the entire corridor, but Hela ignored him.

"Well then, I'll do what I want too," the man hissed, and disappeared in a cascade of turquoise flames.

11. Demon Worshipers

Hugo woke up when the car bumped into the road. He looked around in confusion and realised that he was sitting in the passenger seat.

A thick blanket had been carefully wrapped around him, and his head was resting on a pillow. Someone had helped him to get dressed, and he looked up at Tommy, who was looking intently at the road ahead of them.

"So, you're awake," Tommy said after a while.

He met Hugo's confused gaze and smiled.

"You've been asleep for hours," he continued, looking at the road again. "After what happened, we didn't want to wake you up. We let you keep sleeping while we packed up the camp. Not that it was possible to wake you up anyway, you didn't even wake up when I helped you get dressed."

Hugo turned around and saw Wille sitting in the centre of the back seat with Lovisa leaning over his shoulder.

On the other side of Wille was Váli, curled up with his head and front paws over their knees.

All three looked like they were deeply asleep, and Wille made some heavy snores.

Hugo brought his hand to his throat and felt the searing pain were the demon had gripped him. He saw himself in the rearview mirror and noticed that he still had red marks around his neck where the demon had held him.

"Do you want to talk about it?" Tommy asked worriedly.

Hugo lowered his head and looked at his feet. They were still bloody from the walk through the forest.

"He came to me in the dream," he replied ashamedly. "I didn't know what Váli looked like in his usual form."

"Wille told me what happened," said Tommy. "He also told me that you took a liking to a guy at school."

Hugo felt embarrassed, even though it was true, he didn't want Wille to tell everyone else.

"It's nothing to be ashamed of," Tommy continued calmly as he turned off the forest road, and onto a country road again. "On the contrary, it's brave of you to be yourself."

"I don't care about what Váli has done in the past, I want him to stay with us even when we get there," Hugo said confidently, turning his gaze towards the back seat.

He cast a glance at Váli and saw a tear running down the wolf's cheek. It was clear that he had heard the conversation.

❧

They drove for several hours before reaching a village, and Tommy parked the car deep in the forest. Váli stretched himself so that his body length took up the entire back seat, burying his claws in the knees of Wille, who swore in pain, and Váli shamefully apologised.

"There's an inn up ahead," Tommy said, surveying the forest where they had parked. "We need to eat, but I thought you, Váli, would probably want to get out and move around, so I'll leave the car here, and you can wander outside."

Váli nodded gratefully, jumping over Wille and Lovisa as they opened the car door.

When Tommy locked the car, he had already disappeared into the forest.

"'Noppikoski', what a strange name for a village," said Wille as he read the village sign next to the road.

Lovisa started laughing, and Wille felt confused.

"We are in an area of Dalarna called 'Orsa Forest of the Finns '", Tommy explained, stopping at the door of the restaurant. "A long time ago, people from Finland migrated here to do forestry. They built several villages with Finnish names and settled permanently in the area. Noppikoski, by the way, means 'Bud rapids', referring to a rapid in the forest where we parked the car."

He held the door open for them. Inside the eatery, it was quiet, with only a couple of guests sitting farther in at a table engaged in what looked like a lively discussion.

Tommy walked over and ordered the food, and the others sat down at a table.

"So, how long is it really until we reach your relatives?"

Wille asked and looked at Lovisa.

"Not far at all, we should arrive there later tonight," she replied, and set out napkins and cutlery for them.

Tommy came back and sat down again. He looked tired, Wille thought when the man leaned back against the sofa.

The waiter who served the food looked at Hugo's neck, but without saying anything.

Wille sipped the soda that was in front of him. He looked at Hugo's neck and remembered that Váli had said that the mark would disappear after a while. But the memories of the night's events wouldn't be forgotten anytime soon, he thought, and shivered.

Wille felt around his own neck where the demon had grabbed him. Although there hadn't been the same marks after that as on Hugo, he could still feel the pain.

Lovisa gave him a threatening look, whereupon he stopped rubbing around his neck and went back to his soda.

Neither of them noticed the waiter holding up a newspaper as she talked intensely on the phone, and when she came out with their food, none of them could sense the terror hidden in her eyes.

ᐧᐧ

Váli gently chewed through the rabbit's meat. Even though he had lived as a wolf for so many years, he still couldn't get used to the bloody taste, and he hoped that Hugo brought him something good from the restaurant.

The rabbit's meat was tender, and he ate with a good appetite until only the fur and the bones remained. He licked his lips and turned his attention

118

to the rapids further down in the forest. He pawed over the slippery rocks and began to drink from the clear water.

Suddenly he sniffed the air, and then he turned around and peered into the trees. It could not be possible, that smell was unmistakable and yet impossible.

Someone moved among the trees and came towards him.

Váli growled, it couldn't be who he thought it was.

A figure in a police uniform appeared in front of him. The person was tall and muscular, with dark, spiky hair and a thin stubble of a beard that went behind his chin.

Váli felt as if he had been punched in the stomach, it just couldn't be true.

"Well, I should have guessed that you were their guide," said the person standing in front of him and started laughing. "Is this how you greet your brother?"

Váli was shocked and took a few steps backwards, his eyes tearing up.

"Nari?!" Váli managed to say. "But how? You died!"

He could feel the tears running down his face, and his brother's face pulled into an icy smile.

"Yes, you killed me," Nari replied, baring his fangs, and his eyes blazed with black flames.

At that moment, two other policemen came out of the forest behind Váli, who was terrified.

"No, it can't be! How can you be a demon?" he exclaimed, and turned his head towards the two policemen behind him.

One of the officers pulled out a stun gun, and shot Váli in the abdomen. There was a sizzling sound as he dropped to the ground, shivering as electric shocks passed through his body.

Nari took a step towards them and motioned for the policeman to stop before bending down and removing the wires from Váli's body.

Then he looked deep into the wolf's eyes and smiled, exposing his fangs again.

"Poor little brother, how little you and the others know," said Nari with a smug smile.

Váli felt his consciousness begin to fade. The tears were still flowing from his eyes as his brother reached out and whispered in his ear.

"The dragons have awakened!"

✧

"Have you finished eating?" Tommy asked, looking at the young people who were sitting slumped on their chairs and nodding wearily as he got up to pay.

"Don't forget the pork tenderloin for Váli," Hugo called out.

Tommy turned to the boy and sighed while smiling faintly. That wolf is going to have to start paying for himself soon, he thought as he reached the checkout counter.

He noticed that the other customers were no longer there as he rang the bell at the counter. Nothing happened, and he rang the bell again, but there was still no reaction.

Tommy opened the kitchen door and shouted without any response. He saw a newspaper laying open on a bench next to the checkout counter.

It had the headline 'Children kidnapped', and his face paled when he saw their pictures.

"We have to get out," he shouted, rushing to the table.

"Dad, what happened?" Lovisa asked in shock, looking at her father, whose face was white as chalk.

"Is it a demon?" Wille asked before quickly getting up, looking around in the empty room.

"There's no time to explain," Tommy replied, pushing them out of their chairs.

As they headed for the exit, the door flew open with a bang, and armed police stormed in.

"This way," said Tommy, pushing them through the kitchen entrance.

Shots were fired as all four ran out from the restaurant.

"Don't turn around, just run," Tommy shouted as they ran towards the car while bullets ricocheted around them.

There was a beeping sound as the car was unlocked, and Hugo, who was first to the car, opened the door to the front seat. Tommy threw himself forward and opened the trunk.

"Stop," came a sharp voice from the forest.

Tommy, who was about to take the rifle out of the car, froze when a dark-haired man in a police uniform stepped out of the trees and pointed a gun at him.

Then they were surrounded on all sides by policemen, standing with their guns drawn and aiming at them.

Wille and Lovisa instinctively raised their hands, and a moment later, two policemen were holding their arms.

"Step out of the car," the dark-haired man ordered, waving his free hand at Hugo, who carefully stepped out of the car.

He had barely managed to close the car door, before he was wrestled to the ground by a police officer.

"Drop the gun," the dark-haired man continued, and turned towards Tommy again, who stood shaking all over.

"I'm not going to say it again," the dark-haired man hissed, and unholstered his gun.

Tommy turned his gaze to Lovisa, who was being held by strong arms just three steps away from him. Their eyes met, and he smiled at her before, with a movement of his cloak, he drew his rifle.

The sound of a gunshot echoed in the air, and Tommy fell backwards when his rifle was fired.

Lovisa pulled herself free when the body hit the ground, and lay there with blood flowing from the back of the head.

A red blood stain began to appear on Tommy's chest where the shot had entered his body, and Lovisa's screams echoed in the forest as she buried her face in his chest.

Wille looked at the motionless body in horror before fixing his eyes on the black flames that were the eyes of the demon that had shot Tommy.

"I warned him," the dark-haired man said.

A police officer tried to grab Lovisa, who was struggling and screaming hysterically. After a look from the dark-haired demon, the policeman left her alone.

"What kind of cowardly demons shoot their victims?" Wille asked angrily.

"I'm afraid I'm the only demon here," the dark-haired demon replied, and pointed the gun at Hugo's head.

Hugo closed his eyes as the gun was pressed against his forehead, and he began shaking uncontrollably while sobbing.

"Please, don't shoot me," Hugo begged, and the demon laughed.

"I would have expected more from the son of Bragi," the demon snorted, and turned towards Wille. "But I guess you're the brave one."

"Easy for you to say, pushing your victim down and playing with a gun against his forehead," hissed Wille.

He felt himself boiling with rage and tried to tear himself away from the strong fists that held him.

The demon was now standing in front of Wille, with the gun pointing at his face.

"You're right," the demon hissed, baring his fangs. "Maybe I should start with you instead."

"Go ahead, then," said Wille, staring defiantly into the black, blazing eyes.

Their gazes met for what seemed like an eternity before the demon finally lowered the gun.

"Lucky for you, your father wants you alive, whatever use he sees in you."

Wille felt the anger flowing inside him, of course his father was behind this.

He looked down at Lovisa, who was crouching over Tommy, crying. He would never forgive them for this.

"What do you mean you're the only demon?" Wille asked, and looked around at the police officers. "Why would the police want to cooperate with a demon?"

"Do you really think people only worship gods?" the demon asked sarcastically, and swept his hands out.

Wille looked in confusion at the expressionless faces of the police officers before he realised what the demon meant.

"Demon worshippers," he whispered in amazement.

"That's right!" the demon exclaimed with satisfaction, and walked up to one of the men. "In exchange for various favours, they help us with certain things. Some are even willing to sell their souls to us, right, Thomas?"

"Of course, sir," the policeman replied, as the demon thumped his hand on the man's back.

"Have you sold your soul to that demon?" Wille asked angrily. "Are you crazy?!"

The policeman took a quick step forward and gave Wille a slap with such force that his face was thrown to the side.

The demon quickly grabbed the man's hand.

"Keep in mind that our master wants the boy unharmed," he hissed warningly at the policeman, who immediately muttered an apology.

"Váli!" Hugo began to shout in a desperate voice.

The demon turned towards him and smiled ominously.

"Yes, we must not forget my dear brother!"

"Your brother?" Wille asked in surprise while a dark van backed up towards them. "What do you mean?"

The demon did not answer, but went to the back door of the van and opened it.

Inside there was a large dog cage that covered the entire inside of the van, and in the middle of the cage lay Váli motionless with his legs chained to the floor, and his mouth wrapped in duct tape.

"Váli!" Hugo shouted when he saw the wolf lying motionless.

"What have you done with him?" he hissed at the demon, who looked amused at Hugo's reaction.

"Don't worry, my brother and I were just having a fond reunion," the demon replied with exaggerated delight. "I decided to let him come home with me."

He laughed and slammed the back door of the van.

"But you can join him," he continued, pulling the gun from its holster. "You, Wille, are coming with us – your father will be happy to see you again! And your brother we can probably benefit from taking with us as well."

The demon looked at Lovisa, who was still leaning crying over her father's body.

"However, your girlfriend is probably better off joining her father," he hissed, and raised his gun.

"No," Wille prayed, trembling, while a painful stab went through his chest.

The memory of how he had held Lovisa while her face was buried in his chest made his legs go numb, and he collapsed in the policeman's grip.

"LOVISA!" Wille shouted in despair at the same time as the demon fired the gun.

12. Nari's Portrait

Lovisa heard Wille calling her name, but she was barely aware of her surroundings, and his voice seemed distant.

She turned her head and saw the demon fire his gun, only to feel in the next second that she was being pulled to the ground with a sudden jolt.

Lovisa looked down at her feet in confusion and realised that a tree root had wrapped itself around her calves. She heard screams from the policemen and watched the scene unfold in front of her, as the policemen were pulled up in the sky by the roots of the trees.

A curious sound was heard, and she looked up at the sky at the same time as a large number of birds swooped down on the remaining policemen, attacking them.

The demon swore loudly and started shooting at the birds, which swarmed around them like a whirlwind.

A rumbling roar was heard from the sky as something struck the ground, causing the demon to lose his balance.

Lovisa saw two guys stand out in the swirling sea of feathers as the demon tried to stand up.

One of the guys raised a double-edged axe and slashed at the demon, who conjured a black spear out of thin air to block it, then twisted the axe out of the attacker's hands.

Lovisa turned her head and saw Wille tear himself away from the policeman holding him, and then throw himself over the man who was holding Hugo down on the ground.

They tumbled to the ground, while Hugo threw himself towards the rifle that had landed behind Tommy's body.

Meanwhile, the demon fought the two newcomers. One of the newcomers, a muscular guy with bronze-coloured hair in a ponytail, used a giant hammer and swung it at the demon.

The other guy, who, like his companion, looked fit but seemed younger and had short, combed hair, picked up his double-edged battle-axe again, which he suddenly split into two axes – one gold and one silver.

They attacked the demon from each side, and the demon, whirling with the spear like a dance, parried their attacks.

The sound of a gunshot echoed through the chaos as Hugo fired the rifle. The demon looked down at the bullet hole through his body, and brought his claw-like hand there.

Lovisa watched in horror as the hole healed itself.

The demon held up the bullet in his hand while the two guys swung their weapons against his body.

He laughed as the hammer struck his body without seeming to do any damage, and the axes that penetrated his body were pulled out again before he threw them on the ground, whereupon his wounds healed almost immediately.

Lovisa felt the ground tremble and laid herself over her father's body, as large sinkholes appeared in the ground.

The policemen standing around them screamed as they fell through the holes, and the birds that had attacked them flew back into the forest.

The trees, which held some of the men upside-down in the air, dropped their screaming victims into the holes and then put their roots in the holes, where they returned to their rest.

Lovisa ran up to Wille, who was still wrestling with one of the men. She gave the policeman a hard kick in the ribs, whereupon Wille managed to throw the man into a sinkhole right next to them, where one of the remaining trees crushed the screaming man.

❧

Hugo stared into the demon's dark eyes, and noticed that a black dagger appeared in the demon's hand.

Just as the demon made a lunge at him, one of the guys behind them chopped off the demon's head with one of his axes, and the head bounced down to the ground.

126

Hugo stared in horror at the head, which began to laugh, before the demon's body picked up the head and put it back in place again. He felt the fear creeping into him, as he watched the demon's neck merge with his neck.

"What are you?" Hugo whispered in horror as he lay on the ground with the rifle pointed at the demon.

The demon turned towards him and held the bullet in front of his face.

"I'm complicated," Nari hissed.

The two strangers picked up their weapons again but seemed to hesitate to continue attacking.

"So, where were we?" asked the demon sarcastically, and again raised his hand with the black dagger towards Hugo.

Then the ground rose up in a circle around the demon, which, with a thud, closed into a high hill. Hugo dropped the rifle as the trembling ground rose in front of him, putting one arm over his face for protection.

When he took his arm away, the guy with the combed hair was standing there, reaching his hand down towards him.

After some hesitation, Hugo took the guy's hand, and was pulled back to his feet. Over the guy's shoulder, he saw three more figures coming out of the forest.

A guy and a girl who looked like they were around Wille and Lovisa's age, and a little boy who looked younger than Hugo. All three were red-haired and looked like siblings.

Hugo backed away carefully and looked around in confusion. Wille stood by Tommy's lifeless body, and held Lovisa, who hugged him tightly. She had stopped crying, but instead seemed to go numb in his arms.

Hugo suddenly remembered Váli and rushed to the closed van. He tore the door open and looked at the motionless Váli.

As he was about to open the cage, he was stopped by the pony-tailed guy, who put a hand on his shoulder.

"So, this is the answer to why you've had such a bad time," said the guy, hitting his giant sledgehammer against the cage.

Váli flinched and tried to look up at them, but then sank back with his head on the floor again.

"What are you doing?" Hugo hissed and tried to get around the guy, who stood in his way.

The other stranger peered into the darkness of the van.

"So, that's how it happened," said the guy with the combed hair, and pulled his face back again before turning to Hugo with a grim expression.

"We have to get out of here," he continued, and started to push Hugo away. "We're going to walk, so take only the essentials with you."

"I don't know who you are," said Hugo angrily, "but I'm not going anywhere without Váli."

He slapped the guy's hands away and stood with his arms crossed. The guy with the ponytail looked uncomfortable, and glared at him irritably.

"You don't know what he's done," said the ponytail, pointing angrily with his hand towards the van.

"Yes, we do," said Wille, who appeared next to Hugo.

Hugo turned around and saw Lovisa sitting in the car.

"He's has saved our lives several times in the last few days," Wille continued, crossing his arms. "He saved us from Garmr, and from my father and his soul eaters. If it wasn't for him, we wouldn't be here now."

The ponytail guy's eyes widened at the mention of Garmr and Wayland. The three red-haired youths stood a few steps away and watched them with interest.

"We can't take him with us, or that human for that matter," said the ponytail irritably.

Now it was Wille's turn to be upset.

"She's my girlfriend, and we're *not* leaving her or Váli," he snapped.

A bird landed on the red-haired boy's shoulder. The boy turned to the girl next to him, and whispered something.

"We don't have time to discuss this," the girl said in a firm voice. "The birds say there are several police cars coming this way, and the trees whisper that the wolves are nearby."

The girl looked scrutinizingly at Hugo and Wille before she turned to the ponytail again.

"They're all coming with us," she said firmly. "We'll take the cars to the cottage, where we, in peace and quiet, can discuss this further."

The ponytail guy looked like he was about to protest, but the other guy put a hand on his shoulder and shook his head.

Hugo opened the passenger seat of the black van. He was about to jump in when the little boy came up and asked if he could take a seat with him.

The guy with the combed hair got into the driver's seat and noted with satisfaction that the car keys were still there.

The ponytail guy jumped into the driver's seat of the hunting car, and Wille gave him the keys before jumping into the middle of the back seat, putting his arms around Lovisa.

The older red-haired guy and the red-haired girl also jumped into the hunting car, before both cars started pulling out of the forest road.

Just as they turned onto the highway, the top of the dirt hill behind them cracked. Nari's claw-like hand dug its way through the masses and then disappeared in a haze of darkness.

∽

"My powers are in your hands, Master!"

The small room was covered in shimmering darkness as Wayland let his claw-like hand wander over the pedestal with the black flame wrapped around his hand as he spoke.

A whispering sound was heard from within the flame as its dark light travelled like shadows across the stone walls.

"Master!"

Nari slowly entered and kneeled in front of Wayland while the black flame snaked its way back to the pedestal.

"You failed," Wayland hissed, taking his hand from the flame. "You know that I don't accept failures."

"The elves saved them," said Nari, not daring to look up. "The elves and that damned Thor's kids."

Wayland walked around him, stopped behind his back, and then kicked Nari to the floor.

"You had two days to find them before the others did," Wayland hissed, as he grabbed Nari by the neck and dragged him up the stone steps outside the room and into a large throne room.

At the far end of the hall, he pressed Nari's face against a portrait on the wall.

Nari closed his eyes to avoid seeing the disfigured creature staring back at him.

"I created you," Wayland whispered in his ear. "I enclosed your soul in that portrait and put your body back together again. I didn't give you your powers so that you would fail!"

Nari stared in horror at the grotesque creature. It did not look human, as it pushed the canvas out from the inside. The creature had a torn-up face, its head was hanging down from its shoulder, and it was missing several fingers.

"When you are no longer useful, I will burn the portrait and destroy you. Is that clear?!" Wayland exclaimed.

"Aren't you being too hard on him?" a voice was heard.

Wayland released Nari, and turned around angrily. In the entrance to the hall stood Hela, and watched them with a calm expression. The black staff in her hand shimmered purple as she stepped into the room.

"How did you get in here?" Wayland asked angrily.

Hela walked calmly towards him, and the coughing boy lay on the floor.

Then she looked at the grotesque figure in the portrait.

"Interesting how you use your magic," Hela said nonchalantly, running her hand over the frame of the portrait.

"Stay out of it," Wayland hissed. "Why are you here?"

Ignoring the man's anger, she reached down to Nari to help him up.

"His failure is your failure, too," she replied calmly.

Nari stared in horror at the woman's ghastly, yet beautiful, face as she pulled him up.

"Get out of here," Wayland hissed, looking like he was boiling with anger as he stared into her eye.

"Instead of being angry, you should think about how we can help each other," Hela said coldly, meeting his gaze.

"Your damn wolf tried to kill my son," he almost shouted. "I need him alive."

"For that old sword?" Hela exclaimed, laughing lightly. "You can't forget it, can you?"

She looked amused at the angry man.

"You can have the boy, I'm not interested in him anymore," Hela said softly, brushing a hand over his cheek.

Wayland hastily slapped her hand away but seemed to calm down.

Nari stood terrified and pressed himself against the wall, staring at the two rivals.

"What did you have in mind?" Wayland asked irritably.

"I don't know where you got your new powers," replied the deformed woman, and started walking towards the centre of the hall. "But I do know that we need each other to stop them before they reach the mountain."

Hela stopped and turned around again.

"Your puppy there has control over a large number of demon worshippers, right?" she asked, looking Wayland straight in the eye, who nodded grimly in response.

Nari stood frozen, not daring to utter a word.

"Good," Hela continued. "I will gather a large number of wolves from the Iron Woods. We will meet them at the bottom of the mountain and crush them before they have time to open the gate. Our combined forces will kill the godchildren."

"Very well," Wayland agreed, putting his hand to his chin. "But remember, the boy and his cross belong to me. I don't care what you do with the others, but restrain your wolf when it comes to my son."

The light from Hela's staff burst into purple flames, whereupon she was engulfed by the flames and disappeared.

Wayland turned to Nari, who stood pressed against the wall.

"Don't look so scared," the man snapped menacingly. "Gather the entire Legion, and get them ready to fight."

"The whole Legion? Are you sure, Master?" Nari asked.

"I thought I made it clear not to question me," replied Wayland, and grabbed his collar, whereupon Nari, terrified, found himself hanging over the stone floor.

"You gather the entire Legion, understand?! I will not lose to that hag!"

Nari swallowed hard and nodded.

Wayland let go of his shirt, and Nari hit the floor before getting up and ran away from there.

13. Children of The Gods

They continued driving in silence. Wille was still holding Lovisa, who had fallen asleep in his arms, and the red-haired guy looked at them curiously.

"Who are you?" Wille asked.

"I'm Nyri," the guy answered without meeting Wille's gaze and looked disinterestedly out the side window.

Wille examined the guy and noticed that he seemed thin. His grey pants were coarse and looked to be made of wool, whereas his light green lace-up shirt looked thinner and emphasised his red, shoulder-length hair.

"He's a little shy," said the red-haired girl sitting in the front seat, looking at them in the rearview mirror.

"Are you gods?" Wille asked, turning towards her.

"Yes, just like you," the girl replied, and turned around.

Lovisa turned in his arms and seemed to be fast asleep.

"My name is Tellervo, but you can call me 'Tella'," the girl said, holding out her hand.

Wille hesitated a bit before taking her hand and murmuring "Wille" while shaking her hand.

"I'm trying to learn the customs of the humans and have realised that many of you prefer to greet that way," Tella said, smiling at Wille.

"Nyri is my twin brother," she continued, pointing to the guy sitting next to him. "And the little guy who is travelling with your brother in the other car is our little brother, Tulio."

"And who are you?" Wille asked, turning to the ponytail guy driving the car.

"My name is Magni," the guy replied with a grunt, looking up in the rearview mirror.

Wille looked at him scrutinizingly and noticed that he had three deep scratches on his cheek.

The guy must have noticed Wille staring at his face because he turned the mirror at a different angle.

"I am the brother of Módi, the guy who drives the other car," Magni continued bluntly as he turned off the highway and onto a forest road.

Wille noticed how the other car behind them followed, and he wondered where they were really going.

"Who is your girlfriend?" Tella asked and looked at Lovisa, who was curled up in his arms.

"Lovisa," Wille replied, and was again on his guard.

He noticed how Magni was looking at them through the rearview mirror.

"Was it her father who was shot over there?" Tella asked, without caring about Magni.

Wille turned his face away. It hurt to think of Tommy. The memory of his body lying motionless on the ground made him remember his mother's death.

"He helped us get this far," he said. "Without him and Váli, we wouldn't have made it here."

Tella nodded and seemed to think for a moment.

"Does she have any other family nearby?" she asked.

Wille shook his head and thought about how Lovisa had lost both her father and her brother. He was all she had now, he thought, and hugged her while promising himself never to abandon her.

∽

"So, Módi, where are we going?" Hugo asked, looking at the guy with the short, bronze-coloured hair driving the car.

"There's an old fire lookout tower on a mountain further along this road," Módi replied without taking his eyes off the road. "We'll stop there tonight, so we can catch up and plan our next move."

"What is this?" Tulio asked, taking the ocarina out of Hugo's pocket.

The boy's eyes widened as he examined the instrument.

"Where did you get this?" he asked with a serious voice.

Hugo was surprised by the boy's seriousness.

"It was a gift," he calmly replied. "It was an old man who helped us a few days ago, and he asked me to take care of it."

"Do you know who the man was?" Tulio asked.

Hugo noticed that the boy's eyes were beginning to twinkle, he saw a deep longing in those brown eyes.

"He never told me his name," he replied, carefully taking the ocarina from the boy's hand. "But he had a silver-winged hawk with him and used a golden sword."

Módi stopped the car so sharply that both boys were thrown forward in their belts and turned to Hugo.

"What did you just say?" Módi asked, sounding eager. "Describe him briefly, please."

Hugo described the old man as well as he could remember and saw a smile spread across Módi's face, who closed his eyes and seemed relieved.

"He's back," whispered Tulio with tears in his eyes.

"It seems so," Módi said, and started driving again.

Hugo was waiting for an explanation from Tulio, but the younger boy became absent-minded, looking dreamy.

"Who is he?" Hugo asked, turning to Módi.

"His name is Lódurr," replied the elder god. "He is the Lord of the Elves and Tulio's grandfather."

Tulio's grandfather, Hugo thought, holding up the ocarina.

He thought of the old man with the silver-white beard and the friendly eyes and wondered if the man knew that Váli was going to teach him how to use the instrument.

They came to a turnaround, and Módi parked the van next to the chase car. Magni was unloading the pack, while Wille helped a shaken Lovisa out of the car.

Tulio jumped out and ran to Tella, who was talking to Nyri next to the other car.

The boy bounced eagerly to share what he had learned.

When Tella finally listened to what her little brother had to say, she quickly looked up at Hugo, who had started to open the back doors of the van.

"Váli," Hugo whispered as he opened the door to the cage.

Váli raised his head as best he could and looked up as Hugo crawled into the cage.

He began to pull the tape off Váli's nose, and the wolf let out yelps of whimpering in pain.

"I know it hurts, but we have to get the tape off," Hugo said, looking into his amber coloured eyes. "I'll try to be careful with your fur."

Tufts of wolf fur followed the tape, and Váli groaned, but eventually the tape was gone, and he opened and closed his mouth several times, as if to get rid of the pain.

"Does it hurt a lot?" Hugo asked, and gently put his hand behind one of Vali's ears.

"It will pass," Váli replied with a slight grimace. "Thank you for standing up for me before."

Hugo wrapped his arms around the wolf's neck.

"I told you I'm not leaving you," he said in a trembling voice. "It was lucky we didn't die over there."

"Surely none of the others..." Váli began.

"Tommy," Hugo replied, hugging him. "The demon shot him dead."

He noticed how Váli began to shake at the news.

"Hugo," came Wille's voice from the back door.

Hugo let go of Váli and turned to the door, where he noticed that every-one was watching them.

"If you step out, we'll free him from the chains," Módi said, taking out the silver axe.

Wille nodded to him, and with his eyes fixed on the axe, Hugo crawled out of the cargo hold.

"I promise that's all we'll do," Módi said calmly.

Hugo nodded but still felt unsure as he stood next to Wille, who looked at him inquiringly as Hugo used his arm to wipe his tearful face.

Módi let his axe slowly cut through the cage's bars to create a larger hole where Váli could get out.

Then he split the chains with three quick strokes.

"Argentum," Módi said when he noticed that Hugo and Wille were examining the silver axe. "The axe can cut through almost anything, except darkness."

"The axes seem to suit you," Wille said as he examined Módi's black leather vest and dark wool pants.

Módi laughed and wrapped his beige wool cloak around him as he folded the gold axe and silver axe into the larger, double-edged axe again.

"Don't worry, you'll get similar clothes when we get there," he said, giving Wille a wink.

Váli stood up slowly, and a rattling sound was heard as the chains fell off his legs. He carefully crawled out of the cage, and the others stepped back to give him room as he jumped to the ground on trembling legs.

"You owe an explanation," Magni said, crossing his arms.

Váli nodded and gently limped over to Hugo, who ruffled his fur.

❧

They took as much packing as they could manage, and began to walk along the steep path that led to the tower.

Hugo walked alongside Váli, who carefully limped along on his sore legs, and Wille gently led Lovisa up the slope.

She had not said anything since they left the village, and her eyes looked empty, which worried Wille.

Finally, they arrived at the top of the mountain where a red house loomed up before them. It wasn't big, but it had a tower that was built together at the side of the house.

Near the house there was a water well, and an information board that told them that they were six hundred and forty-four meters above sea level on a mountain called 'Pilkalampinoppi', and it was a mighty sight, Wille thought when he looked out over the vast forest below the mountain.

Magni opened the door to the house and started carrying in the luggage. Wille followed and looked around the small kitchen inside the door. There was a wood stove, a table with benches, and some cabinets. In the next room, there was a landing that seemed to lead up to the tower they had seen outside the house.

"Before we do anything else," Magni said, when they were outside again, "we should talk about what's going on."

"There are certain gaps in the story that need to be filled," he continued, and narrowed his eyes at Váli, who recoiled.

"I guess I'll start then," Váli sighed, and sat down on the ground so everyone could see him.

Nyri, Tella, Tulio, and Módi sat down on a bench. Wille and Lovisa sat on the front steps of the house, and Hugo sat on a stone next to Váli. Magni leaned against the wall of the house, and crossed his arms.

"I told you that my father turned me into a wolf, that I then killed my brother, and that the gods banished me," said Váli, turning to Wille, who nodded.

"But I didn't really tell you how it happened," the wolf continued, and began to tremble again.

Hugo stroked his fur encouragingly, and Váli took a deep breath before he continued.

"My father, Loki, is skilled at manipulating others. He can transform himself into just about anything, and anyone," Váli then said and shivered.

"Anything?" Wille asked in surprise.

"Yes, anything," Váli replied without taking his eyes off him. "And your father, Wille, was not the first of us to let the darkness into his heart."

"What do you mean?" asked Wille, looking at the wolf.

"My father likes to experiment," replied Váli. "He wanted to know if you could create something using the darkness, and he tried to create creatures by mixing darkness with the power of a giantess and elven magic."

Wille looked into his eyes and wondered where their friend was going with his story. Lovisa sat quietly next to him, and he hugged her.

"He created gigantic monsters with such dark magic that the gods had to trap them inside the earth and the sea so that they wouldn't destroy us and the rest of Middle-earth," Váli said, scratching one paw on the ground.

"What kind of monsters?" Hugo asked.

"Garmr, among others," Váli replied sadly.

"He created that beast?" Wille exclaimed in amazement.

"Yes," replied Váli, looking down at the ground again. "He was forbidden to continue his experiments, but was persuaded by a witch to experiment on her daughter."

The wolf shuddered, as if remembering something, and Hugo stood up and gently ran his hand through his fur.

"Loki poured a bottle of darkness into the girl's mouth and made her swallow it. The result was that half of her face rotted away," Váli continued, turning his gaze to the night sky, where the sun was setting over the horizon.

"The other gods saw the darkness growing inside the girl and banished her to the realm of the dead, where she would forever be forced to exist, unable to make it back to the world of the living and unable to move on to the World Spirit," he said without taking his eyes off the sky.

"Who is she?" Wille asked, feeling his anxiety rising.

"Her name is Hela," replied Váli, looking at Wille again. "She is the one who sent Garmr after you."

"Why?" asked Wille.

He was filled with rage, if that woman sent the beast after them, she was also responsible for their mother's death.

"We can answer that later," Magni broke in. "First, I want the wolf to tell his own story without slipping away."

"Anyway," Váli continued, ignoring Magni's threatening look. "After that, the gods confiscated all his experiments, and banished him from Asgard. My mother, however, asked the gods to have mercy on him, so after some time he was allowed to come back again."

"What nobody knew," Magni broke in again, and stood up, "was that the darkness had infected his already evil soul."

"He tricked our uncle into shooting a poisoned arrow through his brother's chest, and as punishment, the gods had Loki shackled inside a rock crevice with poisonous snakes," the god continued, crouching down so that he was sitting across from Váli.

"Before he was captured, he turned me into a wolf," Váli said without meeting Magni's gaze. "He disappeared, and in my eagerness to kill him, I began to follow his tracks. Finally, I found him, and attacked his throat."

Váli was shaking so badly that Hugo put his arm around his back in an attempt to calm him down.

"I was tricked," the wolf continued, tears now appearing on his face. "He had put a curse on Nari, so when I thought I was attacking my father, it was actually my brother's throat I was ripping out."

"You didn't listen when the rest of us told you to wait," Magni said, drawing his hand over the three scratches on his cheek. "It was your hatred, and the fact that it led to your brother's death, that caused you to be banished from Asgard."

"But I didn't know he would come back as a demon," said Váli sadly.

"It doesn't matter," Magni hissed. "I don't know what you thought you could accomplish by leading them there, but you won't be allowed back in, so you might as well leave us."

"If that's the way it's going to be, we're not going there either," Hugo said, glaring angrily at the elder god.

"You can't change this, no matter how much you want to," said Magni, crossing his arms. "They're not going to let him in, no matter how hard you try."

"I think they will," Tella interrupted, and walked up to them with Tulio close behind her.

"Show them the ocarina, Hugo," the boy said expectantly.

Hugo reached into his jacket pocket, and pulled out the strange wind instrument. He held it out to Magni, who was surprised when he received the object.

"What is this?" Magni asked, his eyes widening as he examined the shiny blue surface.

"It can't be," he whispered, turning the ocarina in his hand.

Nyri stood curiously beside them.

"Where did you get this?" Magni asked with an astonished expression, and turned to Hugo.

"It was a gift from a man who helped us a few days ago," Hugo replied confidently. "He helped us when Wille's father threatened me and Lovisa."

"You know what this means," Tella said triumphantly. "If he has authorised both the wolf and the girl to come with us, you and the others will have to let them in."

She took the ocarina from Magni and gave it back to Hugo.

"He took care of me after I was banished," Váli said in a shaky voice. "I've been following him ever since, helping him with various things. It was he who sent me to you that night when Garmr attacked."

"I suspected as much," said Wille, rising to his feet, standing next to the wolf and Hugo.

"As I said, we're not going anywhere without either Lovisa or Váli," Wille continued, and crossed his arms as a signal that this was final.

"Well, I give up," said Magni sourly, and threw up his hands. "But I won't take responsibility for what happens when we get to the gate."

He wrapped his brown wool cloak around him and went back into the house.

Tulio walked up to Váli, and wrapped his hands around the wolf's nose, while muttering something inaudible. The tape wounds were beginning to heal, and new fur was growing out again. He removed his hands and examined the nose for a moment.

"That's better, right?" Tulio asked in her bright voice.

"Thank you," Váli replied, wrinkling his nose as if to feel that the wounds were really gone.

"How old are you really?" Wille asked, looking at Tella, who seemed surprised by the question.

"That's tricky to answer," Tella replied, running her hand through her braided hair. "But with your way of thinking about age, Nyri and I are sixteen, and Tulio is twelve."

"Let's go get some wood," she said quickly, pulling Nyri from the bench, before heading into the surrounding forest.

Módi went into the house to talk to Magni, and the others sat down at the bench outside. Wille picked up Lovisa, who had not moved during the entire conversation.

"Look," said Tulio, pointing to the starry sky.

Wille looked up in the direction the boy was pointing and saw a beautiful meteor shower moving through the dark space. Váli lay down so that he had his head in the arms of Hugo, who gently scratched him behind the ear. All five admired the spectacle that went on for a long time.

Wille saw that even Lovisa smiled faintly, which pleased him. He sincerely hoped that she could get over the terrible events of the last few days.

❧

Lovisa felt empty inside, as if she was just an empty shell. The grief after her father's death was like a hole in her chest, and nothing felt real. She glanced cautiously at Wille, who smiled at her. He was all she had left now, she realised, and looked down at the ground.

Wille gently put his arm around her, and she laid her head on his shoulder.

The warmth he radiated brought tears to her eyes, and despite everything that had happened, she still felt safe with him. Perhaps he could fill some of the void in her heart.

14. The Military Force

Amanda Svedin had just sat down on the sofa with a cup of steaming tea in front of her.

In the armchair next to her, Jörgen, her husband, was sipping from his whisky glass.

It was Friday afternoon, and they were looking forward to a peaceful weekend after the troubled week.

"Have you heard anything more about the kids?" Jörgen asked after a while as he flicked on the TV.

She looked at him and shook her head in response.

"I'm worried about them," she said, sinking into the back of the sofa. "The police told me that I shouldn't talk to anyone, but I can't do it."

"But it's still odd that the police haven't contacted you," said Jörgen, and putting down his glass. "You haven't even been able to give a proper statement yet."

The front doorbell rang, and Amanda headed for the hall.

"Who is it?" called Jörgen when she didn't come back.

There was no answer from the hallway, but he could hear voices talking intensely.

After a while, a man in military uniform appeared in the living room, with Amanda close behind him.

Jörgen stood up, but the man motioned for him to sit.

"My name is Kenneth," the man said, sitting down on a chair. "I am sorry to disturb you, but I must ask you to pack the essentials and come with me."

Jörgen looked as if he had been punched in the stomach.

"Why is that?" he asked in a worried voice, and looked at Amanda, whose face had faded.

"I can't go into details here, but your lives are in danger, and you will be evacuated," Kenneth replied, pulling out a document. "This is a matter of national security."

"Evacuated?!" Jörgen exclaimed in horror. "Why?"

"As I said, your lives are in danger," Kenneth repeated.

Jörgen looked at Amanda again, who nodded, while Kenneth got up and walked past her into the hall.

"Pack the most important things and come out to the courtyard," he said, before he left the house again.

"What's going on?" Jörgen asked in exasperation as Amanda sat down on the couch again.

Her face was pale, and she was slow to answer.

"Jörgen," she finally replied. "There were no real police officers who came to my office the day before yesterday."

He stared at her uncomprehendingly.

"These fake cops, they're good at eliminating their tracks," she continued in a trembling voice. "I'm not expected to come to the police station and give any witness statements, because I'm not expected to survive the weekend."

Jörgen looked at her as if she had gone mad.

"What's going on?" came a voice from the kitchen.

Jessica, their twenty-two-year-old daughter, stuck her head into the room and let her eyes wonder from her father, who was leaning on the edge of the couch, to her mother, who stood worriedly nearby.

"I'll help her," Amanda said. "You start packing."

Jörgen could hear his daughter's agitated voice from inside the kitchen and thought the whole situation seemed surreal. He looked around, wondering where to start, before his eyes settled on the bookshelf, where he kept books and photos from his many travels.

It took an hour to pack, and Kenneth came in several times to hurry them up as well as to support the process.

When they finished, they had filled several bags, and once out in the courtyard, they were greeted by a surprising sight.

The highway around them was full of soldiers and military vehicles.

Several neighbours were talking to the military and seemed concerned.

The bags packed by the family were taken out of the house and loaded into a vehicle.

Kenneth stood a short distance away, and waved to them.

He was wearing a dark blue camouflage suit, clearly distinguishing himself from the rest of the green-clad soldiers in the courtyard.

All three walked towards him, but stopped when he held out his hand as a sign for them to stop, while a deafening clatter was heard, and the wind picked up around them.

Jörgen looked up at the dark sky and saw a large, dark-coloured, helicopter with two mounted machine guns hovering above them.

The helicopter landed about ten metres from them without turning off the engines. Kenneth crouched down and made his way towards the family, with one of his arms to protect his face.

"Follow me," he shouted, waving to them to run towards the helicopter.

They ran crouching towards the helicopter, where a soldier pulled them into the cabin one by one. The sound of the propellers made it impossible to hear what any of them were saying, but Jörgen managed to get Jessica to sit in the middle before he himself sat down next to her.

Amanda sat down on the other side of Jessica, and the military man who had received them sat on their opposite.

Finally, Kenneth came in and handed out helmets with earmuffs to them. While they were putting on the helmets, he signalled for them to press a button on a button on the side of the helmet, before he himself sat down on the last seat.

The headphones on Jörgen's helmet were crackling, and he could hear Kenneth's voice clearly and distinctly. He noticed that a small microphone could be folded out from them helmet next to his chin, that was barely bigger than a thumb.

"Can you hear me?" Kenneth asked, and everyone answered yes.

"Good," he said, signalling for the pilot to take off.

The helicopter shook, and Jörgen grabbed Jessica's hand and squeezed it hard.

"Afraid of heights?" Kenneth asked.

Jörgen nodded silently in response, and Amanda leaned over and put her hand on his knee.

"I promise we'll drive as quietly as we can, but we're in a bit of a hurry, so we'll have to transport you by helicopter," Kenneth continued in an understanding tone.

"What's going on?" Jörgen asked. "Where are we going?"

"I can't tell you where we are going," replied Kenneth. "And I think we wait with explanations until we are there."

They flew at low altitude for several hours, and Jörgen realised that they were heading north. He saw several villages and towns, and from time to time, he noticed several military vehicles driving along the roads. Jessica had fallen asleep on his shoulder, and he himself felt sleepy.

"How far is it?" he asked, looking at Kenneth.

"About an hour," came the voice of the pilot, who was apparently also connected to the common sound system.

Jörgen glanced at Amanda, whose face was turned towards the horizon outside the window, where the last rays of the sun were slowly fading away. He realised that she was worried about the kids, because she was always worrying more for others than for herself.

Jörgen smiled inwardly, and thought about how mentally strong his wife actually was. He himself felt helpless about the situation they were in. He looked at Jessica, who still had her eyes closed where she was lying against his arm, and put his other arm around her in a hug as he closed his eyes.

❧

Amanda Svedin stared into the eyes of Kenneth, who sat opposite her in the small conference room. Jörgen and Jessica sat on either side of her and listened intently to what the officer was saying.

"Is this supposed to be a joke?!" Amanda exclaimed, rising angrily from the table. "You're dragging us off on a Friday night to a military base, God knows where we are, because you say our lives are in danger. Then we get to live in rooms with rock-hard beds, with no dinner. And now you're telling us stories about gods and demons?!"

"Please sit down," said Kenneth, trying to calm them down. "I can assure you that everything I have said is true."

"You can't expect us to believe all this," Jörgen said from his chair. "I demand that you take us home again."

There was a light knock on the door, and a man with a long silver-white beard and flowing clothes entered.

"I'll take it from here," the man said, closing the door.

Kenneth raised one eyebrow before nodding.

"Who are you?" Jörgen asked, eyeing the man's strange woollen clothing. "Is this supposed to be a masquerade?"

"For a religious scholar, you are very sceptical, my friend," the man replied, and sat down in a chair.

"You know who I am?" Jörgen asked in surprise.

The man laughed while sipping from a glass of water.

"Of course," he replied, taking a sip. "Your name is Jörgen Svedin, you're a religious scholar and explorer who has travelled around different countries, where you have collected stories and artefacts that stem from ancient cultures and mythologies. Your work has been rewarded with several awards over the years, and you have held several well-paid jobs. Right now, you are without commissions and you spend your days cataloguing your notes and writings."

Jörgen sank back into his chair in amazement.

Amanda opened her eyes wide, and Jessica still seemed to think she was dreaming.

"So, who are you?" Jörgen asked with greater enthusiasm.

The man took out a strange stringed instrument from an inner pocket and gave it to Jörgen, who accepted it. He examined the strange instrument and, after a while, became more and more excited about what he saw.

"You can tell me who I am," the man said, and watched with amusement as Jörgen took out a magnifying glass from his pocket to examine the inscriptions on the object.

"What is it?" Jessica asked, leaning forward.

Jörgen's expression changed from eagerness to pallor, and then back again, faster than a traffic light.

"This object, it can't be right!" he finally exclaimed, and looked up at the man again.

"If I didn't know better, I'd say it came from Finland, specifically from the Finnish mythology of Kalevala. I have only seen vague sketches of it before," Jörgen continued with fascination as he handed the instrument to the man again.

"You really are as skilled as they say," said the man, putting the instrument away again.

Amanda hesitantly sat down again.

"But that doesn't explain who you are," she said, clasping her hands together. "Or what's happening."

"Do you believe in magic, Amanda?" the old man asked, turning towards her.

She stared into the man's sharp, but kind, eyes and suddenly felt a calmness spread through her body.

Kenneth cleared the table, and the old man placed his hand on the bare surface.

A shimmer of different colours appeared on the table, which made all three members of the family jump in fright.

"In Finland, they call me "Väinö"," the man said with a smile. "But I prefer my original name, Lódurr."

"Lódurr," said Jörgen, looking at the old man in shock. "One of the creators of Norse mythology?"

The man nodded towards him.

"Do you know more about me?" Lódurr asked curiously.

"Not much is known about you," said Jörgen, reaching for his bearded chin. "Apart from the creation myth, you don't appear in any known writings at all."

"It doesn't surprise me that you haven't found much about me, I'm known by many names in the world," said Lódurr.

The shimmer on the table changed in character, and they saw a picture of a forest seen from above. The picture kept moving, and several houses suddenly appeared.

Amanda immediately recognised Wille's and Hugo's house, as the image slowed down above it.

"What you see are memories of my hawk," said Lódurr as the image landed among the trees. "I'm going to show you what actually happened in the last few days, but I must warn you that there will be a lot of unpleasant images."

Kenneth sat down at the table again, and everyone's eyes were fixed on the picture.

They watched the boys leave the house, and the hawk seemed to follow them.

Then the picture changed, and the hawk was in the old theatre.

Amanda gasped when she saw Liam baring his sharp fangs before sending the boys flying across the room. Then Ida was seen to parry the floating ball lightning and send it back towards Liam.

"So, that's what happened," Amanda whispered, squeezing Jörgen's hand.

The images continued to flash by. Jessica screamed as the giant wolf appeared, and darkness swallowed half the wall of the boys' house before the wolf laboriously crawled inside.

Screams were heard from the house before another wolf appeared and pulled the big beast out of the house again.

The big wolf attacked the smaller wolf, while the boys' mother climbed out of the house.

"What kind of a wolf is that?" Jörgen asked, staring at the picture. "It's huge!"

"Garmr," Lódurr replied without taking his eyes off the image. "The Hellwolf."

Just then, Jessica screamed and buried her face in her hands, while Amanda wrapped her arms around her. They had come to the events in the clearing, where Wille put his arms around his dead mother and cried out his anguish.

"Ida, it can't be true," said Amanda, with tears in her eyes.

Jörgen, whose face was pale, squeezed her hand.

"Garmr, the dog tied to the gates of hell," Jörgen murmured, and watched as the two wolves tossed each other around on the ground.

"Not quite," said Lódurr, turning to him.

"What do you mean?" Jörgen asked.

Kenneth went over, and refilled the old man's water glass, and Lódurr gratefully took a sip, before replying with a counter question.

"Have you heard of the Fenris wolf?"

Jörgen hastily looked down at the beast that just disappeared, and the image was replaced with Tommy and the children loading the car.

"The Fenris wolf, the gigantic wolf that was so big that no chain could hold him," said Jörgen, scratching his thinning head. "Not until the dwarves forged a magical rope from which he could not escape, and in revenge, he bit off the hand of the god Tyr."

"Exactly, but it wasn't a rope in the sense you're thinking. We reduced the beast to about a fifth of its size," Lódurr continued. "Then we chained it in the realm of the dead."

"So, you mean that that monster is actually even bigger?!" exclaimed Jörgen, raising his eyebrows.

Lódurr nodded and returned to the slideshow on the table, which now showed Garmr trying to push the car off the road.

They continued watching for a while, and saw the party camped by the lake, and then the battle with the soul eaters.

Amanda and Jessica sat quietly, just staring at the events unfolding before their eyes.

"Who is he?" Jörgen asked, pointing to the man with long, raven-black hair. "Why is he saying that he is Wille's father?"

"His name is Wayland," Lódurr replied with a deep sigh. "He captured Wille's mother at one point, and raped her."

"Wayland, the blacksmith?" Jörgen asked, puzzled.

Lódurr nodded slowly, and watched the scene as they left the forge after the battle.

"I've seen enough," Amanda said fiercely, waving her hand. "Turn off this at once!"

The old man waved his hand, and the images disappeared.

It was a knock on the door, and a man in a dark uniform entered with a silver-winged hawk on his arm.

"Hábrók!" exclaimed Lódurr, and the hawk immediately flew and perched on his shoulder.

He gave the hawk a biscuit, which it quickly gobbled up.

Kenneth walked over and said a few words to the man who had just come in.

The man nodded before saluting and left the room.

"Demons have infiltrated the police, as well as several other institutions in Sweden, Norway, and Finland," Kenneth said before sitting down again.

"If you hadn't gone to the house, you would have been safe, but because they had not secured the traces of the children and do not want witnesses that could risk exposing them, there was a chance that they would have eliminated you and your family," he continued, meeting Amanda's gaze.

"But who are you?" Jörgen asked, sweeping his hand meaningfully around the room. "How is it that you in the military know about this?"

"We are a secret unit within the military intelligence and security service," replied Kenneth, clasping his hands together. "We don't exist officially, and only a handful of people in the government know about us, and even fewer know what we do."

"They work for me," Lódurr broke in. "I have walked among the humans for a long time, but some time ago I noticed that demons began to take over more and more of society. I realised that I had to try to organise a resistance force before the demons got too strong."

Kenneth nodded in agreement. "Lódurr is our contact with the gods, and leads us in our organisation. I act as commander and his right-hand man."

"Where are the children?" Amanda asked excitedly.

She still hadn't let go of Jessica, who now lay with her head in her arms.

"Heading north," Lódurr replied, and a flickering map appeared before them on the table. "They need to get to Flatruet near the Norwegian border, where they can open the gate to Asgard and get to safety."

"Are they okay?" Jörgen asked, leaning forward.

A red dot appeared on the map.

"The children are fine," said Lódurr, examining the dot. "Several of our own children have reached them and are following them the rest of the way. Unfortunately, they lost Tommy yesterday."

"What do you mean?" Jörgen asked, shaking.

The hawk made strange sounds, and Lódurr sighed.

"He was shot trying to protect the children from the police infiltrators, and they shot him dead," he replied, leaning over to Amanda, who had a blank look in her eyes.

"I know this is a lot to take in all at once, but do you know whether Tommy had a plan when he drove them up north?" Lódurr asked Amanda, who was staring at the map.

"He has relatives in a village nearby," said Amanda, pointing to a village not far from the dot.

Lódurr nodded, and the hawk flew out the door before the old man stood up.

"Kenneth," he said, turning around. "Make sure all three of them are as comfortable as possible and properly fed. We'll talk more tomorrow."

15. The Moon God

Wille admired the mighty northern lights.

Tella and Nyri had returned with the firewood, and everyone had gathered to admire the beautiful spectacle that unfolded across the night sky, to the sound of Hugo's ocarina.

Magni had made a crackling fire that warmed the chilly night air, and when they all stood around the fire, Váli had suggested that Hugo should continue practicing his magic.

As Hugo played, the light of the northern lights danced across the sky with the music and Váli's howling, and a warm wind swept down on them.

Wille felt how the wind lifted his hair, and he quickly looked at Lovisa, who sat curled up next to him. Her eyes were still haunted by an emptiness that he couldn't fill. The wind caressed her hair, and a tear ran down her cheek.

The forest around them seemed to be full of life, and Wille saw small balls of light in different colours that seemed to float in there.

One of the balls of light was floating towards them. It flashed in a blue colour as it approached Wille, and was only a couple of decimetres away from him when he gently reached out his hand to the ball of light, which stopped and seemed to hesitate, as if it would dare not approach him.

Wille gently pulled the little light towards him and stared in amazement at a small, smiling, human-like face.

The creature lifted itself from the palm of his hand and floated on to Lovisa, who wiped the tears from her face and watched in amazement as the creature landed on her knee.

A light blue glow surrounded Lovisa like an aura, and Wille noticed with amazement that she was actually smiling and almost laughing.

"Thank you," she said as she hugged him.

Wille did not really understand what was happening, but noticed that the light blue shine now enveloped both of them.

The bright ball floated on and landed on Tulio's head.

The little boy looked up and laughed delightedly as a blue glow swept over him.

"Wille," a voice suddenly appeared in his head.

Wille flinched without letting go of Lovisa.

"Who are you?" he heard himself think.

He looked around at the others, but they still seemed to be entranced by Hugo's magical music. Then Tella slowly turned her head and nodded at him.

"How can you be in my head?" Wille thought.

"Telepathy," replied Tella's voice in his head. "All elves can communicate that way."

"Even me?" Wille thought in surprise as he noticed that Lovisa had fallen asleep in his arms.

"Your father was once one of us," Tella replied. "You have Elvish blood in you, and so you can do what we can do."

"What happened to Lovisa?" Wille asked.

Tella turned to the northern lights again, and ran her hand through her curly hair.

"Fairies," he heard her answer with her mouth this time. "They are secret guardians of the forest, and have magical powers. They can heal almost all wounds, even soul ones."

"Soul wounds," muttered Wille, looking at Lovisa.

"She's been through a lot," Tella said without taking her eyes off him. "She is traumatised by everything that has happened. The fairy helped her to heal some of the grief by focusing her mind on the happy memories instead of the grief, but it will take time for her to be herself."

Hugo stopped playing and opened his eyes. Váli had long since stopped howling, and looked at him in amazement.

"You're getting good at this," the wolf said, smiling.

Magni smiled too, something Wille had not seen him do since they met. He watched as the older guy went to put out the fire.

"I think that's enough for today," Magni said, looking at them. "We need to sleep, and tomorrow we leave again."

Módi picked up Lovisa in his arms. They are really strong, Wille thought as they entered the house.

Magni and Módi had prepared sleeping places for them downstairs. Módi gently laid Lovisa down on a couple of mattresses in the kitchen, before he took out some blankets and gave them to Wille, who gratefully accepted them.

Hugo and Váli joined them in the kitchen, and Módi went out again before Tella, Nyri, and Tulio entered the house.

"We sleep in the tower," Tella said, as her brothers made their way up the stairs. "Magni and Módi are sleeping in tents outside, so you can sleep safely tonight."

"Thank you," said Wille, spreading a blanket over Lovisa.

Tella smiled at him before making her way up the stairs.

Váli settled down by the front door, and Wille noticed that Hugo settled down next to the wolf. He spread a blanket over both of them, and smiled at his brother, who closed his eyes with his face peacefully buried in the wolf's fur.

Váli seemed to have already fallen asleep, letting out a rustling breath.

Before Wille crawled down next to Lovisa, he noticed a faint glow outside the window. The little fairy that had come to them earlier pressed itself against the window pane and seemed to want to come in.

Wille hesitated for a moment but opened the window and let the creature in, and the fairy started floating around the room.

The last thing Wille saw before he put his arm around Lovisa and closed his eyes was how the little fairy floated above them and how a silver-blue dust seemed to fall on all four friends who were huddled together on the floor.

∾

Wille fell through the strange light. His descent slowed, and he began to float in the strange light before feeling an invisible floor under his feet.

Silver-blue dust danced around him when a man with long, dark hair stepped out of the light.

The man smiled kindly, and Wille relaxed when he realised that it was not his father standing in front of him, even though they looked eerily similar.

The man was dressed in a shimmering blue fur jacket with a silver fur trim hood and dark wool pants. The coarse, black hair flowed down past his shoulders, and Wille thought he looked quite young despite the dark beard stubble.

"You've grown up since I last saw you," the man said, giving him a friendly smile.

Wille didn't know how to respond when the man gave an amusing laugh and put a hand on his shoulder.

"Who are you?" Wille asked nervously.

"I am Máni, the god of the moon," the man replied, and ran his hand across Wille's forehead.

"Are you Váli's grandfather?" Wille asked in amazement.

"And your grandfather too," replied Máni, laughing.

"My grandfather," said Wille. "How is that possible?"

"Your father and Váli's mother are half-siblings," Máni replied as he withdrew his hand and scrutinised Wille's reaction. "You and Váli are cousins."

"Does Váli know about this?" Wille asked in amazement.

"I'm sorry I didn't tell you," came a voice from behind Wille, which made him jump.

The dark-haired guy standing behind him seemed to be a bit taller than Hugo and dressed in similar clothes as Máni. He seemed the same age as Wille, with a slim but fit look, and Wille sensed a boldness in his eyes.

"Váli?" Wille asked uncertainly, and the guy nodded in response while he laughed.

"We will let one more into the room," said Máni, whereupon Hugo appeared next to Wille, looking confused.

"Wille, where are we?" Hugo asked before his gaze was fixed on Váli, who was looking amused at him.

Hugo seemed to hesitate for a moment before he ran up to Váli, who laughed as Hugo wrapped his arms around him.

"That took a while," Váli laughed.

Wille saw that Hugo's eyes were tearful.

"Hi cousin," Váli said, as he let go of Hugo to give Wille a hug as well.

"Cousin?" Hugo asked, suddenly looking ashamed.

Wille and Váli looked at each other before both of them burst into laughter. Wille told Hugo what he had just learned, and Hugo looked a little more relieved.

"What's this?" Váli asked, looking amused at Hugo's reaction. "Don't you want to be my cousin too?"

"I…well, I mean…no, it's not like that," Hugo stammered. "I do like you, but…"

He didn't seem to get the words out properly.

"It's okay," Váli laughed, and hugged Hugo again. "I'm just joking with you."

Wille couldn't help but laugh as Váli pulled Hugo to him in what at first seemed to be a hug, and then rubbed Hugo's head with his clenched hand while Hugo tried to tear himself away from Váli's grip.

"Now that all three of you are here," Máni interrupted them, "we need to talk about what's going on around you."

The moon god had stood behind them, watching their greetings with an amused smile.

"What do you mean?" Wille asked, turning to the man again. "Do you know more about what's going on?"

The moon god nodded again.

"I am not allowed to physically intervene in your world, but in this room we can communicate freely," he replied, flapping his arms in the silver-blue haze.

"What do you mean you can't interfere?" Hugo asked, trying to wrestle Váli to the ground.

"I belong to the race of the giants," Máni replied. "A long time ago, we lived in harmony with the other gods, until the darkness began to spread through the worlds."

He now had the attention of all three boys.

"Wayland forged eight magic rings to bind the darkness. After that, the rings were divided among the races of gods, which angered Wayland because he felt entitled to get them back," Máni continued gloomily.

"What happened?" Wille asked.

"Wayland had previously forged a magical sword, which would destroy the darkness when it was bound to the rings. But his hatred took over, and he began to fill the sword with dark magic," Máni replied with a deep sigh. "With the sword, the darkness was freed from the rings and corrupted the races of the gods to fight among themselves. In the war that followed, many of us were killed, and we giants who survived had our magic limited so that we would not be able to influence too much in the human world."

"What can you do then?" asked Hugo.

"I watch over the night and the human dreams. And through the dreams, I try to guide them," replied Máni.

"But now for more important things," he continued, his voice taking on a steely tone as he narrowed his eyes at Wille. "Do you know why you are being hunted?"

"No," Wille replied thoughtfully. "I know that dad wants me for something, but I don't know what for. And then there's that woman Váli told me about who sent Garmr. Are she and my father working together?"

Máni shook his head at his question.

"Your father needs you to get the sword," the moon god replied. "When the gods defeated Wayland, they hid the sword, and sealed it with a magic that can only be broken when light and darkness intertwine. The sword's own magic is bound to Wayland by blood, meaning only he or his descendant can use it."

Wille flinched when he heard this, and understood why his father so desperately pursued him. Wayland's blood flowed in his veins, but also his mother's blood. He was indeed the only one who could free the sword.

"The woman you are talking about, Hela, is after you for other reasons," Máni continued. "She has gathered several outcast gods around her and plans to use the rings to rule the darkness and the world. Therefore, she cannot allow you to seize the sword and destroy the darkness."

"Where are the rings?" Váli asked excitedly.

"The Aesir have one of them, I think," Máni replied, running his fingers through his beard. "I think Hela's group has come across the other rings, but it's unclear because no one knows where they went after the war."

The three boys looked hesitantly at each other.

"Grandfather, Nari has become…" Váli started to say, but Máni cut him off abruptly.

"I know," he said, looking sad again. "After you were banished, your brother's body disappeared under mysterious circumstances. No one knows who or who took it, let alone how they managed to smuggle it out of Asgard."

"Asgard?" Hugo asked, looking at Váli. "What is that?

"Asgard is the abode of the gods, our home," replied Váli. "I was going to tell you about it, but so many other things have happened."

"How do we fight the demons?" Wille interrupted without taking his eyes off the moon god. "So far, it feels like we've been mostly lucky when we've confronted them."

"I'm glad you asked that," Máni replied, turning to him again. "As you've noticed, there are different types of demons, their powers depending on what kind of gods they were before they were swallowed by darkness. What is common to all demons is that they can only be killed by turning their own magic against themselves, by using strong magic against them, or with various magical weapons."

Wille thought about it. Liam had been killed by his own lightning, and the demon who had tried to kill Hugo in his dream had fallen over the bridge, down onto the sharp rocks of the thundering waterfall. If what the demon had said was true, that you died for real if you died in your dream, then the demon would technically have died by its own magic.

"Wait a minute, how did we manage to kill the soul eaters?" Hugo asked and turned to Wille. "The only thing we did to them was to stab them with Tommy's hunting knife."

"Do you still have the knife?" Máni asked.

"Yes," replied Wille, looking as puzzled as Hugo. "After the battle against Nari and the demon worshippers, I took the knife from Tommy's holster. I thought Lovisa might want it when she feels better."

"Good," said Máni. "When you wake up, you can show it to Váli and see if he sees anything strange about it."

"But grandfather," Váli said, and now it was his turn to look confused. "Módi and Magni cut off Nari's head with their weapons, yet he survived and put his head back again."

Máni's gaze now took on a dark hue in his otherwise crystal blue eyes, and for a moment, Wille could sense that his grandfather didn't want to tell them everything.

"As I said, no one knows what happened to your brother after you killed him, but whatever he is now, he is no ordinary demon. There are stronger forces at work than you can imagine," Máni said, putting his hand to his chin, as if he were wondering how much he should tell them.

"Does it have anything to do with the dragons?" Váli asked cautiously.

Máni's eyes widened, obviously surprised by his question.

"Where did you hear that somewhere?" the moon god exclaimed sharply.

"When Nari caught me, he whispered that the dragons had awakened," Váli replied.

Máni sighed, and threw up his hands.

"It's just as well that I'm telling you, even if the others probably will punish me," he said in a complaining tone.

"The dragons were the first creatures to be created by the World Spirit. They were created to serve him, and fed on the eternal magic of the tree. But then some of them rebelled, and tried to take over the creation," Máni said without taking his eyes off Váli. "They were trapped deep beneath the roots of the World Tree, where they had to feed on what little magic was left over from the creation."

"The roots of the World Tree," Wille said, looking at Váli. "Didn't you say that my father went there to create the sword?"

Váli nodded thoughtfully.

"That's what I've been told anyway," he replied, looking questioningly at his grandfather.

"The road to the dragons is sealed from the other worlds," Máni said, running his fingers through his moustache again. "But somehow Wayland found his way there. I suspect that the rings he created to bind the darkness were created with the help of the dragons."

"What does that mean?" Hugo asked, standing silently for a moment and listening to the conversation.

"It means that the magic of the dragons is intertwined with the rings," replied Máni, suddenly looking around.

The silver-blue light around them began to fade, and Máni scratched his head.

"I think that's enough for tonight," he said, looking at them. "The sun will be up soon, and you need to wake up."

"Can't you turn Váli back into himself again?" Hugo asked hopefully.

Máni shook his head.

"They won't allow me to intervene," he replied, looking at Váli. "But there is a way for you to break the curse yourself."

"How?" Váli asked eagerly.

"That is something you must discover for yourself," replied Máni, smiling at his grandson. "If you prove that you are a true god, you will get your body back."

"How do I do that?" Váli asked, as the void they were in faded away.

"The answer to that is within your heart," the moon god replied before the last contours of the room disappeared.

"Follow your hearts!" the moon god's voice was heard one last time before the dream ended.

16. The Wolf Cross

Hugo flinched when Wille shook him.

"How do you feel?" Wille asked worriedly when he saw his little brother's pale face.

"Fine," Hugo replied dully, and leaned against the wall.

Wille put a blanket behind his head and handed him a cup of water.

"Take it easy it will soon pass," said Váli, who was sitting in the corner of the kitchen, watching them.

"What happened?" Hugo asked sleepily.

"You didn't really want to wake up after our dream together," replied Wille, and turned questioningly to Váli.

"That is probably because only those who share blood ties with the moon god master inner soul journeys," said Váli. "The fact that you were invited should be considered an honour, since he probably sees you as family."

Hugo looked at his friend, who was now wearing his wolf skin again, and nodded before drinking the water.

"So, you had a bit of an adventure last night," Módi said, leaning against the kitchen wall. "Do you want to share with the rest of us what was said?"

Wille told them everything the moon god had revealed. When he told them about the dragons, Tella flinched.

"It's worse than we thought," she said, glancing around the room. "What do we do now?"

"We stick to the plan," replied Magni, who had been sitting on the stairs with Nyri and Tulio.

The older guy walked up to the kitchen.

"You have relatives in a nearby village, right?" he asked, looking at Lovisa, who was curled up in Wille's arms.

She nodded in response, not wanting to meet his gaze.

"Do you think they will accept us?" Magni asked.

Lovisa seemed to think for a moment.

"Yes, I think so," she replied. "My uncle and his family live there. They are friendly, and will probably welcome us with open arms."

"Good," said Magni. "We'll leave the cars here and take only the most necessary of the packing. Módi and I will take care of the packing if you clean up and cook breakfast."

Magni and Módi went out to check the pack, while Nyri and Tella went to light a fire. Tulio remained inside the cabin, and watched as Wille, Lovisa, and Hugo started to put away the mattresses.

"Hugo, would you come out for a while?" the boy asked. "There is something that Váli and I want to show you."

Hugo looked in surprise at Tulio and Váli, who stood expectantly at the door, and followed them out of the cottage.

Wille stayed inside with Lovisa, which he thought was nice since they hadn't had much time for themselves.

"How are you feeling?" Wille asked and met Lovisa's gaze. It was not as empty as it had been yesterday, but he could still sense that she was carrying a great sadness inside her.

"I don't know," she replied as she folded a blanket. "I feel empty. I've lost my brother and my father, and I don't know what I have left anymore."

"You have me," Wille said, and gave her a hug. "I love you and will always be here, I promise."

A light blue light shone down upon them as they held each other, and Wille saw the fairy he had let in the night before hovering around them.

They let go of each other and watched the little creature, which made a whistling sound before landing on the kitchen table.

Wille took Tommy's hunting knife out of his bag.

"I thought you might want this," he said, handing the knife to Lovisa, who had difficulty holding back her tears.

Carefully, she clasped her hands around the sharp edge with the white, ornate handle.

"Thank you," she said, and Wille saw in her eyes how much it meant to her.

Wille suddenly remembered what his grandfather had said and tried to memorise the image of the knife in his head before sending the thought to Váli, hoping it would work. If he had elvish blood in him, perhaps Váli had it too.

"Interesting," he heard Váli's voice in his head.

"What is it?" Wille asked, sending the thought away.

"The handle of the knife appears to be made of reindeer horn," Váli replied. "And the way the steel is shaped...I would think that's a shamanic ceremonial knife."

"What does that mean?" asked Wille, confused.

"Shamanism is a form of spiritual magic practiced by the Vanir, our relatives in the north. That explains how you were able to kill the soul eaters," Váli replied.

"Okay, where did you go anyway?" Wille asked.

"We're behind the cabin," Váli replied. "Tulio is teaching Hugo to channel the magic of the forest using the ocarina."

"Is it going well?" Wille asked curiously.

"Come out and see for yourselves," Váli replied happily.

Wille and Lovisa put on their outerwear, and opened the front door. The sun had risen and warmed the morning air.

As they walked around the cottage, they could hear the sound of the ocarina, although it was different from last night. Then the notes had been in a slow, beautiful melody, but now the music was fast, and Wille almost felt like dancing.

Another sound was heard in addition to the notes from the ocarina, like someone else playing music at the same time as Hugo. Lovisa took hold of Wille's arm and pointed a bit into the forest. He had difficulty grasping the sight that met them when they walked up to the place she had pointed to.

Hugo was sitting on a stump in a small clearing, playing the ocarina, while the snow melted on the ground around him, and was replaced by grass and flowers.

The leaves of the trees were burst out, and birds were chirping around them. But that was not the strangest part of the macabre scene. Plenty of animals had gathered in the clearing – Wille could see bears, squirrels, birds, deer, and a wolf that had settled down in the grass.

Then the second sound was heard again, and behind the stump, Váli stepped forward, with Tulio sitting on his back.

The boy also seemed to be playing an instrument, but unlike Hugo's ocarina, Tulio's instrument was a stringed instrument.

Wille held on tight to Lovisa as they nervously walked through the herd of animals, who did not seem to take any notice of them. As they passed the wolves, they began to howl, and Lovisa ran the last bit towards the stump.

One of the bears stood up, and Wille didn't dare go past.

"It's all right," said Tulio, brushing his boyish bangs aside. "They are my friends and are completely harmless."

Wille did not feel completely satisfied with his assurance but still moved carefully towards the stump, where he almost threw himself into the arms of Lovisa.

Hugo continued to play, and the animals seemed to be almost in a trance from the clear notes from the ocarina.

"Do you play an instrument too?" Wille asked, pointing at the object in Tulio's hand.

The boy laughed delightedly and nodded proudly.

"It's a kantele," he replied, and handed the instrument to Wille, who turned it over scrutinizingly.

"It helps me channel my magic," Tulio continued. "My grandfather made it for me when I was little."

"But what is it made of?" Wille asked, running his hand around the bone-white edges.

"It's made from the jawbone of a pike," Tulio answered, laughing at Wille's uncomfortable expression.

Wille had never liked fish, either alive or dead, which was because he had been bitten by a pike when he was little and had been swimming in a lake. One of his feet had bled profusely, and after that, he preferred to avoid being in water.

Hugo stopped playing, and the animals came out of their trance.

A bear walked towards Wille, who felt how he began to sweat and pressed himself against a tree trunk.

"Take it easy, Wille," said Váli, watching the bear. "He won't hurt you. Just let him sniff you."

Wille closed his eyes as the bear's snout brushed past his face, and he could feel the bear's breath against his ear. He slowly opened his eyes again, only to see that the bear's face was right in front of him. He flinched back, but when he met the bear's gaze, he stopped moving and looked into those matte black eyes. He could feel the animal's emotions, its eyes radiated warmth, and he gently reached out his hand to the large animal.

At first, the bear looked as uncertain as he felt, but it bowed its head, and Wille ran his hand through its fur before scratching it behind its ear.

"See, that wasn't so bad," said Váli, watching with amusement as Wille walked around the side of the bear.

The bear lowered its back and Wille looked inquiringly at Váli, who gave him a brief nod of confirmation.

Wille took a firm grip on the bear's fur and swung himself on to its back, whereupon the bear took off at full speed through the forest. He clung desperately to avoid falling off, screaming as the bear increased speed before it turned back.

There was a creak as they passed the last tree, and Wille, who felt dizzy from the run, saw how Tulio tried to keep from laughing as several squirrels climbed up Lovisa's jeans.

Hugo was squatting a little way away, petting one of the wolves that was still lying in the dry grass, and seemed to be enjoying the early spring that had arrived in the clearing.

The bear lowered its back, and Wille tried to get down on the ground in a daze. Hugo went forward, and caught him just as he fell off the bear's back.

"Are you okay?" he asked, but Wille couldn't come up with an answer, only nodding his head.

"Sorry, Wille, I was the one who told the bear you might enjoy a ride,"

Váli said, trying to hold back a laugh. "I didn't think it would run away like that."

"It's okay," said Wille, sitting down on the ground. "Just give me a few minutes to recover."

Suddenly, he felt the bear licking his neck and running its tongue up through his hair.

Hugo and Tulio howled with laughter as Wille hastily stood up, while his hair stood up in a curved arc. Even Lovisa actually laughed, which made him start laughing too.

The bear started to walk back into the forest again, which the other animals seemed to have already done, Wille noted.

Tulio became silent for a moment and seemed to be concentrating on something before he declared in a cheerful voice that breakfast was ready.

They began to walk back towards the cabin, and Wille wondered how Tulio could get along so well with the animals. He sent a thought to Váli, who replied immediately.

"His father is Tapio, god of the forest and king of the forest elves," Váli replied. "As the youngest prince, Tulio is the friend of the animals, and he can communicate with the animals and summon them whenever he wants."

"What about Tella and Nyri?" Wille asked.

"You've already seen what they can do," replied Váli, as they came around the cabin. "Nyri controls the earth and the mountains. He is very skilled at manipulating the land around him. Tella is a tree whisperer. She communicates with the spirits of the trees and can summon their help."

"Hurry up," Tella called out. "The food is getting cold."

∾

"So, can all demons control the darkness?" Hugo asked before taking another bite of the stew.

They were eating from the steaming breakfast casserole that Tella had cooked over the fire, and had started discussing demons.

"No," said Magni, shaking his head. "Demons are not powerful enough to control the darkness, although Nari seems to be an exception. I don't know how he got that power, but he seems to be able to conjure up physical objects made of darkness."

"The only other person powerful enough to control darkness is Wayland," Módi said. "Perhaps Hela and the banished gods she has gathered around her could control the darkness through the magic rings. Even Garmr can control the darkness through the way he was created."

Wille took a bite of his stew and fingered the wolf cross around his neck. It had felt heavier during the last few days, and he could feel how it had begun to steal energy from him.

"What is that?" Módi wondered, looking at the necklace that was half-hidden under Wille's collar.

Wille pulled the wolf cross out so that the entire necklace was clearly visible against his shirt.

Nyri gasped, and Tella seemed to almost choke, while Magni and Módi looked surprised at his necklace.

"Where did you get that?" Tella asked, coughing as she reached out to touch the cross.

"From my mom," Wille replied, looking at Tella's scrutinising eyes. "She told me never to take it off."

"What is it?" Tulio asked, leaning forward to look at the necklace.

"That necklace was forged by Egil, Wille's uncle," replied Tella, looking at the surprised expression on Wille's face. "It is a totem, an emblem of a power animal."

"What is a power animal?" Hugo asked curiously, looking up from his bowl.

"A power animal is a special spirit sent by the World Spirit to watch over one or more people," replied Tella. "Which it usually does through thoughts or emotions when we face difficult choices in life. They can also provide mental strength and help us be brave when we need it."

"What do they look like?" Wille asked.

"That's the thing," Magni replied. "They are usually not visible to the naked eye, but you can sometimes sense their presence or dream about them."

"We call them Fylgjur," Tella continued. "They take the form of different animals depending on who they guard and what path the World Spirit thinks the person should follow in life. It can be anything from a bear, a hawk, a mouse, or, as in your case, a wolf."

"A wolf?" Wille asked, looking up from the jewellery.

"Yes," replied Tulio, squatting down to get a better view of the necklace. "A totem necklace helps you to channel the contact with your totem animal, and the wolf represents leadership, protection, wisdom, and spiritual strength. A totem forms a bond between you and your power animal."

"But how do you know which power animal you have?" Wille asked, as Tulio fingered the necklace.

"Most people don't know what their power animal is," replied Tulio. "To find out, you have to go into deep meditation and merge with your power animal's energy."

"The fact that you can have a wolf totem without it being repelled shows that your power animal really is a wolf, although I've never seen a totem like this," Tulio concluded, looking questioningly up at her sister.

"That's because it's a very unusual totem," said Tella, and looked at Magni and Módi, who were listening quietly. "You two should recognise what it means."

Both brothers nodded, but they still looked puzzled. Módi leaned forward, and examined the necklace more closely.

"That necklace is made from the dust of the World Spirit," Módi replied, and examined Wille from head to toe, as if he had just met him. "As far as I know, only two pieces were made, both for Odin's two squire. That you seem to have a third can only mean that Egil made one in secret, which he kept when he was imprisoned on the island."

"But what can I do with it?" Wille asked.

"Dust from the World Spirit is the only thing that can destroy the darkness," Tella replied. "Unfortunately, you can't just take the dust from the place where the tree is, and bring it to our world. You have to shape the dust into solid objects – which is what your father did with his sword, before he corrupted it with his dark magic."

"My magic," said Wille, looking surprised. "What can I really do?"

"You said that you spirit walked, right?" Tella asked. "That seems to be a primary magic of yours, and the cross helps you to channel your magic."

"How?" Wille asked, looking from Tella to Magni.

"You remember how you focused your energy when you were going to spirit walk into Hugo's dream, right?" Váli asked, and trotted over to Wille, who nodded thoughtfully.

"Okay," Váli continued. "Try to do the same thing while directing your energy into the cross."

Wille tried to remember how he felt when Hugo lay motionless on the ground. In his mind, he drew a picture of the cross and tried to direct his emotions to the image.

"Good," Váli exclaimed, looking enthusiastic. "Hold the image and the feeling in your head when you close your eyes."

Wille did as he was told, and waited. At first, nothing seemed to happen, then he felt a tingling sensation throughout his body. His body grew, and when he opened his eyes, he felt, to his horror, how his clothes tore apart as the cold hit his body. He looked down at one of his hands, but instead of a human hand, he saw a silver-white paw pressed into the snow.

"Welcome to my world, cousin," Váli said, walking towards him with an amused expression.

⁂

Nyri saw how Wille tried to take a few steps forward, to Váli's obvious delight. He didn't know why, but for some reason he felt at ease in their company – which was unusual, as he usually finds it difficult to interact with others without becoming nervous.

He took a bite from his bowl and watched with amusement as Váli tried to teach Wille to walk. Then he turned to Tulio, who smiled back at him.

"They don't seem so bad, do they?" his little brother's voice was heard in his head.

"No…or I don't know," Nyri sent back.

"Relax, and you'll see that you can be good friends," Tulio concluded, and Nyri nodded with a smile in response.

17. Legion

Jessica felt bored in the cramped room with the narrow beds. She struggled to grasp everything, nervously running her fingers through her light brown hair.

The night before last, she had been in her room, getting ready for a party night. She had put on her finest black trousers and the white cardigan she had received for Christmas. Her friends had been waiting, but instead of an evening of music and laughter, she had been forced away to some inaccessible military barracks called 'the Föne Base'.

Her cell phone had been confiscated, and she was not allowed to contact her friends.

She sighed and sat down on the hard mattress when there was a knock on the door, and her father came in.

"Can I sit down?" he asked, and sat down on the edge of the bed without waiting for an answer.

They sat next to each other for a while, hands clasped, without saying a word.

Finally, her father broke the silence.

"You know you can talk to me about anything," he said, stroking her hair.

"I don't want to be here, dad, I want to go home!" Jessica exclaimed, a little more vehemently than she intended, looking up at his tired face.

"I know, sweetie, I know. Your mom and I want nothing more than to come home," he said, sighing. "But until the situation is resolved, we have to stay here."

"But why?" Jessica asked, resting her head on his shoulder. "Why involve us in this strange war?"

"They're just trying to protect us," he replied calmly. "Your mother saw things that she shouldn't have seen, and that's why we're in danger."

"But what about her job and my school?" Jessica asked.

"Your mother has been an assistant principal for ten years and has accumulated a lot of overtime," he replied. "No one thinks it's strange that she wants to take a break."

Jessica sighed, and closed her eyes. She had barely slept properly during her stay, and felt exhausted.

"As far as your education is concerned, we have spoken to your teachers, and, given the circumstances, they have agreed that you can continue to study by distance learning – as long as we submit assignments regularly," he continued.

"But who will be my teacher?" Jessica asked, noticing how her father began to smile. "You don't mean…"

"Yes," he replied with a wry smile. "Who better to teach religious studies than the world's top religious scholar?"

❧

Amanda walked between the large tents at the edge of the forest, trying to find Kenneth to see if he had any new information to share. As she turned the corner at the hangar, she stopped abruptly.

A young man, dressed in a long dark coat, was standing further away by some trees, lifting a soldier by the throat. In his other hand, he was holding a dark sword, sticking it out of the soldier's back.

The man looked quickly in Amanda's direction, before letting go of the soldier, and starting to walk towards her with the sword dragging along the gravel.

Suddenly, someone grabbed her shoulder from behind and pulled her around the corner again. She started to scream, but Kenneth hastily motioned for her to be quiet.

Several soldiers ran past them, and shots were heard being fired from the automatic weapons. Kenneth started running, pulling Amanda away from the battle.

"We are under attack," he said, putting his hands around her face. "You need to get your family, and lead them to the cars at the big hangar – we need to get away from here!"

Amanda was paralysed with fear and couldn't say a word.

"Do you understand?" he asked resignedly.

She nodded, and he let go of her before he started to run back towards the smaller hangar, where more soldiers were joining the battle against the swordsman.

❧

The door to the room burst open, and Jörgen stood up quickly when he saw Amanda's terrified expression. She almost collapsed at the door when he ran towards her.

"Darling, what happened?" Jörgen asked, giving his wife a moment to catch her breath.

"We have to get out of here," she managed to say. "We're under attack."

"What do you mean…" Jörgen started to ask, but stopped himself when he heard guns being fired outside the house.

He quickly waved to Jessica and pulled them both out through the front door.

The sound of fighting thundered through the trees, and Jörgen had difficulty locating a safe path. After a few seconds of hesitation, he pulled them along the right end of the house.

They ran side by side past soldiers rushing in the opposite direction, before Jörgen stopped abruptly.

"Keep going," he shouted. "The big hangar is behind the dining hall. Run, I'll catch up with you soon!"

"What are you going to do?" Jessica asked in horror.

Jörgen leaned over and hugged Amanda.

"I have to get something," he replied calmly. "Don't worry, I'll come back to you."

With those words, he started to run back towards the dormitories, while Jessica screamed after him.

Amanda, who had been frozen, stared after her husband before grabbing Jessica and pulling her towards the hangar.

They ran along the gravelly courtyard and were met with chaos. Around the hangar, men in police uniforms were shooting at soldiers evacuating in military trucks. A whistle was heard from across the yard, and Amanda saw Kenneth waving at them from behind the hangar door.

She grabbed Jessica's arm and pulled her along with her as she crouched in the hail of bullets above their heads.

Kenneth shouted out an order, and the soldiers gave them cover fire before they reached their destination.

"Where is Jörgen?" he asked desperately.

"He's coming," Amanda replied breathlessly.

"We can't wait any longer, we have to go," he said, staring across the courtyard. "We are almost surrounded."

He gestured to the nearest soldiers, who pushed Amanda and Jessica towards a waiting car.

Jessica shouted that they had to wait for her father as she tried to break free, but the soldiers opened the back door of the vehicle and abruptly pushed Jessica inside.

As Amanda was about to jump in through the other back door, the sound of a gunshot was heard, and she collapsed lifelessly on the yard.

Jessica was desperately trying to get out of the car again, while two soldiers jumped into the front seat and started the car, which sped off across the chaotic courtyard.

When they emerged from the compound, there was a deafening explosion, and Jessica saw huge flames shooting up from the place they had just left.

❧

Nari walked across the courtyard, with his sword dragging on the ground, looking at the devastation. The fire was still burning, but the sounds of the battle had subsided.

Two of his demon-worshippers came dragging a soldier, who looked half beaten to death.

"How many did we get?" Nari asked as the men threw the wounded soldier on the ground beside him.

"About two hundred dead, sir," replied one of the men.

"And our losses?" Nari asked.

"About the same number of casualties, sir," the man replied, looking down at the soldier.

Nari squatted down and lifted the soldier's face, so that their eyes met. He bared his fangs, but the man showed no fear despite his predicament.

"How many are you, and where are you going?" Nari asked, his matte black eyes flashing.

"Go to hell," the man replied and spat.

Nari ran a hand over his face, and wiped away the saliva. For a moment, he was filled with rage, but quickly calmed down and leaned towards the man.

"Where do you think I came from?" he whispered in a hissing voice in the man's ear before biting him in the throat.

The man slumped to the ground while the blood flooded out of his throat.

Nari slowly got up, and put his hand over his mouth to wipe away the blood around his mouth. He felt intoxicated, it had been a long time since he last drank blood.

There was a rumbling sound, as Wayland appeared on the roof of the hangar in an inferno of black fire.

Nari took off and threw himself into the air, landing with a thud next to his master. He squatted, swept his dark cloak, and bowed, not daring to meet Wayland's gaze.

"Did I not tell you to gather all of Legion?" Wayland asked in a voice that sounded cold.

"It was not possible to get all the troops here on such short notice," Nari replied without looking up.

"How many do you have here?" Wayland asked, looking down disapprovingly at his apprentice.

"We have eight hundred soldiers, master," replied Nari. "We lost two hundred soldiers in the attack, and eliminated as many of their soldiers."

Wayland walked past him without commenting on the numbers. He stood on the edge of the roof and held up his right hand. Below, the demon worshippers lined up and watched the black-haired man.

"My friends," said Wayland in a thunderous voice. "You have sworn your allegiance to me, now it is time to prove yourselves. It's time to become what you were born to be."

Wayland raised his hand, and a dark fire swept down from the ceiling and formed a ring around the men on the ground.

Some screamed, but most of the men threw out their arms and seemed to embrace the black fire that burned them. Their faces contorted, and their hands grew into great, deformed claws. Huge wings grew out of their backs, and their heads were covered with pointed horns.

"Pursue them, and do not stop until you find them," echoed Wayland's thunderous voice, which drowned out the men from whose mouths there now grew razor-sharp teeth.

"You will feel no pain and no fear," he shouted to drown out the sound of the demonic men on the ground. "You will taste the blood of the children of the gods!"

There was a roar of approval from the ground in response, and Wayland turned to Nari.

"You know I want the boy and his wolf cross," he said. "You can do as you please with your brother."

Nari nodded and smiled an ominous smile.

Wayland stood with his face so close that their noses met.

"Kill the rest," he hissed, disappearing in the dark flames.

Nari stood on the edge and threw out his arms.

"Who are we?" he shouted, and was met with an abysmal roar from the winged creatures.

"LEGION!" they roared in reply.

"Why?" Nari continued to shout.

"WE ARE LEGION, BECAUSE WE ARE MANY!"

❧

"How much longer must I walk like this?" Wille asked, strolling alongside Váli on the path.

"You might as well get used to it," said Váli, laughing. "As a wolf warrior, you need to be able to handle it."

They had been hiking for several hours. Váli and Wille walked at the back, while Hugo and Lovisa walked in front of them. Further ahead were Nyri and Tella, who seemed to be discussing Wille's necklace. Magni and Módi took the lead and led the way through the forest. Tulio, however, was nowhere to be seen.

"But, I don't want to be a wolf," said Wille, whining.

"Would you rather go naked?" Váli asked.

They had left the cars at the cabin to reduce the risk of detection. As a result, they had been forced to limit the amount of luggage they could carry, and of course no one had thought about taking Wille's backpack with clothes.

Wille, who had run off ahead of the others with Váli to get used to his new-found wolf body, had been disappointed that no one had thought of him. He wanted to return, but Magni said that he could get new clothes when they arrived instead.

"But I don't understand," said Wille. "I can transform myself back into a human when I want to, but you can't?"

"That's because, through your totem, you've made a deal with your power animal," Váli replied. "But my transformation is due to a curse that I can't break myself."

Wille nodded thoughtfully, then looked down at the wolf cross that dangled around his neck.

"Can anyone with a totem transform?" he asked, whereupon Váli shook his head.

"A regular totem allows you to communicate with your power animal, and borrow powers from it," Váli replied. "But there are special totems that allow you to transform into the animal that represents your power animal."

"But what does it actually represent?" Wille asked, looking down at the cross again.

The fact that it was shaped like a cross surprised him.

"The cross stands for Naud, the rune of destiny," Váli replied as they dove under a fir tree that was in the way. "It is the strongest rune, associated with the goddesses of fate."

Wille thought for a moment, he had heard about runes before. He had heard that it was some kind of magical written language used by the Vikings in the past.

"The wolf head at the top of the cross, just like your power animal, stands for strength and spiritual wisdom," Váli continued.

They heard Hugo laughing further along the path while they were walking, whereupon Váli became quiet, and looked down at the ground again.

"You know he likes you," said Wille, looking at his cousin, who nodded without looking up.

"I know, but…" Váli started to say and looked at Wille, who smiled, waiting for his answer.

"I like him too, it's just that…I mean, we're both guys," he concluded.

"What does it matter?" Wille asked. "How do you feel about him?"

They looked at Hugo and Lovisa walking in front of them.

"My body tingles when he pats me," Váli replied. "Every time he hugs me, it feels wonderful."

He looked down at the ground again and continued walking.

"Do you think I'm weird?" Váli asked and looked at Wille, who laughed so loudly at the question that both Hugo and Lovisa turned around.

"What are you talking about?" Hugo asked.

Váli looked terrified, and quickly turned his head.

"Nothing in particular," he replied hastily, while Wille looked at his cousin with an amused expression.

Hugo shrugged and continued walking.

"Nervous, cousin?" Wille asked, nudging him.

Váli looked embarrassed, which said more than a thousand words.

"Okay, maybe I am a little nervous, but…I mean, look at me! I'm a wolf!" Váli exclaimed.

"But you won't always be," said Wille, smiling.

"That's just it," said Váli. "He thinks I'm big and tough now, but what if I become human again? Will he see me the same way?"

"You mean when you become human again," Wille replied. "We will not give up until you break the curse."

"And the other thing you don't have to worry about. Hugo senses who you are in here," said Wille, while stopping and putting his paw on Váli's chest.

A shout was heard further down the path, and both of them hurried forward.

The others waited at the edge of the forest, where a village stood out by a large lake.

"We are here," said Lovisa.

They tried to avoid walking on the main road and came to a village sign, which Wille read aloud to himself.

'TANDSJÖBORG'

18. A Family Reunion

Gustav walked along the forest road towards the house. The sun was warming the otherwise snowy landscape, causing the snow to start melting.

He took off his camouflage hunting cap and let the fresh air sweep through his short brown hair. It was the first of April that day, and spring was coming.

The mirror-like surface of the lake was enticing, but he knew that it was still far too cold for a swim.

A movement in the forest caught his attention. There were lots of animals in the forest near the village, he knew that from the hunting trips he and Tommy had taken. Still, it was rare for the animals to venture near the lake.

There was a rustling behind him, and Gustav turned around. He stared in amazement at the girl who stepped out of the forest.

"Lovisa?! What are you doing here? How did…"

He didn't have time to finish the sentence before she threw herself against him and wrapped her arms around his waist. She was crying, which Gustav had never seen her do before.

Another rustling sound was heard, and two wolves stepped out onto the road.

Panicked, Gustav grabbed Lovisa and quickly pushed her behind his back.

"It's all right, Gustav, they're with me," said Lovisa as she wiped away her tears.

"What are you talking about?" Gustav asked in horror. "Lovisa, those are wolves, not pets!"

There were more noises from the forest, and a young man with a ponytail stepped out onto the road behind the wolves, closely followed by another guy with snagged hair.

Gustav got a strange feeling in his body and looked around. Behind Lovisa stood two teenagers, a boy and a girl, with reddish hair and watched them.

"Lovisa, what's going on?" Gustav asked, looking around anxiously with his arms outstretched to try to protect her.

"It's all right I came here with them," she replied, putting her hand on his shoulder.

"With two wolves?" Gustav asked tensely.

"Perhaps it would be better if we talked somewhere else," said the black-furred wolf, taking a step forward.

"It's talking!" Gustav exclaimed, staring at the big wolf.

"Gustav, I know it's a lot to take in, but trust me," said Lovisa calmly. "Can we go somewhere and talk?"

Gustav stared at the wolves.

"The old cottage above the campsite is empty at this time of year, we can talk there," he replied without taking his eyes off Váli. "But I want a good explanation for this."

Lovisa nodded and grabbed his hand, beckoning the others to follow them.

Gustav glanced anxiously behind him as they walked along the forest road, but the wolves kept a safe distance from them along with the rest of the company.

The old cabin stood on a hill above the campsite. Gustav took up a key from his pocket that he put in the lock.

The door creaked open, whereupon Gustav pulled Lovisa behind the door and let the rest of the party go in.

"Okay, Lovisa, now you can tell me what's going on," Gustav said as he closed the door.

The company sat down in a sofa group, and Lovisa pulled out a chair at the old kitchen table.

In a trembling voice, Lovisa began to tell him what had happened in the last few days. How Wille and Hugo had discovered that they were gods, how the demons had attacked them, about their journey, and about Váli's curse.

Gustav listened and oscillated between the feeling that she was making fun of him and that he was dreaming.

When Lovisa started telling him about the demon that had killed her father, her eyes teared up, and she couldn't get the words out. The silver-white wolf approached her, and Gustav stood up quickly, but he stopped when he saw Lovisa sinking to the floor and hugging the wolf.

"Are you trying to tell me that we are in a room full of old Aesir gods?" he exclaimed fiercely.

"Be careful who you call old," Magni said from the couch, causing Gustav to jump.

The rest of the party hadn't said a word because Lovisa had asked them to let her do the explanation.

"I just…I mean…this is ridiculous!" Gustav exclaimed at the same time as he gesticulated wildly. "And in that case, who is the wolf that you are hugging?"

"It's me, Wille," said the wolf calmly.

Gustav felt overwhelmed. He had not seen Wille for several years, not since he and his father had last visited Lovisa's family.

"Wille!" he exclaimed. "But…but how…"

"He discovered yesterday that he can turn into a wolf," Lovisa replied, and stood up.

Gustav looked puzzled at the wolf sitting next to her and wondered if this was all a strange April Fool's joke.

"If you can turn into a wolf, you can turn back, can't you?" he asked. "Do that, and I'll believe this whole story."

The wolf looked down at the floor, and looked ashamed.

"If he turns back, he won't have any clothes," Lovisa replied.

Gustav laughed, and Wille looked offended. Then Gustav struck out with his hands again and shrugged his shoulders.

"So, how are you going to prove this fairy tale?" he asked in a sarcastic tone.

The red-haired girl got up from the couch and sighed, as if she were tired of the conversation. Then she made a few gestures with her hands and closed her eyes.

The kitchen window was shattered, and a tree root entered the cottage. It grabbed around Gustav's waist and lifted him into the air before turning him upside down.

He shrieked in horror as the tree brought him so close to the girl's face that they almost touched.

"Do you believe us now?" she asked, using the same sarcastic tone that Gustav himself had used on Lovisa.

Gustav felt himself starting to sweat and nodded slowly.

The red-haired girl reached out one of her hands and ran it through his bangs, which were hanging down.

"He's quite cute, your cousin," she said, and Gustav felt himself blushing.

"Please, put me down," he begged embarrassedly, and the girl smiled amusedly at her victim.

"Since you ask so nicely," she said, as she waved her hand and the tree put him down again.

The tree let go of his waist and he rubbed his back, while the root of the tree disappeared out the window.

"So, who are you?" Gustav asked, looking nervously at the girl, whose powers had made him hang upside down.

"My name is Tella, and the guy sitting closest to the edge of the couch is my twin brother Nyri. The other two are Magni and Módi," Tella replied.

Gustav turned around and nodded briefly towards the company on the couch, while still rubbing his back.

"I'm sorry," he said, and Lovisa found it hard to contain her laughter.

"So, it really is you, Wille?" Gustav asked, and gently stroked his hand around the silver-white wolf's neck.

"Yes," replied Wille, while closing his eyes, seeming to enjoy being scratched.

"But how did this happen?" Gustav asked, examining him curiously.

"I discovered that I can transform myself into a wolf, and my clothes were torn by the transformation," replied Wille.

"We spent the night in the old firehouse on the mountain," said Lovisa. "We came there with two cars yesterday, but since we were being hunted, we left the cars there."

"And since we couldn't get all the luggage we had in the cars, we had to prioritize," Wille continued. "And there was no one who thought about bringing my clothes."

Gustav laughed again, and Wille looked puzzled.

"Sorry," Gustav said. "If you want, you can get some clothes from me that I have grown out of."

"What happened to Tommy?" he asked, and turned to Lovisa again, who became noticeably gloomy.

"A demon shot Dad," she replied sadly. "The demons pretended to be police officers and stopped us in Noppikoski, that's where Tella and the others saved us."

Gustavs felt his eyes tear up, and turned his face away so as not to show how hard the news was hitting him.

"And Oscar is dead too," sobbed Lovisa, wrapping her arms around his waist.

Gustav grimaced, still in pain from the tree's grip earlier. He gently removed her arms, and placed his palms over her cheeks.

"What are you talking about?" he asked with surprise in his voice. "Oscar is not dead."

"Yes," Lovisa replied. "He was the first to die."

Gustav shook his head, and brought a small smile to his tearful face.

"Oscar came here yesterday afternoon, he's at our house alive and well," he said, looking into her eyes.

No one said anything for a long time. Lovisa looked shocked, and Wille tried to say something.

"Are you sure it's him?" Módi asked, looking at Gustav, who felt puzzled.

"Of course I'm sure," replied Gustav irritably. "I recognise my own cousin!"

"He's alive," said Lovisa, looking at Wille. "He's alive!"

"Can we go and see him?" Wille asked, sounding enthusiastic.

"Yes, of course we'll do that, but..." Gustav began, looking from the two wolves to Módi and Magni, whose large weapons would not be possible to hide.

"But what?" asked Magni, with ill-concealed impatience.

"Well, we usually hunt wolves around here, and now we have two talking wolves as well," Gustav replied, and looked worriedly at Wille and Váli. "And your weapons are not exactly invisible. I'm going to have a hard time selling this to mom and dad."

"I still think I want to meet this Oscar," Magni said, and stood up. "We can try to hide our weapons, and the wolves can wait outside for a while."

Gustav thought for a moment.

"Okay," he said after some hesitation. "But let me and Lovisa do the explaining."

"Sure," said Magni, opening the door. "Shall we go then?"

Módi paused for a moment and took off the gun bag he had been carrying on his back. He took out the rifle, handing it to Gustav along with a small bag containing ammunition.

"Lovisa told me that you used to hunt with her father, so I thought you might want his rifle," Módi said, as Gustav zipped up his camouflage-coloured anorak.

Gustav's hands trembled as he accepted the rifle, and he managed to say thanks before they left the cabin and locked the door. They hurried off after the others, and were in such a hurry that they did not see the glowing red eyes that watched them from the grove behind the cottage.

❧

"Oscar, why are you doing this?"

Mikael was tied up on the floor, next to him was his wife Hanna, whose hands and feet were also tightly bound with the coarse rope. Unlike him, she had also been provided with a rag in her mouth.

Oscar bent down and looked at his uncle, who was sweating profusely.

"I'm sorry, uncle," he replied, and brushed the edge of Mikael's hunting knife across his cheek.

Mikael grimaced as blood began to run down his cheek. He stared in horror as Oscar's eyes began to glow with a strange purple light.

"What happened to you?" Mikael whispered.

Oscar smiled, exposing a row of pointed fangs. He stood up, and made a whistling sound.

Two large wolves slowly lumbered into the living room.

One of the wolves had a blood-red, thick, billowing coat. The other wolf had a coat that resembled a shade of midnight blue and growled softly. What both wolves had in common was that their eyes glowed the same colour as their coats.

The wolves stood on either side of Oscar and almost reached his shoulders. Mikael trembled and stared at the creatures in front of him without making a sound. Hanna twisted and turned, trying to get free, while desperately trying to scream behind the cloth in her mouth.

Then Oscar raised a hand, and Mikael closed his eyes, while the two wolves threw themselves upon them.

His screams echoed in the woods around the house as the wolves sunk their teeth into him, and he finally fell silent as the dark blue wolf tore out his throat.

❧

"What was that?"

Wille stopped and listened to the scream echoing in the forest. Another scream was heard before it became silent.

Magni swore loudly and started running. Gustav had frozen where he stood, seeming paralysed by fear.

"That was my father screaming," he said, before he started to run after Magni.

Lovisa and Wille looked at each other and began running after them.

It had begun to get dark when they arrived at a red house at the edge of the lake, and Magni rushed in, closely followed by Gustav, Lovisa, and Wille.

Tella and Nyri hurried after them, and Módi was the last to enter the kitchen, where everyone stopped short.

At the kitchen table sat Oscar. He looked shocked at them, and brushed his light brown hair out of the way as the group rushed in through the kitchen door.

"Hi," he said, looking surprised to see Lovisa staring at him as if she had seen a ghost.

Lovisa regained her composure and threw herself at him.

"Lovisa, you're suffocating me," said Oscar, as he struggled to get up and put his arms around her.

"I thought you were dead," she said, sobbing.

"What's that noise?" a voice was heard from the doorway on the other side of the room.

A large woman entered the room and stood with her arms crossed, as she surveyed the company.

"Mom!" Gustav exclaimed, and stepped forward.

Magni looked confused, and Módi stood leaning against the doorway to catch his breath. Wille stood between them and stared in amazement.

"We heard Dad screaming," said Gustav. "Where is he?"

"Here I am," another voice was heard from behind the woman.

A muscular man limped into the room, while the woman pulled out a chair and helped him sit down.

"Sorry if you were worried, Gustav, I just fell down the stairs," the man said, grabbing his head.

"Dad, what have I told you about the attic stairs?" Gustav sighed, and squatted down next to the man.

"Yes, yes," muttered the man, and turned to the group.

He stared at Wille and put his hand on his chin.

"So, who are your friends?" the man asked in a confused manner. "And isn't that a wolf?"

Gustav introduced them in turn, but when it came to introducing Wille, he didn't quite know how to explain that there was a silver-white wolf in the kitchen.

Just then, thumps were heard from the front door, and everyone's eyes turned to the hall, where they saw Tulio enter the house, closely followed by Váli and Hugo.

"Where have you guys been?" Wille asked without thinking that maybe he shouldn't talk.

"Wille," whispered Hugo, his eyes wide open. "He's here, he chased us in the forest."

"Who?" asked Wille, though he already knew the answer before Hugo opened his mouth again.

"Garmr, he's outside the house!"

19. The Fire Wolves

There was a panic as Magni and Módi forced their way out of the house, while Gustav's parents demanded to know what was going on.

Bangs were heard from the outside, and Gustav's father headed for the door but was stopped by Tella.

"I know that we are trespassing and that you don't know who we are, but you need to get to safety," she said with a look that brooked no argument. "You are in danger!"

The man looked shocked but nodded slowly, then put his arm around his wife and led her out of the kitchen again.

Tella and Nyri were just about to leave through the front door when Tulio tried to push past them.

"You will have to stay inside," Tella said firmly, and pulled him back into the kitchen under loud protests.

"Everyone, stay inside," she said, before running out of the house. "And watch Tulio."

"What's going on?" Oscar asked, looking horrified.

"I'll tell you everything later," replied Lovisa. "The big wolf that attacked us earlier is here."

"What should we do, Wille?" she asked the white wolf.

"Wille?" Oscar exclaimed in confusion, looking at him.

"That's a long story for later," Váli replied firmly. "We must try to help them in some way."

Oscar looked suspicious at Váli.

"Where is Gustav?" he asked.

No one had noticed that Gustav had disappeared.

"Maybe he went with his parents," Tulio suggested, pointing towards the door on the other side of the kitchen.

Suddenly, the whole house shook so much that Lovisa and Tulio lost their footing. The ceiling beams began to crack, and wood shavings fell on them.

"We can't stay here," said Váli. "Find Gustav and his parents, we must try to get out of here."

The ground continued to shake, and a wooden beam fell down next to them. Lovisa took Oscar in one hand and Tulio in the other and pulled them towards the door where Gustav's parents had disappeared.

Váli ran towards the front door with Hugo and Wille in tow, but stopped abruptly and turned towards them.

"I must help them," he said. "Find another way out, I don't want you to follow me."

"But…" Hugo began to protest, but Váli cut him off.

"Look, he's after you, Wille," Váli said in a sharp voice. "You must not interfere in the battle. And you, Hugo…"

Váli broke off his sentence, as if he didn't quite know what to say, and put his head against Hugo's arm for a moment, before he took a leap out the front door.

"Váli," Hugo shouted, but Wille held him back.

"Hugo, he's right," said Wille. "We must not expose ourselves to the risk. We would probably just be in the way."

Just then the ground shook again, and there were loud bangs from upstairs as walls collapsed.

Wille dragged his brother backwards with his fangs, before Hugo turned around, and they started running through the kitchen towards the other side of the house. They looked around for the others, but could not see them anywhere.

A rifle shot echoed, and they stared at each other.

Wille looked to the left and saw a door ajar. He pushed open the door, and through the vague light of the lamp in the ceiling, he could see a staircase leading down to what appeared to be the basement of the house.

"Hello," he called out. "Is anyone there?"

There was no answer, and he glanced at Hugo, who nodded, and then they carefully made their way down the stairs. Wille felt how it got warmer further down.

Once at the foot of the stairs, they stood and stared at the scene in front of them.

Oscar lay passed out on the floor in the middle of the root cellar. At one end of the room, Lovisa stood with her arm outstretched to protect Tulio. In front of them, Gustav was pointing his rifle at his parents.

"What's going on?" Wille asked in panic, while the ground shook again and several screams were heard from outside. "We have to get out of here."

When Gustav's parents turned around, he took a step backwards in fear. The father's eyes were burning with dark blue flames, and the mother's eyes with blood red ones.

But that wasn't the worst of it; their faces had been twisted into grotesque smiles.

Their clothes were torn, and their bodies twisted unnaturally, whereupon red and blue flames burst around them when they took on the form of two large wolves.

The flames hit the wooden floor of the house, which immediately caught fire. The fire spread fast, and Wille realised that they did not have much time to get out of there.

"Everything went smoothly," said the dark blue wolf.

"It looks that way," said the blood-red wolf, smiling.

"Who are you?" Hugo asked, looking anxiously at the floor beams that were burning at a furious pace.

"He wants to know our names, Sköll," said the blue wolf.

"Funny, isn't it, Hati?" laughed the blood-red wolf. "They haven't realised that they are doomed."

"Where are my parents?" Gustav shouted, pointing his rifle at the dark blue wolf.

Hati snorted at him.

"Do you really think that's going to bite us?" asked the wolf in a contemptuous voice.

A shot was fired and travelled through Hati, and the blue flame around the wolf's aura sealed the bullet hole.

"It will be a pleasure to sink my teeth into you," Hati growled. "Let's see if you're as cowardly as your father was when I ripped out his throat."

Wille thought quickly, the situation didn't look good. He cast a glance at the roof, and formed a picture in his mind while he desperately tried to locate Váli.

"Use the ocarina," a voice suddenly was heard so strong and clear that Wille jumped.

"Hugo, can you use the ocarina?" Wille shouted to drown out the crackling sound of the fire.

"I don't know how to use it properly yet," Hugo replied, picking up the instrument.

Then Hati pounced on Wille and knocked him to the floor. The blue fire burned Wille's fur, and he gave a howl of pain. Hati was worthy of his name, because all Wille could see in his flaming eyes was hate drilling into him.

The fire wolf pressed his paw even harder against Wille, who screamed uncontrollably as the flames burned his skin.

Then the sound of Hugo's ocarina was heard, the clear tones seemed to fill the entire room and drown out the crackling flames. Wille turned his head and could see how the blood-red wolf was getting ready to pounce on his brother, who stood a few metres away from him with his eyes closed and the instrument on his lips.

The moment the wolf pounced on Hugo, it was knocked away by a strong wind that was picking up in the cellar, and that's when Wille saw it. Further away in the cellar stood the old man who had helped them before and held a strange stringed instrument that he played.

The notes from Lódurr's instrument, combined with Hugo's ocarina, created a strong wind that made Sköll fly into the wall.

Hati growled and was about to sink his teeth into Wille when Gustav slammed the wolf with the piston on the rifle.

"At least that bites you," he said triumphantly when the wolf hit the hard floor.

Suddenly, parts of the house foundation collapsed on top of them. Just as a burning beam fell down towards Wille, the wind increased in strength, and seemed to slow down the beam's fall, only to lift it into the air again.

"This way," shouted Lódurr, who had stopped playing and waved at them from the other end of the root cellar.

Gustav threw the rifle strap over his shoulder and grabbed Oscar under the arms, before dragging his unconscious cousin towards the old man.

Lovisa grabbed Tulio, and started to run.

"Hugo!" Wille shouted at Hugo, who was still playing.

Hugo didn't answer, but his gaze went up to the burning rubble above them that still seemed to be held up by the wind, and Wille understood that the moment Hugo stopped playing, everything would come crashing down upon them.

A movement on the stairs caught Wille's attention. Sköll rose laboriously to her feet and growled irritably.

Then Wille turned his head again and had just enough time to throw himself to the side before Hati thudded to the ground where he had just stood.

The wind picked up again and pushed Wille towards the other side of the room where the others had run.

"Hugo!" cried Wille, trying to fight the strong wind.

Someone grabbed him, and the old man lifted him up.

Lódurr carried him away from the battle. The old man seemed to be stronger than he looked, Wille thought when they came to a hatch leading out of the root cellar.

Gustav reached down towards Lódurr, and with their combined strength, they managed to get Wille up through the hatch before Hati grabbed Lódurr's coat and pulled him down into the cellar again.

Gustav swore and threw himself down through the hatch.

Lovisa and Tulio showed up next to Wille, and they dragged him away from the burning house.

The boy put his hands gently over Wille's chest, which felt as if it was still burning from Hati's fire, and he could hear Tulio muttering strange rhymes. Suddenly he felt the pain subside, and the wound began to heal.

"Are you okay?" Lovisa asked worriedly.

"I think so," Wille lied, and Tulio removed his hands.

It still felt like his chest was burning, albeit less intensely.

"Where is Oscar?" Wille asked, looking around.

Lovisa pointed to a tree farther away, where Oscar was sitting half leaning backwards with one hand over his chest.

Tulio was leaning over him, seeming to heal his wounds.

"I have to go back," said Wille. "Hugo is stuck there."

There was a deafening roar as the house suddenly collapsed in front of their eyes.

Wille screamed violently and began to run back towards the house through the thick smoke that lay like a dense fog around them. Then he ran into Lódurr, who was dragging a half unconscious Gustav.

"Turn around!" the man shouted commandingly.

"But what about Hugo?" shouted Wille back, while the old man grabbed the back of his neck and, with great difficulty, dragged both him and Gustav into the forest.

Then the clear tones of Hugo's ocarina were heard again, and when Wille looked up to the fiery red sky, he saw that Hugo was hovering about ten metres above them.

The wind seemed to form a bubble around him as he slowly descended to the ground, where the others were waiting. When Hugo landed, the wind slowed down, as he sank to the ground.

There were creaking noises behind Wille, as Magni and Módi breathlessly appeared, carrying Nyri and Tella in each of their arms, who seemed to be unconscious.

"We have to go," shouted Módi. "Garmr is chasing us! Váli is trying to buy us time, but he can't hold him back."

Blood ran down Módi's face, and Magni limped.

A loud rumbling sound was heard from the burnt-out house, and Wille turned around as a dark blue flame of fire shot up from the ruin and mingled with the red flames.

Lódurr drew his sword and took up a defensive position. Wille could see that the old man looked exhausted and was sweating profusely.

Magni and Módi appeared on either side of them, with drawn weapons.

The flames that leapt up from the house formed two gigantic wolf heads, which descended with a roar upon them.

Lódurr put up his sword for protection, and the flames struck the sword with such force that the old man was pushed backwards. He seemed to falter where he stood, but swung his sword with such force that the fire was dispersed.

The fire gathered on the ground, and the two wolves appeared in the smoke. They threw themselves towards Magni and Módi, who blocked the attacks.

Magni dropped to his knees and held the mace in both hands, while Sköll's jaws wrapped around it. There was a flash of lightning from the giant hammer as the wolf was thrown away, while Magni held his chest.

Meanwhile, Módi had split his double-edged axe and whirled around with the silver axe and the gold axe while being surrounded by blue flames of fire. The sky above them began to rumble, and Módi raised the gold axe above his head as a giant bolt of lightning struck the axe.

Wille held up his paw to protect his eyes. He could see Módi throwing the gold axe around him, and into the blue fire, where it was spinning in a circle, while lightning flashed around it. The blue fire subsided, and with a howl, Hati landed on the ground.

"How sweet," a familiar voice suddenly sounded.

Wille saw Garmr standing some distance away, watching the battle. The giant wolf picked up something with its enormous jaws and threw it on the ground next to Wille, who drew breath when he saw Váli landing, unconscious.

196

"Did you really think this puppy could stop me?" Garmr asked condescendingly. "I should have killed him last time, I won't make the same mistake."

Lódurr stood next to Wille, who noticed that the old man was leaning convulsively on his sword. Garmr laughed delightedly at the sight of the injured man.

"You have lost, old man," the wolf gloated. "You will all die here tonight!"

A sizzling sound was heard above them as blue and red flames of fire struck into the ground on either side of Garmr, and the two fire wolves appeared in the flames.

Wille turned around and saw Modi crouching next to his brother, who had collapsed on the ground. Lovisa had helped Oscar get back on his feet, and they were leaning against a tree in horror. Tulio was bending over his siblings, who were still lying lifeless on the ground next to a large pine tree.

Then Wille realised that they were trapped by Garmr's darkness, which had surrounded them and cut off their escape routes.

"What do we have here, the prodigal son in a new form?" exclaimed Garmr, whose luminous eyes scrutinised Wille.

"Your father will be delighted to see you in your new attire," said the wolf, smiling ominously.

"Wille," Lódurr whispered, not taking his eyes off the wolves. "I need you to trust me."

"Okay," Wille whispered back. "What should I do?"

"You must spirit walk into the wolf cross," Lódurr replied.

"Into the wolf cross?" Wille repeated in confusion while the darkness moved towards them. "How will that help us?"

The old man gasped exhaustedly, not answering him.

Wille could see out of the corner of his eye how Lovisa and Módi were trying to drag the others as far into the centre of the circle as they could. He looked questioningly at Lódurr again, who nodded affirmatively, whereupon Wille closed his eyes and tried to disconnect from the consciousness as when he spirit-walked into Hugo's dream.

Hati threw himself over Lódurr, who blocked the attack, but Wille did not hear. His consciousness was disconnected, and his body now stood up like an empty shell.

Then, suddenly, the wolf cross began to glow with a light so bright that it dazzled everything else around Wille.

Lódurr put up one arm to protect his face, while the fire wolves crouched on the ground and whined, as they tried to cover their faces with their paws.

A huge wave of light energy erupted from the cross, and like a dome, it expanded around them. Garmr howled furiously with rage as the energy field reached the darkness and destroyed it with a sizzling sound before it faded and Wille sank to the ground. He opened his eyes again just as the giant wolf threw himself on top of him.

Then the ground between them opened up like a deep abyss, and Garmr had to slow down to avoid falling.

Wille turned his head, and he could see Nyri standing with one arm outstretched towards him as he leaned against a tree.

Then several tree roots reached out and grabbed Garmr's back legs, and Wille realised that Tella must also be on her feet again. He felt his head filling up with fog, and the last thing he saw before he lost consciousness was how Módi and Magni threw the fire wolves away with two giant lightning bolts.

⁊

Garmr roared with rage as the roots of the trees pulled him backward. Hati and Sköll appeared next to him, splitting the roots with their flames. The wolf got back on his feet and stared at the party on the other side of the gorge. All of them had awakened again and stood ready in battle position.

"There are too many," Sköll hissed, licking her paw. "We can't defeat them now that they are together again."

Garmr let his gaze sweep over the party before a new darkness loomed up behind the three beasts, enveloping them before they disappeared into nothingness.

Lódurr hurried over to Wille and knelt down beside him. He was soon joined by the others, who formed a ring around the silver-white wolf.

"Will he be all right?" Lovisa asked anxiously, looking at Wille's silver-white wolf body.

"Don't worry, he's just unconscious," Lódurr replied, gently lifting up Wille in his arms.

Hugo jumped when he heard a creaking sound behind him. He grabbed Lovisa's hand and pulled her behind his back, while Oscar stood next to him. They exchanged a sympathetic look, and got ready.

Several shadowy figures were moving in the forest and seemed to be coming towards them.

The flames of the destroyed house still lit up the sky and the edge of the forest where they were.

A man appeared among the trees and pointed a rifle at them. Hugo prepared to attack, when he saw several men with rifles coming out of the forest, surrounding them.

The man in front of them pointed the rifle at Oscar, who seemed unusually calm as he stared into the barrel.

20. The Fylgja

They stood petrified in front of the rifle muzzle.

"Lie down," the man hissed, and pressed the rifle against Oscar's chest.

Hugo looked over to the clearing and noticed that the others had also been visited by men with hunting weapons. He saw Váli crouching behind Nyri and Tella, who were trying to protect him, while Lódurr seemed tense about the situation.

"Stop!" came a pleading voice.

In the glow of the flames, Hugo could see how Gustav pushed his way forward, with both arms stretched out and seemed to be trying to calm down the tense situation.

"Gustav?!" exclaimed one of the men, and lowered his rifle as the young man walked towards him with his arms outstretched. "What's happened here?"

"Håkan!" Gustav exclaimed before wrapping his rough arms around the hunter, who seemed to be the leader, and Håkan returned the greeting cordially.

"Where is Mikael?" Håkan asked, looking around. "And your mother, don't tell me that they…"

Gustav began to cry, and Håkan hugged him tighter.

Lovisa was running towards them when one of the men fired a shot at her, and she fell to the ground.

"Don't shoot Lovisa, please!" shouted Hugo, while Håkan shouted out an order for the rest of the men to stop shooting.

"Is that you, Lovisa?" Håkan asked in astonishment, and bent down in front of her.

"Please, Håkan," Lovisa begged, holding her leg. "Tell them to stop shooting, there are no enemies here."

Hugo could hear Lovisa's sobs as she wrapped her arms around Håkan's neck.

"Drop the guns," Håkan commanded. "Don't shoot!"

"There are wolves here!" exclaimed one of the men, pointing his rifle at Váli, who was curled up on the ground.

"Please, stop shooting!" cried Hugo again in despair.

"NO MORE SHOOTING!" Håkan's roaring voice echoed across the area.

It became silent, and the only thing that could be heard was the flames crackling in the remains of the burned down house. Then, one by one, the men laid down their hunting weapons on the ground.

"You were hit," said Håkan, looking at Lovisa.

"It's alright," she said, and grimaced as Håkan ran his hand over her wound.

"It's our friends that you pointed the guns at," Lovisa continued. "They're the ones who saved us from the house, please don't shoot them."

Håkan looked from Módi and Magni, who were standing with their weapons in combat position, to Nyri and Tella standing protectively in front of Tulio and Váli.

"Where are Mikael and Hanna?" he asked again, looking down at Gustav, who was crouching against Lovisa.

"They are dead," Lovisa replied briefly. "Murdered by the same people who set fire to the house."

There was silence around them. Some of the hunters were breathing heavily, and others reached for their weapons again as they looked around the dense forest.

"Murdered?!" Håkan exclaimed after a while, looking at the smoking ruin before looking down at Gustav again, who looked up at him with tears running down his face.

"And how do you explain the wolves?" he asked, looking at Lovisa. "And who is the man holding one of the wolves?"

Håkan pointed at Lódurr, who had started to move towards them.

"I think I can explain myself," said the old man, as he put Wille down on the ground.

"Do you have a cell phone on you?" Lódurr asked and held out a note to Håkan.

Håkan nodded and took out a cell phone from his jacket, while at the same time reaching out and taking the note.

"What is this?" Håkan asked and unfolded the note.

"Call that number," Lódurr replied. "It will answer some questions."

❧

They had been travelling for three hours, and they were about to pass Sveg when his phone rang. Kennet stared in amazement at the number he didn't recognise.

Strange, he thought, no outsider should know this number.

"Hello," Kennet said as he clicked on the call, and listened to the voice on the other side.

The voice sounded almost panicked, and he had a hard time making sense of what the person was saying.

"Wait, calm down," Kennet said. "Did you say an old man with a semi-long silver beard and strange clothes?"

He was listening intently, trying to make sense of what the man on the other side was telling him.

"A fire," Kennet repeated quietly. "And wolves? Several unknown people. Alright, where are you?"

There was silence for a moment before the voice answered. Kennet looked at his driver and motioned for him to turn south.

"Okay," he then said to the unknown person on the other side of the cell phone. "Listen to me very carefully because this is a matter of national security. You must help the man and his companions, take care of them, and make sure they are alright."

Several voices were heard on the phone, expressing dissatisfaction.

"Yes, you heard right!" Kennet exclaimed, in a harsh tone. "You are speaking to the deputy head of the KSI, an organisation within the military security service. This is a matter of national security, and if that man tells you to take care of two wolves, that's exactly what you should do!"

There was a moment's silence before Kennet spoke again, while the car turned off towards Tandsjöborg.

"We are in Sveg right now," he said briefly. "We'll be at Tandsjöborg in two hours, take care of them until then."

With those words, Kennet ended the call and announced their new destination to the rest of the fleet.

სა

Wille looked around the empty space in surprise. A silver-white flame in the centre of the room lit up the darkness and gave off a warm glow. He cautiously approached the flame and extended his hand.

The flame flickered out and undulated through the emptiness that was now bathed in the light from all the colours of the rainbow. Wille saw the outlines of hundreds of animals in the depths of the colours, and wondered where he had ended up when the outline of a silver-white wolf appeared in front of him. He backed away, and the wolf stopped a few metres in front of him.

"Don't be afraid," the wolf said, and sat down in front of him.

"Who are you?" Wille asked and squatted down.

"Your fylgja, of course," replied the wolf, looking at him.

"Where am I?" Wille asked and looked around in the undulating light.

"You almost drained yourself of your powers when you fought the darkness," the wolf replied. "And as a result, you lost consciousness."

"You are in the consciousness of the World Spirit," the wolf continued when he saw Wille's puzzled look.

"The World Spirit...consciousness..." Wille muttered and saw an eagle flying above them.

"Through your necklace, you are united with the World Spirit," said the wolf, looking at his bare chest.

Wille only now realised that he was in his ordinary form, wearing nothing at all but the necklace. He lifted the necklace and looked at it.

"What exactly is the World Spirit?" asked Wille, whereupon the wolf began to laugh.

"The ultimate question," laughed the wolf. "The World Spirit is everything that has been, everything that is, and everything that will exist. The world spirit is that from which everything originated and to which everything will return."

"It's really more than you can understand," the wolf continued, looking at Wille's confused expression. "What you do need to know is that the World Spirit is sick."

"Sick," Wille repeated uncomprehendingly. "How?"

"The first creatures that the World Spirit created were the dragons," the wolf replied. "Some of them rebelled and tried to utilise the power of creation for their own purposes."

"But they were defeated and locked up, right?" Wille asked, and the wolf nodded.

"Yes, they were locked up deep inside the World Spirit's consciousness," the wolf replied. "Unfortunately, it is also from there that they have begun to spread the darkness."

"Are the dragons spreading the darkness?" Wille asked hastily and let go of his grip on the necklace.

"In a way," the wolf replied, and took a couple of quick steps towards Wille so that their eyes met.

"You will face difficult challenges," the wolf continued. "And if you fail, then the darkness will devour all of creation."

"But what can I do against the darkness?" Wille asked.

"You'll discover that in time," the wolf replied, backing away from Wille before turning around with its back to him.

"Be brave, use your strength and wisdom, and you'll be fine."

"Wait," Wille exclaimed as the wolf prepared to step into the light again. "You never told me your name?"

The wolf laughed again and turned his face towards him.

"I have never had a name," he replied.

"But what should I call you?" Wille asked.

"I guess I've never needed a name before," the wolf replied thoughtfully. "We fylgjur never really communicate directly with our protectors."

The wolf seemed to think for a moment, before turning his face to the light again.

"You can name me since I'm your fylgja. Then you have something to think about until the next time we meet."

With these words, the wolf took a leap into the light, and seemed to run up for a road on the other side of the veil.

ᔣ

"Wille, wake up!"

Wille slowly opened his eyes, meting Hugo's worried face

He was lying on a mattress in a large room. Hugo sat next to him, gently stroking his silver-white fur. At the far end of the room, several men could be seen standing, having a lively discussion with Lódurr, and gesticulating wildly. Módi and Magni were each sitting on a chair along one wall, cleaning their weapons.

"Where are we?" Wille asked.

"We are safe, you saved us," replied Hugo. "But try not to talk, the inhabitants here are very nervous."

Wille saw Oscar sitting next to Lovisa, who was in a half-sitting position at the other end of the room.

He sat up sharply when he saw that she had one leg wrapped in a bandage.

"Easy," said Hugo, pushing him down again. "It's all right, a shot scratched her leg."

Wille looked around but couldn't see the others.

"Where are the others?" he asked. "Don't tell me they…"

"They're fine, thanks to you," Hugo replied, and firmly pressed down his head on the mattress again. "Gustav, Nyri, and Tella are helping to extinguish the last remnants of the burned house."

"What about Váli and Tulio?" asked Wille worriedly.

"They are scouting to see if there are any more enemies in the area, although I don't think that there are," replied Hugo. "The wolves left when your light dissolved the darkness."

"Where were you?" Wille asked with a slightly irritated tone. "Why did you disappear before the attack?"

"Tulio ran away when we entered the village," replied Hugo. "I found him talking to a squirrel, and that's when Garmr attacked us. I took Tulio and tried to get us out of there, but Garmr was too fast. If Váli hadn't shown up, we probably wouldn't have made it to the house at all."

"Sounds like you've been through a lot," said a voice beside them, and Wille jumped up.

Oscar had quietly stood beside them and listened.

"Oscar," Wille whispered. "Is it really you?"

"Yes, I think we've established that now," he replied with a laugh, and sat down on the mattress.

"How did this actually happen?" he asked while running his hand through Wille's fur. "Not that it bothers me, you make a good wolf."

Wille felt uncomfortable, he was still struggling to deal with his wolf form, and just wanted to transform back again.

"It's a long story," he replied. "But how did you escape the darkness?"

"I really don't know," Oscar replied, looking thoughtful. "When the darkness pulled me down, it was as if I went numb, and then I woke up in the realm of the dead."

"In the underworld!" Hugo exclaimed, and Oscar nodded.

"It's a terrible place, full of lost souls and demons," said Oscar. "I got help from a god to get out."

"A god?" Wille asked, looking suspiciously at Oscar, who nodded in response.

"A god who was murdered with a mistletoe arrow," replied Oscar affirmatively. "I think your friends know who it is, we can talk about it later."

"But how did you find us?" Hugo asked, continuing to run his hand through Wille's fur.

Wille could sense that his brother was nervous, and he himself was beginning to feel worried himself.

"When I came back, the house was abandoned," replied Oscar, flapping his arms. "I went home and discovered that our house had also been abandoned. I saw that Dad's hunting car was gone, so I put two and two together. The only times he uses it is when he's hunting or when we go up here."

"But how did you get here?" Wille asked, studying his expression.

"By train," Oscar replied. "The Inland Railway passes on the other side of the lake, and since it's only tourist trains that use the line, there's usually no problem asking them to stop, even if there is no natural stop there."

Hugo still looked sceptical. Wille turned his head and looked at Lovisa, who sat slumped against the wall.

"What about her?" he asked worriedly.

"It's just a slight flesh wound, it's nothing to worry about," Oscar replied. "But there seems to be something else that is troubling her. I suspect that you have been through a lot."

Wille turned his head towards Hugo, and their eyes met in agreement. Lovisa had apparently not told him about Tommy, and Wille suspected that it was up to him.

"Oscar," he said quietly, looking up at his friend. "Tommy, your father..."

"Yes, where is he?" Oscar interrupted, looking around. "Wasn't he with you?"

Wille let out a sigh and felt a tear start to run down his cheek. This was not going to be easy, and he knew Oscar would break down.

"He's dead," Hugo replied briefly.

No one said anything for a while, and they could hear the men's lively discussion from across the room.

"What do you mean?" Oscar asked, his face turning pale.

Wille could see how he began to shake.

"They were demon worshippers," Wille replied, lowering his gaze. "They attacked us along the road, disguised as police officers. They were led by a demon who could conjure up things of darkness, and he shot Tommy dead."

Now Oscar was shaking so much and trying to hold back tears, that Hugo had to calm him down. Wille looked at Lovisa, and from her sad expression, he realised that she knew they had told him. A line of tears ran down her face, and he wished so badly to hold her in his arms.

Just then, the front doors opened, and several men in military uniforms came into the room.

Lódurr talked for a while with one of the men, who nodded gravely, and walked away to the corner of the room where Wille, Hugo, and Oscar were.

"So, you are one of the wolves who have been frightening the villagers," said the man, squatting down beside Wille.

"My name is Kenneth, I'm the commander of a group of soldiers who assist the gods," he continued. "Don't worry, we'll help you get to the mountain."

21. A Special Book

Jörgen's head throbbed, and he saw the blurred outline of someone leaning over him.

"Dad, he's waking up now!"

Jörgen tried to sit up but felt a stabbing pain in the back of his head. He put his hand there and leaned back.

"Calm down, Jack, let him regain consciousness before throwing yourself at him," came a sharp male voice.

Jörgen put his head on the pillow and tried to push away the tingling, which cut into his head like knives.

"There you go, take it easy," said the sharp voice again as another figure appeared in his field of vision.

"Where am I?" Jörgen muttered.

The field of vision cleared, and a muscular man with shoulder-length, snow-white hair and silver-white eyes appeared in front of him.

"Looks like he's really coming around now, Dad!"

Jörgen turned his head, seeing a young man standing next to him. He tried to get up, but the pain throbbed in his head.

"Careful," the man said, grabbing Jorgen's neck. "You have a good injury to your head, and you need to rest."

"Where is my family?" Jörgen asked, and the two strangers exchanged menacing looks.

"The military base was attacked by demons," the man replied, while the boy put a blanket over Jörgen. "I'm afraid your wife is gone."

"What do you mean?" Jörgen asked, holding his head.

"She was shot in the chaos of your escape," the man replied, looking down at his hands. Jörgen felt grief mixed with anger. He felt the tears sting his eyes, and clenched his hands in anger.

"Your daughter, on the other hand, survived and is safe," the man continued, putting his hands over Jörgen's fists.

The man's hands felt strange. They were icy cold, but still gave off a strange warmth.

"Who are you?" Jörgen asked, staring at them.

"My name is Ullinn," the man replied. "But you can call me Ullr."

"Ullr, as in the snow god?" Jörgen asked, managing to sit up properly.

"Oh yes, I apologise," exclaimed Ullr, laughing. "I forgot that I was talking to a professor of religion."

"But yes, that's right! And this is my son, Jack," he then said, placing his hand on the boy's shoulder.

Jörgen looked scrutinizingly at the young boy, who looked to be in his fifteenth year. The boy's short hair was the same snow-white shade as Ullr's, and he looked almost like a younger version of the man. Ullr himself looked surprisingly young despite the thick stubble, and Jörgen guessed that he was somewhere around thirty years of age.

"You seem surprised," said Ullr, as if he could guess what Jörgen was thinking. "We gods don't age like you humans, and we can freeze our ageing."

"So, what does that mean?" Jörgen asked.

"It means that we are older than we look," Jack replied. "I know that I look like I'm in my fifteen's and that Dad looks like he's somewhere around thirty. But believe me, with the age of the gods, we are much older."

"Jack, take it easy," said Ullr. "It's too much information for him right now."

"What happened to me?" Jörgen asked.

He still felt dizzy and slightly nauseous.

"We came to help," replied Ull, looking pitifully at Jörgen. "But we were too late, the demons had left by the time we arrived, and we found you on the floor with this."

Ull picked up a thick book from the floor and gave it to Jörgen, who suddenly remembered everything. He had run back to the dormitory to fetch the book, and found himself in the middle of the fighting. Then he remembered a sharp pain and emptiness.

"It's an interesting book about us gods," Ullr continued. "When the time is better, I hope we can improve it."

Jörgen nodded and accepted the book. It was his life's work, and yet the weight of the book was nothing compared to the weight of his sad heart as he pressed the book against his chest.

"You need to rest for a while longer," Ullr continued, and stood up. "We will leave this afternoon."

"Where are we going?" Jörgen asked, placing the book on the mattress.

"To Asgard," Jack replied, smiling as he leaned Jörgen's head against the pillows. "You are safe, and your daughter is with friends, you will see each other again soon."

∽

Jessica looked out over the crowd at the abandoned school. She sat with a blanket wrapped around her and was shaking with sadness. She missed her parents, her father's calm, and her mother's loving hugs.

"You can't be serious?" one boy shouted at the top of his voice, while two older boys held him back.

Jessica didn't understand what was going on, and she saw a silver-white wolf coming out of the building.

An older man walked over to try and calm the situation, but the boy still seemed upset.

Then a black-furred wolf appeared from the edge of the forest. The dark wolf seemed to be talking to the silver-white wolf, and they seemed to come to some kind of conclusion.

Jessica couldn't care less about two wolves talking to each other. Her world had been shattered, and she no longer cared about what was going on around her.

"You look like you need someone to talk to," a voice suddenly spoke next to her, and she turned her head.

A boy with light brown hair sat down next to her and put one arm around her shoulders.

"Who are you?" Jessica asked, but he shushed her.

"My name is Oscar," the boy replied. "You look like you need a friend right now."

"I'm just confused," she said as she watched several soldiers begin to load the trucks with supplies.

"So, what are you doing here with the military guys?" Oscar asked, looking at the crowd in the courtyard.

Jessica felt tears begin to flow down her cheeks as she recalled the events of the past twenty-four hours.

"I'm sorry," he exclaimed, putting one arm around her. "I didn't mean to upset you."

"It's okay," Jessica said, wiping her face. "We were attacked this morning, and my mom was shot before we could evacuate."

"Do you have a father?" Oscar asked, grabbing her hands.

"He disappeared in the chaos just before we evacuated," Jessica replied, looking at him with tearful eyes. "I don't know if he survived or not."

"I'm sorry," Oscar said. "I lost my dad in this war, so I understand what you're going through."

"Thank you," she replied, wiping her tears. "Why are there two wolves here?"

Oscar looked at both wolves and smiled.

"That's actually a good question," he whispered quietly to himself. "Why are there *two* wolves here?"

⁌

"Are you sure about this?" Lovisa asked.

"I don't think we have much of a choice," replied Wille, looking down at the ground.

"You can always turn back," she suggested gently.

"Well," he said, looking around. "There are too many people here, and I have no clothes. Besides, I don't want to abandon Váli."

"Then we'll go with you," said Hugo, standing beside them. "We are a family after all."

Wille looked up at him in surprise. He had never thought about it before, but he realised that Hugo was right, they were all family in a way.

"Out of the question," came Váli's clear voice.

The dark-furred wolf joined them.

"I'm afraid we have to split up for a short time," he continued. "Me and Wille do not fit in the cars in our present form, and if you were to join us, we would be slowed down."

"But Váli," said Hugo, bending down by the wolf. "What if something happens? I don't want to lose you too."

"That's why I'm coming with you," Tulio's voice was suddenly heard, and everyone looked at the boy, who stood silently watching them.

"Tulio…" began Wille, but the boy put up his hand.

"Váli, you can carry me, right?" Tulio asked, looking at the wolf.

"Sure," replied Váli. "But…"

"Váli," Tulio said. "You have to go through the woodland to get to the mountain, and if something happens on the way, my friends in the forest can help you."

"Tulio, you're staying here," came Tella's sharp voice.

She and Nyri came walking towards them.

"Tella!" the boy exclaimed, hugging his big sister.

"I can't let you go with them. It's too dangerous," she said.

"You know I'm their best chance if something happens," he said, and smiled broadly.

"Yes, but that's no reason to…" Tella began, but was interrupted in surprise when Nyri put a hand on her shoulder.

"Tella, you can't protect him forever," he said. "He needs to grow up, and learn to take responsibility."

Nyri leaned down, and looked seriously at his little brother. Then he put his hand on Tulio's shoulder.

"Are you sure about this?" Nyri asked.

Tulio nodded confidently.

"Take care of yourself," Nyri said, and gave him a hug.

Tulio looked at Tella, who now had tears on her face. She nodded in agreement with him as Nyri let go and stood up.

"Take care of him," Nyri said, looking seriously at Váli.

"Here," Módi said, appearing behind Tella. "You might need this."

Módi handed Tulio a small backpack, with his clothes carefully packed along with food and water.

"Thank you," Tulio said, accepting the backpack.

Váli walked over and stood by his side.

"It won't be an easy journey," Váli said, looking at him urgently. "Are you sure?"

Tulio nodded, and Váli turned to Wille.

"We'll leave right away," he said firmly. "We will need to travel fast to catch up with you, so we might as well get a bit of a head start."

✑

Oscar stood a little way into the forest and watched the two wolves leave. The little boy, Tulio, was riding on Váli's back and seemed to be struggling to hold on when the wolves picked up speed. He could see the boy clinging to the dark grey wolf's neck.

Oscar turned, and looked into the white eyes behind the trees. The dark creature loomed up in front of him, and slowly bowed its head.

"You know what you need to do," Oscar commanded, striking out with one hand. "Go!"

The creature grunted and stood up on its hind legs before dashing off through the forest in the same direction as the wolves had just disappeared.

✑

"Are you out of your mind?!!!"

The words echoed between the pillars as a turquoise fire erupted around the circle.

"How could you ally yourself with him?!"

Hades stood completely engulfed in flames and stared furiously at Wayland, who stood in the centre of the circle.

Wayland stretched out one hand, and the turquoise flames were quickly replaced with black flames.

"Enough," said one of the dark-clad figures, rising from his seat.

The figure pointed his claw-like hand at Hades, who dropped to his knees and howled in pain. The dark-clad man twisted his three fingers and struck out with them in a gesture, whereupon Hades immediately got on his feet again.

"What good would that do?" thundered Hades.

"Know your place," replied the dark-clad man. "The only reason you are here is because we need your ring."

"And you," said the man, turning around to face Wayland again. "Put out those flames before I subject you to the same treatment!"

"I doubt you can do that," said Wayland, waving a hand, and the flames disappeared. "But for the sake of politeness, I will do it."

"Are you done with all the drama?"

Another of the dark-clad figures stood up and pulled off her hood.

The old woman who appeared was holding a black wooden stick, which she leaned on as she walked towards them.

"Mother," Hela's voice was heard behind them.

The old woman turned around. Hela had risen from her seat, and stared out at them with her staff in a tight grip.

"We need each other until we have stopped them from reaching the mountain, until then, we are allied with him," Hela said, looking at Wayland. "What happens after that remains to be seen."

"Are your hunters ready?" she asked in a daze.

"We attacked their soldiers early this morning and destroyed a large number of them," Wayland replied.

"Good," Hela said, stepping down to the floor.

Hades still looked furious, but quickly complied as Hela started walking towards them.

"Mother, we need to leave," she said, and the old woman nodded, grabbing Hela's outstretched staff.

Purple flames enveloped the women before they disappeared.

"And where are you going?" Hades asked irritably as Wayland began to walk away.

"Hades," the dark-clad man growled warningly, raising his three claw-like fingers again.

"Where I go is none of your business," Wayland replied, before he was enveloped by black flames and disappeared.

"Hades, we still don't know where he gets his powers from," said another dark-clad figure. "Until we know, we can't get rid of him, he is stronger than us."

The woman pulled off her dark cloak to reveal a lovely pale-skinned female face with snow-white hair.

"How is the plan to rescue him going?" asked the man with three fingers. "We need him to succeed in your part of our plan."

"Don't worry," the woman replied, smiling. "Your granddaughter's puppy has found his way back to his friends again, and when he is released into Asgard, he will release him. I can't wait to see my beloved again."

The woman put one hand behind her head and smiled.

"Don't forget to have the mirror ready," said the three-fingered man. "We can't open the door without it."

"Not to worry, my own puppy is doing puzzles with it right now," the woman said with a laugh, before a white fire surrounded her and she too disappeared.

"Come, my queen," said the three-fingered man, and another darkly dressed figure stood up.

The man with the three fingers grabbed her rotting hand before they faded away and disappeared.

A turquoise veil of fire enveloped Hades, who also disappeared, leaving the hall seemingly empty.

Silence fell before a dark silhouette appeared in the centre of the circle. The man raised his hand, and dark blue flames lit up the room.

Just as the man was enveloped by the flames and disappeared, a gigantic shadow was cast against one wall of the hall. The horned shadow spread its wings and opened its lowering blue eyes, before it too disappeared, leaving the hall in dense darkness.

ↁ

"Are you still angry that I tried to drown you?" asked the old woman, looking at Hela.

They had stopped in front of a large gate of dark iron.

"I won't discuss it," Hela replied coldly.

"Very well," said the woman, banging her wooden staff against the gate three times. "How many do you need?"

"Two hundred," Hela replied as the door opened, and an uncountable number of purple eyes stared at them from within the darkness.

The black wolves that trotted out stood around them. Hela raised her staff, which began to glow with a purple light.

"You know what to do, leave no one alive except the boy," she said, and the wolves scurried off into the darkness, howling.

"Your brothers are impatient," said the old woman. "They wonder when the next phase will begin."

"The next phase begins when we have taken care of the boy and his friends," Hela hissed before walking away.

22. Santa's Sledge

Tulio was coughing and seemed nauseous.

"Please, can we take a break?" he asked.

Wille looked at Váli, who seemed impatient.

"I told you it would not be a pleasant journey," Váli said, looking at the young boy.

They had run half the night and found themselves by a lake. Váli bent down, and drank voraciously from the water.

Tulio tried to get up, but fell against Váli's back.

"Váli, we need to slow down," said Wille, looking at his cousin, who was lifting his head from the water.

"We don't have time for that, Wille!" Váli exclaimed, looking annoyed at them.

"We'll take our time," Wille said firmly, and looked at Tulio, who was still leaning against his back.

Váli sighed and walked towards them. He narrowed his eyes at the boy, who turned his face away.

"I'm sorry," Tulio said, standing up on shaky legs. "I thought I could help."

"Maybe you can," Váli said, looking at the starry sky. "We need to sleep, but someone needs to keep watch."

Tulio nodded and took out his kantele, which he brought to his hands and began to play. It was a lively melody whose mysterious depths reminded Wille of a beautiful summer day, with birds chirping and trees waving.

After a while, several moose emerged from the forest. One of them was chalky white in colour, and Wille thought it looked majestic as it emerged and sank down on its front legs in front of Tulio, who stopped playing. The boy ran his hand along the moose's white fur and scratched it lightly behind the ear.

"Will they stay with us all night?" Wille asked.

"They will watch over us tonight," replied Tulio. "No one will disturb us while we are sleeping."

"Good," said Váli, as he lay down on the ground.

Wille lay down next to him and watched as the moose formed a ring around them.

"Uhm, Váli," said Tulio, looking uncertainly at the dark-furred wolf.

"What is it?" the wolf asked impatiently. "Go to sleep!"

"Yes, but I need to…you know…go," Tulio stammered nervously.

"Then go do your business," Váli hissed irritably.

"Yes, but…" Tulio said, looking into the dark forest. "I'm afraid of the dark."

"Are you serious? You're a forest god!" Váli exclaimed vehemently.

The boy nodded, looking down at the ground in shame.

Váli sighed and stood up.

"Let's go then," he said, and followed Tulio into the forest.

Wille lay down, and listened when they disappeared in to the forest. He remembered himself when he and Oscar were younger, and both were afraid to go home in the evenings. Perhaps gods and humans were not so different after all.

Wille heard the creaking when they came out of the woods again, he was still having trouble getting used to the sharp hearing that he had gotten with the transformation.

Váli lay down in the same place again, but Tulio was still standing there, looking uncertain.

"What is it now?" asked Váli, sighing as the boy looked around nervously.

"Tulio," said Wille. "You must trust the moose to protect us, that's why you asked them to come here."

"Besides, there's another one watching over us," said Váli, looking up at the moon, which appeared as a faint streak behind the clouds.

"Yes, but…can I sleep between you guys?" Tulio asked hastily, looking at them pleadingly.

The wolves looked at each other before they moved away, and Váli motioned for Tulio to lie down between them.

Wille watched in fascination as the young boy curled up like a ball and lay down close to Váli. He smiled at Váli, who watched the boy in amazement, and guessed that his cousin was not used to that kind of closeness.

Váli saw the smiling expression on Wille's face and seemed unable to keep from smiling himself before laying his head on the ground.

As all three fell asleep, a pair of large white eyes stared at them from further away in the forest.

〜

"Why so gloomy?" Módi asked, looking at Hugo.

They had been travelling for two hours, but Hugo hadn't noticed much of the journey. He and Módi sat in the back seat of a military car and hadn't said a word to each other.

"I'm turning fifteen tomorrow, and I have neither Wille nor Váli with me," Hugo said, and sighed.

"Fifteen then," Módi said, pulling on his chin. "That's something special for a god."

"What do you mean?" Hugo asked.

"Well, when a god turns fifteen, he is usually given a test to see if he is ready to become an adult," replied Módi. "As for your brother, it is a little late for that, of course, but you might be ready for your test."

"What kind of test?" Hugo asked nervously.

"Don't worry," the young man replied, smiling lightly at him. "I think you'll pass it."

"What are you two talking about?" Tella asked, leaning back from the passenger seat.

"Nothing," Hugo exclaimed, curling up in his seat.

Tella looked at him questioningly, while Módi smiled.

"He's nervous because he's turning fifteen tomorrow!"

Tella opened her eyes and looked at him.

"You're not going to…" Tella began in astonishment, as Módi nodded in satisfaction.

"His brother is already over fifteen, but we still have a chance here," he continued in a purring voice.

Tella stared at Módi and then looked at Hugo, who was curled up like a ball where he sat.

"See, you've got him worried," she said angrily. "This is up to you, I won't be a part of this."

"We will stop at the village of Hede and ask if there is any good place to stay nearby," their driver interrupted, looking at them curiously.

Tella nodded as the car in front of them turned into a fuel station. She saw Oscar, Magni, and Lódurr jump out of the car, along with the driver. She opened her own car door, and walked towards them.

"Grandpa, what's going on?" Tella asked, looking at Lódurr, who was watching Magni and Oscar as they entered the shop together.

"We need to see if there is a good place where we can camp for the night," he replied, looking at her.

"That's not what I meant," said Tella, looking towards the shop. "Something is bothering you, isn't it?"

"You can't be fooled," her grandfather replied, crossing his arms. "There is something about him."

Tella watched through the window as Magni and Oscar talked intensively with the shopkeeper.

"But hadn't Magni checked him?" she asked, looking at her grandfather, who nodded slowly.

"Of course he has, but there are some things that Magni hasn't been taught yet," Lódurr replied.

"Do you want us to keep an eye on him?" Tella asked.

"Keep a close eye on him," replied her grandfather, as Magni and Oscar came out of the shop.

"There is a tarn along our route, which apparently is very suitable," said Oscar, looking at Lódurr.

"That's right," Magni continued, lowering his voice slightly. "There is a perfect campsite where we can fit all the cars and tents."

"But?" Tella asked, looking at Magni, who seemed unusually nervous.

"There is a legend about the tarn that says that a treasure is buried at its bottom," he replied, looking at Lódurr. "And those who search for the treasure do not return."

"Probably just an old tale," said Oscar, shrugging his shoulders. "Besides, we're not on a treasure hunt, are we?"

Lódurr looked at them and turned to Magni.

"How far from here is this place?" the old man asked.

"About half an hour away," Magni replied. "There seems to be plenty of room for all of us there, and we could really use a rest."

Lódurr nodded, but said nothing.

Tella looked inquiringly at her grandfather, but she knew better than to disturb him when he was thinking.

"Can you and your brother handle this?" Lódurr asked, giving Magni a tense look.

"Sure, but…" Magni started to answer, but was interrupted by Tella, who was looking angry.

"Are you leaving us again?" she asked, meeting his gaze.

"I have to prepare the other gods for our arrival because we should reach the mountain in the next twenty-four hours," Lódurr replied. "I also want to see that we have no unpleasant surprises waiting for us there."

"We can lead them the last bit," Magni said firmly. "But can you manage alone?"

"Don't worry about me," Lódurr replied, laughing.

He took out his stringed instrument and put it in his hand.

"Is that a kantele?" asked Hugo, who had joined them.

"Yes, it is," replied Lódurr, running his fingers over the strings. "I suppose Tulio showed you his kantele?"

"Yes, he can attract animals with it," Hugo confirmed, looking curiously at the old man's instrument.

"This kantele is a bit different," said Lódurr, and began to play the strings.

A wind lifted the man high into the air. It was so strong that the others held their arms in front of their faces for protection as the old man disappeared in the wind.

"What just happened?" Hugo asked, looking at Magni.

"Don't worry," Magni replied, signalling them to go back to the cars. "He does that sometimes."

❧

He slowly opened his eyes and shrugged.

"Afraid of heights?" Jack asked teasingly, as Jörgen opened his eyes in fear.

They were just above the treetops, travelling at high speed along the ice track Jack had created in front of them. The boy with the bright blue wool coat seemed fully focused, and Jörgen watched in amazement as the ice disappeared again behind the sledge.

"I know it's hard for you," Ullr said from the front seat. "But we don't have time to get there on foot."

He pulled on the reins, and the reindeer pulling the sledge swung quickly to the left, with Jörgen thrown to the side.

The edges of the sledge were so high that it was impossible to fall out, but it did not make the experience more pleasant. If Jörgen had not been so terrified, the experience would probably have fascinated him more.

"You should feel honoured," Jack said proudly. "Not many people get the honour of riding in Santa's sleigh."

"You mean you're Santa Claus too?" asked Jörgen, who was beginning to feel motion sickness.

"In a way," replied Ullr, laughing.

Jack ran his hand over Ullr's face, and Jörgen gasped as snow-white frost grew over the man's short stubble, forming a coarse snow-white beard. In combination with his dark blue wool coat, he certainly looked like Santa Claus.

"I guess we can say we're keeping the tradition alive," Jack said, looking amused at Jörgen's expression.

"We are part of a network that tries to spread joy among people," Ullr continued, flicking the reins. "Even if the darkness prevents us from showing ourselves as gods, we still want to try to keep the magic alive within you."

"So, the reindeer are?" Jörgen asked tentatively.

"Blitzen, Comet, Cupid, Dancer, Dasher, Donder, Prancer, and Vixen," Jack replied proudly. "I have named them."

"No Rudolph?" Jörgen asked, and Ullr laughed.

"You can tell him, Jack. It's your reindeer after all," he said, smacking the reins. "It's getting hard to see, so we might need some extra light."

Jack let out a whistling sound, and Jörgen saw something coming towards them from above their heads. He looked up and saw a reindeer that seemed to be running in the air.

"Rudolph is the only one of the reindeer that can actually fly," said Jack, as a red light began to shine above them.

"Is that your reindeer?" Jörgen asked, looking at Jack, who nodded sombrely.

"Actually, it's my mother's reindeer," he replied, and sat down with his arms around his legs.

"Who's your mother?" Jörgen asked, noticing how Jack began to shake where he was sitting.

"I don't think that's a good topic for discussion," said Ullr encouragingly.

"I'm sorry," said Jörgen. "I didn't mean to be rude."

"It's all right," said Jack, looking smilingly at Jörgen, who could see that the boy had tears in his eyes. "I just miss her."

"No need to apologise," said Jörgen. "Do you want to tell me what happened?"

"We don't know what happened to her," interjected Ullr. "She was one of the three goddesses who were kidnapped by the blacksmiths when they were held prisoner on the island. After their escape, both Jack's mother, Hulda, and the blacksmith Hjúki, have disappeared."

"I have heard of Hjúki," said Jörgen. "But not Hulda."

"Hulda is known by several names, including Holle and Bil," said Ullr, looking worriedly at Jack.

Jörgen took his arm out of the blanket that was wrapped around him, and pulled Jack close to him. The boy hugged him, and Jörgen gently wrapped the blanket around him.

"Bil is the child of the moon, isn't it?" Jörgen asked, and Ullr nodded.

"Long ago, during the last war against darkness, Máni the Moon God discovered two children outside a house that the creatures of darkness had attacked," the snow god replied seriously. "He felt compassion for the children, who had been orphans, so he raised them as his own children."

"But doesn't that mean that both Jack and his mother are human?" Jörgen asked, looking down at the boy in his arms, who seemed to have fallen asleep.

Ullr shook his head.

"Hulda was indeed a human when she and her brother Hjúki came to our world, but they were elevated to gods by the World Spirit," he replied, looking sadly at Jörgen.

"She was my everything, the love of my life," Ullr continued, sighing. "But now there are only me and Jack."

Jörgen felt compassion for the younger man, for he knew exactly how he must feel. His chest tightened when he thought about Amanda. If he hadn't run back, he might have been able to protect her.

A screeching sound was heard, and Jörgen looked up just in time to see a silver-winged hawk landing next to Ullr.

"Hábrók," said the god in surprise. "What are you doing here?"

The hawk flapped wildly and seemed to be trying to say something.

"It seems he wants us to follow," said Jörgen, looking after the hawk disappearing into the night.

Ullr nodded in agreement and suddenly pulled the reins so that the reindeer swung off in the same direction as the hawk had just disappeared.

Jörgen saw from the red light that Rudolph had understood, continuing to light the way for them.

"Where do you think it takes us?" Jörgen asked, looking at the sleeping boy again.

"I don't know," replied Ullr. "But wherever it is, it seems that we are in a hurry."

"Wait a minute," exclaimed Jörgen, noticing how they had begun to sink into the treetops. "How can we still be in the air without Jack's ice?"

"Look under the sledge again," replied Ull, laughing.

Jörgen cautiously raised looked down and saw an enormous swirl of snow that was slowly lowering the sledge to the ground.

"I may be a winter god, but my magic is limited to snow," said Ull. "Jack is the only one of us who can make ice, and the sledge is too heavy for my snow to hold it up. We will have to travel on the ground for now, until he wakes up again."

23. The Monster in The Tarn

The tarn they camped at was certainly different. Oscar had been told that it was called 'the Eggshell Tarn', or 'the Edgeshell Tarn', and he understood why, as the oval tarn was only a few square metres in size. Moreover, it was located next to a ridge, and the alternative name referred to the intersecting edge between the tarn and the ridge.

"Let's go on a treasure hunt," chirped Hugo, who threw off his shirt and plunged past Oscar towards the small tarn.

"Stop!" Magni and Módi shouted before Hugo got there.

"No one goes into that tarn until we've examined it," said Módi, and walked up to the water's edge.

"What do you think?" he asked, looking at his older brother and feeling the water in the small tarn.

"I'm not sure," Magni replied, looking inquiringly at the mirror-like water.

"The trees are worried," said Tella, who came and stood beside them. "Something about this place is bothering them."

She waved to Nyri, who joined them as they watched Kenneth take command of the campsite, where the military soldiers began raising large tents with stoves below the ridge.

"Can you feel anything here?" Tella asked.

Nyri bent down to the ground and put one hand near the waterline. He closed his eyes, and seemed lost in thought.

"There really are gold and precious metals buried in the bottom of the tarn," he replied after a while, and let his eyes wander along the inlet of the tarn that ran down from the ridge and under the road. "But there is something more."

"Can you feel what it is?" Tella asked urgently, but he shook his head.

"I'm afraid not," he replied, shaking his head as he stood up again. "But whatever it is, it is aware of our presence."

"That settles it," Magni said, and walked over to Kenneth, who was standing directing the soldiers.

Oscar could see how Magni pointed to the tarn and how the military leader looked in their direction, while he nodded and crossed his arms.

"What are you going to do?" Oscar asked, walking towards them.

"We divide our cars so that we form a wall both in front of the tarn and at both ends of the road," replied Kenneth, giving the order to one of his men. "That way we are protected both from the road and from the tarn."

"And no one will leave the camp alone," he continued, looking urgently at the youths, who nodded in agreement.

The rest of the evening was spent preparing the large military tents with sleeping bags. Before they went to bed, the soldiers served a steaming stew for supper, and everyone ate with a good appetite.

It was decided that a rotating shift schedule of two soldiers and one of the young people would keep watch for two hours each throughout the night.

"I can take the first watch," said Oscar, standing up. "I'm still alert."

"Don't you need to rest?" Lovisa asked, looking up anxiously from her food bowl.

"Don't worry, I'll be fine for a few more hours," replied Oscar, smiling confidently at his sister.

He watched as Hugo placed the bowl at the makeshift sink and crawled into a tent, closely followed by Gustav, Nyri, Magni, Módi, and Kenneth, as well as ten soldiers.

The girls were given their own smaller tent in the centre of the camp, and the other tents along the road were quickly filled by tired men who crawled into their sleeping bags.

Oscar remained seated on one of the makeshift benches around the campfire, and he were joined by three soldiers.

"Can you manage to sleep by yourself?" Gustav's voice was heard in the tent.

"It's unusual when Wille and Váli aren't around, I miss them," Hugo replied, turning to the tent canvas.

"I'm sure they're fine," said Gustav. "Váli seems used to the forest, and your brother is tough, I wouldn't worry if I were you. Besides, we'll see them again soon."

The boys' conversation was soon replaced by loud snoring. Oscar looked out over the tarn and the steep ridge, while laughing in approval at the military guys' jokes. How ignorant they were, he thought, smiling to himself. He could feel what was in the tarn and in the soil behind the ridge. The remnants of people who had come here over the years, but who had never been allowed to leave the area alive.

The tarn was bubbling up and Oscar grinned with satisfaction – he couldn't have planned it better himself!

☙

Hugo had a nightmare, he dreamed that he was standing outside the tent when he saw a strange hare scampering up the steep ridge, which was now covered with dried hay. The snow-white hare had strange horns protruding from its head, and as he followed it up the ridge, it unfolded coarse capercaillie wings and flew away, whereupon Hugo suddenly found himself under water, surrounded by gold and valuables, but were unable to breathe, and the ground pulled him slowly downwards like a dyke.

Then he saw a large creature swimming towards him with seaweed swirling around it. The creature opened its mouth, and revealed gleaming fangs. Hugo tried to scream, but only drew water in through his mouth. Just as the creature was about to sink its teeth into him, everything went black.

☙

Hugo opened his eyes in panic and gasped for breath. He looked around, but discovered that everyone else was still fast asleep. From the opening of the tent, however, he could see a strange light shining in through the night.

Cautiously, he crawled out of his sleeping bag and listened nervously for sounds from outside. Nothing could be heard but the rustling sound of the breeze blowing through the leaves. Hugo cautiously opened the tent canvas and peered out over the camp. He could see neither Oscar nor the soldiers, but the strange light gave the night darkness a golden-white hue.

The bright light penetrated the trees that covered the ridge, and Hugo felt himself being drawn to the strange glow as he passed by the cars. Nervously, he looked around – it was far too quiet in the forest around the camp.

A feeling of being watched ran through him, and he looked around. Hugo was shocked to find himself face-to-face with a glittering white horse, the same shade as the light illuminating the ridge. The horse looked very beautiful, almost enchanting, as it bowed its head before him.

Hugo carefully reached out with one hand and gently stroked it along the horse's mane. The fur felt wet and sticky, but the horse seemed to appreciate his touch, so he continued to run his hand over its back.

The horse whinnied and lowered its back towards him.

Hugo hesitated for a moment as he looked into the horse's dark eyes. He had never ridden a horse before. He carefully mounted the animal's back and sat down.

The horse stood up, and Hugo held its neck tightly to prevent himself from falling off. Then he heard someone calling his name, and when Hugo turned his head, he saw Lovisa standing with her hands over her mouth.

The horse snorted again, and when Hugo turned his face back, he was no longer staring at a golden-white horse but at a green, scaly face with a mane made of seaweed.

At the same moment that fear gripped him, Hugo felt his body stuck in the sticky fur. He could sense the creature sneering at him, and he cursed himself for being so gullible.

Hugo heard Lovisa screaming for help, but it was too late. The horse stepped up on its hind legs before taking a big leap towards the illuminated ridge.

❧

"Help! Help!"

Gustav woke up with a jolt, and immediately sat up when he heard Lovisa's desperate cries for help outside the tents.

He quickly grabbed his pants and rushed out of the tent, while shouting at the others to wake up.

"Lovisa, what's going on?" Gustav asked when he reached the ridge where she was screaming hysterically.

He shook her, whereupon she pointed with a trembling hand to the other side of the ridge.

"It took Hugo," she screamed in despair as Magni and Módi rushed past them.

By now, the whole camp had come to life, and several soldiers rushed over the ridge as Kenneth came panting.

"What's going on?" he asked in a daze.

"A big horse took Hugo," answered Lovisa, without lowering her hand. "It is trying to drown him in a tarn."

Gustav swore and let go of her before he started to run the last bit over the ridge, with Kenneth panting behind him.

Once over the wooded crest, they saw an almost dried-up tarn where a marsh spread out. There was chaos at the tarn, with several soldiers pointing their rifles at the deeper part of the marsh, whose surface gave off waves from the struggle.

"Don't shoot!" Kenneth roared. "You might hit the boy."

"Can't you do something?" Gustav asked, and looked at Magni, who was looking out over the water surface.

"We don't have time," replied Módi behind him. "Before we have time to use our magic, he has already drowned."

Gustav pulled off his pants and threw his shirt away. He was just about to dive in when Magni stopped him.

"What are you doing?" the young god asked, looking at him sternly. "Do you want to die too?"

"I'm not going to stand by and watch him die," Gustav replied, before wading into the icy water, swimming towards the place where it was bubbling.

It was difficult to see anything in the murky water, but Gustav was an experienced swimmer and had no problem with the temperature of the water. He had to strain his eyes to the limit to see anything, but he could sense strong movements in the water a little further ahead.

Suddenly, he saw Hugo slowly sinking towards the bottom of the tarn.

Gustav took a few vigorous strokes and caught him at the same time as he perceived movements in the corners of his eyes. He had to make an effort not to open his mouth and scream when he saw the creature coming towards them with a wide, open mouth, and its fangs bared.

Then Oscar appeared and pushed a knife into the creature's abdomen, whereupon it seemed to lose its orientation.

Oscar pointed to the surface of the water before grabbing Hugo's arm.

They swam upwards with Hugo as fast as they could, but Gustav sensed that the creature was after them.

They broke the surface of the water with a loud splash, and Gustav immediately lay on his back, dragging Hugo towards the edge of the wetland.

He saw how Oscar came swimming behind them, at the same time as the surface of the water cracked and an enormous, scaly head loomed up.

There were screams from the others standing around the marsh, while the horse creature threw itself upon Oscar and began to drag him under the water.

Gustav reached some of the soldiers and got help to pull Hugo up on land, before he threw himself into the water again. He reached the splashing Oscar, who was fighting the creature, and grabbed his hand just as Oscar's head disappeared beneath the surface of the water.

Gustav suddenly saw a large tree root appear next to them. He glanced to the side and saw how Tella focused on directing the tree root, which dived below the surface of the water where it grabbed Oscar around the waist.

Just as the tree root dragged Oscar above the waterline, Gustav also grabbed it and the tree root brought them towards the shore, while the horse creature threw itself upwards towards their legs.

Then there was a rumbling roar from the sky. Gustav squinted his eyes and saw how Magni and Módi stood with their respective weapons pointed towards the sky, which was now pitch black.

Lightning illuminated the weapons, and travelled up to the sky, while at the same time, a powerful lightning bolt zigzagged down from the dark clouds and hit the tarn.

There was a terrible roar from the horse creature as millions of volts of electricity coursed through its body and seemed to fry it alive. A loud splash was heard as the lightning subsided, and the creature collapsed into the water.

Gustav saw the waves of the heavy body lying motionless on the surface of the water, as the tree root dropped them back onto solid ground.

"Are you okay?" Kenneth shouted, running towards them.

"I think so," replied Gustav, looking at Oscar, who nodded in agreement. "What about Hugo?"

Kenneth made a gesture with his hand towards the trees, some distance away. Magni, Módi, and Nyri stood bent over Hugo, who still seemed unconscious.

The soldiers had formed a ring around them with their rifles pointed both towards the tarn and the forest. Gustav rushed towards Hugo and, to his great relief, could see that he had regained consciousness. Hugo seemed to have just coughed up water from his lungs and looked exhausted.

"Are you okay?" Gustav asked worriedly.

"I'm fine," Hugo replied. "Thanks for saving me."

"What the hell were you doing anyway?" Magni asked, sounding angry. "You could have died! What did we say about leaving the camp alone?"

"Sorry," replied Hugo, looking ashamed. "It was so beautiful, and it seemed kind."

"What was that thing?" Jessica asked, pointing at the tarn where the large creature's body was floating.

"A water horse," Módi replied, looking at the body.

"I don't suppose any of you have heard of the Bäckahäst?" he asked, whereupon all shook their heads except Gustav.

"Well, isn't the Bäckahäst a legend about a horse that enchants children into wanting to ride on its back until the horse drowns them?" he asked, looking at Módi.

"That's right," Módi replied. "Water horses are known by other names around the world, such as 'Ceffyl' or 'Kelpie'. What water horses have in common is that throughout history, humans, in their foolhardiness, have tried to tame them, but they almost always end up drowning their victims, whereupon they feed on their bodies."

"Do you realise how lucky you are?" Magni hissed and narrowed his eyes at Hugo, who nodded and swallowed hard.

Hugo tried to stand up, but fell back to the ground again. Módi quickly caught him, whereupon the god picked Hugo up in his arms and carried him back over the ridge, closely followed by Gustav and Oscar.

"You're really strong," Hugo coughed.

"You have no idea," Módi said, smiling. "Try not to talk."

"By the way," Módi continued, looking at the boy in his arms. "Now that the water horse is gone, perhaps you want to look for the treasure?"

Hugo shook his head, looking both scared and nauseous.

Gustav and Módi laughed, and as they came to the small tarn by the tents, they stopped, starring in amazement.

The water in the tarn was sinking away, while at the same time the earth expanded, revealing a shimmering treasure.

They went forward to examine the treasure, which consisted of gold and silver objects, a black dagger, and a strange stone that shimmered in a crystal blue colour.

Módi picked up the dagger and the stone. Hugo leaned forward to get a better look at the stone, which had a gold casting in the centre and ran in perfect symmetry along the centre of the triangle shaped stone.

Módi held out the stone to him.

234

"Congratulations! You have passed your test," he said, smiling. "Even though it didn't turn out exactly as I thought."

"What do you mean?" Hugo asked, puzzled.

"When a god turns fifteen, he or she is usually given a test to prove themselves worthy," Módi replied, placing the stone in Hugo's palm. "Very few who do not master magic survive an encounter with a water horse. Through your ignorance, you have hopefully learned caution and thereby gained wisdom. I think the stone is a perfect reward for you."

"What do I do with it?" Hugo asked with a cough, examining the glowing stone in his hand.

"I can show you tomorrow," Módi replied, before helping Hugo into the tent and into the sleeping bag.

"Módi?" Hugo asked with a cough.

"What is it?" Módi asked back.

"How old are you and Magni?"

Módi laughed for a moment and delayed his answer.

"What is it with people in this world anyway?! You are so curious about others ages!" he exclaimed.

"I'm just curious," Hugo coughed.

"With your way of looking at age, Magni is twenty-one years old, and I'm nineteen years old," replied Módi. "Try to sleep now, and don't talk so much."

Gustav, who had been watching them from the opening of the tent, let the tent cloth fall again before he joined Kenneth and Magni, who were inspecting the golden treasure.

❧

"Why did you save them?" asked the dark-clad figure, crossing his arms. "You had a wonderful opportunity to get rid of them, but instead you helped them."

"I had to do it," replied Oscar, looking towards the campsite where the soldiers began to crawl back into their tents again. "Magni and Módi suspect me, so I had to prove myself trustworthy to them."

"I just hope they didn't mistake it for foolhardiness," the figure replied with a sarcastic tone, before disappearing in dark blue flames.

Oscar watched Kenneth and Magni, who were standing a bit away. It was important that he gain their trust before they reached the mountain if their plan was to succeed.

ↄ

"Will he recover?" Jessica asked, looking anxiously towards the tent where Módi had brought Hugo.

"Hopefully," replied Tella, walking beside her. "Módi will take care of him, he knows what he's doing."

"You gods are really special," Jessica said, scrutinising her. "Did you say you and your brother were elves?"

"That's right," Tella answered, stopping in front of the tent. "I suppose you expected pointed ears?"

"That's what you've heard," Jessica replied, embarrassed.

"It's a modern invention," said Tella, laughing. "But we have extremely good hearing."

Just then, Lovisa opened the canvas with a questioning look on her face. She rubbed her bandaged leg and grimaced.

"Will you ever come in?" she asked, whereupon all three girls crowded into the small tent.

"Why do guys always have to put themselves in danger?" Lovisa asked and closed the zipper on the tent fabric.

"Good question," replied Jessica, crawling into her sleeping bag. "Guys are always supposed to be cool, but they're not very smart."

"There's not much difference between guys in our worlds," said Tella, lying down on the pillow. "Our guys play tough, but have trouble showing emotion."

"I've never experienced Wille or Hugo like that," said Lovisa, and crawled into her sleeping bag. "Wille has always been tender and loving, and Hugo… well, he's Hugo!"

"Wille is your boyfriend, right?" Jessica asked and smiled broadly, whereupon Lovisa blushed.

"Yes, that's right," she replied, managing a smile. "I miss him already."

"We'll see them again soon," Tella said encouragingly. "How do you feel about his transformation?"

"He's still my Wille, if that's what you mean," Lovisa replied. "I know he can change back whenever he wants."

"I'm curious about the other wolf," Jessica said, stretching. "Who is he? Hugo seems to like him."

"Váli is one of our younger gods, who has run into some difficulties," Tella replied. "He is kind, but he needs to find himself in order to break the curse."

"Hugo is more attracted to boys," Lovisa continued, smiling as she thought about her friend. "I guess that's what makes him who he is. Although, I had never imagined that he would be attracted to a wolf."

All three of them laughed, and Jessica felt safe. It was really nice having two girls to talk to.

⁊

"What should we do with the treasure?" Gustav asked, examining the pile of gold coins and silver objects that the soldiers had picked up and put in one of the vehicles.

"Some of the objects belong to the world of the gods," Magni replied looking at the treasure. "Among other things, the stone and the dagger that Módi took. These things will be returned to our world."

"But the rest of the treasure belongs in this world," Kenneth continued, and closed the door to the trunk. "We will find a good use for it."

Gustav nodded before crawling into the tent where Hugo lay coughing, while Módi tried to put Hugo's head in a higher position.

Gustav pulled his own sleeping bag and lay down on Hugo's side. He looked worriedly at the younger boy, who couldn't stop coughing, and laid one palm over Hugo's head.

24. A creature of darkness

Someone called his name. The voice sounded familiar, and when Wille opened his eyes, he saw Máni standing over him, surrounded by a blue light.

Wille stood up on unsteady legs and looked around in the silver-blue light.

"Grandfather…" Wille started to say, but stopped when Máni held up his hand.

His grandfather made a gesture with his hand, and Váli appeared beside them.

"Grandpa, what's going on?" Váli asked uncertainly.

"Please listen," Máni replied without lowering his hand. "You are in great danger."

"Danger," said Váli. "In what way?"

"The Mörksugga," his grandfather replied, looking seriously at Váli, who recoiled.

"Where is it?" Váli asked, alarmed.

"It's watching you right now," the moon god replied. "But it probably won't wait long to attack."

"What should we do?" Váli continued, looking worried.

"You must try to leave at once," replied Máni. "Help is coming, but it will not reach you in time."

"What is the Mörksugga?" Wille asked in confusion.

"We don't have time for explanations," Váli replied in a panic. "We have to escape! Grandpa, send us back!"

Máni nodded and closed his eyes, and the silver-blue light faded away.

❧

Wille opened his eyes. It was still dark outside, and the moose were still in their circular formation around them.

Tulio rolled over in his sleep and seemed to be sleeping deeply.

"Wille," said Váli, who was sitting at the edge of the circle, looking at the dark forest. "Wake Tulio up, but do it calmly and without looking panicked."

Wille didn't understand what was going on but nudged Tulio a few times, whereupon the boy opened his eyes.

"Wille, what…" the boy began to mumble, but was quickly shushed by Váli.

"Tulio," Váli said, looking at the boy. "Listen very carefully, we are in great danger."

"What kind of danger?" Tulio asked in surprise and looked at Wille, who answered the question with an equally questioning look.

"You are a forest god," said Váli. "Can you sense if there is anything unusual near us?"

"Sure," replied Tulio. "But to do that, I need to play."

Váli nodded without saying anything, while Tulio took out his kantele and began to draw along the taut strings. The moose woke up to the clear tones of his kantele, and they stood up without leaving the circle, scratching their hooves anxiously.

Suddenly, Tulio opened his eyes and looked terrified. He took a couple of steps backwards and let the instrument fall to the ground as he leaned towards Wille.

"What is it?" Wille asked as the boy grabbed his fur.

"Wille, I'm afraid," replied Tulio, and Wille could see the fear in the boy's eyes. "It…it's staring at us."

"What is staring at us, Tulio?" Wille asked, looking uncertainly into the forest's darkness. "What can you see?"

"Darkness," the boy replied. "A creature of darkness."

"Darkness," Wille repeated, and looked at Váli in surprise, while Tulio carefully bent down on trembling legs and picked up his kantele.

"The Mörksugga," Váli said. "One of my father's experiments, a creature of darkness."

"Why is it watching us?" Wille asked, but immediately changed his mind and realised that he did not want to know the answer.

"What do you think?" Váli hissed irritably.

Wille felt stupid, but Váli didn't wait for an answer.

"The only reason why it hasn't attacked us yet is because we have the moose watching us, there are too many of us," he continued. "But that won't stop it for long, because now it's planning and calculating the risks."

"You mean it's intelligent?" Wille asked in surprise, to which Váli nodded in response.

"Almost as intelligent as Garmr, another of my father's creatures," Váli replied, looking out into the forest again.

"Garmr, a creature of darkness?" Wille murmured questioningly and looked at Tulio, who hugged him shakily.

"They are creatures whose souls have been numbed by the darkness," Váli replied. "As I told you before, darkness devours the souls of men and eclipses the souls of gods. But my father came up with a third way for the darkness to take over creatures."

"How?" Wille asked without taking his eyes off the forest.

"I didn't know it then," Váli replied. "But now that I know that the dragons are involved, I understand better."

Váli lowered his voice slightly before continuing.

"I think my father figured out a way to put the souls of creatures to sleep by using the magic of the dragons," Váli said. "Then the darkness can take over the creatures without having to attack their souls, thus allowing the darkness to exploit the emotions and personalities of its victims."

Wille nervously looked around for an escape route, and his gaze was fixed on the shining lake behind them. For a moment, he thought they could swim away from there.

However, a quick glance at the trembling Tulio made him abandon that idea.

"The question is how we're going to get out of here," Váli continued, and turned towards them.

"Can't we run away from it?" Wille asked, but Váli shook his head.

"It's way too fast for that," he replied. "Besides, we have Tulio with us."

Wille looked at Tulio again, who was curled up against his fur, and wondered what they would do.

Before either of them could say anything else, the forest exploded in a deafening roar as an enormous creature burst out of its darkness and ran straight towards them.

The white moose roared and lowered its horns to meet the attack.

Wille tried to understand what he was seeing, the creature that the white moose knocked over with its horns was a huge, black boar with a spiny back and coarse tusks.

The great beast attacked the white moose again, while Váli brusquely tore Tulio from Wille's side with his mouth, signalling him to jump on his back.

The two wolves rushed from the fight, while Tulio struggled to hold on around Váli's neck.

"This way," Váli shouted as they ran back along the road. "I saw a wolf den as we ran past, we'll take cover there."

They came to a large pit dug out from under a hill, and Váli brusquely threw Tulio towards it.

"Into the den!" he commanded, getting into a fighting stance.

Tulio crawled into the pit, and Wille was just about to follow when Váli began to growl. The white moose appeared among the trees again, but Wille could see that something was wrong. Blood was dripping from the moose's thighs, and the white colour of its fur had taken on an ugly, dark hue.

The moose scraped its hooves before lowering its horns and attacked Váli, who stood still without moving. Wille shouted that he should move but was dumbfounded by what happened next.

The moose stopped in front of them, and although Wille could see how it tensed its muscles, clearly wanted to catch Váli, it could not take another step forward.

Wille took a few steps forward and gasped when he saw why the moose did not move. A shadow stretched out from Váli's body and merged with the moose's shadow.

Váli took a step backwards, and the moose did the same, which resulted in the fact that the closer Váli got to the den, the further away the moose got.

Then the shadow released its grip on the moose, which immediately lunged towards them again, before a new shadow meandered along the ground and grabbed the moose's body.

Wille looked fascinated at his cousin, who seemed to be to the utmost to keep the moose under control.

～

Tulio heard a faint whine in the dark den as he crawled in. He didn't like the dark, and he had trouble seeing clearly.

Suddenly, he bumped against something soft with one hand and recoiled in horror when he realised that it was a dead wolf body lying in front of him. The body was torn, and something seemed to have cut it open. Its innards were spread out, and the stench made him gag.

The whining sound was heard again, and he saw a wolf cub lying further into the cave, watching him. Tulio crawled past the rotting body and reached for the puppy, which growled and bared its teeth.

He hesitated and withdrew his hands again before picking up the kantele and began to play.

The wolf cub stopped growling, then sat up and looked uncertainly at Tulio before carefully crawling forward and sniffing him curiously.

The puppy started licking his arm, and Tulio laughed as he scratched the pup behind his ear.

～

The big wild boar stormed out of the forest and threw itself at Wille, who barely managed to jump away. Váli was busy trying to keep the white moose pressed against the ground and could not help him.

"Wille, don't let it hurt you," cried Váli. "The slightest scratch from the tusks, and you will be infected by the darkness."

Wille didn't have time to answer, as he was busy avoiding the Mörksugga's wild attacks. He hastily looked around and realised that the random attacks from the creature didn't seem random after all, since it had managed to corner him against a stone cairn.

Wille realised that he was trapped, he would not be able to jump away from the next attack because there were large boulders around him. The dark boar looked at him triumphantly with its white, glowing eyes and lowered its head while scratching the ground with one of its claws.

Just as the gigantic boar threw itself upon him, the night sky was illuminated by a strange red light, and Wille heard how the creature roared angrily when a young boy appeared between them, and a wall of ice was formed, which the Mörksugga angrily banged its head against.

The boy grimaced, it was clear that the creature was strong and that the ice would not last long.

A snowflake landed on the tip of Wille's nose, then another and another. The snow increased, and a strong wind swept a wave of snow, throwing it against the dark creature.

Through the wall of ice, Wille saw the outline of a man waving his hands as the snow seemed to swirl around him, blinding the Mörksugga, who tried to attack the man instead.

"Dad!" the boy shouted as the ice wall broke and rushed towards the man who was trying to catch the dark boar in a giant snow vortex.

"Stay where you are," the man shouted tensely. "I can't hold it much longer."

Then, suddenly, the dark boar lunged out of the snow vortex, knocking the man to the ground. The man struggled against the tusks that were trying to tear open his belly.

The younger boy shouted and was about to run towards them when Wille stood in his way.

"Wait," he said. "I have an idea, take off my necklace."

"Why?" the guy exclaimed in despair.

"Just do as I say," said Wille impatiently, whereupon the guy took off the necklace.

Wille felt a wave wash through his body like the first time he transformed. He felt how the fur disappeared and how his claws were pulled in. His wolf ears disappeared, and his nose was replaced by his usual face again, whereupon he stood up and saw the guy staring at him in shock.

"You can make ice, right?" Wille asked, and the guy nodded without answering.

"Good," he continued. "Make a spear out of ice with the necklace frozen in the tip."

The guy continued to stare at him without moving, but when his father shouted, the guy woke up from his trance and formed a long shaft of ice with the necklace in its point.

Wille tore the finished spear from him and took a leap towards the man who was struggling against the giant boar.

Just as the Mörksugga turned around and roared at his onslaught, Wille drove the spear through its mouth.

For a second, everything seemed to stop around them.

Váli stared at the scene unfolding and seemed not to notice that his shadow was loosening its grip on the moose. The guy who made the ice spear still stood in shock and didn't move. Tulio, who had just gotten out of the den, looked wide-eyed at Wille, where he stood with both arms in a firm grip on the spear that pierced the big beast.

Then a growl was heard from the Mörksugga, followed by a hissing sound, before it collapsed to the ground. The creature's body began to smoke as the darkness inside it dissolved, leaving behind a body that looked more like a regular boar as the spines on its back disappeared.

The guy who had made the spear rushed forward and wrapped his arms around his dad, who stood up on trembling legs. Váli stood next to Wille, staring at him so wide-eyed that it felt like he was looking at him for the first time.

"Wille," said Váli at last. "That was a very brave thing to do! Foolhardy, but brave at the same time!"

"Thank you," said Wille, who still hadn't taken his eyes off the Mörksugga's body.

"You saved my life," said the man, walking over to them.

The man was still trembling, and the young guy walked beside him in support.

Wille felt himself freezing and suddenly realised that he was naked. Instinctively, he tried to cover himself with his hands, while at the same time he looked embarrassingly at Váli, who burst out laughing.

"I think it's a little too late to think about that now, Wille," Váli said with amusement. "You may have been brave when you killed the Mörksugga, but you didn't seem to think of what would happen when you took off your necklace and broke the connection with your power animal."

"Here," said the man, picking up the remnants of his coarse wool coat from the ground, before handing it to Wille.

The ice-blue coat had been torn apart in the struggle but seemed to have protected the man from more serious injuries. The sleeves were ripped, but Wille managed to tie the coat around his waist so that he at least felt less naked.

"I have an extra coat in our sledge that you can borrow," the man continued, and smiled kindly. "It's parked a bit from here, we thought we'd give you a lift the last bit."

"That's nice of you, Ullr," said Váli. "Then we don't have to be too late to the rendezvous point."

"Nothing to speak of," said the white-haired man, amused. "We were on our way anyway, and a little company is always welcome."

"Wille, this is Ullr," Váli said by way of introduction. "He's our cousin."

"Hello," Wille said briefly, looking at the smiling man.

"And I'm Jack, his son," the young man interrupted, reaching out his hand in greeting.

Wille felt insecure in his predicament but finally took his hand, which

Jack shook so hard that the pieces of cloth around Wille's waist fell down into the snow again.

"Can you get the necklace out of the spear, please?" Wille asked, and nodded to the boar's body, while trying to keep the remains of his coat around his waist.

"I think we can get the necklace out," Ullr answered, casting a glance at the dead beast. "But I'm afraid you'll have to wait to turn into a wolf for a while, even though our sledge is big, we won't be able to fit two wolves in it."

"Not even a small wolf?" Tulio asked.

All eyes turned to the young boy, who was quietly standing next to them with a wolf pup in his arms.

"Tulio, put the cub back immediately," said Váli angrily. "It belongs here with its mother."

"His mother is dead," Tulio said sadly. "She's lying dead in the hole in the ground with her belly ripped open."

"The Mörksugga must have caused it," said Ullr, scratching his head. "She was probably trying to protect her baby, and when her abdomen was ripped open, she probably died from blood loss before the darkness took over."

"Please, Váli," Tulio said, gently hugging the little animal. "It is partly our fault that his mother is dead, because we led the Mörksugga here."

Váli looked at the boy and the little wolf cub in his arms.

The cub whimpered and curled up against Tulio's chest, as if it felt safe there.

"Are you okay with this, Ullr?" Váli asked, turning to the snow god again, who nodded in agreement.

"You'll have to take care of it yourself," said Váli, looking sternly at Tulio. "You feed it and raise it all by yourself, do you agree to those terms?"

The boy nodded in response, and Váli turned to the white moose still lying on the ground some distance away.

"But first, you must help the moose," he said. "You are the only one of us who knows the art of healing."

"But isn't it infected by the darkness?" Tulio asked, looking uncertain.

"When Wille killed the Mörksugga, the darkness disappeared from all the creatures that it infected," replied Váli. "But hurry up, it has lost a lot of blood."

Tulio hurried to the moose and gently bent down at its thigh. He murmured for a long time, and a golden light shone from his hand over the wound. It wasn't long before it was healed, and the moose got back on its feet.

Tulio bowed politely to the moose to show his gratitude, and the moose answered the bow by elegantly lowering itself on one of its front legs with its head down before getting up again and walking back into the forest.

"Uhm, I don't want to stress you," said Wille, shivering, while he tried to hold up the remains of the coat. "But could we go to that sledge now?"

Everyone turned and looked at him. Jack and Váli started laughing, and Wille felt himself blushing. Not even Tulio seemed to be able to keep from smiling at him as he struggled to fasten the coat around his waist.

❧

"It's getting interesting, Master," the young man said, glancing down at the company. "Are you going to try to soul-walk into him again?"

"No, Ítrek," the man next to him replied in a low voice. "Let the groups play their cards out, the boy's soul will be ours soon enough."

Ítrek made a slight bow and disappeared in a cloud of darkness. The darkly clad figure looked after the party as they moved towards the snow god's sledge, smiling viciously.

25. Jack's Origin

Wille noticed how the man in the sleigh stared at them as they approached, and he could not blame him. A boy with a wolf cub in his arms, a large black wolf, and he himself walking almost naked, except for the remains of Ullr's wool coat.

"Did you find what you were looking for?" asked the man as Ullr and Jack came towards the sleigh with the others in tow.

"We found some lost friends," replied Ullr, waving his hand at them.

"And we had to rescue them from a monster," added Jack, looking proud of his efforts.

"So, uh, why isn't he wearing any clothes?" the man asked and looked at Wille, whose cheeks were flaming red.

Wille felt like he wanted to sink through the earth and disappear when Jack grinned at him.

"It's a long story," Váli replied, eyeing the sledge.

"It talks!" the man exclaimed in horror.

"We'll get the explanations when we're in the air," said Ullr. "Will you take my extra coat out of the drawer for Wille here, please? I think Jack has embarrassed him long enough."

The man called Jörgen pulled the heavy coat out of a drawer, which he carefully wrapped around Wille, before helping him up on the sledge.

Wille sat down at the far end towards the driver's seat, and Jörgen settled next to him against the outer edge of the sledge.

Finally, Váli climbed aboard, and settled at their feet.

"Where should I sit?" Tulio asked, looking worried.

"You and the puppy can sit on the floor with me," replied Váli. "You will probably fall asleep, so that's fine."

Tulio hesitantly curled up next to Váli with the wolf cub.

"Is everyone ready?" Jack asked, closing the sledge.

Without waiting for an answer, he sat down in the driver's seat next to his father, with his head right next to Wille.

"Do you feel better now, cousin?" Jack asked teasingly.

"Did you just call me cousin?" Wille asked in surprise and met his gaze nervously.

He sensed that Jack was something of the teasing type when Jack laughed at his nervous expression.

"We're almost cousins anyway," he replied, turning forward again. "I thought it was easier than saying I'm your cousin's child, we're the same age after all."

"Jack, do you think you can continue the discussion when we are in the air?" Ullr asked, giving him an impatient look.

"Sorry, Dad," said Jack, putting his hands together.

An ice rink appeared in front of them, and Ullr smacked the reins. The reindeer began to run, and Wille watched fascinated as the sledge moved up the sloping ice track when the ice behind them disappeared.

"How does this happen?" he asked, looking out over the edge of the sledge.

"Those are my snow particles," Ullr replied, as the sledge veered sharply to the right. "Jack is freezing them so that an ice track forms in front of us."

"But shouldn't the ice fall to the ground?" Wille asked.

"I can keep the ice up for a short time," Jack replied, smiling. "When I let go of control of the ice behind the sledge, Dad controls the particles by bringing them into snow form in front of the sledge, whereupon I freeze them again. This way, it looks like we're flying in the air, but we're actually riding on an invisible ice track."

The red light appeared again, illuminating the dark surroundings. Wille spotted a reindeer flying above them, and it slowly descended so that it flew beside the sledge.

Wille gently reached out his hand, and let the reindeer sniff his fingers. After a while, he gently stroked its palm along the reindeer's neck, whereupon it gave a faint growl and seemed to appreciate the gesture.

"He seems to like you," Jack said, looking surprised. "He doesn't usually like strangers."

"What's his name?" Wille asked, and Jack laughed.

"Haven't you figured it out yet?" he asked, without answering the question. "It's a flying reindeer with a red muzzle, does that sound familiar?"

Wille was astonished when he realised what Jack was talking about.

"Is it…Rudolph?" Wille asked in surprise.

"You are in Santa's sleigh, so you should already know the answer," Jack replied.

Wille stared at him as if he had gone mad, but Jack just laughed and smiled at his unexpected reaction.

"I guess you're not very smart after all," he said sarcastically. "You are on a sledge driven by reindeer, which makes its way through the air, where the driver is a snow god, and one of the reindeer has a muzzle that glows red – but the thought didn't even occur to you! No wonder you can't keep your clothes on your body!"

Wille suddenly felt annoyed by Jack's attitude. He had thought it was strange that they would be travelling in a flying sledge, but after everything that had happened in the last week, he thought no more about it.

"Jack," Ullr said sharply. "Show some respect and kindness, he's our cousin, and he saved my life back there."

Jack looked scared as his father looked at him.

"I'm sorry," Jack said ashamedly. "I didn't mean what I said."

Wille looked into his eyes and could sense that Jack was feeling both scared and insecure.

"Don't worry," Wille said, seeing a tear form in one of Jack's eyes.

"Jack isn't used to having friends his own age," said Ullr, without minding that everyone could hear him. "He has spent most of his time with me since his mother was kidnapped and has never met anyone his own age."

There was a grunt of disapproval from Váli, and Ullr laughed.

"Except you, of course, Váli," he said, glancing over his shoulder.

"Kidnapped?" Wille exclaimed in surprise.

"By your uncle," continued Ullr. "I haven't seen her for fifteen years, and Jack has grown up without her."

Wille felt a knot in his stomach. He knew exactly how Jack must feel, having lost his mother still hurt terribly.

The knowledge that it was his uncle who had caused the suffering made Wille sad. He put a hand on Jack's shoulder and noticed that he was shaking.

"Jörgen," said Ullr, looking at the man who had been sitting quietly watching the discussion. "Would you mind switching places with Jack for a moment? I think the boys have some things they'd like to talk about."

"Ehm," Jörgen replied uncertainly. "I don't know…"

"I promise it will be fine," said Ullr. "You won't notice the height at all."

Jörgen still seemed sceptical, but carefully stood up. Jack stood up as well, and Wille helped him over the edge, whereupon he and Jörgen exchanged places with each other.

Jörgen staggered, and grabbed the edge in fear as he tentatively put his foot on the driver's seat. Ullr let go of one of the reins, and pulled him down so that he hit his back on the edge of the sledge.

"Relax, Professor," said Ullr kindly. "There's no difference sitting here compared to sitting in the back."

"Professor?" Wille asked, looking at the well-built man.

"That's right, I never told you who I am," replied Jörgen, turning around. "My name is Jörgen Svedin, professor of religious studies."

"Svedin," said Wille in surprise. "It's the same surname…"

"Like Amanda," Jörgen finished the sentence with a sigh. "Your teacher, and my wife."

"How is she involved in this?" Wille asked, puzzled.

He noticed that Jörgen put his hands over his face, and leaned forward, whereupon Ullr put one arm around him.

"She died, Wille," replied Ullr in Jorgen's place. "They were attacked by your father's demons, and she was shot. Nari was the one who led the demons."

"Nari?!" exclaimed Váli, raising his head. "Are you sure?"

Ullr nodded, and Váli lowered his head again in concern and sighed, closing his eyes.

Wille looked at Váli and felt dizzy. So much sadness and misery caused by his father made him feel sick. He looked at Tulio, who was sleeping deeply, curled up against Váli, and at the wolf cub lying by the boy's face. They were really the only ones that made up for the grief in the company at the moment, the boy and the wolf-cub who had found each other through a series of strange circumstances.

A sob next to him reminded him that Jack was sitting at his side. Wille gently put an arm around him, and to his surprise, Jack sank into his shoulder.

"Sorry," Jack said after a while, and sat up again. "I don't usually break down like this."

"It's all right," said Wille, looking at him sympathetically. "But don't be so spiteful, okay?"

"Sorry about that," Jack replied, without meeting his gaze. "I was just wondering if…could we be friends?"

For a moment, Wille looked surprised by the question, then he burst out into laughter. Jack looked distressed.

"Sorry," Wille replied, giving Jack a pat on the shoulder. "Of course we can be friends, you just had to ask."

Jack looked up at him, and for a moment, Wille could sense a smile in him. Wille looked deeply into his eyes, and it almost felt as if he saw himself in a mirror image.

There were loud snores from Váli, and the boys exchanged a meaningful look before laughing.

"You're cold," said Jack, who saw Wille shivering.

He took off his coarse leather boots and handed them to Wille, who gratefully accepted them. They felt heavenly when he stepped into them, and he could feel the stinging in his toes as the warmth slowly began to return to his feet.

"Thank you," Wille said, as Jack found an extra blanket and wrapped it around him.

"So, tell me about your brother and your friends," Jack said. "Dad has told me already, but I want to hear from you."

⁓

"What do you mean Jack has never met anyone his own age?" Jörgen asked, trying not to look down. "Don't you have any gods of his age in Asgard?"

Jörgen was trying to keep his eyes straight ahead and had asked Ullr not to do any fierce dives, which the laughing snow god had agreed to. He had even slowed down slightly, which made Jörgen relax more.

"Jack has never been to Asgard," Ullr replied in a composed manner. "The other gods are unaware of his existence."

"How is that possible?" Jörgen asked in surprise.

"Hulda's magic is based on people's dreams," replied Ullr, sighing. "She helps those who have severe grief, fulfilling their innermost dreams and desires."

"Their innermost desires?" Jörgen asked.

"Hulda has a dream world of her own, where those who are deeply unhappy can come and live with her for a while," replied Ullr, turning gently to the right. "Depending on who the unhappy person is, Hulda appears in the guise of either a teenager, a middle-aged mother, or an elderly grandmother."

"I've never heard of this," said Jörgen in surprise.

"Nice to be able to surprise a professor of religion with something," said Ullr, laughing.

"Tell me more about her," asked Jörgen curiously.

"Well," said Ullr. "I can tell you about the first person she helped, a young girl who was tormented by her stepmother, who made her work on their farm. The poor girl had to sit by a well every day and spin so much yarn that the skin cracked under her nails. One day she dropped one of her balls of yarn, and it fell into the well. Fearing the punishment she would receive from her stepmother, the girl bent down and tried to catch the ball of yarn, but she ended up falling into the well herself. When no one heard her cries for help, she sank into the cold water and thought she was going to die."

Ullr paused for a moment before continuing.

"She woke up in a meadow with thousands of flowers and the sun shining on her. Hulda showed herself to her as an old woman, and the girl stayed with her in her house for several days, where she was properly fed for the first time in her life. The girl saw many magical things, but eventually began to feel homesick. Hulda, who could see that the girl was feeling better, led her back to the meadow where she had woken up. Golden snowflakes fell on her before she again found herself in front of the well where she had fallen, and when she looked at her clothes, they were covered with golden glitter. With the help of the golden flakes, she was able to move away from home and eventually marry happily," Ullr concluded the story.

"A nice story," said Jörgen. "But how does Jack fit in?"

"I've always wanted a son," Ullr replied, looking at him. "But I had a hard time finding a woman that I loved."

Ullr looked over his shoulder at the two boys laughing behind him.

"I love him more than anything else, and I wouldn't forgive myself if anything happened to him," he said, looking suddenly sad.

"What do you mean?" Jörgen asked, following his gaze. "Why should something happen to him?"

"Because Jack isn't supposed to exist," said Ullr, turning forward again. "Both he and Rudolph are born in Hulda's dream world, created by the dream world. And when the other gods find out about it, I'm afraid they won't accept it."

"You don't mean that they..." Jörgen began, and opened his eyes wide when Ullr nodded in confirmation.

"I'm afraid they're not going to let him live," he said, smacking the straps again.

"Does Jack know about this?" Jörgen asked, and was even more surprised when the snow god shook his head.

"I can't keep him a secret any longer, he's so big now, and it's not right to hide him. But I don't want to worry him before we arrive there," Ullr replied. "I'd appreciate it if you didn't say anything to the boys."

～

"So, your brother likes boys. Is that normal in the human world?" asked Jack curiously.

"What do you mean?" Wille asked back, looking at him suspiciously.

"Sorry," Jack replied, regretting the question. "It's just that I thought that guys liked girls, and vice versa."

"It's not abnormal," Wille replied, leaning back. "But it is a little more… unusual."

"Unusual?" Jack asked curiously.

"Some people find it embarrassing," replied Wille. "I guess it's expected that guys should like girls. That's why some people judge Hugo and others who like people of the same sex."

"I meant no offence to your brother," said Jack anxiously.

"I know that," said Wille, stretching. "In that case, I would have pushed you out of the sledge."

Both boys laughed, and the mood lightened again. The wolf cub had woken up and was whimpering gently in front of the boys. Jack got up and took something out from under the seat. He unfolded the content and handed it to the wolf cub, who sniffed uncertainly.

"It's dried reindeer meat," said Jack, seeing Wille's surprise. "The wolf looks to be big enough to eat meat."

Sure enough, after a little hesitation, the wolf took the meat from his hand and began to chew on the piece of meat.

Tulio brushed his hand across the wolf cub's back, and Váli turned his head, watching them with interest.

"So, Váli, are you like Hugo's boyfriend?" Jack asked.

Váli's posture revealed how uncomfortable the question was for him.

"You like him, right?" Wille asked teasingly.

Váli looked at them in panic as they smiled amusedly at him.

"He really does," Tulio replied, turning to Váli. "I have heard them talk when they think no one is listening."

"Shut up and go to sleep," Váli hissed at Tulio, who looked defiant.

"Aww," said Wille. "Is the tough wolf getting uncomfortable?"

Váli looked from Wille to Jack and finally down at Tulio, all of whom were smilingly waiting for his confession. Then he lowered his head and realised that he was defeated.

"Yes, I like Hugo," he said, looking up at Wille. "But do you have to tell everyone?"

"Sorry," replied Wille, who continued to smile. "But you shouldn't try to keep it a secret, and you should tell Hugo properly."

"I know," said Váli, sighing, before resting his head on his paws again.

Tulio, who continued to pet the wolf cub, reached out his other hand, and gently stroked Váli's back.

Ullr and Jörgen exchanged an understanding smile before returning to their own discussion.

Jack felt a feeling he had never felt before, a sense of belonging. His stomach tickled as he laughed with the others at Váli's expense. His cousin seemed embarrassed at having to admit his feelings, which Jack found strange. Although he hadn't expected that two boys could feel that way about each other, he didn't think those feelings would be something to be ashamed of.

His father had talked a lot about Asgard and the human world, but it was something different to actually experience it. Jack sighed heavily and looked longingly to the north. He couldn't wait until he got the chance to step through the gate.

26. The Traitor

Módi firmly pushed Hugo's head back against the pillows and looked at him anxiously. Hugo had been coughing all night, and despite Módi's attempts to keep his head in a high position, the cough had only gotten worse.

"I'm sorry," Hugo managed to cough out.

"Stop apologising," Módi sighed. "Just try to lie still."

"How is he?" Kenneth asked, entering the tent.

Outside, Módi could hear the military demolishing the camp.

"The bridges that cross the creeks ahead are too narrow for our vehicles, we have to go around, which means it will take longer to arrive," said Kenneth, seeing his puzzled look.

"Hugo has pneumonia," Módi replied, standing up as Hugo coughed. "He won't be able to travel."

"But can't one of you cure him?" Kenneth asked as Módi pulled him out of the tent.

"Neither I nor Magni have that kind of magic," Módi replied, looking out over the campsite. "Possibly Tella or Nyri could do it, but Tella went in the first car with Jessica and Lovisa."

"And Nyri?" Kenneth asked, looking around.

"I don't know where he is," replied Módi. "But we must try to find him, otherwise, I'm afraid we'll have to split the group again."

☙

"Tell the truth," Magni said, crossing his arms.

Oscar stood tied to a tree and stared at him defiantly as the self-winding rope held him in place.

"So, you want me to believe that you managed to escape the darkness, that you magically appeared in Tandsjöborg after several days, and didn't have anything to do with the events of last night?" Magni asked, looking at the angry face.

"You've had your answer," Oscar hissed irritably in reply. "How long are you going to harass me?"

"Until I'm satisfied," Magni replied impatiently. "So, you had nothing to do with the water horse?"

"I've already told you that," said Oscar irritably. "I had gone away to attend to my needs, and when I came back, that thing was drowning them. I jumped in because I wanted to save my friend and my cousin."

"Brave of you, then," said Magni, drawing his fingers on his chin. "And the three men who were supposed to be on guard with you, where did they go?"

"How should I know?" hissed Oscar, trying to break free from the ropes that were tightening around him the more he tried. "They were sitting by the fire when I left, I have no idea where they went."

"How long were you gone?" Magni asked without taking his eyes off him.

"It was maybe ten to fifteen minutes," Oscar replied exhaustedly, and seemed unable to resist the rope any longer.

"That long?" Magni asked, tightening the rope more.

"Please don't do that," exclaimed Oscar with tears in his eyes. "It hurts!"

"Why were you gone so long?" Magni asked without paying attention to his whining.

"I said I had to do some needs," gasped Oscar, his face turning red. "Let go of me now!"

"I have a better idea," Magni said grimly. "I think I'll leave you here and come back in a couple of days. If you're still here, then I'll take you to the others, if not…well, then we know you've been helped."

"You don't dare leave me behind," Oscar hissed. "Wille, Lovisa, and Hugo would never allow it!"

"They won't know anything until we're gone," said Magni, and he could sense the panic in the boy's eyes.

Oscar again tried to break free before he fell forward, panting, with the rope pressing against his waist.

"The more you tug and pull, the more it tightens," Magni said, crossing his arms. "Laedingr was forged by my father to turn the strength of his prey against itself, so without the help of magic, you don't stand a chance."

"Magni, let him go," called a voice behind them.

Módi walked up and threw one of his axes, splitting the rope against the tree trunk, and Oscar dropped to his knees.

"I have to check him," Magni said grimly.

"You've already done that, and you won't get a better answer by tormenting him," said Módi, helping Oscar up.

"I apologise for this," he continued, brushing off leaves from Oscar's shirt.

"It's okay," Oscar said, not meeting Módi's gaze.

"I suppose I owe you an apology," Magni said, extending his hand towards him.

"Like I said, no problem, " said Oscar, taking his hand.

Magni locked eyes with him before letting go.

"Good," Módi said. "Have you seen Nyri?"

"I'm here," Nyri's voice was heard from within the forest.

The young god came out of the forest, looking uncertain.

"Where did you go?" Magni asked in surprise. "You were right behind us when we got here."

"I didn't want to be in the way when you…eh, talked," Nyri replied, looking nervously at Oscar. "Are you okay?"

Oscar seemed surprised by the question but didn't bother to answer, and turned to face Módi again.

"What happened?" he asked, as if he could read Módi's expression.

"Hugo has caught pneumonia," Módi replied. "I hope that you, Nyri, can cure it with your elvish ability."

"I would love to," Nyri said, looking distressed. "Unfortunately, neither I nor Tella have mastered such magic. We can heal injuries and cure simple poisoning, but viruses and bacteria are something else."

"So, what should we do?" Oscar asked. "We can't just leave him."

"Of course not," Módi replied. "We have to come up with a plan because we can't move him in his current state."

"Tulio!" Nyri exclaimed. "Grandfather has taught him such things, if we can get him here, he can help Hugo."

"But he is far from here with Váli and Wille," said Magni. "How can we get in touch with them?"

"Through him," replied Nyri, pointing to the sky.

Everyone looked up and saw the silver-winged hawk circling above the camp. Nyri put his fingers to his mouth and made a whistling sound, and the hawk dived down towards them and sat on his arm.

"We have to show him to make him understand," Nyri said, pointing to the camp. "Will you come with me?"

"You go," Módi said, looking at Nyri and Oscar. "We'll be there in a moment."

Magni stood there hesitantly and watched the boys walking towards the camp as Módi handed him the rope that had effectively repaired itself.

"What do you think of him?" Módi asked.

"I don't know what it is," Magni replied. "But he is hiding something from us."

"But there's no point in continuing the interrogation," said Módi. "He will not reveal it to you."

"I know," Magni sighed. "But I feel compelled to try."

They stood in silence for a while before Módi started walking towards the camp.

"Are you staying with him?" Magni asked.

"Yes," Módi replied, and stopped. "I have become attached to him, and I don't want to leave him alone."

❧

"Hugo?" Oscar said questioningly, entering the tent.

There were deep coughs as Hugo tried to get up from his half-sleeping position. Then he collapsed on the ground and lay down, still coughing.

Oscar leaned him back into a sitting position again.

"You're not going to get up anytime soon," Oscar said firmly, while Nyri entered the tent with Hábrók.

The silver-winged hawk let out a scream before flying from Nyri's arm and landing next to Hugo, who recoiled slightly before he started coughing again.

"You'll cough up your lungs if you try to get up again," said Nyri, who sat down next to them.

"But we have to go," Hugo managed to say as he coughed.

"You should wait here for help," Nyri said. "I'll send Hábrók to try to alert Tulio, he's the only one who can help you get better."

"But I don't want to be here alone," Hugo pleaded, coughing. "Please, don't leave me here!"

"I'm staying with you," a voice was heard at the opening.

Módi came into the tent and joined them, looking at Hábrók thoughtfully.

"How are we going to make him understand?" he asked.

Nyri made a few hand signals to the hawk and pointed at Hugo before he took something out of his backpack, and Hábrók gave a sharp cry.

The forest god placed the soft object on Hugo's chest, and made a sweeping gesture across his chest.

The silver-winged hawk made a shrill, screeching sound and flew back outside again.

"I think he understands," Nyri said, smiling.

"I'm staying too," Oscar said, crossing his arms.

"I don't think that's a good idea," Módi said, giving him a scrutinising look. "I won't be able to take all three of you out of here after the healing is done."

"I said I'm staying," Oscar said, fixing his gaze on Módi's face. "It wasn't a question."

Módi looked at him thoughtfully for a moment before nodding in agreement and standing up.

"Well," the elder god said before walking out of the tent. "Maybe it will be good after all."

Oscar looked after Módi as he walked out, before he sat down next to Hugo, who couldn't stop coughing.

"Hugo," he said, putting one hand on his sleeping bag. "Some things have happened that I would like to tell you."

"What kind of things?" Hugo asked tensely.

"I want to tell you, but I can't – not right now," replied Oscar, feeling depressed. "I just want you to know that no matter what happens, I am always here for you."

"I already know that," Hugo said, trying to smile as he coughed. "And whatever it is, you know you can tell me."

"How sentimental!" came a dark voice from inside the tent, and Oscar whirled around.

The man who was watching them pulled off his dark hood and revealed a youthful face with short-cropped, raven-black hair. In one hand, he held a black staff that seemed to be bathed in a dark blue light.

"Velnias," Oscar said, trembling. "I was just..."

"You were just going to what?" hissed the man, who took a couple of steps forward and grabbed him by the collar.

Oscar was lifted into the air by the man, while Hugo tried to stand up but fell to the ground again.

A roar was heard from the tent opening, and Oscar saw Magni rush towards them, followed by Módi and Kenneth.

Magni raised his mace, but Velnias threw Oscar at him, resulting in both of them falling to the ground.

Módi raised his axe and aimed a blow at Velnias, who blocked the strike with his staff. As the weapons of the two combatants met, there was an enormous flash of lightning and dark blue fire that set the tent canvas on fire.

Kenneth rushed forward and dragged Hugo out of his sleeping bag, then rushed out of the tent with him.

Oscar struggled to his feet and threw himself at Velnias, who gave him a strong kick, whereupon Oscar landed powerless on the ground again.

"I should have realised you were involved," Módi said, pressing the axe against the staff. "You've never been a match for me, so why don't you just give up?"

"Things change, my friend," replied Velnias with a smirk.

A huge shadow appeared in the fire behind them. The big head with the huge horns stared at them with grotesque blue eyes, whereupon Módi lost his footing from the shock and landed on the ground.

Velnias laughed as he waved his staff.

"I could not imagine a better fate for you than to serve my master," he said, pushing the blue flames close to Módi's terrified face. "Did you really think you could compete against the powers of the dragons? You are pathetic!"

Oscar raised one arm and punched the ground with his fist, and a wave of darkness hit Velnias, who roared in anger as he lost his footing and fell backwards.

"What do you think you're doing?" Velnias hissed, staring furiously at Oscar, while the tent was engulfed in blue flames. "Do you really think they will accept you now that they know what you are? You will come back to us, and you will complete your mission."

With those words, Velnias disappeared into the flames.

Oscar crawled to Módi, who was still on the ground. He grabbed the god's black leather vest, and turned to Magni, who was kneeling at his brother's side.

He met the wrathful god's gaze nervously before letting the darkness teleport them outside, as the burning tent collapsed.

❧

"Magni, calm down," Módi said, and put his arm around his brother.

Magni threw his arm away and rushed towards Oscar, who was on his knees, whereupon Kenneth threw himself upon the young god and wrestled him to the ground.

"I don't know how you do things in Asgard," Kenneth said. "But this is not the right way to handle this."

Oscar sat on the ground, pressing his hands into the soft grass. The blue fire had burned down the entire tent, and the remains were now smouldering on the ground.

All around him, soldiers were pointing their guns at him, ready to shoot.

Magni calmed down, and Kenneth let go of him. He stared angrily at Oscar, who did not dare to meet his gaze.

"Take him to the car," Kenneth ordered, and two soldiers lifted Oscar up, who didn't seem to want to struggle.

"Módi," Hugo said weakly from the ground.

Módi turned around and sank down next to the sick boy.

"Please," Hugo begged, coughing. "I want him to stay."

"Do you realise the danger he put us through?" asked Módi in a serious tone.

"Please," Hugo begged again. "I need him!"

"What is that?" Módi asked, looking at the object that Nyri had placed on Hugo's chest earlier.

"Nyri told me it's Tulio's stuffed animal," Hugo replied, gasping for breath. "He thought I should hold it until Tulio came to us."

Módi looked at the young guy lying on the ground, hugging the stuffed animal, which seemed to be a wolf. He felt someone put their hand on his shoulder, and he discovered Nyri standing next to him with a sad face.

Módi felt a pang in his stomach, and turned around as the cars began to drive away. He made a quick decision and plunged forward in front of the military vehicles. There was a braking screech from the wheels as the cars came to a stop, and Magni flew out of the passenger door of the car in front.

"What are you doing?" he exclaimed frantically.

"Magni, this is not right," Módi said firmly, as Kenneth joined them.

"Not right?" his brother asked angrily. "What do you think we should do with him then?"

"Leave him with me," Módi replied, turning to Kenneth. "I'll take responsibility for him."

Kenneth sighed before opening the door of the nearest car and helped Oscar out of the car again. Módi could see that his hands had been tied up.

Without a word, he untied the ropes, and Oscar tenderly rubbed his wrists.

"You better be sure about this," Magni said irritably.

"Trust me," Módi said calmly, and led Oscar back to the campsite again.

Nyri helped Hugo sit up as Oscar sank to his knees next to him.

"Oscar," Hugo said as he coughed and gave him a hug.

"I'm sorry, Hugo," said Oscar, crying as he returned the hug. "And thank you for believing in me."

"Relax, it's okay," Hugo said, coughing. "Just don't make me regret it."

Módi looked at them for a moment and turned back to the cars. Magni and Nyri raised their hands in a farewell salute before getting into their cars and closing the doors.

As the cars rolled away, Módi wondered if he had really made the right decision. A glance at the two boys hugging each other made him realise the magnitude of his decision. He had rarely seen such a strong bond between friends, and it would be interesting to see how strong the friendship was.

"That's a powerful weapon you have that can match Velnias staff," Oscar said, examining the axe on Módi's back as he let go of Hugo.

"Perun," Módi replied, pulling out the axe. "Its strength matches Magni's hammer, and it allows me to create and control electricity."

Oscar wiped his face and looked mesmerised as Módi demonstratively split Perun into two smaller axes, a gold axe and a silver axe, before he put them back together.

"Now," Módi continued, sitting down on a stump. "Tell me everything."

27. Váli's Confession

When the sledge landed on the mountain plateau, Wille assumed that they had finally arrived, but Ullr had dashed his hopes by telling him that they were not on Flatruet – but on the nearby Sonnefjället and that they had about a day's journey left to Flatruet.

They had been travelling most of the night, and although the sun would soon rise, they made camp because Jack needed to rest, ending up with him and Jörgen falling asleep in the sledge with Tulio and the wolf cub.

Ullr made a campfire next to the sledge, and he, Wille, and Váli sat there and talked while the first rays of the sun began to appear in the sky.

"Váli, what kind of magic did you use before?" Wille asked and looked at his cousin.

"Shadow magic," Váli replied without meeting his gaze. "I can manipulate my shadow, and make it solid."

"Awesome," Wille said, staring into the flames while putting his feet against the fire to warm them. "But how did you get the moose to freeze like that?"

"When my shadow touches someone else's shadow, it temporarily takes over that person's shadow," Váli replied, looking down at the ground. "I can then control that person, or the animal for that matter, for a short time."

"I think you should tell him the whole truth," said Ullr, leaning forward towards them. "He deserves to know."

"Know what, Váli?" Wille asked in confusion.

Váli sighed heavily, as he always did when he was keeping something to himself that he didn't want to tell anyone.

"Do you remember I told you that the darkness has entered your hearts?" he asked, looking at Wille, who nodded. "I don't know if you have noticed, but Ullr has no shadow."

Wille turned to Ullr and was astonished to see that Váli was right – the snow god had no shadow.

"But what does that mean?" he asked in surprise.

"Gods have no shadows because shadows are a reflection of darkness in the hearts of beings," replied Ullr.

"But that's not true," said Wille, turning around. "I have a shadow."

"That's because your father provided you with darkness when you were little," Ullr said. "Not much, but enough for it to settle in your heart."

"And Hugo?" Wille asked doubtfully.

"In the same way that your father brought the darkness over to you, he also brought it to your brother," replied Ullr again. "Namely, through your mother."

"What do you mean?" Wille asked in horror. "How could my mother have transmitted the darkness?"

"Wayland's soul is darkened," replied Váli, sinking down on his paws. "When he raped your mother, he also transferred some of his darkness to her. Virtually any other person would have succumbed to the darkness, but your mother was special."

"She was much loved in our world," Ullr interjected. "Your mother was a very popular goddess."

"In what way was she special?" Wille asked, and felt himself trembling inside.

He had wondered what kind of goddess his mother really was but had been too afraid to ask.

"You knew your mother as Ida," Váli replied. "But to us, she was Idun, the guardian of the tree."

"The guardian of the tree?" Wille asked, looking thoughtfully at Ullr for an explanation.

"Váli has told you about the World Tree, or the World Spirit, I suppose?" asked the snow god back, and Wille nodded.

"The World Spirit is the great Cosmos that surrounds us," Ullr continued. "It gives us life, and maintains the balance of life. But it does not do it alone. Three powerful goddesses help the spirit in the physical world."

"The three goddesses of fate," Váli interjected. "The three are the goddess of necessity, Skuld, who governs the actions and consequences of every being, the goddess of visions, Verdandi, who rules over the future possibilities of all beings, and Urdr, the most powerful of them, who rules over the fate of all."

"But what does that have to do with mom?" Wille asked, looking at them. "Was my mother a goddess of fate too?"

"Not really," replied Ullr. "But she was their high priestess, and as such, she was commissioned to provide the family of the gods with the World Spirit's immortality."

"In Asgard, there is a tree that reflects the World Tree," Váli continued. "We call it the tree of life, and by eating the apples from the tree, we can stay young and healthy."

Wille felt a sudden burst of inspiration.

"The apple lemonade," he whispered, staring at Váli, who nodded in agreement.

"You've never had to be sick once, have you?" Ullr asked and laughed. "Those apples contain the dust of the World Spirit, and can cure just about basically everything."

Wille felt his eyes tear up. The longing for his mother ached in his chest. Váli walked up to Wille and put his head over Wille's shoulder as if in a hug.

"I know how it feels," he said. "But it gets easier."

"I guess so," said Wille, wiping his face. "But now tell me about why you have a shadow."

Váli sat down sadly again, and Wille leaned forward, gently caressing him behind the ear.

"Váli," he said firmly. "I know it's hard for you, but you'll feel better getting it out of you."

Váli looked up at him in astonishment, and Wille realised that he had never spoken so seriously to him before.

"Remember I told you that my father turned me into a wolf?" Váli asked, and Wille nodded in response.

"Do you also remember that I told you that he came up with a way to put creatures' souls to sleep to make it easier for the darkness to take over them?" he continued, with his eyes tearing up.

"Váli, what are you trying to say?" Wille asked in surprise and leaned back again.

"Out with it now," urged Ullr. "You've almost said it."

"Wille," Váli replied sadly. "I am a creature of darkness like Garmr, and like the Mörksugga you killed last night."

There was complete silence around the fire, and no one said anything for a long time before Ull got up.

"I'll go and wake the others so we can get going," he said. "It's already in the middle of the day, and I want to cover a bit of the route before it gets dark again."

Ullr looked at his cousin and put his hand on the wolf's back.

"The worst is over," he said, giving Váli a look of sympathy. "You go on and tell him the last thing."

Wille looked after Ullr, who went to wakeup Jörgen, who seemed to sleep deeply despite the chilly air.

"Váli," Wille said, and turned forward again. "What exactly do you mean by "dark creature"?"

Váli took a deep breath before continuing.

"When I say that he sedates the souls of his victims, I don't mean it literally," he said. "What he was doing was sealing the body's connection with the soul."

"Explain," Wille said, crossing his arms.

"A being's soul is a separate part of the World Spirit," Váli continued. "When a creature dies, the soul is supposed to return, but as you know, the darkness stops it."

"Yes, you said the souls of the gods are darkened, and they turn into demons," said Wille. "And that human souls are eaten."

"That's right," said Váli. "But the gods strengthened the hearts of the humans, which led to their souls escaping the darkness in their hearts and returning to the World Spirit, as long as they are not exposed to more darkness from outside."

"But what does that have to do with this?" wondered Wille, who still had his arms crossed.

"The heart acts as a door to the soul," replied Váli. "What my father did was to seal that door, and cut the link between the person and its soul."

"What happens to the person?" Wille asked.

"The darkness takes over their consciousness but leaves the soul intact," Váli replied. "Because the bond between the soul and the person is severed, and the soul cannot resist, the person becomes a slave to the will of darkness."

"And that is what has happened to Garmr and you?" Wille asked, feeling angry.

Váli nodded without saying anything else.

"When we first met after Garmr killed my mother, I asked you if you and he were of the same kind, were you lying to me then?" asked Wille in a sharp voice, and narrowed his eyes at his cousin, who looked scared.

"Wille, I didn't lie, not directly anyway," he replied, bowing his head.

"NOT DIRECTLY!" exclaimed Wille, and stood up so violently that Váli recoiled. "What do you mean by that?"

Wille seethed with anger and measured a blow at Váli before he felt how someone grabbed his hand. He looked up and met Ullr's sad look, while Váli gave a plaintive howl and ran into the forest.

Ullr shouted for Váli, but to no avail, while Jörgen and Jack came up to them.

"Come," said Ullr, as he put out the fire. "Let's go."

"What about Váli?" asked Jack, looking for the wolf's footprints in the snow. "We can't just leave him here."

"We have to," replied Ullr, harnessing the reindeer. "We don't have time to look for him. With luck, he'll make it to the rendezvous point on his own."

Just then, Hábrók swept down and landed on the edge of the sledge. The silver-winged hawk screamed incessantly and seemed upset. Tulio, who had just rested the wolf cub, listened intently to the hawk.

"Wille," he said worriedly. "It's Hugo, he's sick."

"What do you mean?" Wille asked tensely, and made his way to the edge of the sledge. "What has happened?"

"They stayed at a tarn northeast of us last night," replied Tulio. "If I understood correctly, they were attacked by…"

He broke off as the hawk raised its wings.

"By what?" asked Wille impatiently. "What happened to my brother?"

"He was almost drowned in the tarn," replied Tulio. "By a water horse."

Ullr put a hand on his shoulder, and Wille got a lump in his stomach when he met his cousin's worried gaze.

"What is a water horse?" he asked anxiously.

"There's no time to explain," replied Tulio. "Hugo has got pneumonia, and I'm the only one who can cure it."

"Ullr, please, can we get there?" Wille asked desperately.

"Is everyone else still there with them?" Ullr asked, looking at Tulio, who was shaking his head.

"Módi and Oscar are still with him, the others went on to the meeting place," replied the boy.

Ullr traced his fingers along his chin and met Wille's despairing gaze, before turning to Jack.

"Can Tulio hitch a ride with Rudolph?" Ullr asked, looking at the red-nosed reindeer.

"Absolutely," replied Jack. "But is Tulio really going to fly alone? I mean, he's still so young."

"We can't risk being late for the rendezvous point," Ullr replied. "I have a feeling that an unpleasant surprise awaits when the others get there."

"Can't you go with him, Jack?" Jörgen asked, looking at Tulio, who seemed terrified by the very idea of flying alone on the reindeer.

"Sure, but then the sledge stays on the ground," Jack replied. "My ice is needed to get us into the air."

"I'll go with Tulio," said Wille, looking at Ullr. "I'm worried about Hugo."

"But you can't fly on Rudolph with nothing but the coat on you," said Ullr. "It will flap around, and give no protection at all against the wind. Besides, it will be very uncomfortable to sit on his back without pants."

"I think I have a solution to that problem," said Wille, looking at Jack scrutinizingly.

Ullr followed his gaze, and after a while, the Snow God seemed to understand what he meant. Jack looked anxiously from one to the other, and when he realised what it was that Wille was referring to, he looked frightened.

"Wille, you don't mean…" Jack began, and automatically took a step backwards. "Dad, you're not going to…"

"It's the only way," said Wille, taking a step towards him.

Jack made an effort to run away, but Ullr grabbed him.

"Look on the bright side, cousin," said Wille, looking amused at Jack's terrified expression. "You'll learn that you can't always keep your clothes on."

❧

A moment later, Wille had gotten the clothes on and helped Tulio up onto Rudolph's back.

"Be careful," Ullr said, when both boys were properly seated. "It can be a bit scary the first time."

"Thank you," said Wille, feeling tears in his eyes.

"Calm down," said Ullr, and gently put his hand on Wille's arm. "I know you regret what you did, it was wrong. But he'll come back, you'll see."

Wille nodded and grabbed the reins.

"Wille," called Jack from the sledge, where he sat wrapped in Ullr's big coat. "You promise to send my clothes back with Rudolph, right?"

"Isn't it fun to be naked?" Wille asked teasingly.

"Please," said Jack, looking embarrassed.

"Don't worry. When we get there, I'll turn into a wolf and send the clothes back in the saddlebag," replied Wille, laughing as he grabbed the reins.

"Take care of Akela in the meantime," Tulio called out to Jörgen, who waved affirmatively and held up the wolf cub.

"Remember that Rudolph flies by himself," Ullr called out as they lifted off the ground and took to the sky. "The hawk will lead him, all you have to do is hold on tight."

❧

Váli watched both parties leave and felt abandoned.

Wille had raised his hand against him and had intended to strike him if Ullr had not intervened. The anger and disgust that he had seen in Wille's eyes had both frightened him and made him desperate. He felt the tears running down his cheek and let out a howl.

A feeling of being watched made him turn around. A flash of light appeared between the trees, and Váli stood up with tears still flowing from his eyes.

"Who's there?" he growled, feeling exposed in his condition. "Show yourself!"

A woman with long, flowing hair stepped out from behind the trees. The strange glow came from the light, yellow hair that shone in a warm glow against her white dress.

"Don't be afraid," the woman said, taking a few steps forward.

"Who are you?" Váli asked, taking a step backwards.

"You have grown up since the last time I saw you," said the woman with a smile. "Don't you recognise me?"

Váli stared at her uncertainly for a moment before opening his eyes in recognition.

The woman took the last few steps towards him and sank to her knees. The snow around her melted away, exposing the thin grass hidden under the snow cover. As she wrapped her arms around him, it was as if he couldn't hold back his emotions any longer, and the tears ran down his cheeks as he began to shake.

"I've missed you, Sunna," he sobbed.

"And I you," the woman said in a soft voice. "Don't be sad, it came as a shock to him, and he didn't mean to react like that."

"I miss them," Váli sobbed.

"You'll see them again soon," she promised, brushing her hand across his cheek. "But there is one thing you must do first."

"What do you mean?" Váli asked uncertainly.

"Come, I have my wagon further away," Sunna said without answering the question. "I'll give you a ride the rest of the way."

"But I thought you weren't allowed to intervene in this world anymore?" Váli asked, wondering.

"Things have changed," Sunna replied. "Both me and your grandfather have insisted on helping you."

"Grandfather too?" Váli asked, feeling a little happier. "Will I get to meet him for real soon?"

"Sooner than you think," replied Sunna. "The enemy has gathered at the mountain, and you will need all the help you can get. That's why you and I are going on a special mission before we continue there."

They had begun to walk towards the place the woman had pointed to, and came to a golden chariot pulled by two winged yellow horses, with tails and manes made of fire.

A woman in a light blue dress was waiting for them.

"Bea!" Váli exclaimed, running forward to greet her.

The fire horses stamped nervously as he rushed past, but calmed down when Sunna extended her hand to them.

"Did you miss us?" Bea asked, laughing as Váli threw himself against her.

"Of course I have," he replied, standing on his back legs while hugging the woman.

"We have to go," Sunna said, and Váli sat down in the wagon. "We have much to do."

274

"What exactly are we going to do?" Váli asked curiously.

"We're going to get help," Bea replied mysteriously, and gave Sunna a kiss.

"This one is for you," Sunna said, threading a necklace with a yellow-green stone around Váli's neck.

"What is it?" Váli asked, looking down at the strange stone, which was shaped like the leaves of a rose.

"It is a Peridot, a sun pearl," Sunna replied with a smile.

"You'll understand in time," said Bea, laughing as she saw his uncomprehending expression.

Váli watched as they left the ground on a wave of blue fire. He had really missed his great-aunt and her wife.

❧

"I miss him, Tulio," Wille said sadly.

They had been flying for what seemed like an eternity, but Hábrók still didn't seem to think they had arrived.

"I shouldn't have raised my voice to him," he continued, feeling his anxiety building.

"It's good that you feel remorse," said Tulio. "It shows you care about him."

"I should look for him," said Wille. "I want him back."

"He will come back," said Tulio, smiling boyishly.

"How do you know?" Wille asked, wiping a tear.

"Let's just say that I have a strong hunch that we'll see him at the mountain," replied the boy, looking at the rising sun.

Suddenly Hábrók began to dive downward, and Rudolph followed. They landed in a clearing on the cold snow cover.

"Hábrók says we have arrived," said Tulio. "Hugo and the others are a hundred metres ahead of us."

"Okay," said Wille, stepping off the reindeer's back. "Could you…you know, turn around?"

He waited until the smiling boy turned his back on him before he began to undress. Still, Wille couldn't help but feel like he was being watched as he folded his clothes and put them in the saddle bag. He closed the bag, and the reindeer ran off into the sky again.

Before Wille could turn into a wolf, a snowball hit him in the back. When he turned around, he saw that Tulio was grinning with several snowballs in his arms.

Wille immediately felt embarrassed, but before he could protest, the boy showered him with snowballs and started running away.

Wille focused, and he felt the wolf's form take shape inside him again. The wolf's paws felt wonderful in the soft snow, and he stopped shivering.

He started running after Tulio and threw himself at the young boy, whom he wrestled down and showered with snow before running on.

✧

Tulio howled with laughter as he ran away from Wille, but it wasn't as funny when the older boy caught up with him and wrestled him into the snow.

He looked after the silver-white wolf, who disappeared in the dark air in front of him, and quickly got back on his feet. He didn't want to be left behind in the dark.

Tulio missed his siblings but still felt a sense of security as he ran to catch the wolf that had stopped to wait for him.

A wonderful feeling spread through his body when Wille lowered his back for him to jump up. He knew that they had become friends.

As Wille ran across the wet snow towards the tent in front of them, Tulio turned his head and looked east. He wondered what his parents were doing and if they missed him before laughing to himself, realising that he was homesick.

28. Gargoyles

The huge beast rose up on its front legs, and a cloud of smoke steamed out of its nostrils. There was a clang as several gold coins fell from the huge pile of gold under its feet and hit the stony floor. The dragon looked at Nari, who nervously stood at the back of the chamber's entrance.

"If you help us, we will help you," Hela said, standing at the foot of the pile of gold.

"The ring can turn you back again," said Wayland, taking a step forward out of the darkness.

"You're the one with my ring, aren't you?" the dragon asked, stretching his head over Hela and Wayland. "Why don't you ask me for this yourself?"

"My lord, Fáfnir, I humbly apologise," replied Nari, and sank to the ground in a deep bow.

"The boy is subordinate to me," said Wayland confidently. "You of all people know of my powers."

The dragon turned to Wayland and Hela. Black and purple flames billowed out around them, but he didn't seem to care.

"It was you two who tricked me into this," Fáfnir hissed contemptuously. "Now I understand how it happened."

"Then we agree?" Hela interrupted him. "You help us, and in return, we will lift the curse of the ring on you."

Fafnir stared again at Nari, who stood trembling in panic.

The great dragon crawled forward and coiled around him like a snake. The beast strained its eyes on Nari and scrutinised him for a long time.

"Are we agreed?" Hela asked irritably.

Fáfnir turned to Wayland and smiled slyly.

"So, the great and powerful Wayland needs help from a lower dragon," Fáfnir snorted. "Well, I have two conditions."

"Name them," said Wayland without pretending the insult.

"I am not interested in reversing my transformation," continued Fáfnir.

"I and my servants will help you on the condition that I get one of the girls as my queen."

"And the other condition?" Hela asked impatiently.

"The second condition is that from now on the boy belongs to me," Fafnir replied, without taking his eyes off Wayland. "Including the portrait that you think no one else knows about."

If Wayland was shocked that Fáfnir knew about the portrait of Nari's soul, he didn't show it. Instead, he cast a long glance at Nari and scratched his chin.

"Very well," he said, flapping his arms. "Help us in this battle, and both the boy and his portrait belong to you."

There was a clang as several gold coins rolled away down the stony floor. One coin spun, and landed flat at Nari's feet.

He stared with a terrified look at the coin's golden reflection before the dragon's fire was extinguished and the stone hall was plunged into a dull darkness, which was broken when dark blue flames appeared at the entrance.

Velnias appeared in the flames, but took no notice of either Fáfnir or Nari. Instead, he walked up to Hela, where he made a deep bow.

"Velnias," Hela said delightedly, running her hand over his cheek. "That's not necessary."

"The newcomer joins us," Wayland said delightedly.

Velnias made a move to attack Wayland, but Hela stopped him with a kiss.

"No need for jealousy," she said, smiling. "We need each other right now, that's all."

"I'll be here when you're ready, Velnias," Wayland said with amusement. "Just say the word."

"Do you have something to report?" Hela interrupted.

"We have lost control of the boy," Velnias replied with ill-concealed irritation. "His heart is too strong, the soul is winning over the darkness."

Hela's expression suddenly turned to rage, and Wayland let out an eerie laugh.

"Have you begun to lose the spark, Hela?" he exclaimed, watching with amusement as she surrounded him with her purple flames.

The purple flames mingled with Wayland's black fire, which eventually devoured the last purple colours in the fire.

"Your powers were indeed overwhelming before, darling," he said sharply. "But it's different now."

Wayland's knuckles hardened as he revealed his black ring, holding it before her angry face. The black ring glinted from the glow of Velnias blue flames, and Wayland flexed his hand demonstratively.

"This ring, the ninth ring, is stronger than the other rings," he said menacingly. "Even with all the other eight rings, you and your little family wouldn't be able to stand up to me now."

Hela looked furious and turned to Nari, who was still standing and trembling.

"Don't just stand there shaking," she hissed. "If you are going to work with us instead of for us, you can start doing some good. Get the boy and bring him to me!"

Nari stared from the angry woman to Wayland, who stood with his arms crossed, and finally at Velnias grim expression. Then he turned his head and noticed that Fáfnir was carefully observing his reaction. With trembling hands, Nari enveloped himself in darkness and disappeared.

Fáfnir ostentatiously wrapped his wings around his face, it was clear that he considered the meeting to be over. A mixture of blue and purple flames surrounded Hela and Velnias, and they too disappeared from the cave.

"You know you don't have a chance to control that power," the dragon said softly. "Not even the real dragons could fully master him."

"Thank you for your concern," Wayland said, laughing. "I have what it takes for my protection."

With those words, Wayland disappeared into the black flames.

"Your arrogance will be your downfall," said the dragon, closing his eyes.

ও

"What is that?" Jack asked, looking puzzled at the dark contours in the sky.

He turned to his father, who looked terrified, and clapped his hands with the reins.

"Dad, what is it?" Jack asked worriedly.

He had never seen his father so frightened before.

"Trouble," replied Ullr.

He stopped the sledge, and turned to Jack.

"You must quickly build a pillar of ice beneath us from the ground," said Ullr, looking at the dark outlines coming closer. "We can't get away, we have to fight them."

Jack peered out from the sledge and managed to make out the first outlines of the creatures coming towards them.

Jörgen, who had stood up to get a better view, gasped in horror and sat back down in terror.

"Don't worry, Professor, we'll defend ourselves," said Ullr, looking down at the column of ice that was beginning to form beneath them.

It grew rapidly, and Jack formed an oblong plateau where they could land the sledge.

"Are you ready, Jack?" Ullr asked, looking at him.

"I think so, father," Jack replied anxiously.

"Protect the reindeer and the professor," said Ullr seriously. "And try not to let them hurt you."

Jack looked nervously at the creatures coming closer to the plateau. He wrapped his coat around him and felt himself beginning to perspire as they waited for the coming attack.

The first creature crashed into the ice pillar and began to climb up towards them. It was soon followed by more, and Jack could see the grotesque fangs and pointed horns protruding from their heads.

Then the battle broke out as the creatures made their way over the edge of the ice and ran towards the sledge. Ullr waved his hands, and huge snowdrifts enveloped the sledge and the reindeer.

Jack held up his hands, and a huge hailstorm fell on the demons, driving them back towards the edge of the pillar again. He pointed his hands to the side and sent large, pointed pieces of ice flying in all directions as he spun around in the sledge.

Jörgen dove so as not to be in the line of fire and curled up on the floor of the sledge.

Suddenly, one of the demons threw itself at the sledge and slammed Ullr with its claws. The snow god landed on the icy plateau, whereupon the demons threw themselves upon him, and the snow vortex around the sledge diminished.

"Dad!" cried Jack, pointing the ice spikes at the demons around Ullr.

More demons ran across the ice plateau towards them, and Jack realised they were way too many for him.

Then several blue fireballs fell from the sky, hitting the demons clawing furiously in front of them.

Jack saw countless fireballs falling over the large swarm circling the ice pillar, whereupon the demons broke up their formation and began to fly away.

One of the remaining demons had climbed onto the sledge and grabbed Jack around the waist, pushing him down to the floor of the sledge.

The demon opened its mouth and bared its fangs as Jack desperately tried to push it away.

A howl caused the demon to look up, and Jack watched in amazement as Váli ripped the demon down on the ice again.

Jack carefully peeked over the edge of the sledge and could see a woman in a blue dress crossing the ice, piercing the demons with a huge blue fire spear.

As the woman pierced the last of the demons on the ice plateau, Váli tore the throat of the demon he fought and threw the winged creature over the edge.

The woman with the spear put one hand at its base and the other at the tip, squeezing the spear to disappear into nothingness.

"Váli," said Jörgen in surprise, and got out of the sledge. "How did you get here?"

"I got a ride," replied the wolf, and looked over to the edge of the ice, where two fire horses landed with a golden carriage.

At the bow stood a beautiful woman in a golden-white dress, her hair glittering like the sun.

"Who is that?" Jörgen asked curiously.

The woman walked towards the sledge, her braided golden yellow hair dragging on the ground.

"My name is Sunna," replied the woman, making a light-hearted gesture with one hand in greeting. "And the woman over there is Bea, my wife."

The other woman helped Ullr get back on his feet. Her silver-blue dress was matched by her silver-white hair, which, like Sunna's, was long and braided.

"Sunna?" Jörgen exclaimed in surprise. "The sun goddess?"

"That's right, Professor," she replied, laughing. "Can you place my wife too?"

Jörgen looked puzzled and shook his head.

"What if I say that 'Bea' is a nickname for Beaivi?" Sunna asked in a sly voice.

"Beaivi!" Jörgen exclaimed, looking at the woman in the blue dress who had just arrived at the sledge with Ullr.

The woman smiled warmly and crossed her arms.

"Am I being talked about already?" she asked, laughing.

"I was just telling the professor who you are, sweetheart," Sunna said, giving her a quick kiss.

"So, this is the professor I've heard so much about," said Bea, and extended her right hand in greeting.

Jörgen held out his hand and shook hers.

"You belong to the family of the Vanir gods, don't you?" he asked.

"You really know your history," Bea replied, seeming delighted to be recognised.

Jack had been sitting quietly in the sledge, observing the conversation. He felt nervous in front of the two strangers and tried to wrap the coat as best he could around his naked body as he rose from the floor.

"Jörgen," he said gently. "Can you help me up?"

"Oh, I'm sorry, Jack," Jörgen replied, reaching down to pull him up.

"And who do we have here?" Bea asked excitedly, scrutinising Jack, who shyly wrapped the coat around him.

"My name is Jack," he replied, and felt himself blushing. "I am Ullr's son."

"Really?" Bea asked, looking wonderingly at Ullr.

"Are you okay, Dad?" Jack asked worriedly, looking at his father, who was leaning against the edge of the sledge.

"I'm fine," Ullr replied, and stood up straight. "I just need to rest for a while."

His coarse woollen sweater was torn by the demons' claws, and he was bleeding profusely from the wounds.

"What was that all about, anyway?" Jörgen asked, looking in the direction that the creatures had disappeared.

"Gargoyles," replied Sunna with a grim face. "They call themselves 'the Legion', and are part of Wayland's army."

"Gargoyles?!" Jörgen exclaimed in confusion. "I didn't think any such creatures existed in real life?"

"They do," Sunna replied, and began warming Jack's feet. "But Wayland hasn't used them since the last war."

"But I thought demons couldn't fly?" Jörgen asked and sat down in the sledge.

"You'd be surprised to know how many different kinds of demons there are with unique characteristics," replied Bea as she examined Ullr's wound. "But to answer your question, Gargoyles are still unique, they are people whose souls have been torn out of their bodies before the darkness takes over."

"Torn out?" Jörgen asked, looking at her inquiringly. "How does that work?"

"The magic of Wayland," Sunna replied. "Even before Wayland became involved with the dragons, he had the ability to manipulate souls, and with his newfound powers, his abilities have increased to the point where he can, among other things, rip the souls out of his victims' bodies."

Jack shuddered, and made a moaning sound as the veins in his feet slowly warmed up. Bea, who seemed satisfied that Ullr's injuries were not serious, put her hands on his shoulders, and a silver-blue light shone from her hands, warming him up.

A reddish glow revealed how Rudolph descended to land on the edge of the plateau.

Ullr greeted him and opened the saddlebag.

"You're lucky, Jack," said his father. "The clothes are here, so you don't have to wrap yourself in the coat anymore."

"Thank you," said Jack, accepting the clothes.

He cleared his throat, and he looked at them nervously.

"Could you give me some privacy?" he asked, looking pleadingly at his father.

"We can go away for a bit," Sunna replied, smiling as she motioned for Ullr and Bea to follow her.

"Can I stay then?" Váli asked, sitting down next to him.

"Yes, all right," replied Jack, and put his clothes away again while letting his hand run through the fur of the wolf, who laid his head on his knee.

"I heard what happened," said Jörgen, walking around the sledge. "Do you want to talk about it?"

The dark-furred wolf let out a sob.

"I wanted to tell you, but I didn't know how," Váli replied. "The moment never turned out well."

"I can understand that," said Jörgen. "But how does that work?"

Jack could see that Váli was crying, which he had never seen him do before. To Jack, his cousin was tough, and he didn't know how to deal with the fact that he was now sobbing into his lap.

"As you have probably heard, my father's method is to close the heart's opening to the soul, making it easier for the darkness to take over the victim's body without having to overcome the soul," Váli said. "But the method has a flaw."

Váli gave the professor a sad look.

"Human hearts reacted differently to the gods' attempts to make them more resilient, which led to some people having a greater chance of survival than others. If a person with extra resilience is subjected to an attempt to close the door of the soul, that seal does not hold, and the soul breaks through and overcomes the darkness," he said quietly.

"Okay, but what you've described applies to humans, and you're a god, so what's the difference?" Jörgen asked.

"Just like human hearts, the hearts of gods are different, some are stronger than others," Váli replied. "When the darkness attacks us, it takes over our souls instead of destroying them, as the darkness does with the souls of humans. But it takes time and energy for the darkness to do that, and the stronger the heart, the longer it takes to turn us into demons. That's why Dad developed the method that instead of the darkness having to conquer the soul, it can be locked up, and the darkness can conquer only the body."

"And how come you are not taken over?" Jörgen asked, examining Váli.

"When my father turned me into a wolf, he sealed my soul and forced a bottle of darkness into me. What he didn't count on was that my heart was too strong for the darkness and his magic to overcome," Váli replied. "The darkness made me mean and ferocious for a short time, before the strength of the soul crushed my father's magic and overcame the darkness. Unfortunately, I had already killed my brother."

Váli put his head back on his lap again and closed his eyes. Jack gently put his hand behind the wolf's ear.

"Uh, Váli," Jack said gently. "You know that I like you, and that you can talk to me about things but could I be allowed to put on my clothes now?"

❦

"Is he really your son?" Bea asked, looking at Jack, who continued to get dressed. "Who is the mother?"

"Hulda," replied Ullr, sighing heavily.

"What!" Bea exclaimed. "Why haven't you told us?"

She looked at Sunna, who was standing with her arms crossed. "Did you know about this?"

Sunna looked at him for a long time. Ullr started to sweat and tried hard not to look too nervous.

"I see," she said after a while. "How were you going to tell this to everyone else?"

"Tell what?" asked Bea, looking confused.

She stared first at Sunna's determined expression, then at Ullr's sad look, before glancing over at Jack again, examining his slender but supple and fit torso.

"Don't tell me…," Bea began, putting her hand over her mouth before staring at Ullr again, who nodded.

"I love him," he said quietly. "I thought you of all people would understand the feeling of being different."

"It's not that, Ullr," said Sunna. "We understand, but I don't think the others would."

The fire horses began to scrape their hooves on the ice, and she made a gesture with her hand to reassure them.

"We'll discuss it later," she continued, suddenly looking serious again. "We have more urgent problems."

"What have you seen?" Ullr asked.

"In addition to the demons of Wayland, who are heading for the mountain, two hundred hellwolves from Járnvidr are waiting for you there," replied Sunna. "As well as Garmr, Hati, and Sköll."

Ullr swore and started walking towards the sledge again, but was stopped by Bea, who put one hand on his upper arm.

"There's more," she said worriedly. "Wayland and Hela have allied themselves with Fáfnir and his minions from Trollhammer Mountain."

"We are in no position to fight a dragon!" Ullr exclaimed in panic.

"That's why we go for help," said Sunna patiently. "Váli is going to get help from the mountains, and another god is on his way to help against the dragon."

"What other god?" Ullr asked.

"That, my friend, is going to be a surprise," she replied with a secretive smile.

29. Di Inferi

Módi stared into the crackling flames. The fire gave off a pleasant heat, but the smoke made Hugo cough more intensely. He had put the boy as close to the fire as possible to keep him warm, and now Módi tried to set up a temporary shelter for him.

"So, Velnias and Hela are working together?" Módi asked, casting a glance at Oscar, who was sitting next to the fire.

"It's a bit more...intimate than that," Oscar replied. "They seem to have some kind of love affair."

"And the fire wolves are their creation?" Módi asked.

"Hati and Sköll," confirmed Oscar. "Hela and Velnias mixed the magic from Garmr with darkness and fire from their respective dragons to create the fire wolves as a symbol of their desire."

"Interesting," Módi said, spreading his coarse woollen cloak over Hugo, who was coughing frantically.

"Can't we do more for him?" Oscar asked anxiously.

"I'm afraid not," replied Módi. "He has fever, and we have to wait for Tulio to arrive."

Módi smiled when he saw Oscar's concerned look.

"It's nice to see that you care about him," he continued. "It has probably helped you overcome the darkness."

Oscar looked down at his hands and started shaking.

"You're not the first to wake up from the darkness and realise what you've done," Módi said, looking into his eyes.

"I killed my uncle," Oscar said, shaking. "I was the one who gave the fire wolves the order to devour them."

Módi saw the tears on his face and grabbed his hands.

"It wasn't your fault," he said, looking compassionately into Oscar's eyes. "Don't ever take the blame for it, because then the guilt will eat you up from within."

Oscar nodded and pulled his shirt sleeve over his face.

"Tell me about the other gods who are with Hela, what do you know about them?" Módi asked.

"They call themselves 'Di Inferi', the lower gods, and there are seven of them," Oscar replied. "Hela is the leader, but one of the others seems to take command over her to some extent."

"Who?" Módi asked, sitting down. "As far as I know, none of our enemies are more powerful than Hela, except for Wayland, of course."

"I don't know who he is," replied Oscar. "But he stands out from the others. His cloak is torn, and flutters like rags around him, and instead of hands, he has three-fingered claws protruding from his mutilated arms."

Módi stood up abruptly, his face paled, and he felt the fear wash over him.

"Módi?" Oscar asked in amazement. "Are you all right?"

"Tuoni," Módi whispered quietly. "His name is Tuoni."

"Who is he?" Oscar asked. "You seem scared."

"The question you should be asking is what he is," replied Módi. "Unfortunately, there is no easy answer to that question. In life, his name was Koshchei, and he was one of the shamans of the Vanir, who practiced necromancy, a conjurer who brings the souls of the dead back to our world. He was good at what he did, until he brought darkness instead of souls."

"What happened to him?" Oscar asked, and Módi could see that he had scared him.

"He turned into a lich, an immortal ghost," Módi replied, shivering. "He's also known as the 'Death Conjurer', because he can't be killed. He has given rise to what you humans call the Grim Reaper."

"What do you mean he can't be killed?" Oscar asked in horror. "I thought even gods could die?"

"That's the problem," replied Módi. "He's dead! When the darkness took him, he spirit-walked out of his body."

Módi turned and peered nervously into the forest.

"Is he a ghost?" Oscar asked.

"Worse," replied Módi, shivering. "As you know, the souls of the gods cannot be destroyed by the darkness in normal cases, but they are darkened and trapped in the body."

"Normally?" Oscar asked.

"When Tuoni's soul left his body, the darkness probably mistook it for the fact that he had a weaker soul than a god, a human's soul, because the darkness broke apart his body," Módi continued. "His soul, in that case, would have been able to return to the World Spirit if the darkness had not infected his soul in the process."

"So, you mean he is a darkened soul without a body?" Oscar asked. "But can't your magical weapons kill him as with other demons?"

"Not when he has no body to which his soul is bound," replied Módi, shaking his head. "After he and his children spread horrible wars and diseases in your world, we locked him up in the underworld, but if what you say is true, he has been helped to break free from the shackles."

"His children," Oscar said quietly, seeming to think. "One of the other gods, which I never saw the face of, was called 'queen' by Tuoni."

"Tuonetar," Módi replied, sitting down again. "She was originally called 'Baba Yaga', and belonged to the race of giants. She was a witch, who practiced such evil magic by bewitching people's minds, that we had difficult to kill her."

"So, what happened to her?" Oscar asked curiously.

"Three times we tried to kill her," Módi replied. "The first two times we used our weapons, but Tuoni helped her soul to leave her body, and she reappeared in her body with her magic. The third time we burned her body, so that the soul would have no place to return, but her wicked soul was not welcomed by the World Spirit. Instead, it was Tuoni who welcomed her with open arms into the realm of the dead."

"So, a darkened soul and a wicked soul," Oscar observed, looking at Hugo, who, coughing, hugged the stuffed animal.

"Who else did you see?" asked Módi, who calmed down.

"A blind woman with dark red hair," replied Oscar.

"Louhi," Módi sighed, and leaned forward. "She is the daughter of Tuoni and Tuonetar, and she is a skilled sorceress. She in turn gave birth to ten children, nine demons that haunt your world, and Hela – the worst of plagues!"

"You already know about Velnias," Oscar continued. "The sixth is a temperamental god called Hades."

Módi swore so loudly that Oscar jumped.

"Hades belongs to one of the families of the giants," he explained when he saw Oscar's surprised expression.

"During the last war, our warriors killed almost their entire race because they had been taken over by the darkness. But they did not find Hades, because he has a magical helmet that makes him invisible, even to us," Módi sighed heavily, and got up from his stump.

"Who is the last member?" he asked sadly.

"I don't know," replied Oscar. "She always has her hood up, but my mission was to free someone for her."

"Wait a minute!" Módi exclaimed, feeling a shiver run through his body. "How many of the rings does Hela's group actually have?"

"I think all seven have one ring each," Oscar replied. "Where the eighth ring is, I don't know."

"I can answer that," said a voice behind them.

Módi grabbed the axe and whirled around, but did not have time to meet the blow from Nari's sword, which slashed him across the back. He went down to the ground and remained there, unable to get up, while Oscar grabbed the sword and tried to push it away.

"So, it's you they've lost control of?" Nari asked sarcastically.

"You!" Oscar exclaimed angrily. "You killed my father!"

"And now I'm going to drag you back to your mistress," Nari replied, smirking. "I wonder what she will do with you."

"What makes you think I would go with you?" Oscar asked, putting all his weight on the sword.

"You think you have a choice?" Nari countered snidely.

Módi tried to get up, but it was useless. He could feel the darkness bubbling up from his back.

"So, what do you choose to do?" Nari asked, grinning at Oscar. "If you choose to pull the darkness out of him, I'll knock you down. If you choose to keep pushing away my sword, we will soon have another demon joining us."

Then there was an explosion from the forest, and something threw itself at Nari with such force that the demon flew several metres. There was a ringing sound as the sword struck the ground in front of the growling silver-white wolf.

"Wille!" Oscar exclaimed.

The angry wolf stood between them and the demon, who rose to his feet and brushed off his coat.

Módi heard running footsteps behind him, and turned around just in time to see Tulio kneeling at his side.

"Stop!" Oscar shouted. "He is infected by the darkness."

"But how are we going to save him?" Tulio asked.

"I can pull the darkness out of him," replied Oscar.

"How?" Tulio asked, looking into Módi's dark eyes.

Módi felt the darkness move in his chest and had to make an effort not to lose consciousness.

"So, they don't know," Nari hissed in delight.

The demon held out one hand, and the dark sword returned to his hand again.

"Isn't it about time you told them what you really are?" he asked in a triumphant voice.

"What does he mean, Oscar?" Wille asked.

"I'm a creature of darkness just like him," replied Oscar, pointing at Nari. "And like your friend, Váli."

"Yes, my dear little brother," hissed Nari. "Where is he?"

"You'll never get hold of him," replied Wille with a growl.

Nari lunged at Wille with the great sword, and a wall of darkness rose between them. The demon swung the sword and cleaved the wall in half before Oscar threw himself on top of him, and both of them tumbled around on the ground.

"So, you sacrifice Thor's son to try to save your friend," Nari hissed. "Interesting choice."

"Wille, your necklace," cried Tulio.

Wille rushed forward and looked down at the dark wound that was growing larger over Módi's back.

"Wille," Módi whispered, noticing his vision going numb.

"Give me the necklace," Tulio said sharply.

"But..." Wille began to protest.

"We don't have time for that now," the boy said firmly, prying the necklace loose.

As Wille transformed back into himself, Tulio pushed the necklace as far down as he could into the wound.

Módi felt a searing pain and let out a painful roar, at the same time as a hissing sound was heard. Tulio also screamed, and it was clear that it also affected him.

Slowly, Módi regained his vision and watched in horror as Nari impaled Oscar with the dark sword. He met the boy's terrified look, while Wille started running towards them. A darkness enveloped Oscar and the demon, who disappeared before Wille could get to them.

Módi pushed Tulio aside and took the necklace from him before he stood up on unsteady legs. He staggered over to Wille, who had sunk to his knees on the cold ground, and he could see that the boy was devastated.

"I couldn't save him either," said Wille, banging his fists on the ground. His eyes were red with tears.

"You'll find him, I'm sure of it," Módi said, putting his hand on Wille's shoulder.

Wille met his gaze and pulled his arm across his face, while Módi held out the necklace to him.

☙

"Oscar," said Hugo, coughing.

"Shh," said Tulio meaningfully. "Don't talk so much."

The young god placed both his hands over Hugo's chest, and a golden light flowed out of the boy's hands. For Hugo, it felt like liberation, his coughs subsided, and his lungs began to feel lighter. The fever subsided, and he could clearly see the contours of his surroundings again.

He heard Wille crying somewhere and tried to sit up, but Tulio firmly pushed him back to the ground.

"Lay still," the boy urged.

The golden light continued to embrace Hugo, and he felt his energy returning. After a while, the light faded, and Tulio sat down on the ground, exhausted.

Hugo laboriously got up, while Wille, in his wolf form, and Módi came walking towards them.

"Are you okay, Hugo?" Wille asked.

"Yes, I feel much better thanks to Tulio," replied Hugo, giving his brother a hug.

"He took Oscar," said Wille, with tearful eyes.

"We'll get him back," Hugo said confidently.

"Hugo, I've done something terrible," Wille continued, sobbing. "I drove Váli away." Hugo felt an icy cold spreading down his spine and let go of Wille.

"Why?" he asked, getting teary-eyed.

"He told me that he was a creature of darkness, and I didn't take it well," Wille replied sadly. "I didn't let him finish explaining, and I drove him away. I almost hit him."

Hugo sank back to the ground again.

"Váli," he whispered quietly, and began to tremble.

"Forgive me," said Wille. "I want him back with us."

"He soon will be again," interjected Tulio.

"How can you be so sure?" Wille asked.

"He was picked up by our friends after we left," replied Tulio. "Hábrók told me."

"What friends?" Wille asked.

"You'll see when we get to the mountain," the boy replied with a wink. "Don't worry, Váli will be there."

"Thanks for your help," said Hugo, giving Tulio a hug.

"You're welcome," said the young god, overwhelmed by the sudden hug.

"Well, Tulio," Hugo continued, letting go of the boy. "Thank you for the…uhm…loan."

He held out the stuffed wolf and handed it to Tulio, who carefully received it.

"Silver!" he exclaimed. "Thank you, I've missed him. But why do you have my stuffed animal?"

"I have trouble sleeping, so I usually sleep with a stuffed animal," Hugo replied. "Nyri gave it to me so that I would have something to cuddle when I was ill."

He felt uncomfortable and looked awkwardly at Wille, who smiled.

"Guys, we need to get going if we're going to catch up with the others," shouted a voice behind them.

All three turned around and looked in surprise at Módi, who swung himself up on a golden yellow horse. Hugo automatically flinched and stared at the magnificent horse.

"It's okay," Módi said, reaching down towards him. "This is Gullfaxi, and he is a real horse."

Hugo hesitated, but took hold of Módi's outstretched hand and swung himself up in front of him on horseback.

"Can Tulio ride on your back, Wille?" Módi asked, and the wolf nodded.

"Good," he continued. "Gullfaxi is one of our fastest horses, so I hope you can keep up with the pace."

Módi paused in a sweeping motion.

"Before we leave, though, there's one thing we need to do," he said, looking at Hugo. "Can you take out the stone?"

Hugo looked puzzled at him but took the crystal blue stone out of his pocket.

"Take out the ocarina," Módi instructed. "Look underneath it."

Hugo stared in amazement at the hole underneath the instrument, which was in the same shape as the stone. He took the stone and carefully placed it in the hole, after which he heard a clicking sound.

"Keep your thumb on the stone and try playing," Módi said, as Gullfaxi gently led them up the ridge.

Hugo let his consciousness disconnect, as he had done several times before. His fingers moved on their own accord, but this time the thumb was pressed against the stone.

A rumble was heard, and dark clouds loomed above them. The rain began to fall to the tune of the ocarina, it increased and poured down on them. Hugo noticed that the larger tarn started to fill with water again as large amounts of rain poured into the swampy wetland.

After what seemed like an eternity, Módi put his hand on Hugo's ocarina, and he stopped playing.

The rain slowed down, and Hugo was shocked when he looked around.

The filthy wetland had filled up, and the mirror-like surface of the water stood out beautifully against the dense forest around them.

"What really happened?" Wille asked, looking fascinated at the restored tarn.

"Lapis Manalis, the storm stone," Módi replied with a smile. "It has been disappeared for ages."

"But how come Hugo can use it?" asked Tulio curiously.

"Summoning rain is actually a form of magic that can only be used by a few gods," replied Módi, looking at Hugo's surprised expression. "But the ocarina is special, it's designed to enhance your ability to copy the magic of other gods."

"Tell me more," Hugo asked, looking up from the ocarina.

"Like your father, you have the ability to copy the magic of other gods," Módi replied patiently. "But some kinds of magic cannot be copied because they are too advanced, such as Lódurr's ability to move with the wind."

"So, how does that explain the rain?" Wille asked.

"The ability to create rain cannot be copied," Módi replied. "However, the ocarina can be combined with certain magical objects, such as that stone. The stone was made for the humans so that they could conjure rain during extreme droughts, but it disappeared several hundred years ago, and I didn't expect to find it here."

He looked out over the tarn.

"The magic of the water horse, which clogged the inflow to the big tarn, is gone, so now the tarn will remain full of water," he continued, grabbing the horse's reins. "But now we have to go on, we have lost a lot of time already!"

"Are you ready, Tulio?" Wille asked.

Tulio nodded and had barely time to swing himself up onto Wille's back before Gullfaxi dashed off at a run.

30. Trollhammer Mountain

They had been travelling for an hour, and their driver had announced that they would arrive at nightfall.

Jessica sat in the back seat and tried to sleep, but every time she closed her eyes, the images of her mother sinking down outside the car door came back. A tear made its way down her cheek when she thought of her father and his obsession with gods. He would have loved this, she thought.

Tella put a jacket over her, and Jessica smiled faintly.

Suddenly, the car swerved so hard that she was thrown forward, momentarily losing her breath as the belt caught her. Jessica opened her eyes wide as she saw dozens of small creatures with black, unkempt hair and beards around the car.

The driver got out and loaded his gun, but before he could do anything, one of the creatures threw a pointed object that penetrated the man's chest.

The man collapsed on the ground, and a pool of blood formed under his body.

Jessica turned to Tella, who seemed to be in some kind of daze, whereupon the trees beside the road rose up from the ground and began to whip the creatures with their branches.

The front passenger door was torn open, and Lovisa was dragged out of the car.

Jessica watched her squirm and scream while several tree roots grabbed the creatures and threw them away.

Jessica lunged forward and grabbed Lovisa's arm in an attempt to keep her in the car, but the creatures were too numerous, and before she knew it, Lovisa was dragged away screaming through the forest.

Jessica started to open her own door, but Tella's sharp voice stopped her.

"Don't open the door, they'll get you too!"

The trees outside the car continued to toss the creatures, which seemed endless in number. Finally, the sky above them began to rumble, and a ball of lightning swept down in front of the car, travelling through the crowd of creatures.

Jessica could see how the creatures retreated into the forest until the road before them was empty and deserted.

Her door opened, and Magni stuck his head in.

"Are you okay?" he asked, looking worried.

"I think so," Jessica replied, looking at the god's tense expression. "What were those things?"

"Dwarves," Tella replied, unbuckling her seatbelt before turning to Magni. "They took Lovisa."

He turned his head in the direction Tella was pointing and scratched the back of his head with concern.

Kenneth came up to them and sank down next to the driver, who was lying lifeless on the ground.

"He is dead," said the military leader, and two soldiers carried the body into the forest.

"You know what this means," said Tella, looking at Magni, who was still scratching his head.

"There's no point in jumping to conclusions," the god replied. "He has been asleep for several hundred years."

"They wouldn't attack us in the middle of the day if he hadn't ordered it," Tella said. "They usually hate daylight."

"Who?" Kenneth asked. "Who had ordered the attack?"

"Fáfnir," she replied. "The dragon in Trollhammer Mountain."

"A dragon?!" Jessica exclaimed in disbelief. "There are such things? And why would a dragon want Lovisa?"

"There are dragons," replied Tella. "They look just like the ones in your legends. Most of the dragons lived peacefully with us in the beginning, but eight of them tried to take over the creation from the World Spirit and were imprisoned deep down in its roots, which was the prelude to this war."

"Most of the dragons died in that battle," Magni continued. "And those who survived, both peaceful ones and evil ones, were plunged into deep sleep."

298

"So, there are peaceful dragons and less peaceful dragons," Tella summarized. "And then there are the seven dragons who are imprisoned and who are tied to the

the magic rings."

"Wait a minute," Kenneth said suddenly. "I thought there were eight rings, and therefore eight dragons?"

"Originally, there were eight dragons," Magni replied. "But during the first war, a group of magicians managed to summon one of them from its prison. Those magicians were destroyed, and one of our gods managed to slay the dragon."

"But what happened to the ring?" Jessica asked, puzzled. "Wasn't it destroyed along with the dragon?"

"At that time, the gods did not know that the rings were connected to the dragons, only that they possessed powerful magic," replied Magni. "This was just after the rings were created and before the gods had time to bind the darkness."

"To answer the question, it seems that the magic in the rings is not dependent on the dragons," Tella continued.

"So, who is this Fáfnir?" Kenneth asked as the two soldiers came out of the forest again. "Is he one of the evil dragons that created the rings?"

"No," replied Magni, shaking his head. "Fáfnir was originally a dwarf and the son of the dwarf king. After the rings were used for the first time, the one ring that was no longer connected to a dragon, the ring called 'Andvari', was hidden with the dwarves who were supposed to guard it."

"But their prince, Fáfnir, was blinded by the power the ring held, and he murdered his father to take it for himself," Tella continued. "His greed awakened the full power of the ring and turned him into a dragon.

The elder gods sealed him inside their mountain, along with the rest of the dwarf king's vast treasure." "But it seems that he has awakened," Tella concluded, looking at Magni, who seemed indecisive.

"We have to save her somehow," said Jessica.

"We're not in a good position to fight a dragon," Magni replied, shaking his head. "Even if I had Módi with me, our magic wouldn't be enough, Fáfnir would fry us alive."

"We can't just abandon her," Jessica said in despair.

Magni seemed to think for a moment and glanced back at the convoy of vehicles behind them. The soldiers seemed both restless and anxious as they stood outside their cars, waiting for a decision to be made. Then he turned to Nyri, who stood next to Kenneth.

"Nyri," he finally said. "You master earth magic, do you think you could use your magic under the mountain?"

"Yes," the younger god replied hesitantly. "Why?"

"You and I will try to rescue her, while the others continue towards the meeting place," Magni replied, looking at the soldiers. "There is no point to risking their lives."

"Nonsense!" Kenneth exclaimed. "We're not going to let you go on a suicide mission!"

"Kenneth, I am grateful for everything you have done for us," said Magni. "But this is a matter for us gods to deal with. If you came with us, you would put yourself in unnecessary danger. We met you at Flatruet afterwards."

"Very well," said Kenneth grimly. "Just make sure you get back in one piece, preferably without a dragon after you."

"Don't worry," said Magni. "He's trapped in that mountain and can't get out!"

Nyri walked up to Tella, who had turned around, and pulled her into her arms.

"I don't want to lose you," Tella sobbed. "I'm already worried about Tulio."

"You'll see us again soon," Nyri said, hugging his sister.

"All right," Kenneth said, and gestured for his men to get back in the cars.

"Wait, I'll come with you," came a sharp voice, and Jessica could see Gustav pushing towards them.

"Gustav, this is not for you," Magni said, looking at the young man, who came walking with his rifle in his hands. "He will devour you in a flash!"

"My cousin has been kidnapped," said Gustav, taking the safety off the rifle. "I'm going with you!"

"You're seventeen years old and still a minor, and since you're not one of the children of the god's, you are my responsibility," said Kenneth sternly. "And I don't like the idea of you heading off to that mountain."

"Magni, please don't leave me," Gustav urged.

Magni seemed to think about it, but shook his head.

"It's too dangerous, Gustav," he said, turning around.

"I have lost my parents in this war," Gustav exclaimed in despair, and sank to his knees. "I have fought with you, I saved Hugo and Oscar from the water horse. Please don't deny me the opportunity to help my cousin."

Magni looked down at the young man, who had tears in his eyes, and seemed to be impressed by his stubborn courage. Then he looked up at Kenneth again.

"It's up to you, Kenneth," he said finally.

The military leader looked from Gustav, who was kneeling, to Magni, who stood with his arms crossed.

"Can you protect him?" he asked, sighing.

"We can try, but I don't know if we can make it out of there at all," Magni replied.

"Please!" Gustav exclaimed pleadingly.

"You do as they say, and don't put yourself in unnecessary danger," said Kenneth, who narrowed his eyes at him. "If it becomes too dangerous, you withdraw, understand?"

Gustav nodded and got up from the ground.

"You are brave," Kenneth continued. "Just make sure your courage doesn't become recklessness."

"All right," said Magni. "We must go, we've wasted enough time already."

☙

"Let go of me!" Lovisa shouted at the dark-haired creatures, who carried her over their heads.

She screamed and tried to break free, but was abruptly carried deeper into the forest.

The forest was dense, and the branches of the trees scratched her face and arms.

After a while, she gave up and let herself be carried away. Her energy was gone, and she couldn't fight anymore, there were too many of them.

They continued through the forest for several hours, and after what seemed like an eternity, they finally arrived at a green-covered mountain. Lovisa made a quick lunge and rolled down to the ground, but she didn't even have time to stand up before the creatures pounced on her.

They carried her up the mountain and through a rocky crevice. She had been afraid of cramped spaces since she was little and had to bite her lip to keep from screaming.

Suddenly, the creatures threw her to the ground. Lovisa sat down, while one of the creatures put a pointed object against her neck and pointed at something behind her. She turned her head and saw a narrow stone staircase winding its way up along the rocky crevice.

"Climb," growled the pale-skinned creature behind her.

Realising she had no choice, Lovisa began to climb the narrow steps. Her fingers were scratched up, and her hands chafed from the hard boulders.

They came to a ledge, and the creatures guided her towards the mountain wall. One of them whispered something inaudible, and the outline of a stone door with carved symbols appeared.

The door opened with a scratching sound, and the creatures abruptly pushed Lovisa into the darkness of the mountain. Her eyes could not get used to the darkness fast enough, and she saw nothing as she was led down the steep staircase that winded its way through the mountain.

Knocking sounds were heard echoing, and she became aware of a flash of light further down the passage.

As they stepped down the last step and into the strange light, Lovisa couldn't believe what she saw.

She found herself on a ledge in front of a hollow void with stone pillars and huge vaulted ceilings. The strange light came from the solid walls of the hall, which seemed to be bathed in the glow of torches, the light of which dazzled against piles of gold that lay like a sea in the mountain.

Everywhere she looked, she could see the same strange creatures that had captured her. Some ran around with various tools, while others sat by small fireplaces and seemed to be busy forging.

The air in the mountain was hot, and the smoke from the furnaces seemed to be carried away by the dizzying paths.

One of the creatures nudged Lovisa with its pointed object as a sign for her to continue walking, and she began to make her way down the landing to the shimmering gold floor.

❧

"But how could they have kept such a huge treasure trove hidden from humans for so long?" asked Gustav as they entered the narrow, rocky crevice. "Shouldn't people have discovered it with satellites or other modern technology?"

"You have no idea how skilled the dwarves are at hiding things from you with magic," Nyri replied, looking up at the steep stone staircase. "There are more gold and precious stones in the bowels of the earth than you know, but the dwarves guard most of it with their magic. Your technology, which you are so proud of, is very easy to manipulate and hide things from."

"So, what's really in there?" Gustav asked, and started climbing up the narrow staircase.

"Gold!" replied Magni. "A sea of gold! And, of course, Fáfnir and his dwarves."

Gustav looked at him in amazement but listened attentively as he loaded his rifle.

"It is said that when the oldest of the gods were young, they wandered around in your world to admire the beauty they had created," Nyri said. "One day they were passing a stream outside the place you call Sveg and saw an otter.

Loki, who had joined the gods, caught the otter to prepare it as an evening meal for them. What they did not know was that the otter was, in fact, a dwarf who had transformed himself into an otter. A few days later, when they visited the dwarves in Trollhammer Mountain, the dwarf king had them imprisoned because it was his one son they had killed."

"Loki, who was the one who killed the dwarf, was given the task of re-placing the king's loss in gold," Magni continued. "He went back to the rapids and managed to catch another dwarf from whom he stole gold to pay the dwarf king. But the gold was cursed."

"A curse?" Gustav asked in a nervous tone.

"Yes," replied Magni. "The gold brings misfortune to all who possess it, so even the dragons ring 'Andvara'."

"But what does the dragon want with Lovisa?" Gustav asked while Nyri walked up to the mountain wall, put his ear to the stone, and began to knock with a metal object.

"It is not the first time that Fáfnir has tried to take a young girl to make his queen," Magni replied. "Before we sedated him, he tried to kidnap a girl who lived in a lonely house nearby. His dwarves visited her two times, and gave her wonderful jewellery as a gift. When they visited her a third time, they brought with them a golden bridal crown and tried to kidnap her. The girl tried to escape, but was overpowered, and the horse she was riding on broke free. The horse was then found by the people of the village of Tännäs, who quickly came to her rescue and managed to rescue the girl before the dwarves had time to take her into the mountain."

"I have found it, Magni," Nyri interrupted, and pointed to a place along the mountain wall.

Magni raised his huge hammer, and Nyri took a few steps backwards. The hammer began to glow with electrical charges, and small flashes of lightning came from it. A loud bang could be heard as he drove the hammer so hard into the rock that a portion of the rock wall collapsed, exposing an opening that seemed to lead into the interior of the mountain.

"It's called 'Ukko'," Magni said when he saw Gustav's fascinated look. "Its strength is immense, and with it I control thunder, lightning, and magnetism."

"This is the last chance for you to repent," he continued warningly, and looked scrutinizingly at Gustav, who held the rifle in a firm grip. "You have nothing to be ashamed of if you choose to wait for us here."

"I said I'm coming," Gustav said, loading the rifle.

"Very well," said Magni, and started walking into the darkness. "But stick with us, and don't touch any of the gold in there!"

Gustav put the ammunition in his backpack and followed the two gods into the darkness of the mountain.

None of the boys saw the two ravens sitting on a rock some distance away, now flying away. Their eyes flickered as they flew, cawing, over the military vehicles and away towards Flatruet.

❧

"No, please!" the man shouted before the giant wolf tore his throat out.

Everywhere in the village, there were screams from people trying to find shelter as the black wolves mercilessly attacked them. Some men tried to shoot the wolves, but there were too many, and the men were soon overpowered, and they were torn to pieces.

The blood turned the snow red, and several of the bitten ones turned into black wolves, while others were eaten alive, and the agonised screams cut through the night.

Garmr smiled in amusement to himself. They might as well have some fun while they waited for the military vehicles to arrive at the scene.

31. Silver

Oscar cried out and writhed in pain on the floor of the circle while the figure with the torn cap pointed his three claw-like fingers at him.

Around them, in addition to the god with the tattered robe, the other gods were watching the torture. Nari smiled, and seemed to enjoy watching Oscar suffer.

"Enough," came Hela's voice from behind the circle.

The god with the three claws made a gesture with his hand. Oscar stopped screaming, gasping for breath.

The circle split up as Hela and Wayland walked towards Oscar, who tremblingly sat on his knees. Hela bent down and gently lifted his chin with one hand.

"So, your soul was too strong for my magic," said Hela, as she smiled a sly smile.

"You want me to pull his soul out?" Wayland asked, raising one hand.

"No, that's not necessary," she replied, fixing her eyes on Oscar. "I have a better idea!"

"What are you going to do with me?" Oscar asked nervously.

Hela stood up and whispered something to Wayland, who immediately brightened up.

He raised both hands, and a silver light enveloped Oscar, mixed with dark flames.

Oscar felt as if his soul was being pierced by thousands of knives. He screamed as the black flames burned his soul from the inside, and was about to lose consciousness as the pain quickly subsided. Confused, he tried to get up, but found that he could no longer stand up properly.

Several of the evil gods gasped as the great coal-black wolf rose unsteadily on his four legs.

"Incredible!" one of the gods exclaimed. "He is almost a copy of Garmr!"

"Yes, both in appearance and size," said Wayland, with a satisfied smile.

Hela met Oscar's despairing gaze and smiled softly.

"If you want to become human again, you will complete the mission," she said, and a purple fire flared in one of her eyes. "Only then will we consider turning you back."

"What should we call him?" the red-haired older woman wondered. "We must be able to distinguish him from Garmr."

"The magic of the moon helped create him," Wayland replied expressively. "So, my new creation will be called Mánagarmr."

A black fire enveloped Wayland and Oscar before they disappeared. Hela turned to the others with a smile.

"Continue preparations for the next phase," she said, disappearing in purple flames. "Leave this battle to us."

☙

"There are so many of them," Wille whispered, looking down at the hundreds of hellwolves gathered below them.

They had arrived at Flatruet from the east earlier in the day and had been careful around the mountain to avoid the wolves. Now they sat on a ledge and looked out over the sea of wolves below them.

"What are they?" Hugo asked. "They are bigger than Váli."

"Bigger than Váli, but smaller than Garmr," observed Tulio, who let his eyes wander over the wolves.

"They are hellwolves from Járnvidr, the forest of the lost souls, which is an ancient dead forest located between the world of the living and the realm of the dead," Módi answered Hugo's question. "They feed on evil souls that have been rejected by the World Spirit. They are made up of dark magic that they transfer to other creatures by coming into contact with their blood, after which they also turn into hellwolves."

"I think you humans call them 'werewolves'," Tulio said, shaking next to Wille.

"So, what do we do now?" Wille asked.

"You wait here," replied Módi firmly. "I will ride ahead to Asgard to get help."

"But the others are coming from the south, straight into the wolves," said Wille. "Shouldn't we try to help them?"

"It's too dangerous," replied Módi, swinging himself onto Gullfaxi. "Wait here, and stay hidden."

He smacked his mouth lightly and pulled the horse's reins, whereupon Gullfaxi set off at a gallop.

Wille felt how tired he was, he had not slept anything that night, and despite the fact that they were surrounded by enemies, he felt his eyelids start to become heavy.

"Hugo," Wille said, stifling a yawn. "Can you keep watch for a while? I need to rest a bit while we wait for Módi."

Hugo looked worried but nodded briefly in response.

"Just don't snore, or you'll give away our hiding place," said Tulio, nudging Wille teasingly.

"I don't snore, do I?" he heard himself mutter as he fell asleep on the ground.

Wille fell back into the dark void with the silver flame. He moved forward, and to his surprise, he noticed that the flame widened and formed a ring around him. Like the last time, the darkness above him lit up like a mighty aurora borealis, and he could hear the calls of various animals in the beautiful colours.

The silver-white wolf stepped out of the flames and stood in front of him in the ring.

"You have sorrow in your heart," the wolf said, trying to make eye contact with Wille, but he averted his gaze.

"I did something unforgivable," Wille said, without meeting the wolf's gaze. "I drove Váli away, even though he is our friend, I…I almost hit him."

"And why did you do that?" asked the wolf calmly, without taking his eyes from Wille.

"He told me that he was dark-born and that he was partially infected with darkness," Wille replied. "I was angry that he hadn't told me from the beginning. I didn't understand and did not let him explain."

"I see," said the wolf. "What are you going to do about it?

"I want him back," replied Wille. "He is our friend, and…"

He paused to take in what he was about to say.

"And?" the wolf asked tenderly.

"I think Hugo loves him," replied Wille, meeting the wolf's gaze.

The wolf smiled and took a few steps towards Wille.

"Love can come from the most unexpected places," said the wolf. "Not even darkness can defeat it."

"Can love overcome darkness?" Wille asked in amazement.

"No power created by the World Spirit is as strong as the power of love," replied the wolf. "It unites the souls of beings across time and space, even death."

The wolf bowed his nose to the ground and closed his eyes. A shimmer of light began to form between them, and Wille stared in astonishment as a red crystal floated in the air in front of him.

"What is that?" Wille asked in astonishment, staring at the beautiful stone in front of him.

It was no bigger than it could fit in the palm of his hand, and yet he could not tear his eyes away from its shimmering.

"A soul stone," the wolf replied. "In your world, you would call it a 'red diamond'."

Wille held out his hand, and the stone sank into his palm.

"What do I do with it?" he asked, looking at the wolf.

"A soul stone reflects the true soul of a being," the wolf replied. "A creature with a pure soul wouldn't notice anything, but a creature infected by the darkness…"

Wille saw a dark spot float inside the stone.

"The darker the soul is, the darker the stone becomes when you hold it in front of a creature," the wolf continued. "You have darkness in your heart, but not so much that it has taken over the soul."

"What happens if the stone becomes completely dark?" Wille asked.

"The darker the stone is, the less there is left of the creature's soul," replied the wolf. "The darker the stone, the more likely it is that the creature either has no control over its soul or that the soul no longer exists."

"You mean like a demon?" Wille asked uncertainly, and the wolf nodded.

"If you are ever unsure who you can trust, let the stone decide," said the wolf. "It locks the darkness in creatures, and unlike your cross, it doesn't need direct contact with the darkness to do so."

"But what does this have to do with the Váli?" Wille asked. "His darkness is still there."

"Just like your darkness is within you," the wolf replied calmly. "Váli's soul has overcome the darkness that infected his heart, but not eradicated it."

"But how do I get the stone out of here?" Wille asked. "This is just a dream."

"Is it?" replied the wolf, and looked around. "I have never thought about what it is or isn't, I just realised that it is."

Wille stared questioningly at the wolf, who smiled.

"Before your adventures are over, you will have broadened your perception of reality," the wolf said enigmatically, as the room around them began to fade.

"Wait!" shouted Wille. "Can I call you Silver?"

The wolf looked puzzled, but then laughed.

"I guess that name suits me," the wolf replied, and seemed to be thinking about it.

"That's fine," he finally confirmed. "I like it."

"Can I see you again?" Wille asked as the last contours of the wolf's face faded away.

"I'm always with you," he heard the wolf reply. "If you don't think that it's just a dream, of course."

જી

"So, what do you think of Magni?" Tella asked and looked smilingly at Jessica, who immediately began to blush.

Jessica turned her head uncertainly without answering.

"I saw how you looked at him," Tella continued, amused.

"Yes…well…I mean," Jessica began to mumble.

She had indeed been fascinated by him, but didn't really know how she felt about it.

They didn't get any further in their discussion before the girls were thrown forward as the driver hit the brakes. In front of them, people came running, and Kenneth got out of the car to meet them. Jessica and Tella unbuckled their belts, and they got out of the car to hear what was going on.

"Calm down," Kenneth said, trying to drown out the panicked people gathered around him. "What's going on?"

"Wolves!" a woman screamed in despair. "Hundreds of giant wolves attacked our village."

She cried hysterically, and told him that the wolves had killed her husband and one son.

At that moment, Kenneth's cell phone rang, and when he answered it, he had a hard time hearing what the voice on the other end was trying to say.

"Establish a no-fly zone over the whole of Härjedalen immediately," Kenneth ordered. "Tell our Norwegian colleagues to mobilise their units and contact the boss, tell him it's code black and that I need air support. Give him the position at the village next to the lake Messlingen."

He ended the call and gave orders to his soldiers to start setting up an evacuation camp some distance away.

"What's going on?" Jessica asked, looking anxiously at the people gathered in front of them.

"The road up to Flatruet is blocked," Kenneth replied grimly. "Hundreds of giant wolves have gathered at the foot of the mountain, and flying demons swarm over the northern parts of the mountain."

He swore and kicked a rock on the ground.

"What's worse," Kennet continued, " is that the public has been made aware that something is going on up here. We're doing our best to limit the flow of information, but the fact that these wolves have attacked a village means that there are many witnesses to these giant wolves."

"What is it, Tella?" Jessica asked, noticing that her friend's face had gone pale.

"Kenneth, please describe the wolves," said Tella.

The military leader gave a brief account of the description that had been reported, whereupon she began to tremble.

"Kenneth," she said, tugging hard on the man's arm. "Immediately evacuate people out of here and seal off all roads in and out of the area leading to the mountain. And make sure that the reinforcements speed up!"

"Why?" asked Kenneth. "We have the situation under control."

"No, you don't!" Tella exclaimed vehemently. "I don't know what kind of flying demons there are at the mountain, but those wolves…"

She looked as if she were going to faint, and Jessica took a few quick steps forward to keep her upright.

"What about the wolves?" Jessica asked, startled.

"You would call them 'werewolves'," replied Tella. "Those who survive their bites turn into the same kind of monster that bit them."

She looked at Kenneth in panic.

"If there are hundreds of them at the mountain, they can destroy all life within as many miles away," she whispered.

Kenneth looked as if someone had punched him in the face. He stood frozen for what seemed like an eternity before running away and shouting out orders to his men.

&

"Surrender, old man!"

Lódurr stood leaning on his sword. Hati and Sköll circled around him, and Garmr stood beside them.

"We have outmanoeuvred you," Garmr hissed gloatingly.

"Our wolves from Járnvidr guard the mountain, as do the gargoyles of Wayland – you'll never get past us!"

"Besides, Fáfnir has reduced your party, the godchildren are staying behind at Trollhammer Mountain," added Hati.

Hati and Sköll prepared to throw themselves at Lódurr, and he raised his sword desperately to protect himself.

"Stop!" came a dark voice behind them.

Wayland approached with casual steps and stopped in front of Lódurr.

"We meet again, old friend," he said, smiling ominously.

"You?!" exclaimed Lódurr. "What do you gain by aligning yourself with them?"

"The enemy of my enemy is my friend, you know," Wayland replied sarcastically, and leaned forward so that their faces met. "And I think you will be surprised by this."

He took a step to the side and made a gesture with one hand towards the woman who had appeared behind him.

Lódurr opened his eyes and stared at the woman.

"It's not true," Lódurr whispered. "How?!"

"With my magic, of course," Wayland replied, smiling at Hela, who approached the old man.

"I guess you remember me, old man," said Hela, smiling softly at Lódurr, who was sweating profusely. "Did you really think that you could keep me locked up in the realm of the dead forever?"

"Hela, you…" Lódurr began, but stopped himself when he saw the flame that flared up in her empty eye socket.

"I have a perfect destiny for you," she said.

‹›

"Come on, just a little more!"

Gullfaxi galloped so fast that Módi found it difficult to stay on the horse's back, and the Gargoyles chasing them were only a few metres behind the horse.

"FATHER!" cried the young god in despair. "HELP ME!"

One of the gargoyles hit Módi so hard that he flew off his horse and landed with a hard thud on the rocky ground.

Blood ran down his head as he tried to get up on his wobbly legs. Everything was spinning around him, and he realised he had a concussion from the impact.

The gargoyles landed in a ring around him, while Gullfaxi continued to gallop away. One of the demons struck out with one hand, and Módi saw the razor-sharp claws gleaming in the evening sun.

Then the sky above them was illuminated by a bright light, so bright that Módi had to hold his arm over his face to protect his eyes. In the next moment, the gargoyles were surprised by several men with swords and axes.

The fight turned violent as the bewildered gargoyles tried to escape from the overwhelming attack. Módi had trouble seeing properly after the hard impact, and he was about to pass out when strong hands grabbed him.

"Dad," Módi muttered as the huge man looked down at him. "Forgive me, I failed!"

"You did great," the man said, smiling.

"They're here," Módi managed to say as his vision went black. "They need help!"

"I know, don't worry! Huginn and Muninn have been keeping tabs on you for a while. They have told us everything," the man said, and two ravens landed on the man's shoulders.

The muscular man with the wispy moustache smiled at Módi, who was slowly losing consciousness, and the man carried him over the hill. As the battle raged around them, they stepped through the gate of light and disappeared.

꿏

Váli felt nervous as he stood before the pack leader, who walked around and examined him carefully. He had been let into the pack's territory, but knew that he must not appear weak or his fate would quickly be decided.

The leader stopped next to him and looked into his eyes.

Váli felt himself beginning to sweat and had to make an effort not to avert his eyes.

The leader yelped at the rest of the pack, who one by one began to howl at the sky before bowing his head slightly, and Váli exhaled – it had worked!

Váli yelped three quick signals, and the leader and the strongest males in the pack began to trot after him.

"Don't worry, Hugo," he whispered quietly to himself as he ran across the thick blanket of snow. "I'm on my way!"

32. Fáfnir's Prisoner

The dwarves threw Lovisa roughly to the ground, and she fumbled with her hands in the darkness. A movement in the darkness caused her to jump in horror, as something large moved along the walls of the hall.

"I apologise for my dwarves," a voice rumbled above her. "They can be a bit rough."

Lovisa couldn't tell where the voice came from. She had been led through the sea of gold to a gigantic pile of gold coins, where the dwarves had left her.

"Who are you?" she asked nervously, looking around the dark void.

Then suddenly the dark void was lit up by great flames of fire, and Lovisa screamed when she saw the terrifying face staring down at her with a sly smile.

❦

They crept through the narrow opening that led into the cave. Below the plateau, a sea of shimmering gold opened up before their eyes. Gustav stared in amazement at the little dwarves running through the sea of gold coins, seemingly occupied with various errands. Magni motioned for him to follow, as they slowly made their way down a carved stone staircase.

The huge stone pillars that stretched so far into the cave were meticulously carved with intricate symbols and rune writings. When they reached the foot of the stairs, Gustav could not take his eyes off the gold coins clinking lightly under his shoes.

"Don't touch the gold, it's cursed," Magni reminded him in a whisper.

Nyri motioned for them to stay as close to the mountain wall as possible to avoid detection. They clambered over piles of coins and crouched down cautiously as the dwarves scurried further down the vast hall.

Then they spotted five dwarves carrying a seemingly unconscious Lovisa over their heads. Gustav made an effort to run forward, but Magni held him back.

"If you run forward, every single dwarf in the whole cave will know that we are here and chase after us," said Magni. "We will follow carefully and see where they take her."

They crept on in the same direction as the five dwarves had disappeared, and were careful to stay close to the mountain wall.

Suddenly, Nyri pulled Gustav down to the ground and covered his mouth. A dwarf came walking a couple of metres from them and stopped next to a pile of coins. The dwarf looked around suspiciously before pouring more coins onto the pile and moving on.

Magni, who had been crouching behind the pile, stood up, and Gustav could see that he was holding tightly to the huge battle hammer.

"Did you see where they went?" Nyri whispered when they arrived at the place where Magni was.

"They disappeared down a flight of stairs over there," he replied, pointing to a stone vault further ahead.

ↄ

Lovisa felt someone caressing her face.

"Wille…" she murmured, and tried to grab the hand that was caressing her cheek.

When she didn't feel a hand, she opened her eyes and stared around the illuminated chamber. She tried to get up but noticed that her foot was chained to the floor.

A scraping sound made her look around the seemingly empty room.

"Who's there?" Lovisa whispered incoherently and slowly pulled herself towards the wall.

"Please don't be afraid," said a voice in front of her.

"Who are you?" Lovisa asked, looking around the small chamber in confusion.

The air in front of her flickered, and a thin guy appeared.

"I'm a friend," he replied, looking at her with pity as she backed away from him in horror.

Lovisa stared at him in shock as he bent down next to her.

The guy's short, dark blond hair looked unkempt, and his bushy eyebrows and rough stubble didn't help matters.

"Who are you?" Lovisa asked again.

She had crawled as far against the wall as the chain allowed, and it was uncomfortable that he was so close.

The guy pulled a sword from his scabbard that was strapped around his waist. Lovisa screamed and put her arm up to protect herself as the guy delivered a very strong blow towards her.

There was a dull clang as the sword split the chain right at her ankle. Lovisa looked surprised at the guy, who reached out his hand to help her up. His blue eyes looked friendly, and he smiled at her.

"My name is Siegfried," the guy replied, putting the sword in the scabbard. "I was sent here to help you against the dragon."

"What can you do against that beast?" Lovisa asked, and shuddered at the memory of the dragon's cruel face.

"My sword, Gramr, can cleave almost anything, and with it I intend to pierce Fáfnir's heart," replied Siegfried, pulling out his sword again, as if to show it properly.

Lovisa looked at the black steel blade with the strange symbols etched into the metal.

"They are magic runes," he said, seeing her fascinated look. "A gift to my father from Odin himself."

"But how did you find me?" Lovisa asked, looking anxiously through the opening that led out of the chamber.

"I saw the dwarves carry you into the cave and followed," Siegfried replied, sliding his sword back into its scabbard. "My foster father was killed by one of Fáfnir's assassins, and I swore to avenge him. But I had no idea where the dragon's mountain lay. During my search, I met the sun goddess Bea, who showed me the way here in exchange for my help."

"Okay, I believe you. Do you know how we can get out of here?" Lovisa asked anxiously.

Siegfried pulled out something that hung over his pearly white shirt.

He pulled the strange object over him and disappeared.

Shortly thereafter, he reappeared right where he had been standing before.

"How does that work?" Lovisa asked in amazement.

"It's my invisibility cloak," replied Siegfried, smiling. "We can use it to sneak out of here undetected, just like I got in."

"Can I fit under it too?" Lovisa asked hesitantly as he wrapped the cloak around them.

"Of course," Siegfried replied, laughing. "Just try to be quiet, because it doesn't block out sound."

✲

"What do you think?" Magni asked, holding up the broken chain for Nyri to examine.

"It seems to have happened quite recently," replied Nyri, running his hand over the iron chain. "Someone has helped her to escape."

"But who?" Gustav asked curiously.

Suddenly, Nyri became rigid and seemed focused. He turned around and stared towards the entrance.

"We don't have time to think about that," he replied, taking a fighting stance. "We have company!"

No sooner had he finished the sentence than the chamber they were in was stormed by dwarves. Gustav stood paralysed with shock as the small, dark-haired creatures pounced on them with picks and sticks.

It was a fierce battle. Nyri raised his hands, and sharp stones flew towards the charging dwarves, who were pierced by the projectiles.

Magni wielded his gigantic hammer and knocked away the dwarves who were closest. Gustav awoke from his trance and began shooting the dwarves, who fell one by one.

"There are too many," Magni shouted. "Nyri, we need an exit!"

Nyri nodded and made a gesture with one hand. The rock wall behind Gustav began to shake and collapse. A cavity was revealed that seemed to lead behind the stone corridor outside the room. Magni grabbed Gustav's jacket and pulled him towards the opening, while Nyri let the ceiling of the chamber crack open and fall down on the wild dwarves.

⁊

"Are you sure?" Fáfnir asked, looking down at the little dwarf who stood shaking.

"Y…yes, your highness," the dwarf stammered. "One of the smiths saw them coming down the stairs at the entrance."

The huge dragon stood up, and hundreds of gold coins rained down from his back as Fafnir sniffed the air.

"Well, thief, what do you think of my queen?" the dragon asked, while Siegfried and Lovisa did their best to stand still. "I can smell you!"

The gold-coloured dragon swept its head above them, and its eye seemed to pierce the invisibility cloak.

"I can hear your breathing," he continued, and wrapped his head around them like a snake. "Where are you?"

Siegfried glanced at Lovisa, who nodded in horror, and before she could blink, he had lifted her up in his arms and was running over the sea of gold coins.

Fáfnir pushed his way through the piles of coins towards them, and they dove behind a stone pillar.

"Don't be shy," said Fáfnir, with ill-concealed delight. "Step out into the light so I can welcome you to our halls."

Siegfried tried to back up against the stone pillar as Fáfnir's head came ever closer. He stumbled and fell backwards, at the same time losing his grip on Lovisa, who in turn tore off his invisibility cloak.

"There you are," said Fáfnir with a broad smile.

"I…I didn't come to steal from you," Siegfried stammered.

"No, you didn't," snorted Fáfnir. "The sword speaks its language. Tell me, how is my brother Regin?"

"You know that," Siegfried replied angrily. "You murdered him."

"So, he was special to you," said Fáfnir, raising his overwhelming body high above him.

"He was my foster father," Siegfried roared, echoing through the vast hall.

"And now you want your revenge," said Fáfnir slyly. "Do you think you can survive it?"

"Probably not," Siegfried replied defiantly.

"No, that's right!" Fáfnir exclaimed triumphantly. "He was your foster father, you say, and yet I have never heard of you. Who are you, if I may ask?"

Siegfried thought quickly. He noticed that Lovisa had cautiously hurried away towards the mountain wall, and he could see a staircase that seemed to lead away from there.

"I am Siegfried, son of Sigmund of Valhalla," he answered defiantly. "This is Gramr, Odin's gift to my father, which after it was broken off was made whole again by Regin – your brother and my foster father."

Siegfried drew the dark sword, and held it firmly in front of him. The sword began to glow with a red aura, and the runes on the blade also glowed bright red.

"And with this sword, I will slay you, Jabberwocky," Siegfried concluded.

Fáfnir roared with laughter and looked at the sword with fascination.

"Really?!" he exclaimed in a lukewarm voice. "Tell me, Siegfried the sword avenger, when my beloved brother taught you my nickname, did he also tell you that I am always one step ahead of my opponents?"

Fáfnir brought his tail in front of him, and Siegfried could see that the tail was holding Lovisa around her waist. He glanced around and saw the invisibility cloak lying some distance away.

Lovisa squirmed desperately to get free, and Siegfried held back his anger as he didn't want to risk her getting hurt.

"And what about your other little god friends?" Fáfnir asked sarcastically. "Where are they hiding?"

Siegfried looked at the dragon in amazement.

"It's just me here," he replied uncertainly.

"I don't think so, sword avenger," said Fáfnir. "They sent you in here to fetch her, didn't they?"

"I don't know what you're talking about," Siegfried replied.

"LIAR!" Fáfnir exclaimed so loudly that the hall shook. "I know the smell of the Asgardians, how the flesh of the Vanir tastes, and how the fear of the Elves feels!"

"The girl is mine," the dragon continued, and began to step over the piles of gold towards the pillar where Siegfried stood. "I can kill you when I want, where I want, and how I want – do you really think that you have any chance?!" roared Fáfnir.

Siegfried ran to the stairs and cast a terrified glance over his shoulder.

"It's Thor's son, isn't it?" exclaimed Fáfnir. "The vile god's offspring cannot be mistaken by smell. He sent you in to pick up the girl."

"I don't know what you're talking about!" Siegfried exclaimed. "I am here to avenge my foster father."

"And yet you freed the girl, didn't you?" exclaimed the dragon. "There's no point in you denying it!"

"But it doesn't matter," continued Fáfnir, bending over the landing where Siegfried was hiding. "Your little adventure here will not make any difference. The darkness is spreading fast – not even the gods will escape this time."

Siegfried breathed heavily as he looked into the gigantic golden eyes that stared down at him from the landing.

"I think our little game ends here," whispered Fáfnir, lowering his head towards him. "Tell me, sword avenger, how do you want to die?"

☙

"It's down there," said Bea, pointing at the mountain. "Trollhammer Mountain."

"So, what happens now?" Jörgen asked when both wagons landed at the foot of the mountain.

"You and the wolf cub will stay with the wagons, make sure the puppy gets some moving," Sunna replied as she fed the fire horses.

Good, thought Jörgen, looking nervously up at the mountain. He was not sure that he wanted to meet a dragon after all.

33. The Magic Fire

Nyris' attempt to bring the roof down on the dwarves had only partially succeeded, and scores of dwarves rushed after them through the newly made opening.

"This way," Magni shouted, and pulled Gustav in through an archway, where both of them stopped.

"What are you doing?" cried Nyri, and ran in after them. "The dwarves are coming, we have to get out of here!"

Nyri stopped when he saw why they weren't moving.

"So, it's true – we have guests!"

Nari stepped down from the dark throne, which seemed to be made of shimmering darkness. The gold coins below rattled as he stepped down from the glittering pile of coins.

"Did you really think you could free the girl and get out of here?" Nari asked with a smug smile.

"You, you…" Magni began and took a step forward.

"Take it easy," said Nari delightedly, holding up his hand.

The dwarves had come into the room and stood menacingly with their weapons aimed at Nyri and Gustav.

Gustav was holding his rifle pointed at the nearest dwarves, and Nyri stood with his hands in combat position.

"What will you do now, Thunder God?" Nari asked with amusement.

Hardly had he uttered the words before Magni ripped open his enormous sledgehammer and lunged at the demon, who laughed at the approaching god.

At the same time, the dwarves attacked Nyri and Gustav, who struggled against the attacking wave.

Nari held out his hands, and a dark shield was conjured out of thin air in front of him. Magni's hammer struck the shield with such force that lightning flashed around them, while a deafening roar was heard.

"Can't you do better than that, son of Thor?" asked Nari, looking with amusement at the raging god through the sea of lightning.

Meanwhile, one of the dwarves had managed to wrestle Gustav to the ground. As he was trying to push away the dwarf with his rifle, a sharp stone flew through the air and impaled the dwarf.

"Leave now!" Nyri shouted, using the remains of a stone pillar as a sledge-hammer against the crowd of dwarves storming into the room.

Gustav stood up while looking for another exit. He thought he saw the outline of an opening behind the black throne and began to run, only to be thrown back down to the ground as Magni and the demon flew through the air in a cascade of lightning and darkness. He cautiously crawled towards the opening, while the battle between the opponents continued in the air when Magni swung his hammer, only to be blocked by the demon's dark sword.

Gustav finally reached the opening and threw himself in, as a giant bolt of lightning shot past him. He sat down behind one wall of the opening and closed his eyes while catching his breath. When he opened his eyes again and took note of his surroundings, he was greeted by an astonishing sight.

In front of him was a huge rectangular altar, and a sword floated above each end of the altar. The swords seemed to be held up by a mysterious ball of fire, which hovered at the centre of the altar.

Gustav stood up as he felt himself being pulled towards the mysterious fireball. Behind him, he could hear the battle continuing in the other room. The strange fireball seemed to increase its energy pulse as he approached the altar.

His thoughts oscillated between fear and curiosity as he slowly reached out his hand towards the fireball, which seemed to be drawn towards him. The fireball touched Gustav's hand and began to envelop his arm. Terrified, he pulled his hand back but relaxed when he felt a pleasant warmth from the fire enveloping him.

There was a rattling sound as the two swords stopped hovering and hit the altar. The globe of fire had moved completely away from the altar and enveloped Gustav like a luminous aura. The fear that he had felt before was gone and was replaced by a pleasant warmth and a strange calmness.

The fire disappeared, and Gustav stared at himself in bewilderment and twisted his arms in surprise. An enormous spear of fire shot out from one of his hands, and he took a step backwards in shock as he continued to study his hands.

Suddenly Gustav heard a scraping sound behind the altar, and looked in horror. Behind the altar was a strange portrait with a greyish frame. A grey sign was attached to the top of the frame, with text that read 'Orandi'.

But it was what was on the canvas that made him shiver. On the canvas of the portrait, a hideous creature was staring at him. It had human features, but the hair was torn and half the face was hanging down in great sludge. The wounds on the creature's face were rotten, and Gustav was disgusted when he saw larvae crawling out of the wounds.

There was a strange darkness around the creature, which seemed to surge like waves in the portrait. But for Gustav, the worst thing was its eyes, from which dark tears flowed.

He recoiled when the creature put up its torn hands, and it seemed to push the canvas out from within. Then he saw how it tried to form words with its grotesque mouth.

Gustav felt he wanted to run away when he saw the razor-sharp teeth in the creature's mouth, but he still forced himself to stare at the portrait, trying to read its lips.

"Help…me…" Gustav muttered uncomprehendingly.

The creature nodded enthusiastically and leaned against the canvas.

"Who are you?" Gustav asked uncertainly. "Are you a demon?"

The creature eagerly shook its head and pointed at itself before it started forming words with its mouth again.

"Nari…soul…" Gustav muttered again, looking unsure as the creature pointed to the entrance.

He turned in the direction the creature was pointing and saw the battle continuing in the other room, where Magni was on his knees with his large sledgehammer, and blocked a blow from the sword that the demon pressed against him.

Gustav turned to the portrait again and tried to interpret the words that the creature was forming with its mouth.

"Nari…demon…can…not…be…killed…" he muttered, while the creature kept pointing to the other room.

"So, how can I help you?" Gustav asked in confusion and looked helplessly at the painting.

There were screams from the other room, and he turned around frantically. A yellowish fire flared up around the combatants, and Gustav made a dash to run back to his friends when he heard the scraping sound again.

He whirled around and saw the creature waving its arms to get attention while pointing at Gustav's hands. The creature held up its own hands and made a motion, as if it were stabbing itself in the chest.

Gustav's hands began to glow from the warming light again, and he looked uncomprehendingly at the creature in the canvas, who eagerly repeated the same movement over and over again.

✌

The yellow fire spread in a circle around Magni and Nari. The demon laughed and held up the golden ring from which the yellow flames were conjured.

"Is something wrong, son of Thor?" Nari asked with a smile. "Have you lost the will to fight?"

Magni, surrounded by the flames, trembled and looked at the golden treasure.

"Magni, pull yourself together!" Nyri roared as the dwarves held him down on the ground.

Magni continued to stare at the gold coins in his hand as the demon approached him.

"Do you feel the gold calling out to you, thunder god?" Nari asked while a black spear was conjured in his hands.

"Don't worry, you will soon admire it even more, as a demon," he continued, and raised the spear with both arms.

Suddenly, Nari dropped the spear and roared as the skin on his face peeled off and large flesh wounds appeared.

Nyri saw Gustav standing further away with a large portrait, which he pierced with a fire spear.

The demon rushed, roaring towards Gustav, who let the fire spear tear the painting apart.

Nari threw out his arms as a wave of darkness surged from the small part of the portrait that still remained and entered through his mouth.

The dwarves stared in horror as the last part of the portrait burned up, and the demon fell lifelessly to the ground.

The moment Nari's screams ceased, the dwarves began to scream instead, as large chunks of ice flew over Nyri's head and knocked away the last of the dwarves, who crashed into the mountain wall.

He turned his head as a young man reached out his hand to help him up. Meanwhile, a cold wind began to sweep through the cave, putting a blanket of snow over the last fire.

A man wearing a coarse wool coat suddenly stood in front of Magni and pulled him to his feet again.

"Glad we didn't miss all the fun," said the guy as he helped Nyri up.

"Thank you," Nyri said gently, and looked away.

"Are you shy?" the guy asked amusedly, bending over to try to regain eye contact with Nyri. "I saved you, so why don't you at least talk to me?"

"Who are you?" Nyri asked cautiously.

"My name is Jack," Jack replied with a smile, and extended his hand to Nyri, who reluctantly accepted it.

"So, you fought a demon before we came?" Jack asked.

"We?" Nyri asked back nervously, looking up at the spot where Magni and the strange man were standing.

"It's Ullr, my father," replied Jack, laughing, as he grabbed Nyri's arm and pulled him up through the pile of coins.

❧

"How is he?" asked Gustav, and looked worriedly at Magni, who was crawling around among the gold coins.

"He has suffered the curse of the gold," replied Ullr, sighing. "That fire that the demon used must somehow have triggered the desire for the gold."

Gustav looked down with distaste at the demon lying lifeless at his feet.

The demon's face had been transformed into something disgusting, with large, festering wounds and slabs of flesh hanging down his cheeks.

"Look!" exclaimed Ullr, pointing at the spot where the remains of the portrait lay smouldering on the ground.

Gustav looked around and was astonished to see a shimmering figure taking form next to the burnt-out frame.

The figure smiling at them looked exactly as the demon had done before it took on that hideous appearance, and Gustav understood what it meant.

Nari's soul put its hand on its chest and nodded, forming a silent 'thank you' with its mouth.

Gustav returned the greeting before the soul dissolved and disappeared.

"Are you okay?" a voice was heard behind them.

Gustav turned around and saw a strange guy walking towards them, along with Nyri.

"I'm fine," Gustav replied. "But who are you?"

"My name is Jack," the guy replied, taking his hand in greeting. "Ullr here is my father."

"Ullr!" Nyri exclaimed, as if he had just realised who the man was. "The Snow God?"

"That's right," said Ullr, laughing. "You are Tapio's boy, aren't you? It's many years since I visited your family, so it's not surprising that you don't remember me."

They were interrupted by the sound of Magni, who was trying to swim around among the coins. Ullr sighed as he grabbed Magni's arms and tried to raise him up.

"Let me go!" Magni shouted, looking ferocious. "I have to take the gold from here!"

"Nyri, please help me," begged Ullr.

They bent down, and together they tried to pull the young god up in a standing position, which was easier said than done as Magni was struggling.

"How long before the effect wears off?" Nyri asked. "It won't be fun if we have to carry him out of the mountain."

"If we can get him away from the immediate vicinity of the gold, it shouldn't take more than a few minutes," replied Ullr, while he and Nyri dragged Magni out of the room.

"Are you coming?" Jack asked as he watched Gustav bend over the demon.

"Just wait a minute," Gustav replied, and pulled the ring from the demon's claw-like hand.

"What is that?" Jack asked curiously.

"If I've guessed right, it's a very important ring that we should take with us," replied Gustav, picking up the two swords from the ground that he had dragged with him from the next room. "I found these two swords at a magic altar in the next room, will you help me carry them?"

Jack nodded and accepted the swords, and both boys started to move towards the exit. They didn't see how the hand that Gustav had taken the ring from began to move.

꿍

"Wille, wake up!"

He cautiously opened his eyes, and saw Tulio leaning over him with a frightened look.

"How long did I sleep?" Wille asked sleepily.

"About an hour," replied Hugo, and tried to calm Hábrók, who had landed next to them, shouting loudly.

"He'll give us away!" Wille exclaimed and stood up.

"Wille," said Tulio, starting to cry. "Hábrók says that the enemy has captured grandfather."

Wille felt a cold chill run down his spine as the news sank in. He stood for a long time without saying anything, while Tulio hugged him.

"Please, help me save him!" the boy pleaded desperately.

Wille met his tearful eyes and knew he couldn't say no. He thought of the old man who had helped them during the journey, he couldn't say no when the man needed their help.

"Does Hábrók know where your grandfather is?" Wille asked, looking at the hawk, who began to scream again.

"He is being held prisoner some distance from here," replied Tulio, wiping his face while pointing to the west. "Please, Wille, we must help him!"

Wille nodded and peered anxiously down at the werewolves, who were a few hundred metres below the shelf. They didn't seem to have noticed Hábrók's screaming.

"Wille, what is that?" Hugo asked and pointed to the place where he had been sleeping a moment earlier.

Wille turned around, and to his surprise, he noticed something lying in the snow, shining with a reddish glow.

"That can't be possible!" he exclaimed, and started digging away the snow with his nose.

"What is it, Wille?" asked Tulio, who stood beside him to observe the object.

"A gift from Silver," replied Wille, looking at his uncomprehending gaze.

"Silver?" Hugo asked in confusion.

"My fylgja," replied Wille, smiling. "Can you carry it for me, Tulio?"

The boy nodded affirmatively and picked up the red diamond that glittered in the white snow.

"But what does he want you to do with it?" Hugo asked, looking at the beautiful gemstone.

"I'll tell you later," Wille replied briefly. "Now we have to find Tulio's grandfather!"

"But what about Módi?" Hugo asked, looking in the direction where the older god had disappeared.

"He'll find us," replied Wille, more confidently than he actually meant.

Just then, Hábrók let out a shrill scream, and Tulio froze.

"Wille, the werewolves have discovered us!" he exclaimed in horror. "Ten of them are on their way up here."

"I'll lead them away," said Wille hastily, and took a leap in the direction that Tulio pointed. "You follow Hábrók and save Tulio's grandfather!"

Before Tulio and Hugo could protest, Wille had disappeared over the ridge and out of sight.

34. The Half-brother

Lovisa struggled desperately to free herself from the dragon's tail. She had attempted to crawl to safety under the protection of the invisibility cloak, but had been snatched from the ground by the giant dragon, who was now chasing her rescuer through the vast treasure chamber.

Now she watched the dragon crawl down the stone staircase behind which Siegfried was hiding.

Suddenly, a ball of blue fire was thrown at the dragon.

Fáfnir lost his balance and fell heavily to the gold-covered floor, and Lovisa hit the ground with a nasty thud as the tail loosened its grip on her.

"Intruders," hissed Fáfnir. "You will all burn."

Siegfried looked up hastily to see Bea and Sunna standing on the ledge just above him. From Bea's blue fire spear, enormous flames appeared, and she threw more fireballs at Fáfnir, who opened his mouth.

A storm of fire raced towards the sun goddess, who summoned a huge fire shield and blocked the attack.

"Take the girl and run!" shouted Bea as she was pushed backwards by the enormous force of the dragon's fire. "I can't hold him off forever."

Siegfried nodded and ran to Lovisa, who had just reached the stairs. He grabbed her arm and pulled her along with him, just as the landing gave way, and began to collapse under the enormous pressure.

Bea and Sunna ran behind them, shouting for them to continue down the stairs to the floor below.

Fáfnir roared angrily and sent a huge ball of fire after them as they ran down the narrow staircase. Just as they reached the next floor, the fireball caught up with them, and Siegfried screamed in pain as the huge flames hit him.

"He's burning!" Lovisa shouted, and Sunna rushed forward to help Siegfried with the burning wool coat.

There was a whirring sound, and then Siegfried was covered with an enormous blanket of snow, which effectively extinguished the hot flames, and the young man looked up in surprise as another party came running towards them.

"Ullr!" Sunna exclaimed in relief as the man in the coarse coat bent down and helped Siegfried to his feet again.

"You couldn't wait for us before you started the party?" Ullr asked, smiling amusedly.

"Gustav!" Lovisa exclaimed in astonishment and looked at her cousin, who, with the help of Nyri, was supporting Magni. "What has happened to him?!"

"He was cursed with the gold disease," Nyri replied briefly. "He will soon be recovered."

"We fought Nari," Magni said with heavy breaths. "He had one of the rings, with which he got me off balance."

"I think it was a little more than 'off balance'," said Gustav, smiling as he received an angry look from Magni and took out the gold ring. "Here it is, by the way."

"You took it off him?!" Nyri gasped.

"I thought we might need it," Gustav replied gently, while Ullr quickly took the ring from his hand.

"Jack," Ullr said to a young guy standing a little behind them. "Freeze it immediately!"

Jack nodded and held out his hands. An ice cube formed in Ullr's hand, with the ring in the centre, and the snow god threw the ice cube to Jack, who put it in one of his pockets.

"That ring is dangerous," said Ullr grimly. "You must wear it until we arrive in Asgard."

"Ullr…and Jack!" Siegfried whispered in amazement and looked at them.

"Who do we have here?" asked the Snow God, examining him from top to bottom.

Siegfried did not answer but walked towards the man in a trance and wrapped his arms around him.

Ullr looked down in amazement at the crying guy, who was holding his arms around him, before he met the smiling faces of Sunna and Bea.

"Dad, who is he?" Jack asked, looking puzzled.

Siegfried let go of Ullr and turned to Jack.

"My name is Siegfried," he said. "I am your half-brother."

Jack looked shocked, and Ullr looked again in confusion at the sun goddesses, who nodded smilingly at him.

"My...half-brother," Jack managed to say.

"Hulda was my mother," Siegfried said sadly.

"Was?" Ullr asked in amazement.

Before Siegfried could answer, the room began to shake violently, and they could hear the dragon's angry roar from the floor above as he attempted to bring down their ceiling.

"We'll explain later," said Sunna. "We have to get out of here."

Ullr nodded, and the party began to run out of the room and down the long corridor to find another way out as the ceiling began to collapse into the room.

∾

The wolf cub whined as he gently led it back from the forest. Jörgen had had many dogs earlier in life, so he didn't feel completely unfamiliar with taking the wolf cub for a walk, even though it felt a little different. The wolf cub began to whine, and Jörgen decided to carry it in his arms the last bit to the sledge.

Suddenly the puppy began to wriggle anxiously in his arms, and Jörgen tried to calm it down as he stiffened up and looked towards the sledge, where someone was sitting in the driver's seat watching him.

"Good evening!" Jörgen said uncertainly as he came up to the sledge with the wolf cub bouncing in his arms.

"Good evening!" the strange woman returned the greeting. "Is this your sledge?"

"Well, not really," Jörgen replied, and dropped the wolf cub into the sledge's back seat. "I'm just guarding it."

Jörgen looked uncertainly at the reindeer. The woman followed his gaze and laughed delightedly.

"Isn't it a bit early to play Santa Claus?" she asked.

"Well, it's not quite what it looks like," replied Jörgen. "Who are you, by the way?"

"Hanna," she replied, holding out her hand.

"Jörgen," said Jörgen, and took the woman's hand in greeting.

Her hand felt unusually warm, Jörgen thought as he let go of it and rubbed his right hand against his knee.

"So, you're guarding the sled, you say?" Hanna asked, smiling again. "Are you and someone else out for a little romantic adventure?"

"No...it's not like that," Jörgen replied uncomfortably.

"Come on, professor, it's nothing to be ashamed of," Hanna said, still smiling broadly.

"How do you know I'm a professor?" Jörgen asked, beginning to feel scared as he surveyed his surroundings.

The woman fell silent, and the smile disappeared for a moment before her face burst into a nasty, wide grin.

"But how clumsy of me!" she exclaimed. "I thought we could talk a little before I continued with the mission."

"Who are you?" Jörgen asked again, feeling scared.

The woman's face grew unnaturally large as she stood up and did a backward flip out of the sledge. Her clothes were ripped apart, and huge flames erupted from her body.

Jörgen stared in horror at the enormous fire wolf that towered beside the sledge, and growled at him.

"I'm sorry, Professor," hissed the blood-red wolf. "But if you want to survive the night, I suggest you do as I say!"

⁂

"Are you okay?" Gustav asked, casting a quick glance back at Lovisa.

"I think so," Lovisa replied, slowing her pace.

They had run for several minutes and managed to find their way up to the floor above, but were instead lost.

"I think we've lost him," said Magni, who, together with Sunna and Bea, had taken the lead.

"But we're lost, aren't we?" Jack asked, looking out over the huge hall with bridges and stairs.

"This way," whispered Sunna, motioning for them to follow. "Be quiet!"

They crept slowly across one of the stone bridges. Lovisa looked anxiously out into the vast hall with its sea of gold, as if she expected to see the dragon jump out from behind a pillar at any moment.

Suddenly, something pinged at her feet, and the whole group came to a stop as the gold coin spun around several times before settling on the stone bridge with a rattling sound. They looked up slowly, just in time to see the tail of Fáfnir crawling on the bridges above them.

Sunna motioned for them to be quiet, while at the same time she waved for them to continue forward.

"Can't we kill him somehow?" Jack asked.

"If I get the chance, I'll drive my sword into his heart," Siegfried replied.

"His scales are as thick as armour," said Nyri. "I don't think any ordinary sword will work on him."

"Good thing this isn't an ordinary sword, then," said Siegfried, and pulled the dark sword from its scabbard.

Ullr gasped. "Isn't that…"

"Gramr," Bea replied. "One half of the avenger sword."

"How did you get it?" Magni asked in amazement. "It was hidden deep inside the roots of the world tree!"

"My father pulled it out," Siegfried replied proudly. "After a challenge from Odin himself!"

"That sword pierces almost everything, even the dragon's scales," said Sunna. "And in the right hands, it swings itself."

"But that's not all," Bea continued. "The magic of the sword requires constant souls, on which it feeds. If that is not provided, the sword absorbs the wearer's magic, until the wearer has no magic left and the wearer is left defenceless."

"So, does that mean we can defeat the dragon?" Lovisa asked, looking at the sword with fascination.

"If only we had something to help us catch him," Magni replied, rubbing his chin.

"My fire can hold him for a while," said Bea, letting a blue fire sweep from her hands. "But I'm afraid that alone is not strong enough for us to slay him."

"It is similar to the fire I found," said Gustav, and conjured up a red fire spear in his hands.

Bea and Sunna gasped.

"My fire!" Sunna exclaimed. "Where did you find it?" Gustav gave a summary of his discovery, and how he had destroyed the demon's painting with the help of the fire.

"That you can even carry the fire without being consumed is incredible," said Bea. "Very few gods can do that, and you're not even a god!"

"Wait a minute, didn't you kill the demon?" Magni exclaimed, and Gustav looked puzzled.

"I thought I did it by destroying the painting," Gustav replied, but Magni shook his head.

"You freed his soul and returned the darkness to the demon's physical body. By doing so, you made it possible to kill him, but then you would have had to pierce him with the spear," Magni said, and Gustav suddenly looked ashamed.

"It's too late to think about that now," said Ullr. "We have other worries to deal with."

"My fire," Sunna whispered. "It was stolen many years ago, I thought I'd never see it again. Can I get it back?"

"Of course," Gustav replied. "But...how?"

"Hold out your hands, palms down," replied Sunna.

Gustav did as she said, and Sunna placed her own palms under Gustav's.

"Nothing is happening," said Gustav.

"You must give the power to me," said Sunna. "I can't take it from you."

"And how do I do that?" Gustav asked, puzzled.

"Focus the heat to your palms," Sunna replied.

Gustav tried to conjure up the warm feeling in his body again, and focused. He felt how the heat left his body and flowed into the sun goddess's hands.

Suddenly, Gustav felt exhausted and fell backward. Bea caught him before he hit the ground.

"Take it easy," she said. "It's natural to feel exhausted after a handover."

Gustav looked at Sunna, who seemed to be bathed in fire. The flames enveloped the goddess, and she smiled at him.

"Thank you!" she said, and Gustav nodded in response.

"Does this improve the situation?" Jack asked uncertainly.

"It certainly does!" Sunna replied emphatically. "Together, I think we can hold him long enough for the rest of you to pierce him with the sword."

Bea nodded, and Magni put his hand to his chin.

"But we need a plan," he said. "Anyone have an idea?"

കൗ

"Calm down!"

Kenneth struggled to try to drown out the noise from the journalists who had gathered in front of him.

"Have wolves attacked a village?" one journalist asked.

"How many are injured?" asked another journalist.

"What will happen to the wolves?" asked a third.

Jessica watched from her folding chair as Kenneth struggled to gain control of the situation.

Several military units had arrived, and blocked off all the roads leading up to Flatruet, and evacuated people who had fled from the neighbouring villages to a central location in the larger town of Funäsdalen, a couple of miles to the west – where journalists had also found their way. A hastily organised press conference was taking place in the evening darkness.

"We don't yet know exactly what has happened," said Kenneth. "We have several injured people being treated by our special units for injuries that are similar to bear attacks."

A nearby movement caught Jessica's attention, and she instinctively put her elbow up for protection.

"Sorry, honey," said a woman, bending down from where she was sitting. "I didn't mean to scare you!"

"Who are you?" Jessica asked in confusion.

The woman gave her name and held out a card showing that she was a journalist for a major newspaper.

"So, are you one of the victims of the attack?" the woman asked, hastily picking up a notebook.

"Not exactly," Jessica replied, curling up in her chair.

"Did you lose anyone?" the woman asked as she clicked out the tip of her ink pen.

"My mom," Jessica replied, her eyes beginning to tear. "And maybe my dad."

The woman seemed even more interested and was just about to ask another question when Tella came walking towards them with quick steps, accompanied by a young man in a military uniform.

"Leave her alone!" Tella shouted as the soldier pushed away the journalist, who loudly protested that it was her right to conduct the interview.

"Do you want to talk about it?" Tella asked, sitting down next to Jessica, who was wiping her face.

"I miss them," she replied sadly.

"I understand that," said Tella. "We got a message from our friends that your father is with them."

"He's alive?!" exclaimed Jessica, brightening up.

"Yes, he is," Tella replied, smiling, before standing up again. "I must get to Flatruet, Wille and the others who are with him may need my help."

"Of course!" Jessica said. "How do we get there?"

Tella shook her head and looked over at Kenneth, who was still trying to keep order at the press conference.

Jessica followed her gaze and suddenly became upset.

"You're not going to leave me here?" she exclaimed in despair. "I don't accept it!"

"You would be safe here waiting for your father," said Tella, looking at her friend inquiringly. "Besides, I don't think Kenneth will allow me to take you away from here."

"I won't be left here," Jessica said firmly.

"Well, then," said Tella, looking around. "But it's not going to be an easy journey, and I can't guarantee your safety."

Jessica swallowed hard and nodded, whereupon Tella signalled for her to follow her as quietly as she could, as they carefully made their way further behind the military vehicles and into the barren landscape leading towards Flatruet.

The dark-blue wolf that stood some distance away, watching them from his hilltop, smiled ominously, before starting the hunt for the two girls.

35. Twin Swords

The enormous fireball lit up the road ahead of them as Ullr, Jack, Lovisa, and Nyri ran across the bridge. The face of the dragon met them halfway, as another fireball hit the beast's back.

Fáfnir roared and struck fiercely with his enormous tail against a plateau above them, where Sunna stood.

A huge pillar of blue fire appeared from the floor and swatted the tail away just before it hit the goddess.

Ullr and the others took the opportunity to run the last bit across the stone bridge, while Fáfnir glared angrily at Bea, who stood below him.

Just as the dragon was getting ready to spray its massive inferno of fire, Jack and Ullr jointly formed a gigantic lump of ice and dropped it on the dragon's tail.

Fáfnir roared and let a cascade of fire sweep across the bridge and into the corridors where Ullr and the others had disappeared.

"I didn't expect you to be so easily fooled, you overgrown lizard," Magni's voice suddenly echoed in the hall.

Fáfnir turned his head again and stared at a ledge high up in the ceiling of the cave, where the young thunder god stood leaning on his huge hammer.

"You!" the dragon shouted, fixing his eyes at Magni.

"Have you become lazy?" Magni asked sarcastically.

Fáfnir roared with rage and let a wall of hot inferno be thrown up against Magni, who immediately took cover behind a rocky crevice.

The force of the dragon's attack struck the roof of the cave, which immediately began to shake, causing large boulders to rain down on the dragon.

Fáfnir tried to move away, but discovered that his feet were suddenly stuck to the ground. Angrily, the big dragon tried to pull his feet up, but before he could even get one foot up, the huge boulders pushed him down to the ground.

"I can't believe we managed to do that!" exclaimed Gustav, who stood behind Bea.

"Magni managed to create deep cracks in the roof with his lightning," Bea replied, and looked around as Ullr, Lovisa, Jack, and Nyri came running towards them. "After that, we just needed to get him to a good place where Nyri could use his earth magic in combination with our fire magic and Jack and Ullr's ability to create ice and snow. That way, we could melt the ground around his feet and make it solidify again."

"Is he dead?" Lovisa asked, looking anxiously at the huge pile of rocks in front of them.

Before anyone could answer, a terrible roar was heard as the pile of stones was blown, and Fáfnir's huge face stared down at them.

Sunna and Bea clasped their hands, and blue and red flames closed around the dragon's neck. Fáfnir's head and torso were pressed to the ground, exposing the dragon's golden chest. He roared angrily, trying to tear himself free. The dragon's wings burst out of the rock, and the sun goddesses struggled to hold him to the ground.

With a roar, Magni and Siegfried threw themselves down from the ledge with their respective weapons. Fáfnir roared angrily and tore at the elderly rope holding him captive, whereupon the sun goddesses were thrown away and lost their prey. Just as the dragon was about to fight his way free from the massive boulders, a huge flash of light appeared in the air as Magni hurled his huge hammer at its head.

Fáfnir roared again as Ukko struck him with a violent force on the forehead and slammed his head into the ground.

Before the dragon could make any attempt to get up again, Siegfried pierced his chest with the black sword.

The dragon howled in horror as the sword began to suck the soul from his heart. Even Siegfried roared and struck twice more with the sword, until he had pierced through the dragon's heart.

"Sword...avenger..." Fáfnir hissed, clawing at the chest in a desperate attempt to stop Siegfried.

Then the dragon fell silent and collapsed to the ground with a loud bang, whereupon silence settled like a heavy blanket in the dim hall.

Siegfried drew the sword from the dragon's chest and was about to faint, whereupon Magni quickly caught him.

"Thank you!" he whispered and smiled broadly.

"You'll have to return the favour sometime," Magni said jokingly, and supported Siegfried as they made their way down from the dragon's body.

Just then there was a low rumbling, and several boulders began to fall from the roof.

"We have to get out of here!" shouted Sunna, waving at them from across the hall. "The roof is collapsing!"

The whole party rushed towards the stone staircase leading out of the cave as the boulders came crashing down behind them.

Magni turned around as he ran and saw the body of the great dragon get buried in stones.

"Faster!" he shouted to drown out the roar of the roof crashing down over them.

He could feel the panic growing as they rushed towards the stone staircase and had to use the hammer to break the stones that came too close to them.

Jack turned around and stretched out his hands towards the ceiling, whereupon an ice shield emerged from his hands and cushioned the fall of the boulders.

"Jack, hurry up!" Ullr shouted from the landing, where Magni was helping the rest of the party get out of the hall.

Jack let go of the shield, which immediately began to fall to the ground. Ullr conjured up an enormous swirl of snow to hold up the ice shield while Jack ran towards the stairs.

"Hurry up, Jack!" cried Ullr. "I can't hold it for long!"

Jack struck out with his hands again, and a path of ice was formed as he glided the last bit to the stairs.

Just as he reached the ledge of the stairs, the swirl of snow subsided, and the heavy formation of ice and rock plummeted the last bit to the ground.

Jack threw himself against the landing just as the stairs gave way and fell to the ground.

Ullr grabbed his outstretched hand, and Jack was left hanging from the platform.

"Pull me up," he cried in despair.

Ullr seemed exhausted by the effort and was unable to pull him up all the way to the plateau.

Magni rushed forward and reached down with his long hammer towards Jack. With joint forces, the two gods managed to get him onto the plateau, just as it began to crack beneath them.

All three of them threw themselves into the passage just as the stone plateau collapsed among the rocks.

As they ran up the dizzying staircase towards the cave's exit, they could hear the mountain collapsing around them.

They came out of the mountain, where the others anxiously waited for them, before the whole party descended down the carved stone steps, and ran towards safety.

A deafening roar was heard, and the party turned around just in time to see the mountain collapse.

"Too bad we didn't get some gold from there, right, Magni?" asked Gustav and smiled teasingly at Magni, who replied with a sour look.

"At least we made it out alive," said Ullr. "That must make up for the fact that we didn't get anything with us from there."

"I wouldn't say we didn't get anything, would you, Jack?" Gustav asked, turning towards him.

Jack loosened the two swords he had strapped across his back. He put both swords over his arms and held them out for the whole group to see.

Sunna stared in astonishment, while Magni frowned at the identical swords, whose intricate gold decorations snaked out on the shiny mirrored sword blades.

"Two swords, what's so special about them?" he asked, giving Gustav a questioning look.

"They were floating in the air above the altar, where I found Sunna's fire and Nari's portrait," Gustav replied, scratching his neck. "I thought they might be important."

"Unbelievable!" Sunna exclaimed, reaching forward.

"What is it?" Bea asked, looking inquiringly at one of the swords, which Sunna examined carefully.

"Ridill and Hrotti," she replied, without taking her eyes off the sword. "These twin swords were forged during the first war by the dwarves, who competed against Wayland to forge the Master Sword, a contest that Wayland won."

"So, can these swords defeat darkness just like the Avenging Sword?" Magni asked eagerly.

"Unfortunately, no," Sunna replied. "Just as Gramr is a part of the Avenger's Sword, Ridill and Hrotti can be joined together into a single sword. However, unlike the parts of the Avenger's Sword, these swords lack the crucial ingredient from the World Tree and cannot destroy the darkness."

"So, what can we use them for?" Magni muttered.

"Ridill is also called the 'Sword of Truth'," Sunna replied patiently. "It can penetrate the most powerful magic and is filled with emotional strength when the wearer wants to protect someone."

"And the other sword?" Gustav asked.

"Hrotti is the Sword of Wrath," Sunna continued. "If the bearer of the sword considers someone to be evil, the bearer is filled with the sword's hungry anger. This can be dangerous because the bearer can attack anyone in anger, friend or foe."

"So, how does that help us?" Nyri asked, standing at the side of the group.

"Only people with intertwined hearts can use the swords," concluded Sunna, handing the sword back to Jack, who hung both swords on his back. "They won't help us right now, but it's safest that they follow us back to Asgard."

"Do you still have the ring, Jack?" Gustav asked, looking curiously at the young god.

Jack put his hand inside the pocket of his coat and pulled out the ice cube with the ring. The ring shimmered so brightly that its light shone through the cube.

"Put that away," Magni said firmly, and put one arm over his face to protect himself.

"Afraid of a little ring, Magni," Gustav asked teasingly, while Jack put the ice cube back in his pocket.

"That 'little ring', as you call it, almost cost us our lives down there," Magni hissed irritably in reply. "It is to be locked up in Asgard as soon as we get there."

"Everyone," Lovisa's voice was suddenly heard behind them, whereupon everyone turned towards her, where she stood scraping one shoe on the ground. "Thank you for saving me from there."

"It's okay, sweetheart," Sunna said, giving her a hug.

"I thought I was going to die down there," sobbed Lovisa, burying her face in the goddess's arms.

"We couldn't leave you," said Nyri. "Gustav was the bravest of us, he insisted on coming along, and without him, we wouldn't have been able to deal with the demon."

Nyri nudged Magni, who grunted in approval.

"Thank you, Gustav," said Lovisa, hugging her cousin.

"I'm always there for you, I've told you that many times," Gustav said, and put his arms around her.

"Are you okay down there?" a voice was heard from above them.

"Professor, what are you doing on Rudolph?" Ullr asked, staring up at the flying reindeer that Jörgen was sitting on.

"I was attacked and had to flee," replied Jörgen, while the reindeer landed softly with the rest of the party.

"Attacked?" asked Magni, and immediately drew the hammer from his back. "By what?"

"A fire wolf of some kind," replied Jörgen, who got down from Rudolph's back. "A woman met me at the sledge, and transformed herself into a huge fire wolf."

"Was the wolf red or blue?" Bea asked hastily.

"I would say it was blood red," replied Jörgen. "It emitted red flames from its body."

"Sköll," said Sunna, before quickly turning around and peering into the forest. "Hela's fire wolves have the ability to take on the appearance of the people they devour, do you know where it is now?"

"It told me to sit still in the sledge and went to your fire horses. I took the chance and threw myself on Rudolph's back before the fire-wolf had a chance to attack me for real," Jörgen replied, shaking his head.

"Okay," said Sunna, not taking her eyes off the forest. "We'll go back to the sledge together, calmly and quietly. We stick together, no one deviates from the group!"

The party moved slowly in the direction where they had left the sledge and the chariot. When they came within sight, everything seemed the same, except that the reindeer had run off with Ull's sledge some distance away.

"Shh," said Jack, patting Blixte reassuringly.

Ullr inspected the sledge before turning to the sun goddesses and giving a thumbs up. The goddesses inspected their chariot, and they seemed to find nothing wrong with it.

Lovisa, Siegfried, Gustav, Nyri, and Jörgen crowded into Ullr's sledge, while Magni joined Sunna and Bea in the smaller chariot that had no driver's seat.

Sunna slapped the reins, and the two fire horses took off up in the darkness of the night on a fireball.

"Strange," said Magni, when they were in the air. "I had expected an attack from that monster."

"Maybe she followed the professor and lost him?" Bea suggested.

"Not likely," replied Sunna. "Those fire wolves are too intelligent for that. But I agree that it's strange. What could Hela's fire wolf have here to do? The battle is at Flatruet."

"Is it?" a voice suddenly thundered in front of them.

Magni watched in horror as one of the fire horses turned its head, forming a nasty smile, before both horses merged into a huge fire wolf, and Sköll's satisfied gaze stared at them.

ↄ

"Can't we slow down a bit?" Jessica asked in alarm.

"I told you it wouldn't be an easy trip," replied Tella.

The tree that carried them rushed forward across the barren landscape, while Jessica clung to the tree branch.

Tella sat on a higher tree branch and laughed delightedly as the tree carried them on towards Flatruet.

"Do you often travel like this?" Jessica asked in horror, looking up at the young goddess.

"Only when I'm in a hurry," Tella replied, laughing. "Well, don't worry, we'll be at Flatruet sooner than you think."

No sooner had she said that than the tree snapped, as a huge wall of blue flames erupted, blocking their path.

Jessica watched in horror as the enormous wolf head lunged at them from the flames.

Tella shouted something at the tree that started to run to the right, but the blue flames surrounded them.

"Not smart to run away from the military, right?" hissed the fire wolf head, who starred down at them.

"Hati," Tella whispered in horror.

The giant fire-head lunged at them, and Jessica let out a scream before they suddenly found themselves behind the fire wolf.

Both Jessica and Tella looked around in surprise. Even Hati seemed confused, and he slowly shrank to his normal size.

"Aren't you going to play with me instead, wolf?" a muffled voice was heard from the forest, and a fair-haired boy wearing a dark coat with red swirling patterns and a rough leather vest emerged from the forest.

"Ítrek," Tella whispered in terror.

"Hi Tella," the guy said excitedly. "It's been a long time!"

"Ítrek, what...how...?"

Tella's voice trailed off as she stared in shock at the guy who had appeared in front of them.

"Tella, who is that?" Jessica asked anxiously.

"I'd like to know that too!" Hati growled angrily. "How dare you come between me and my prey?!"

The young man called Ítrek took no notice of the fire wolf. Instead, he began to walk with determined steps towards the tree, where the girls were still sitting.

With a low growl, Hati lunged at him, but Ítrek snapped with his fingers and disappeared just before the wolf struck the spot where he just stood.

"Are you that eager to play, wolf?" Ítrek's voice was heard as the guy appeared behind the wolf instead.

Hati roared in anger and once again tried to throw himself at Ítrek, only to fail again.

"Weren't you going somewhere?" Ítrek asked, giving Tella a quick glance as he appeared beside the tree.

"Ítrek, what are you doing here? And how...?" Tella started to ask, but was interrupted by Hati's angry roar.

"We'll take all the questions later," Ítrek replied. "Go, and leave the wolf to me."

Tella nodded and made a whistling sound, and the tree began to run again.

"You're not going anywhere!" Hati roared and made an effort to throw himself on top of them.

Ítrek snapped his fingers again, and the wolf was suddenly behind the young man instead, leaving the way clear for Tella and Jessica to continue their journey.

Jessica glanced back and saw how the angry wolf repeatedly tried to attack the guy, until the tree was so far away that the fight was no longer distinguishable.

"Who was that, Tella?" she asked, looking up at the young goddess.

Tella still seemed shocked.

"His name is Ítrek," she replied softly. "He…he was my boyfriend."

36. Thrúd

Magni raised his sledgehammer and aimed a blow at the fire wolf, but before he could complete his attack, Sköll struck the chariot with such force that Magni was thrown off.

As he fell from the chariot, a red light flashed through the air and caught him.

"Thank you, Rudolph," he said, patting the reindeer as he sat down on its back.

"Magni!" shouted Ullr from his sledge, which was a good way down towards the ground. "What shall we do?"

"Stay close, but don't intervene!" Magni shouted back. "If we attack the fire wolf recklessly, the chariot may fall!"

Ullr nodded affirmatively, and Magni called to Rudolph, who headed off after the sun goddesses' chariot again.

❧

"Look what I got in my trap," said Sköll triumphantly. "Not just one, but two sun goddesses!"

Bea let the blue fire burst from her hands and wrap itself around the fire wolf, who laughed and absorbed her fire.

"You'll think your fire work?" Sköll asked, amused.

The wolf stopped the chariot and turned towards the goddesses before she attacked. Sunna and Bea put up their hands and formed a shield to meet the attack.

As the wolf's fire met the goddesses' fire shield, the chariot began to fall to the ground. The wolf sneered at them as they realised the trap. If they didn't try to break the fall, they would hit the ground with such force that they wouldn't survive, but if they tried to break their fall, they wouldn't be able to resist the wolf's attack at the same time.

Sunna met Bea's terrified gaze and smiled at her wife. She gave her a kiss, before pushing her out of the chariot.

"Sunna!" Bea screamed in despair and fell handles, while Sköll's fire enveloped the chariot, which now resembled an enormous fireball crashing to the ground.

Sunna glanced to the side and had time to see how Jörgen caught Bea from the edge of the snow sled.

She was now surrounded by the blazing heat of Sköll as the chariot approached the ground at tremendous speed.

"So, you chose to save her and sacrifice yourself," Sköll hissed as the flames began to scorch Sunna's arms.

The wolf smiled mockingly as the sun goddess howled in pain from the wolf's fire while she desperately tried to protect herself from the overwhelming flames.

"It's almost a pity he can't save you in time," Sköll continued, looking up at the sky above them.

Magni and Rudolph came hurtling towards them, but from the look in Magni's eyes, Sunna realised that the fire wolf was right – he wouldn't make it in time.

"No," she replied calmly, and stopped fighting the wolf's flames. "It is perfect!"

The wolf's smile disappeared as Sunna began to be surrounded by a brilliant aura.

The fire that surrounded the goddess began to be absorbed into her body, and Sköll let out an angry roar as the fire wolf tried to throw herself of the chariot.

The light that surrounded Sunna grew in strength, and Sköll began to be involuntarily drawn to the goddess as the wolf's body was absorbed. The wolf let out a final howl as its flaming face was drawn into the goddess's body.

Sunna met Magni's despairing gaze the second before the light around her exploded, and the chariot hit the ground with a deafening roar.

∽

"I'm sorry," said Ullr, wrapping his coarse wool coat around Bea, who nodded gratefully as she sat on the ground.

The sun goddesses' chariot was still in flames, and Jack was struggling to extinguish the fire.

Magni sat on a stone next to Ullr's sledge and talked to Lovisa, who put one arm around the despairing god.

Siegfried and Jörgen went to check the surroundings to see if more enemies were nearby.

"What do I do now?" Bea asked in despair, looking towards the remains of the chariot, which Jack had frozen.

"I can't tell you what to do," Ullr replied, sitting down next to her. "The grief will take time to process." Ullr put his arm around her.

"You have a child, right?" he asked, and Bea lifted her head as she nodded and wiped her face.

"Sól, our daughter," Bea replied sadly. "I don't know how to tell her about this."

"You'll know it when we get there," said Ullr compassionately, helping her to stand up.

Bea looked into Ull's kind eyes and nodded gratefully at the Snow God, who gently led her to the sledge.

"What happened to the wolf cub?" Ullr asked as Jörgen and Siegfried returned to the sledge.

"I really don't know," replied Jörgen, sighing heavily. "When I escaped, I didn't have time to take him with me."

"It was probably just as well," said Ullr, preparing the sledge. "We're heading into battle, that's no place for a pup."

"Tulio will be disappointed," said Jörgen heavily, and settled down beside Bea in the sledge.

"We've already lost many," Ullr reminded him, looking at the company that was crowded in the sledge. "We must hurry before we lose more."

"Is it all right for you to ride Rudolph?" Jack asked, looking at Gustav, who nodded nervously.

"Don't worry," said Ullr. "Hold on tight, he'll follow us."

With those words, he snapped the reins, and the reindeer began to run up the newly created ice track in front of them.

☙

Akela sat at the edge of the forest and watched them disappear into the great darkness again. He had watched the battle with the fire wolf, and desperately tried to call for attention, but he was too far away and no one had heard him. In despair, he lay down on the ground and curled up into a ball. The cold that bites began to gnaw at his fur, and he shivered. He missed the kind boy who had saved him and kept him warm during their journey.

Suddenly, he heard a noise and turned around. A tailless male was standing behind him, but it was not one of the tailless that he had been travelling with and who had left him here. The tailless aimed at him with a hard stick that made bad noises. Akela began to whine nervously, and the tailless slowly lowered the stick without making a bad noise.

The young tailless looked around and suddenly seemed calmer, but Akela stood up and bared his teeth.

The tailless sat down in front of him and took out a piece of dried meat. Akela, who could feel his stomach burning, calmed down and carefully took the piece of meat.

The tailless said something strange in the language of the tailless and gently lifted Akela into his arms. He felt the fear disappear as the tailless carried him into the forest again.

☙

"Where…am I?" Módi murmured, and opened his eyes.

His head throbbed as he tried to sit up in bed.

"Take it easy, sweetheart," came a familiar female voice, and he felt warm hands wrapping around him.

"Mom?" Módi exclaimed as his vision cleared.

"You've had a terrible blow to the head," the woman said, kissing his forehead. "You need to rest."

"The gargoyles!" Módi exclaimed, standing up quickly.

"Calm down!" she said. "The warriors are fighting them."

"They need my help," Módi said, pulling on his pants. "There are hell wolves from Járnvidr there too."

"And how are you going to help them in your condition?" his mother asked, giving him an admonishing look.

"I will take a battalion of warriors and lead them against the wolves," Módi replied, leaning against the wall.

"You're not in a position to lead anyone right now," she said, pushing him down on the bed. "Besides, there are too many people out there, we risk exposing ourselves."

"But I have to go back, my friends are out there," Módi protested. "I promised to return to them."

"Maybe I can help?" a voice was heard, and a young girl appeared in the doorway.

"Thrúd," Módi exclaimed, trying to stand up again.

"It's not every day we see you get beaten up, big brother," Thrúd said as she walked towards them.

"It was just a little slap," Módi tried to excuse himself while hugging his sister.

"Sure," Thrúd said, smiling. "We'll say it!"

"I brought you some apple lemonade," she continued, and pulled out a small glass bottle from her pocket.

Módi nodded gratefully and pulled the cork off the bottle before emptying the entire contents in a single swallow.

"Will you help me?" he asked, and sat down on the bed to wait for the magic of the lemonade to take effect.

"I guess I have no choice, you don't seem to be able to handle things without me being there to look after you," Thrúd replied, laughing.

"Leave the gargoyles to your father," their mother said sharply. "Focus on helping your friends, understand?"

"Yes, Mom," Módi replied, sighing as he looked worriedly at his smiling little sister.

⁊

Wille ran as fast as he could, with the big hellwolves close behind. He didn't know how long he could keep running, but his pursuers wouldn't give up the chase. One of them was right behind him, closing the distance.

Then Wille heard something in front of him, a low howl that sounded familiar. The ground beneath his feet began to shake violently, and just as the werewolf lunged at him from the side, the sound grew into a deafening roar when several ordinary wolves suddenly ran past him.

There was a howl as the black hellwolf was thrown to the side and landed on the ground. Wille could not believe his eyes as he met Váli's smiling face while hundreds of wolves rushed past and threw themselves over the hellwolves.

"Váli!" Wille exclaimed, taking a couple of quick steps towards his cousin, who laughed at his confused expression.

"We meet again, cousin," said Váli, smiling.

"I'm sorry, Váli," Wille said, without meeting his cousin's gaze. "I'm sorry I yelled at you, and drove you away!"

Váli said nothing but calmly laid his head on his shoulder.

"I've missed you," Wille continued, unable to hold back the tears that ran down his cheek.

"And I missed you," Váli said calmly. "Where are the others?"

"They are in danger," replied Wille. "We must hurry!"

37. The Battle

The young man grabbed his leader's arm.

"My lord, they are too many for us!"

The muscular man with the thick beard swore and struck out with his arm so that the youth fell to the ground.

"You are the best warriors in Asgard!" he roared. "Why?"

The youngster looked at his leader in horror, while the roar of the flying gargoyles and the rattle of the men's weapons echoed around them.

"WHY?" the man repeated irritably.

"Because…we are your soldiers, my lord," the youth stammered.

"Prove it!" exclaimed the man with the scraggly beard, throwing a gigantic hammer that cracked the head of one of the gargoyles before it returned to its owner's hand.

The youth quickly got to his feet before tremblingly reaching for his sword and throwing himself back into the battle.

Thor!" roared another man, throwing himself in front of the leader as one of the gargoyles plunged towards them.

There was a violent crash as the gargoyle plunged its horns into the man's chest. Thor roared with rage and drove his hammer through the gargoyle's body, before the demon dissolved with a hissing sound.

"Heidar," said Thor, and fell to his knees beside the dazed man who had thrown himself in front of him.

"There are…too many of them," the man called Heidar managed to get out while blood welled up from his mouth.

Thor gently placed a hand over the man's mouth as a sign for him to be quiet, before the man became lifeless in his arms. He gently put the man down again and reached for his huge hammer.

A rumbling roar was heard as the clouds above them darkened and pulled together like a vortex. Thor raised the hammer towards the clouds, and a gigantic lightning struck the hammer and spread in a circle around the battlefield.

The gargoyles roared with rage as several of them fell lifeless to the ground.

"No matter how much rage you unleash, it's not enough for all of them, is it?" a dark voice was heard behind Thor.

Wayland's smile met the angry face of the thunder god.

"You!" Thor exclaimed angrily. "I should have killed you earlier and spared us this misery!"

"As temperamental as ever, I see," said Wayland, laughing unpleasantly.

Thor roared and threw his hammer at Wayland.

A huge wall of darkness shot up from the ground like a wall, and the hammer flew into the darkness and disappeared before flying out in the same direction and back into Thor's hand again.

"Be careful with your toy, my friend," Wayland said wickedly. "It would be a pity if you lost it!"

There were screams from the battlefield as the warriors of Asgard fell, while the number of gargoyles killed was nowhere near the number of the fallen warriors.

"Your Einherjar have grown weaker over the years," Wayland mused, looking around. "Don't you agree?"

Thor roared and slammed his hammer into the ground, causing a crack to form in the ground beneath Wayland.

The blacksmith chuckled in amusement, and disappeared into a sea of darkness. Then he reappeared behind the god of thunder and sent a cascade of dark flames that surrounded Thor, who in turn swung the hammer around, and a sea of lightning dissolved the dark flames.

"You cannot win this battle," Wayland hissed. "I suggest that you run away with your tail between your legs."

Just as Wayland uttered those words, an explosion was heard above them, and several gargoyles fell from the sky.

Then there was the hovering sound of several military helicopters, which appeared behind a hillside and fired machine guns at the demons.

The gargoyles fell from the sky, and although the bullets were not enough to kill them, Thor's Einherjar waited for them on the ground, stabbing the demons to death.

Wayland roared with rage and pointed his hands at one of the helicopters. A darkness spread over the machine, which exploded in the air, and the scrap metal rained down on the fighting Einherjar.

"Your battle is with me!" roared Thor, throwing his hammer at him.

Wayland threw himself backwards and barely managed to avoid the hammer that went over his head before he was again enveloped in darkness and disappeared.

∽

"Do you see anything?" Hugo asked, looking around anxiously.

Hugo and Tulio had followed Hábrók, who had led them down the mountain. They had managed to avoid the werewolves roaming around at the bottom of the ridge but had instead lost the silver-winged hawk.

"Nothing," the boy answered.

"Can't you play your instrument and attract him again?" Hugo asked urgently.

"If I do that, I risk giving away our position to both the werewolves and the gargoyles," replied Tulio, looking at Hugo. "We don't want that, do we?"

"No, I didn't think of that," Hugo replied, and sighed. "What do you think we should do?"

Tulio seemed to think for a moment before answering.

"Hábrók has been leading us in the same direction all along, we should continue in that way," he replied. "But be careful, if the werewolves find us, they'll tear us apart!"

Hugo swallowed hard and nodded.

Tulio looked around anxiously in the dark evening that was lit up by the moonlight.

"What is it, Tulio?" Hugo asked, looking at the young god, who suddenly seemed afraid.

"I...don't like the dark," replied Tulio, looking uncertainly at Hugo, who smiled back.

"Are you afraid of the dark?" Hugo asked, putting his hand on his shoulder.

Tulio nodded in response and looked down at the ground in shame.

"It's okay," said Hugo. "I don't like the dark either. Stay close to me, and we'll fix this together."

They began to move cautiously along the rugged ridge, but they did not get very far before Hugo stopped and put his arm out in front of Tulio.

"What is it, Hugo?" Tulio asked, looking at his terrified expression.

Hugo pointed to a place a bit ahead of them, and Tulio followed his gaze.

"Grandpa!" Tulio shouted and tried to run forward, but was held back by Hugo, who pulled the boy backwards.

A bit ahead of them, Tulio's grandfather was hanging upside down from a sturdy tree. His body seemed to be held up by darkness that wrapped like rope around the man's legs, arms, and neck. Lódurr looked exhausted and half unconscious, and he seemed not to have heard Tulio's cries. On the other hand, another figure below the tree had done so.

Both boys stared in horror as the disfigured woman with the dark hair turned her smiling face towards them.

"Well, we have guests!" the woman exclaimed gloatingly. "Come over here, and don't be shy!"

Just as Hugo turned to drag Tulio away, he stared into the familiar face of a wolf.

The gigantic wolf suddenly came face-to-face with Hugo, who was trembling and holding Tulio close to him.

"He won't hurt you if you come here and do as I say," the woman purred contentedly.

Hugo took hold of Tulio, who pressed himself tightly against his arms, and led him slowly towards the woman without taking his eyes off the big wolf.

The wolf seemed amused by their reaction and slowly followed them until they were in front of the tree.

"Who do we have here?" the woman asked playfully, examining them closely.

"M...my name is Hugo," Hugo replied haltingly, trying to avoid the woman's gaze as it bore into him.

"Yes, the son of Bragi," said the woman sarcastically. "Tell me, what did you think of my dream demon?"

Hugo felt himself shivering with fear as he remembered the terrible night on the suspension bridge.

"Who are you?" he whispered, holding Tulio tight to him.

The woman laughed at the question, and a barking reply was heard in the darkness around them. Hugo looked around and realised, to his horror, that they were surrounded by the

by large, coal-black hellish wolves. He saw the familiar face of Garmr, the larger wolf that had just scared them, standing in front of the werewolves. But there was something strange about the wolf's face.

"My name is Hela, and you better remember it, boy," Hela hissed, and a cold chill ran down Hugo's spine.

The pressure from Tulio's arms suddenly became even tighter around Hugo's waist as Hela lowered her face to meet the smaller boy's frightened gaze.

"And who do we have here?" Hela asked.

"He's my friend," Hugo replied, more forcefully than he had intended, and put one hand around Tulio's head.

"I think I heard your friend call out "grandpa" just now, didn't I?" Hela asked, looking searchingly into Tulio's eyes.

"No, he didn't," Hugo replied defiantly.

"Don't lie to me!" Hela hissed as purple flames shot up into her empty eye socket.

She pulled Tulio out of Hugo's arms and held the boy with her hand around his throat. Hugo could see the fear wash over Tulio's face and made an effort to lunge himself at Hela, but stopped when he saw Garmr standing beside him.

"You think I don't know an elf when I see one?" Hela hissed and tightened his grip around Tulio's neck. "You're Tapio's youngest son, aren't you?"

"You're choking him!" Hugo shouted desperately.

Garmr growled warningly at Hugo, who recoiled before the wolf's huge jaws.

"I'm not going to choke him…yet," said Hela, turning Tulio around so that the boy's face met Lódurr's. "Not until he has seen his dear grandfather die!"

"Hela…let them…go," gasped the old man, without opening his eyes.

"What's wrong, old man?" Hela whispered softly. "Don't you want your grandchild to join you?"

She leaned towards the old man.

"His grandmother has already gone ahead," Hela whispered triumphantly.

Lódurr opened his eyes in disbelief and tried to tear himself away from the darkness that held him in a firm grip.

"She was the last victim of my firewolf," Hela said sharply. "A fitting end that fire destroys fire."

"Grandmother," whispered Tulio, looking at his grandfather with wide eyes.

"I guess you never told your grandchildren who their grandmother was," Hela purred softly. "One wonders why?"

Hugo threw himself at the disfigured woman, but was immediately knocked to the ground by the huge wolf, who stood with one paw over his chest. Now Hugo saw what was wrong with Garmr's face. The wolf's eyes were no longer red but more like human eyes.

Hela took no notice of them but continued to mock Lódurr.

"Isn't it a fitting end?" she asked rhetorically. "Your brother hanged himself likewise to achieve perfect knowledge, and your disciple was nailed to a tree. There is only one thing missing to complete the parable," Hela said, pulling a pointed object from her robe.

"Both your brother and your disciple were stabbed with spears, therefore, it is only right that you too should feel that too," she hissed, placing the point of the spear in front of Lódurr's face.

Hugo tried to wriggle free from the wolf's paw, but stopped himself when the wolf bared his teeth in warning.

"This is made from the tooth of one of my wolves," Hela whispered happily. "You shall spend the rest of your miserable life as my servant, forever trapped in the form of a werewolf."

Tulio writhed in the goddess' grip, trying in vain to grasp the spearhead.

"Farewell, old man!" Hela cried triumphantly.

Just as she was about to thrust the spearhead into the side of Lódurr, something unexpected happened. Out of nowhere, a young girl appeared and blocked the blow with an axe.

Hugo stared in amazement at the young girl with the wavy, amber-coloured hair standing in front of Hela. Sparks erupted from their weapons as they met, and Hugo thought it looked like Hela was trembling.

A rumbling roar was heard above them, and a huge ball of lightning shot through the air and hit Garmr, whereupon the wolf fell to the ground, and Hugo was able to get up again.

He saw Módi standing on a shelf of rock above them and seemed to be directing his ball of lightning, which struck the tree with such force that the darkness let go of Lódurr.

Then another rumbling sound was heard, and when Hugo turned around he could not believe his eyes. From a hill further away, hundreds of wolves rushed down towards them, throwing themselves over the werewolves.

There was great turmoil as the werewolves and wolves tumbled around on the ground in the fight that followed, and then suddenly Váli stood in front of Hugo.

"Váli!" Hugo exclaimed, hugging the wolf.

"Good to see you too," Váli said. "But we'll talk more later when we get out of here."

Hugo nodded and turned to the tree again.

Tulio had crawled up to his grandfather and tried to get the half-unconscious god to stand up.

Meanwhile, a duel was being fought between Hela and the strange girl. Purple flames erupted around them, but the girl seemed to be incredibly fast, flying forward as she ran around Hela and delivered blow after blow with her axe, which the evil goddess seemed to have a hard time avoiding.

Hela lashed out with both arms, and the purple flames blended with a sea of darkness. The darkness slowed the girl's progress, but it seemed to take a lot of Hela's energy.

"How sweet!" a familiar voice was suddenly heard behind Hugo and Váli.

Hugo whirled around to see the familiar face of Garmr appearing behind them. The red eyes lit up the evening darkness, and Hugo automatically took a step backwards.

"I must say, I didn't expect this," the wolf said, smiling ominously at them.

"But…but how…" Hugo began to stutter and turned around towards the place where the other giant wolf stood up again after Módi's lightning attack.

"Confused?" Garmr asked with delight.

Váli stood up and got into a fighting stance, while the two giant wolves began to circle around them.

"I guess friendship is only superficial after all," said Garmr, and laughed as the other wolf pounced on Hugo.

Váli made an effort to protect Hugo but was effectively blocked by Garmr, who attacked him from the side. The two wolves rolled around on the ground, tearing at each other, while the other giant wolf stood over Hugo with open jaws.

Out of nowhere, Wille appeared and pushed the wolf away from Hugo.

"Wille!" Hugo exclaimed and stood up. "I thought the werewolves had gotten hold of you!"

"I ran into Váli and his friends," replied Wille, while at the same time he threw himself away from the giant wolf. "Since when are there two Garmr anyway?"

"I don't know," replied Hugo, digging in his pocket for his ocarina. "But I don't think that wolf and Garmr are so similar after all, look at his eyes!"

They stared into the eyes of the giant wolf. Unlike Garmr, this wolf's eyes weren't red, they weren't even purple like the smaller werewolves. Instead, they looked like human eyes.

"Who are you?" Wille asked without taking his eyes off the giant wolf.

The wolf did not answer but threw itself over Wille.

A strong wind grabbed the wolf when it was in the air, throwing it off balance. The giant wolf tumbled around on the ground and suddenly stared at Hugo, who was playing his ocarina, surrounded by a strong wind.

Meanwhile, Váli's wolf pack was fighting the werewolves. The werewolves had initially been caught off guard by the sudden attack, but were gaining the upper hand through their advantage of their numerical superiority and were slowly but surely multiplying as they spread their transformation to the wolf pack.

Hela had succeeded in slowing down the young girl's progress considerably with the help of the darkness and the purple flames. The young girl warrior stood surrounded by the purple flames and seemed to falter in her steps.

"What's wrong, child?" Hela asked with amusement. "You're not tired, are you? You who had so much energy!"

She laughed at her helpless victim, while Módi, with a roar of rage, threw himself down from the rock shelf with the double-edged axe exposed in a blow, aiming at Hela.

Just as Módi was about to deliver the blow, the strange giant wolf lunged forward, knocking the young god away, who fell to the ground with a dull thud.

Váli cried out in pain as Garmr grabbed his leg and threw him into the mountain wall.

"You won't get away this time!" Garmr shouted and threw himself on top of Váli again, who lay helpless on the ground.

Just as Garmr was about to sink his teeth into Váli's throat, he was ripped away by a giant tree, which rushed into the battle and grabbed the giant wolf's legs with its roots.

The tree drove the wolf so hard into the mountain wall that stones came loose and crashed down. Hugo turned his wind in that direction and brought the stones to a halt just before they were about to fall on Tulio and Lódurr, who still had not regained consciousness despite Tulio's healing magic

When the stones stopped in the air, they suddenly flew towards the werewolves instead.

There were howls of rage as the rocks hit the werewolves, and when Hugo looked up at the rocky shelf where Módi had just been, he saw Tella and Nyri standing next to each other with their arms outstretched.

Several trees rushed into the battle and grabbed the werewolves, sending them flying. Nyri let the ground swallow up several of them while trying not to harm the wolves that had not yet been infected by their curse.

An explosion was heard somewhere in the sky above them. The flash of light from the exploding military helicopter revealed that the sky was filled with flying demons.

A sledge travelled across the sky on what appeared to be an ice rink, as the darkness of the night was filled with swirling snow that knocked down the flying demons.

"HUGO!"

Hugo turned his head again, just as the strange giant wolf threw himself on top of him. He put up his arms for protection and prepared for the worst.

Then Magni was standing between him and the wolf. The anger in the god's face was horrifying as he slammed his huge hammer into the side of the giant wolf, which crashed into the mountain wall.

"Are you okay?" he asked helping Hugo to his feet, while at the same time holding out a sword for him.

"Who are you?" Wille interrupted angrily, standing between them and the giant wolf.

"Don't you recognise your best friend anymore?" the wolf asked sarcastically and stared defiantly into Wille's eyes.

"Oscar!" Wille exclaimed. "What have they done to you?"

"Actually, his name is Mánagarmr now, and he belongs to me!" a dark voice echoed along the mountain wall.

Hugo turned his gaze to the edge of the mountain to meet the unpleasant voice he recognised so well. There, on a ledge a little above the place where Nyri and Tella were, Wayland stood watching the battle with an amused expression.

"Don't worry," Wayland said. "You'll have plenty of time to get to know his new self once you have joined me!"

38. The Night of The Werewolves

Jessica ran into the small cave and wrapped her arms around her father.

"Oh, darling, I thought I had lost you!" Jörgen exclaimed as she began to cry.

"Dad, I was scared, Mom…" Jessica started to sob, but was interrupted by her father, who comfortingly stroked his hand through her hair.

"I promise never to leave you again," he said, letting their eyes meet as they put their arms around each other again.

Gustav stood hesitantly at one wall of the cave, feeling that he didn't want to interrupt the reunion. At the same time, he felt his eyes tear up when he saw Jessica hugging her father, and was reminded of his own parents.

He would have given anything to see them one last time, and tell them how much they meant to him.

"Dad, this is Gustav," Jessica said, turning to look at him.

Jörgen greeted Gustav, who quickly wiped his face and leaned his rifle against a stone, before joining them by the fire. Then they began to tell about their respective adventures that they had experienced.

It was difficult to decide who was most impressed – Jörgen, who, as a professor of religion, was told about the thunder gods Magni and Módi, the forest fairies, and the Bäckahäst, or Jessica, who was told about the snow god and his flying reindeer. But both of them were amazed when Gustav told them about the events at Trollhammer mountain.

"Is it really safe here?" Jörgen asked, looking anxiously towards the mouth of the cave. "Can't the enemy find us?"

"Don't worry, Professor!" a voice spoke from the entrance.

A guy appeared at the entrance, and Jörgen automatically extended his arms in front of Jessica and Gustav.

"Wait, Professor," said Gustav, standing up. "It's all right, he's a friend!"

"My name is Siegfried," Siegfried greeted, and walked towards them. "You needn't worry, the caves here, like the mountain top, are protected with the magic of Asgard."

He pointed to the rock paintings that surrounded them, and Gustav realised what the primitive paintings actually represented. Moose, reindeer, and bears were mixed in several places with the occasional human.

"This mountain was the first place in Middle-earth where the gods created the passages between our worlds," Siegfried continued. "Your ancestors used the magic they learned from the gods, and created a protective barrier around the top of Flatruet to protect the gateway from evil forces."

"Wait a minute!" Jörgen exclaimed enthusiastically. "Siegfried, son of Sigmund, am I right?"

"You know about my father?" Siegfried asked in surprise.

"Your father is a well-known mythological figure among us," Jörgen replied with a smile. "You forget that I am a professor of religion."

"I was warned that you knew a lot about human religions and mythologies, but I didn't think you were so good," said Siegfried, and sat down on the ground beside them.

"But there is one thing I don't understand," Jörgen continued, looking puzzled. "We have stories and ballads written about you, but you're just a boy. According to our stories, you have already slain the dragon Fáfnir, but Gustav told us that you did it on your journey here."

"I don't know much about your stories," said Siegfried, leaning back against a rock. "But the only explanation I can think of is that your historiography is not based on historical events but rather on prophecies that will happen."

"Please, don't talk about changing the concept of time," Gustav said. "I already have a headache."

"You're not a god, are you?" Jörgen exclaimed, laughing.

"No, not really," replied Gustav, scratching the back of his neck. "I'm a cousin to Oscar and Lovisa."

"Are you as brave as them?" Jörgen asked kindly.

"I hope so," replied Gustav, while shyly scraping with his foot on the ground.

"Don't be shy," said Siegfried, nudging him with his elbow. "I may have killed a dragon in that other mountain, but I heard you defeated a demon."

"A demon and a dragon, then," said Jörgen, sounding impressed. "Then I feel confident that you will protect us."

"Don't worry, Professor, only humans and gods from Asgard can get through the protective barrier created by the magic of Asgard," Siegfried said with a smile.

"EXACTLY!" a sharp voice echoed in the cave.

Gustav reached for his rifle, but a black spear flew past him and landed warningly next to the rifle.

"You should have killed me when you had the chance, boy!" Nari exclaimed sarcastically, walking towards the party. "Well, what am I going to do with you now?"

৩৹

"Unit three, report!"

Kenneth kept the button pressed on the communication radio, desperately trying to reach his men. It had been a little over an hour since he hastily interrupted the press conference to join the attack on the mountain.

Some helicopters had flown ahead to scout but then lost contact with the rest of the army. He swore loudly at the crackling radio and slammed his fist into the side of the helicopter's fuselage. The rotating rotor blades muffled his voice as they raced towards Flatruet.

"Sir! In front of us!" the pilot's voice was suddenly heard.

Kenneth stared in amazement at the scene unfolding before them. Heavy columns of smoke were billowing up from the ground below the mountain, and a great battle seemed to be being fought down there. But it was what was waiting for them in the air above the mountain that made him shiver. The sky in front of them was filled with a gigantic swarm of winged demons.

"Sir, what should we do?" the pilot asked anxiously.

Kenneth clutched the communications radio tightly before calling the other thirty helicopters.

"Attention! This is "Daddy Dragon" speaking! Prepare to fire on the targets. Enter coordinates 5-2-1, I repeat: 5-2-1!" he commanded. "Our goal is to eliminate as many of the flying demons as possible!"

As the first machine gun began firing its shots, Kenneth felt a sense of hopelessness take hold of him as the first helicopter was attacked by the winged demons and exploded.

℘

"Thrúd!"

Módi was bent over his sister, desperately trying to get her to stand up. Around them, the battle between the werewolves and the wolves raged. The wolves were trying to rip out the throats of the werewolves, but they had much more difficulty defending themselves from the werewolves, who, by biting the wolves, turned the wolves into new werewolves.

Several explosions were heard in the air above them, and Módi could see the military helicopters attacking the winged gargoyles swarming above the mountain.

"It seems I couldn't take care of you," Thrúd said softly.

"What a touching scene!"

Hela walked slowly towards them through the tangle of wolves and were-wolves. One of the wolves tried to attack her but was immediately repelled by the darkness that loomed around the disfigured goddess.

"Such love between a brother and sister," she said, smiling. "Don't worry, boy, I'll put you to sleep too before I make demons of you both."

Just as she was raising her hand, Wille appeared from the side and threw himself over Hela, who was knocked to the ground. Her empty eye socket flared with rage as she directed the attack at him instead.

As the purple flames lunged at Wille, a wall of black fire erupted between them and swallowed the purple flames.

Hela turned to Wayland, who appeared behind her.

"I thought I made it clear that I would not tolerate you attacking him, Hela," Wayland hissed.

"Did you really think I was going to let you have the boy?" Hela snapped back.

A sea of darkness enveloped the two like a cocoon.

"Wille!"

Hugo shouted his name just as Garmr threw himself on top of him. The giant wolf pushed Wille down to the ground and smiled triumphantly before he too was thrown aside by Mánagarmr, who attacked him from the side.

Both of the giant wolves rolled around on the ground and out of sight from Wille, who got up to orient himself.

Magni stood in front of his siblings and struck with his huge hammer as a battle club over the werewolves, who came towards them like waves.

Tulio and Hugo had dragged the half-unconscious Lódurr to the protective mountain wall behind Magni. Tella was standing next to Magni, directing her trees, who were trying to help the remaining wolves.

"Wille!" a voice was suddenly heard next to him.

Nyri dragged Váli across the ground towards the mountain wall. One of the wolf's legs was bleeding profusely from Garmr's attack and looked horrible. Wille quickly grabbed Váli, and with joint forces, they managed to drag him the last bit to the others.

One of the wolves let out a powerful roar, and the remaining wolves began to retreat towards the mountain wall. Wille could sense the darkness in the aura of the werewolves when the beasts' disgusting jaws opened and they made attacks against the wolves.

"Módi!" Magni shouted loudly while swinging the huge battle club.

Módi came up on wobbly legs, stood next to his brother, and shared the double-edged axe.

The wolves stood in front of them like a wall, but were no match for the overwhelming number of werewolves that were gathering for a final attack.

Wille sensed a flash of light behind the approaching werewolves. He opened his eyes to understand what he was really seeing. More balls of light in different colours approached the scene, and before the werewolves could perceive the danger, the fairies rolled over them like a wave.

The werewolves threw themselves, stabbing and tearing in the air to chase away the intruders.

Then several cascades of blue fire whizzed through the air and seemed to pierce the werewolves, who one by one fell lifeless to the ground before their bodies disintegrated.

Wille could see a woman in a blue dress some distance away who conjured up the blue flames like projectiles. A swift movement caught his attention as Garmr came rushing across the battlefield towards the woman. Wille started to run forward to try to stop him, but his path was blocked by Mánagarmr.

"I can't let you interfere," said the wolf, and Wille could see the wolf's eyes begin to turn into black flames of fire.

A sharp scream cut through the night as Garmr threw himself upon the woman, who summoned a fire spear for protection. The wolf tried to tear the spear from the woman's grasp, and several of Tella's trees rushed forward to help her.

A wall of darkness rose up around Garmr and the woman, and the trees stopped, unable to penetrate it.

"Oscar, if you're still in there, please – I have to help them!" Wille begged, staring into the dark eyes.

Mánagarmr suddenly seemed to freeze, and opened his mouth. But this time it was not the demon's eerie voice that answered Wille, it was the softer voice of his friend.

"Wille," said the wolf in a shaky voice. "Kill me, please! I can't hold it back, the darkness is too strong. It has almost taken control of me completely!"

Mánagarmr's terrifying figure seemed to struggle against itself as it writhed in agony.

A flash of lightning went through Wille's mind, and suddenly he understood the meaning of what Silver had said.

"Tulio!" Wille shouted in his mind, searching frantically for the boy's consciousness. "I need the stone!"

❧

Tulio sat petrified with his arms around his grandfather, who lay in his arms.

All around them, the fighting was raging, and he saw to his horror how Módi desperately trying to protect his sister as the werewolves pounced on them.

In front of him was Nyri, who was throwing rocks in a flurry around him. There could be heard wailing as the pile-like rocks pierced the werewolves that hit the ground.

Suddenly, he heard Wille's voice in his head. He stared out over the chaotic battlefield, and finally caught sight of him.

Tulio drew a nervous breath when he saw Mánagarmr's enormous form a few metres in front of Wille.

"Nyri!" he shouted, and the older god turned around. "I must get to Wille!"

"Are you crazy?" exclaimed his brother as he hurled a cascade of stones that rained down on the battlefield. "If you go out there, I can't protect you!"

"He needs this," Tulio said, holding up the red gemstone.

"What does he need it for?" Nyri asked in surprise.

"He didn't say," replied Tulio. "But considering he's standing in front of the giant wolf, I don't think he's going to use it to play with!"

Nyri glanced to his left at Wille and Mánagarmr.

"But how are you going to get there?" he asked. "It's on the other side of the battlefield!"

Tulio swallowed hard, hastily looking down at the ground, before he carefully looked up at his big brother again.

"You don't mean…" Nyri began, and Tulio nodded.

"You've done it with me many times before," said Tulio.

"Yes," said Nyri. "But then it was just for fun."

"Nyri, I have to go!" Tulio exclaimed and stood up.

❧

Tella found it difficult to maintain her concentration, she had never handled so many trees before for so long. The battlefield was one big chaos, with wolves, werewolves, and fairies swirling around the flat surface. The only advantage they had was that Hela and Wayland seemed preoccupied with their own dispute, she thought, looking towards the dark bubble where dark lightning struck out and thunderous sounds were heard.

A roar was heard next to her, and suddenly she saw Hugo piercing a werewolf with a sword.

The terrifying beast had just opened its jaws to attack her.

"Thank you!" Tella exclaimed in shock as the werewolf dissolved on the ground. "Where did you get the sword?"

"I got it from Magni," Hugo replied dully.

A werewolf lunged at them, but this time Tella was ready, and one of her trees drove the werewolf so hard into the edge of the mountain that stones rained down on it.

"I must find Váli," said Hugo, rising unsteadily to his feet. "He was injured by Garmr and won't last long."

"Don't push yourself too hard!" Tella admonished him as another explosion was heard above them. "We're outnumbered here!"

"I'm not leaving him!" Hugo exclaimed, and rushed off along the mountainside.

Just then, a howl was heard above them, and Tella couldn't believe her eyes. High above their heads, Tulio was flying through the air on a huge boulder. She swore loudly, and jumped up onto one of the trees, which carried her through the sea of wolves and werewolves.

❧

"We need a miracle!" Magni exclaimed and leaned exhaustedly against the battle club. "We can't hold out much longer!"

Módi nodded as the axes returned to his hands. They were almost encircled, the remaining wolves were few, and the werewolves were approaching from all directions.

"What we need is a plan!" a voice was heard behind them.

Thrúd carefully got up on shaky legs and stood next to her brothers.

"Are you okay?" Módi asked anxiously.

"Were you worried about me?" she asked teasingly, giving both brothers a menacing look.

"You always push yourself too hard," Magni replied without taking his eyes away from the werewolves.

"You are the one to talk," Thrúd countered.

"We don't have time to argue!" Módi exclaimed, looking out over the sea of werewolves. "What do we do?"

Thrúd looked out over the battlefield and saw the fairies trying to stall the werewolves. Suddenly her face lit up, and she smiled broadly.

"I know exactly what we are going to do!" she exclaimed, and whispered something in Magni's ear.

☙

"Isn't it time for you to give up, darling?"

Hela stood slumped over her black staff. In front of her stood Wayland, with a smile. The darkness that surrounded them began to fade, and he bent down so their faces met.

"You will always be number two," Wayland whispered.

Just then, several howls were heard echoing in the night, and he seemed suddenly to become aware of his surroundings.

"It looks like your werewolves are getting a match after all!" Wayland exclaimed, looking out over the battle.

"As do your demons," Hela countered slyly, pointing up to the mountaintop.

"I don't care what happens to that trash!" Wayland hissed impatiently and clenched his fist in front of her face. "All I want is the boy!"

He stood up and wrapped the cloak around him.

"But I know how much your beloved puppies mean to you," Wayland said before disappearing into the darkness.

Hela stood up and let her gaze wander across the battle before her staff began to glow, and purple flames once again erupted around her, spreading among the remaining wolves.

39. Showdown

Kenneth swore loudly and looked at the swarm of demons around the mountain. They had shot down countless numbers of them, which the warriors on the ground had effectively destroyed. The problem was that it never seemed to end, and now they had only three helicopters left at their disposal.

"This is 'Daddy Dragon' speaking," he said, fingering the communications radio. "Units nineteen and seven, return to base immediately!"

"Sir?" asked the pilot looking out over the swarming demons, who were approaching the helicopter.

"Do you know how to use a parachute, Olle?" Kenneth asked and pushed a bag up into the man's chest as he pulled the pilot out of the driver's seat.

"But, sir, what…" the terrified pilot began to protest as he strapped the bag over his back.

"Jump, that's an order!" Kenneth shouted, and shook the helicopter so hard that the pilot threw himself out.

Kenneth fiddled with the settings on the device and set the timer for two minutes. He had hoped not to have to use it, but he no longer had a choice.

Just as the first demons collided with the helicopter's nose, the sky in front of him was lit up by huge flashes of lightning, and Kenneth saw a muscular man flying through the swarm of demons, knocking them to the ground.

The man grabbed the helicopter's driver's door and ripped it from its fastenings. Kenneth stared in shock at the man, who ripped the device out of his grip.

"I will never understand what drives you humans to sacrifice your lives so easily," the man said, before picking up the shocked Kenneth and throwing themself out.

The gargoyles swarmed around them as they dropped to the ground and tried to grab them, but the strange man raised what seemed to be a powerful sledgehammer, whereupon tremendous lightning struck around them and destroyed the nearest demons.

Kenneth watched in horrified delight as he and the strange man sank through a sea of lightning and screaming demons.

"Don't worry!" the man shouted to drown out the roar of the lightning. "You are safe with me!"

The man raised the huge sledgehammer, and directed the lightning at the helicopter, which now looked more like a huge ball of lightning.

"Hold on to me!" the man shouted, steering the ball of light into the centre of the demon swarm. "And don't look into the light!"

Kenneth gripped the man's waist tightly and closed his eyes. A deafening explosion shook the entire mountainside, and a huge flash of light illuminated the night sky as the helicopter exploded.

"You can look now," the man shouted.

Kenneth opened his eyes and couldn't believe his eyes. The light from the explosion still illuminated the sky for what seemed like miles.

All around them, hundreds of demons fell through the air and dissolved into nothingness before their bodies reached the ground.

Kenneth looked down and saw how he and the man slowly descended towards the ground, surrounded by lightning. He looked in amazement at the man who was holding him in a firm grip and was met with ferocious yet friendly eyes.

"Thank you!" Kenneth exclaimed nervously as they reached the ground.

"No, thank you," said the strange man, laughing. "It is true that you humans are foolish, but this time your foolishness still came in handy. My lightning bolts and your primitive device reinforced each other, knocking out virtually the entire enemy force."

"Who are you?" Kenneth asked, standing up shakily.

"The name is Thor," replied the man, smiling. "In your world, I am known as the god of thunder and battle. I suppose you have already met my sons, Magni and Módi?"

Kenneth nodded nervously. The warriors they saw from the helicopters began to gather around them. They were dressed in strange leather clothing and heavy wool coats. Their weapons consisted of long swords and battle axes.

"Don't worry," said Thor, laughing when he saw Kenneth's nervous look. "They are my warriors and will not attack you."

Kenneth still looked sceptical but nodded weakly without taking his eyes off the men.

Thor laughed and put one arm around his shoulder.

"This man is a true warrior!" Thor shouted. "He was going to sacrifice his own life against the gargoyles!"

The other men raised their weapons and roared in victory.

"What is your name, warrior?" Thor asked, pushing the stunned Kenneth in front of him.

"K…Kenneth," he stammered, half terrified.

"Okay, Kenneth, do you want to be one of my Einherjar?" Thor asked, shaking him lightly.

"My lord!" one of the men exclaimed. "There is still a battle going on at the foot of the mountain!"

"You're right, Vil," said Thor, sighing. "We'll do the initiation rite later."

The warriors began to make their way down the mountainside, and Thor looked smilingly at Kenneth, who stood speechless beside him.

"Kenneth," Thor said, punching him lightly in the back. "Feel free to entertain me on the way down by telling me how your human warriors have gotten into this mess."

✸

"Ítrek, why did you help the girls?"

The dark-clad figure stood hunched on the rocky ledge, watching the battle at the foot of the mountain. The wolves had been almost completely wiped out by the werewolves' infection and turned into bloodthirsty beasts.

"Master," said Ítrek, standing beside him. "I just gave them a nudge forward."

A loud roar was heard at the top of the mountain, and the sky was illuminated by a huge flash of light that illuminated the night sky as far as Ítrek could see. He had to hold his arm up in front of his face to avoid being blinded.

"Don't let it happen again," the man said in a dark voice, not caring about the lightning. "Stick to the plan, and make sure that as many of them as possible die before they reach the gate, except the boy and his brother."

"Yes, Master," Ítrek said, bowing slightly. "I have already taken steps to bring the weaker members of the group together with a certain demon."

"And what did you do with the fire wolf after your little game?" the man asked, turning his face towards him.

"It's back in the underworld, Master," Ítrek replied, not daring to meet the man's gaze.

"Good," said the man, turning his head back again. "Make sure there are no more incidents, we must not reveal ourselves!"

Ítrek bowed deeply before the darkness enveloped him, and he disappeared.

The man ran his fingers through his short, silver-white beard and smiled a cunning, sly smile before he too was enveloped by the darkness and disappeared.

⌘

"Did you really think you had a chance against us?"

The werewolf walked slowly towards the wolf with his teeth bared. The huge beast's eyes glowed with purple flames as it approached Váli, who was motionless on the ground.

"Your wolf army will soon be destroyed, and my mistress is destroying the godchildren," hissed the werewolf, bending over him. "Why do you resist? I can feel the darkness spreading in you, you will soon be a demon wolf yourself."

"I will never be like you," Váli gasped exhaustedly.

The werewolf laughed and stared into his eyes.

"No, of course not!" the beast exclaimed. "You'll be a miniature version of Garmr, with a mind of pure darkness!"

A shadow rose up on the ridge, and just as the werewolf turned its head, Hugo roared and cut off its head with a sword that shone like nacre.

"Hugo!" Váli exclaimed, getting up with a limp. "You shouldn't be here!"

"You are injured," said Hugo, reaching towards him.

"What is that sword?" Váli asked, looking surprised at the sword in Hugo's hand, whose glow was beginning to fade.

"Ridill," Hugo replied, lifting the sword so that Váli could examine it properly. "It's also known as the Sword of Truth, the others found it when they rescued Lovisa in Trollhammer Mountain."

"Ridill and Hrotti!" Váli gasped. "I've heard about the twin swords, but I thought they were just a fairy tale."

"Do you tell each other fairy tales?" Hugo asked in surprise.

"Yes, but our children's stories are not quite what you are used to," replied Váli, smiling wryly.

Suddenly, he sank to the ground in agony.

Hugo bent down over him, but the wolf turned his face and growled warningly.

"Stay away!" he hissed at Hugo, who immediately recoiled in shock.

"Váli, what…" Hugo began, but was interrupted by Váli making a lunge at him.

"Go away!" growled the wolf. "I don't want to hurt you!"

"But what's going on?" Hugo asked, trembling.

Váli tossed his head back and forth, scratching the ground and looking ravaged.

"The darkness is penetrating my soul again," he replied. "I cannot hold it back."

"But you have defeated the darkness," Hugo said hesitantly. "You said it could not penetrate your heart again."

Then he felt a cold chill go through his back.

"Don't tell me the werewolves bit you?" Hugo asked in horror.

"We creatures of darkness are immune to werewolf bites because the darkness in us neutralises the infection," replied Váli, writhing in agony. "The contagion comes from Hela's magic and shapes creatures into blood-thirsty monsters, but it has nothing to do with the darkness."

"Then what is happening?" Hugo asked anxiously.

"Garmr's bite," replied Váli, throwing himself upside down on the ground. "He has bitten me three times, his darkness has amplified my own darkness, and it is taking over me."

"Let me help you," Hugo begged, putting his hand on his head.

"No!" Váli exclaimed, pushing Hugo, who landed on his back.

"But Váli, I..." Hugo started sobbing while the wolf stood over him.

"What?" hissed Váli, pressing his paw down on his chest. "Are you going to tell me that you love me? That you want to be with me? I am a wolf, get it through your dull head!"

Hugo trembled with fear as he lay on the ground with Váli standing over him. Tears streamed down his cheeks as he stared into the wolf's eyes. The amber eyes he loved so much had become darker and more ferocious.

"You're just a little boy who misses his mother and can't fend for himself!" Váli hissed, slapping his paw on the ground next to Hugo's terrified face. "You don't even dare to sleep at night without something to hug!"

"No, I...Váli..." said Hugo in a trembling voice.

"Get out of here," Váli hissed, and gave him a swipe of his paw across his arm before limping off up a steep mountain path. "Take your brother and your friends to Asgard if you like, but don't even think of following me!"

Hugo curled up against the rock wall and sobbed uncontrollably, while Váli disappeared up the mountainside.

⁂

"Dad, look!"

Jack pointed down to the ground, and Ullr glanced in the same direction.

Below them, they could see the outline of a person lying lifelessly on the ground.

"Hold on!" Ullr exclaimed and pulled hard on the reins, whereupon the reindeer made a sharp turn and went down to the ground.

The ice rink flattened out, and the reindeer slowed down a few metres from the place where they had seen the person.

Jack quickly jumped out of the sledge and made his way to the lifeless body.

"Dad, it's Lovisa!" he exclaimed in amazement.

Ullr bent down and gently felt her pulse.

"Quickly, unpack all the blankets you can find and put her in the sled!" he commanded as he picked up the girl and rushed back to the sledge. "She's very cold!"

Jack put Lovisa down, and she slowly opened her eyes.

"Jack, where are we?" she asked.

"You are safe in our sledge," Jack replied, grabbing her hand. "What has happened? Why aren't you with the others?"

"I went to look for more wood for the fire," she replied, coughing. "As I was returning, I heard the sound of battle and sought shelter behind a rock crevice near the cave."

"Did you see the others?" Ullr asked, turning his head as the sledge lurched forward.

Lovisa nodded and looked terrified.

"It was that demon, Nari," she replied, shivering. "Siegfried fought him, but the demon was too strong."

Ullr swore loudly and slapped the reins.

"Just what we need," he said, frowning. "More trouble."

"What happened?" Jack asked worriedly.

"Nari hurt Siegfried badly," Lovisa replied. "The demon forced them up the mountain. I tried to get down to you to get help."

"You could have died!" Jack exclaimed angrily. "Or even worse, run into a werewolf!"

"Take it easy, Jack," said Ullr admonishingly. "She's safe now, make sure you get us back in the air so *we* don't run into any werewolves!"

Jack sighed and held out one hand, whereupon the familiar ice rink formed in front of them, and the reindeer began to pull the sledge up into the dark night sky.

༼༽

"Tulio!"

He opened his eyes slowly and saw Wille struggling against the beast, who was pushing him to the ground.

"Tulio, the stone!" shouted the silver-white wolf in despair as Mánagarmr's paws pressed against Wille's throat.

Tulio got to his feet and started digging in his pocket.

"Well, well, well, who do we have here?"

Wayland stepped towards them from a portal of darkness. The man's evil gaze caused Tulio to fall backward in fear.

"So, the big help my son is relying on is a little baby elf," Wayland said coldly, and grinned smugly at Tulio. "What do you have in your pocket, really?"

Just then, there was a deafening roar, and the sky was illuminated by an enormous flash of light. There was a furious roar from Mánagarmr, who was crouching on the ground, and Wayland put up his arms to protect his face.

Then Wille stood next to Tulio and stubbornly scratched his paw against his pocket.

"Take out the stone!" Wille shouted impatiently.

Tulio dug out the red diamond and held it up in front of Wille, who, without hesitation, grabbed it with his mouth and rushed towards Mánagarmr, who was getting up again.

Wille stopped in front of the furious beast and closed his eyes. Just as Mánagarmr raised his paw, and aimed a blow at Wille, the red gemstone began to glow, and the big wolf put his paw in front of his face instead.

The diamond suddenly took on a darker hue as the darkness of the beast's heart reflected in its red shimmer, and Wille pushed the diamond into the giant wolf's chest.

There was an angry roar from Mánagarmr, after which the glow from the gemstone grew intensity until the beast collapsed on the ground, seemingly lifeless.

"What have you done with my wolf, boy?" Wayland hissed, holding Tulio in the air.

On the ground beneath Tulio, sticky darkness began climbing up his feet.

"Take that stone away from my wolf, boy, and give yourself up. Then I let your friend go!" Wayland hissed, narrowing his eyes at Wille.

"Don't do it, Wille!" gasped Tulio, trying to wriggle free.

He stared in horror at the darkness creeping up his legs.

Wayland smiled and met Wille's gaze.

"It's remarkable that in less than a week you've managed to make such loyal friends," he said enthusiastically.

"Let him go!" Wille growled and stood up.

"Or else?" Wayland asked sarcastically. "You have nothing to oppose! You're weak, and dependent on your friends to get by, but this time no one can save you!"

"Let's make a bet!" a muffled voice was heard behind Wille.

Oscar's huge wolf figure stood up on wobbly legs. In the beast's chest, the red gemstone remained, but it had darkened considerably.

"You can take the stone out, Wille," he said calmly.

"How do I know I can trust you?" Wille asked suspiciously.

"How did you know you could trust the stone?" the giant wolf asked back, giving him a menacing look.

"Mánagarmr, what are you waiting for? Attack him!" Wayland hissed.

"Wille!" cried Tulio in terror as the darkness climbed over his waist.

Wille grabbed the stone and managed to pry it from Oscar's chest as the darkness began to reach Tulio's neck.

Oscar threw himself at Wayland, who released his grip on Tulio. Wayland roared with rage as the great beast knocked him to the ground, and then both of them disappeared into the darkness.

"Wille, help me!" Tulio shouted in despair, trying to crawl out of the darkness that pressed him down.

Wille rushed up to him and closed his eyes, while the darkness settled over both of them like a cocoon.

✌

Bea stared in horror into Garmr's giant eyes as she lay on the ground with the beast above her, with only her fire spear separating them.

"Don't worry," the beast hissed slyly. "Your death will be quick and painless."

Bea closed her eyes as her powers finally faded, and the spear disappeared.

The last thing she heard was Garmr's jaws closing around her neck.

40. The Last Stand

Tella screamed in despair as Tulio and Wille disappeared in the darkness. The tree that carried her rushed through the fighting, and she was almost to them when a strange red light began to shine before her.

The red glow grew in intensity until the darkness faded, and the silhouettes of Tulio and Wille appeared in the light.

Wille was sitting on the ground with Tulio next to him, holding his arms tightly around the wolf's neck.

"Tulio!" Tella exclaimed as she jumped off the tree and ran to them. "Are you okay?"

"I'm fine," the boy replied, wrapping his arms around his sister as they both sank into a sitting position.

"How touching!" a familiar voice was heard behind Wille.

Garmr walked towards them with leisurely steps. The dark bubble that had enveloped him and the woman with the fire was gone, but the woman was nowhere to be seen.

"So, you betrayed your father," Garmr said with delight. "I guess you prefer death after all!"

"Stop!" Wille exclaimed and picked up the red diamond.

The wolf laughed and started walking in a circle around them.

"I don't know what's more surprising," Garmr said slyly. "That you have a soul stone, or that he didn't know what it was."

"What have you done with Bea?" Tulio asked in horror, while Tella pulled him closer to her.

Garmr laughed delightedly as he walked past the siblings, so close that he brushed his fur against Tulio's back.

"What do you think?" asked the wolf, stopping with his head over the huddled siblings. "She fought bravely, just like your mother, Wille!"

Wille had followed Garmr closely with his eyes, as the hell wolf circled around them. He was still holding the diamond in a firm grip with his mouth, and had his body tensed so that at any moment he could throw himself over the giant wolf.

"Before you do something you regret," Garmr said ominously, "you should know that stone doesn't work on me. It may lock the darkness that are in creatures, but if you think about it one more time, you will realise that it only helps when the darkness has not fully taken over the creature."

Wille realised that the hellwolf was probably right. If the stone really locked the darkness that were in creatures' bodies, it meant that the darkness could not continue to grow, but what use was it to him with creatures that were already fully taken over?

"Well," Garmr said smugly. "With that realisation in mind, my offer is this – you sacrifice yourself to my mistress, and in return, I will let your friends go!"

"And if he refuses?" a sharp voice was heard behind the wolf.

Garmr turned his head just as Magni's hammer swung through the air and hit the beast with such force that the giant wolf flew several metres away.

A rumbling sound was heard, and Wille dropped the stone in astonishment when hundreds of men with swords and axes threw themselves into the battle.

The werewolves were brutally struck down by the sudden onslaught, and the few wolves that remained retreated to the mountain wall, where Nyri was creating a protective moat around the unconscious Lódurr.

The fairies gathered in an enormous sea above the werewolves, and the mysterious girl warrior Wille had seen earlier ran around the monsters so fast that he had difficulty seeing her.

A movement off to the side caught Wille's attention, and he saw Módi standing with his axes pointed at the sky. A thunderous sound was heard as the axes began to float from his hands into the air above the werewolves.

An angry roar was heard from somewhere, and Wille could see the goddess with the disfigured face forming a huge purple fireball, which she threw at Módi, only to have the attack parried by a muscular man with a thick amber beard and moustache, wielding a giant hammer.

"Wille!" a familiar voice was heard behind him.

He turned around and saw Kenneth running from the other side of the ridge. The military leader looked terrified as he made his way towards them.

"Wille, get your friends and follow me!" Kenneth shouted and made a waving gesture with his hand.

Wille nodded and cast a quick glance to the side at Tella, who was trying to make Tulio get up. He didn't hesitate, but abruptly picked up the boy and dragged him towards Kenneth, while Tella ran alongside them.

Suddenly, Tella screamed as a werewolf attacked them from the side. The sound of several shots echoed in the night, and Wille saw the werewolf collapse on the ground. They reached Kenneth, who stood with his gun drawn, aiming at the werewolf, who was getting up again.

"Follow me!" Kenneth shouted as he picked up Tulio in his arms and began to run.

A deafening bang was heard behind them as they ran away from the battle.

⁊

"My darlings!" Hela roared, as the huge bolt of lightning struck from the sky, and, with the help of the fairies, spread like a filter over the werewolves.

"Oh, what a pity that mom can't be there to comfort them!" Thor said sarcastically and delivered another blow to the goddess with his hammer.

He floated in the air using his lightning bolts. Hela enveloped herself in purple fire and sent cascades of darkness towards the god of thunder, which he easily avoided by constantly moving in the air.

"Isn't it time for you to go home and lick your wounds while you still have a chance?" Thor asked ironically.

Hela looked around. Most of the werewolves had been struck by the lightning attack, and had disintegrated into ashes one by one, and those who had managed to escape were effectively slayed by the warriors.

An angry roar made her turn around. Garmr and Magni found themselves in a fierce battle, with Magni, like his father, floating on lightning in the air, and the wolf's darkness having difficulty reaching him.

"It looks like your favourite wolf is in trouble too," Thor said with a laugh.

"This isn't over!" Hela hissed and turned around again. "The dragons have returned to crush you once and for all, so enjoy this victory – it's the only one you will get!"

With an eerie laugh, the goddess was enveloped in a mixture of purple flames and sticky darkness before disappearing. A roar caused Thor to look up at the hill where Magni threw himself at Garmr, who, like his mistress, disappeared into darkness.

Thor sighed and turned to his soldiers, who were slaying the last of the werewolves.

"A fine victory, my lord!" Vil said, joining him as he wiped his sword clean of werewolf blood.

"I have a feeling we're getting ahead of ourselves, my friend," Thor muttered, and made his way through the sea of soldiers and wolves.

Ↄ

Nyri was kneeling, breathing heavily. The moonlight lay like a silver-white glow above them, and he could see the Einherjar chasing the last of the werewolves and how Magni, Módi, and Trud embraced their father.

"Nyri," someone whispered behind him.

He turned around and was surprised to see his grandfather sitting up, leaning against a rock. Next to him, Hábrók was sitting on the ground, shouting loudly.

"Grandfather, you shouldn't get up yet," said Nyri, sinking to his knees next to the old man.

"Nyri, listen to me – it's urgent!" gasped the old man. "Váli is being taken over by the darkness, he has hurt Hugo!"

"Where are they, Grandfather?" Nyri asked as the hawk screamed louder and louder.

"Hugo is on the ground a little way from here," said Lódurr, pointing to the left while coughing. "Váli is on his way to the Grave of Eva."

"The Grave of Eva," Nyri whispered in horror.

"You must stop him," said Lódurr, rising on trembling legs. "Before it's too late!"

Nyri turned, and started running towards Thor, while Ullr's reindeer ran down the ice track and landed the sledge next to the thunder gods.

⁓

"So, you decided to return!"

Thor fixed his eyes on the snow god, who was sweating and tried to look away from the wrath of the thunder god.

"Forgive me," muttered Ullr quietly.

"We don't have time for this," said Jack, helping Lovisa off the sled. "He has taken our friends!"

"And who are you?" Thor asked angrily.

"I am Ullr's son," Jack snapped back. "Who are you?"

"Your son?" Thor asked, turning to Ullr again.

"Yes, father," replied Ullr, putting his arm around Jack's shoulder. "And your grandson."

"My…grandson…" Thor muttered in astonishment and stared at Jack, who looked equally astonished.

"Grandpa…" Jack whispered, and walked slowly towards the thunder god.

Thor and Jack looked at each other in astonishment for a moment before they embraced each other in a hug.

"What do you mean 'he's taken our friends'?" Módi asked.

"I can explain," said Lovisa, trembling.

She recounted in detail what had happened on the ridge.

Magni swore loudly when he learned that it was Nari who had captured them.

"We'll just have to find them and defeat that demon once and for all," said Thor, looking around. "We'll leave at once!"

"I'm afraid we have more problems," said Nyri, who had been standing next to them. "Several of our friends have disappeared, and one of them is making a big mistake!"

❧

"Hugo!"

Wille ran up to his brother, who lay on the ground with his face buried in his arms.

"Hugo, what happened?" Wille asked, examining the wound on his left arm.

"Váli," said Hugo, sobbing. "The darkness is taking over him."

"And you too, if we don't hurry!" exclaimed Tella, who had caught up with them.

Wille could see how the darkness was spreading from the wound through the veins. Soon, it would reach Hugo's heart.

"The necklace, Wille!" Tulio's voice was heard behind them.

Kenneth stood behind them with the boy in his arms, and Tulio's face looked sadly at Wille.

Tella leaned forward to try to loosen the necklace around Wille's neck when she suddenly stopped and stared at a figure appearing behind Kenneth.

Wille turned around and saw a young man appear behind Kenneth, who nervously turned around to face the stranger.

The red runes shone around the young man's vest as he slowly, but confidently, approached them.

"That's taking too long," the guy said, holding out something.

Wille was stunned when he saw the red diamond in the stranger's hand and suddenly went cold – he had dropped it when they fled the battle!

"A fine gem you have received, Wille," said the young man, turning the diamond in his hand, pretending to examine it. "I hope you are more careful with it in the future!"

"Give it back!" Wille exclaimed.

The guy smiled and walked calmly towards Wille, who stood up protectively in front of Hugo. The stranger looked amused at the reaction, and crouched down on his knees next to Wille with the diamond in front of his face.

"Who are you?" Wille asked nervously.

"How about we rescue your brother first and answer questions later?" the guy asked, without answering.

Just then, Hugo let out a heartbreaking scream and collapsed on the ground. Wille could see how the darkness had reached his chest.

"Well?" the guy asked patiently. "You don't have time to use your cross this time."

Without answering, Wille grabbed the gemstone with his mouth and pushed the tip into Hugo's chest, just as he had done with Oscar earlier.

Wille stared in amazement as Hugo's convulsive twitching subsided, and the stone seemed to darken as its magic locked the darkness in his brother's body.

"Ítrek," Tella whispered. "What are you doing here?"

"Besides saving you again, you mean?" Ítrek asked ironically. "Seriously, Tella, you and the others are losing control of the situation!"

"Do you know him?" Wille asked, looking at Tella.

"We're old friends," she said, looking uncertainly at Ítrek.

"We're more than that, my Lotus Flower," he said with a smile.

"My Lotus Flower?" Wille asked, smiling wryly at Tella, who was turning bright red in her face.

"Well…well…he's…we used to be together," she stammered, and tried to turn her face away.

"Come on, Tella," Ítrek said, laughing. "You don't have to be ashamed of having been together with an outcast!"

"Outcast?" Wille asked uncertainly, looking at him.

"It's complicated!" Tella hastily interrupted. "Can we get back to more important things now, like your brother, for example?"

"I'm fine," said Hugo, rising unsteadily to his feet.

Wille saw how the dark contours in his veins seemed to have returned to a more normal colour. The sorrow on Hugo's face, however, could not be hidden.

"Hugo," Wille whispered as Hugo bent down and wrapped his arms around him.

"Please help me find him," Hugo begged sadly.

"Okay," said Wille, smiling. "If that's what you want to do, I'll help you."

"Fascinating how you gods deal with this kind of things," Kenneth said behind them.

The military leader stood with his arms crossed, looking amused. Tulio stood beside him and gave Tella a questioning look that she stubbornly refused to meet.

"You need a guide," Ítrek said, looking at Hugo with amusement. "Your boyfriend is on his way to the Grave of Eva."

"The Grave of Eva!" Tella exclaimed. "Are you sure?"

"What is that?" Kenneth interrupted, looking incredulous.

"The Grave of Eva is a ravine up in Flatruet," replied Ítrek, turning his eyes towards the mountain. "Long ago, a shamanic woman died there, and her spirit haunts the ravine."

"Why do I get the feeling that this is not good?" Kenneth sighed.

"Because the ravine is cursed," replied Tella, drawing her green woollen cloak around Tulio. "The souls of those who perish in the ravine will be stuck down there forever."

"Gods are strong, but not immortal," Ítrek continued, turning to face them again. "Your friend intends to throw himself off the cliff and die before the darkness takes over his soul, but if the darkness still manages to take over the soul even though the body dies from the fall, the soul cannot leave the ravine."

"Please, help me save him!" Hugo sobbed and looked at them.

Just then, Kenneth's cell phone rang. He dug into the pocket of his camouflage suit and looked at the display.

"It's my boss," he said, sighing heavily. "Keep going, I'll catch up with you later!"

"Shall we go then?" asked Ítrek, gesturing to the path in front of them.

Wille looked at Tella, who nodded in agreement.

"Eh, Wille?" Tulio asked shamefully, looking around nervously in the moonlight. "Could I ride on your back?"

&

Váli struggled up the mountain as his chest ached with grief. The Grave of Eva was only a few dozen metres ahead of him, but it was hard to make out in the dim moonlight. He moved convulsively forward and realised that he did not have much time left.

Suddenly, he stopped and sniffed the air, noticing a faint scent that reminded him of something. In the faint glow of the moonlight, he could make out four figures that seemed to be hanging over the deep ravine. Three of the figures seemed to be moving and twitching violently in the darkness that held them up, while the fourth figure hung motionless.

Váli froze as he recognised Gustav and the young woman he had seen with the soldiers earlier. The faint odour grew stronger and stronger, and there was no longer any doubt. He turned around, only to be greeted by a wave of darkness that knocked him to the ground.

"Welcome, little brother," came a rustling voice, while a shadowy figure stood over the wolf.

Váli gasped when he saw the disfigured face leaning over him.

"Did you really think it would be that easy?" Nari hissed, smiling.

41. The Grave of Eva

Máni was kneeling with one hand in front of his face. Ullr came walking towards him.

"I promised to protect you, forgive me, sister," the moon god prayed by Bea's lifeless body.

Ullr placed one hand gently on his shoulder.

"Máni," he said compassionately. "They fought bravely."

"I should have been here!" Máni exclaimed sadly. "I should have protected them, and you!"

"What happened?" Ullr asked, sinking to one knee.

"I don't know!" Máni exclaimed in despair and slammed his clenched hands on the ground. "I...I can't remember what I did in the last twenty-four hours! It's as if a fog has settled over my consciousness!"

Ullr scratched his chin thoughtfully.

"You don't think someone has been playing with your memory, do you?" he asked. "Who could it be?"

"Does it matter?" Máni asked, slightly annoyed. "I was not there when you needed me, neither at Trollhammer Mountain nor here at Flatruet!"

"You are here now," said Ullr. "And we need your help."

ფ

"So, Kenneth was it?"

Thor gave him a heavy thump on the back, and he looked out over the field where his soldiers had begun to clean up after the fighting. The wolves that had survived the fighting had gathered against the mountain wall and were watching the nervous men, who were cordoning off the area.

Magni and the warriors were gathered behind Thor, and smiled at Kenneth, who flickered his eyes nervously.

"Are you ready to become one of us?" the thunder god asked urgently.

"Well…" Kenneth began, but was interrupted by a man in a fancy uniform walking towards them.

"Kenneth, you're not going to desert, are you?" the man asked with a mixture of joking and seriousness in his tone.

"N…no, boss," Kenneth stuttered and looked nervously at Thor, who laughed amusedly.

"I can assume that you are Kenneth's leader?" Thor asked, and extended his hand to greet him.

"That's right," replied the man, returning the greeting. "My name is Bill, and I am not pleased that you are trying to recruit my soldiers!"

"You've got a soldier you can be proud of," Thor said quickly, giving Kenneth another painful slap on the back.

"I already know that," said Bill, smiling faintly. "But shouldn't you be leaving? You have more trouble at the top of the mountain, don't you?"

"I'm sure the kids can handle it," replied Thor. "We have several seriously injured warriors that we have to carry to the gate, so we sent the youths ahead of us to the gorge."

Bill nodded and turned to Kenneth.

"I'll expect a full report when you've cleaned this place up," he said brusquely. "Then the whole incident will be classified, the media has taken the bait about a terrorist cell with chemical weapons, and that's the official version!"

Bill started to walk away, but suddenly stopped.

"Are there any non-gods left up there that need to be brought home?" he asked, looking over his shoulder.

Kenneth glanced at Thor, who in turn glanced at Magni. The young god looked pleadingly at his father, who sighed heavily and shook his head.

"No, sir," Kenneth said confidently.

"Good," said Bill, and continued walking. "Because if that were the case, they would have to be put under supervision."

Once his boss was out of sight, Kenneth turned to Thor and Magni.

"Can you really take care of them?" he asked.

"They are our friends," Magni replied confidently. "If they don't want to come with us, we'll make sure they get home."

"Magni, we have strict restrictions on who can enter Asgard," Thor reminded him, and looked sharply at his son.

"Please, Dad," Magni pleaded "This is a special situation."

"Kids," Thor said with a sigh, flapping his arms. "Well, we'll talk about it when you are all safe at home."

"Will master Lódurr be okay?" Kenneth asked, looking anxiously at the old man being carried away by the Einherjar.

"He and the other wounded will be restored when we get home," Thor replied. "I'm sure he'll be in touch with you again soon."

Just then, Hábrók's shrill cry was heard behind them, and Kenneth turned around. The silver-winged hawk seemed to be communicating with one of the wolves, who made a slight bow to the hawk before all the wolves took off, sprinting away across the smooth ground.

Kenneth could see how his soldiers nervously stepped aside to let the wolves through, watching them as they disappeared into the darkness.

He suddenly looked around in confusion for the gods and the warriors, who had disappeared.

A note stuck out of Kenneth's breast pocket. He unfolded the note and stood amazed as he read: *"When you are ready!"*

❧

"What do you think?" Módi asked, bending down.

Nyri examined the ground with his hands.

"They've been here," he said, standing up. "A battle was fought here, and I can sense the darkness, but…"

"But what?" asked Thrúd, standing beside them.

"There is another energy here too, one that I haven't felt in a long time…" Nyri replied, his face turning pale.

"Would you like to tell us?" Módi asked, crossing his arms.

"Ítrek," Nyri replied quietly. "Ítrek Sióð has been here!"

Móði's axe fell to the ground with a thud. Þrúd gasped and looked around anxiously.

"Are you sure?" Móði asked, grabbing him.

"I would recognise that energy from miles away," replied Nyri.

"Then we're in a hurry!" Þrúd exclaimed and began to make his way up the mountain path. "Stop fooling around and get moving!"

℘

"Calm down!" Jack exclaimed, scratching Rudolph's ear.

He had persuaded his father to use Rudolph to search for their friends. The reindeer's red muzzle gave off a welcome glow in the otherwise dark night, but it was difficult to ride in the strong wind.

Rudolph made a screeching sound when a strong gust of wind made Jack lose his balance. He fell through the dark night and tried to focus his hands on the ground when he was suddenly stopped above the ground.

A silver-white dust enveloped Jack, and brought him back into the air again, where Rudolph was waiting for him. A dark-haired man was standing in the air, holding the reindeer in a firm grip.

"You must be careful when you ride," the man said.

"Who are you?" Jack asked, looking at the man in surprise as the silvery-white dust settled him on the reindeer's back.

"My name is Máni," the man replied. "I am an old friend of your father and the other gods."

"The moon god," whispered Jack, his face lighting up.

"That's right," Máni replied. "And now I think we should look for your friends!"

℘

Nari laughed as Váli's body flew through the air, smashing into the rock wall.

"Get up!" the demon commanded, kicking him.

Váli whimpered, the darkness burned in his body, and he could barely feel the pain of the beating anymore.

"What's wrong, little brother?", Nari asked sarcastically. "Are you too kind and tame to defend yourself? Or do you not have the strength to fight the darkness anymore?"

Váli looked up sadly at the disfigured demon. His body was exhausted with grief, and the pain of the darkness was beginning to reach his heart. Nari raised the dark sword above him.

"No!" a cry was heard echoing over the ridge.

Váli saw the blurred outline of a wolf and three other people, who were slowly making their way to their place.

"Váli!" the call was heard again, and suddenly he was flooded with warmth inside.

"Hugo," Váli whispered, as the menacing figure of Nari loomed above him.

Just as Nari was about to deliver the blow, a wave of ice surged up from the ground towards the demon.

"You don't touch my friends!" Jack roared, throwing himself off a nearby cliff towards Nari.

The demon laughed delightedly and raised his hands, while a wave of darkness formed above them and descended towards Jack.

As the darkness approached him, Jack was covered in a silver-white glow that enveloped him like a cocoon.

Nari looked around, before his gaze settled on Máni, who was soaring in the air above them, waving teasingly.

The disfigured demon roared angrily, sending darkness shaped like pointed stakes towards the moon god, only to see Jack's ice knock the stakes away into the Grave of Eva.

Jack hurled a wave of pointed ice cubes at Nari, who began to float on a dark plateau in the air between him and the moon god. The demon threw a glance over his shoulder and spun around so that a cascade of darkness went past the ice crystals and continued towards Jack.

A huge swirl of snow threw Jack to the ground a short distance from where Váli lay motionless. Jack looked up in horror at his father, who was in the same place where he had just been, pierced by black spears.

"Dad!" he shouted, as the snow god fell to the ground.

He started to run towards his father, but was prevented by a cascade of darkness that rose like a wall between them.

"I'm sorry," Nari said as the grotesque demonic figure emerged from the dark wall. "I understand that you feel lost and outcast."

"What are you talking about?" Jack asked in despair, sending a block of ice into the air, which the demon blocked with darkness.

"An outcast who doesn't know that he's an outcast," Nari replied amusedly, waving with one hand.

Through the darkness, Ullr's heavy body emerged and landed between them.

"Dad!" cried Jack, making a start to run forward but stopped when he saw the demon's outstretched hand.

"Your father has a secret he hasn't told you," said Nari, who bent down and lifted Ullr's face so that Jack could see his father's gaze. "Right, Snow God?"

"What are you talking about?" Jack asked, trembling.

"Come on, Santa," said Nari, slapping Ullr's cheek with his hand. "You've been naughty, it's time to ease your heart!"

❦

"Váli!"

Hugo sank to his knees next to the dark-furred wolf and tried to shake him up.

"Hugo," Wille said gently. "I think he's…"

"He's not dead!" Hugo roared and buried his face in the wolf's fur. "He can't be dead!"

"He's not dead," said a calm voice behind them.

Máni appeared behind them and sank to his knees.

"His soul is almost completely taken over," said the moon god, and put his hands over Váli's chest. "That is why he is still, it is the final phase before the soul dies."

"Help him!" Hugo pleaded in tears. "He can't die!"

"I can try to halt the process," said Máni, and a silver-white light began to shine from his hands into Váli's body. "But I don't know how long I manage. And even if I manage to hold back the darkness, he will die from his injuries."

Wille examined Váli's abdomen and saw that his cousin was losing a lot of blood.

"Where is Tulio?" Hugo asked desperately, looking around in despair.

"Tella thought he should wait further away, remember?" Wille replied sadly.

"Can't you contact him?" Hugo asked meaningfully. "We need him!"

"I can try," replied Wille, closing his eyes.

A scream cut through the night from the other side of the dark wall, and everyone jumped.

"Wille," said Máni. "While we're waiting for your friend, you must try to help Ullr. He was impaled by the demon's weapon and needs you and your cross."

"But Wille is needed here with his cross," said Hugo, looking pleadingly at his brother.

"We still can't save Váli until Tulio gets here and heals the wound," Máni reminded him, pressing the silver-white light against the wolf's chest. "Go now! I'll hold back the darkness until you get back."

૮૭

"Dad," Jack whispered with a shudder. "Is this true?"

"Forgive me, Jack," begged Ullr, who writhed in agony as the darkness penetrated through his body.

"Now you know the truth," said Nari gloatingly. "You will never be allowed to set foot in Asgard, just like my beloved little brother. But I understand how you feel…"

"You understand nothing!" Jack roared, throwing chunk after chunk of ice at the demon.

"No? You think I don't know what it's like to be an outcast?" Nari roared back, unleashing a wave of darkness.

Jack conjured up an ice shield, which forced the darkness away and hurled itself into the air. A cascade of darkness and ice exploded in the air before he landed back on the ground.

"To not be trusted?" Nari hissed. "To long for a family?"

Jack looked at the grotesque face in horror, not knowing what to answer.

"Since you robbed me of my soul, I have longed for someone to talk to who, like me, understands what it is to be an outcast. I thought that my little brother would understand, but all he cared about was his friends," Nari continued. "Then I heard about you, the dream boy who wouldn't exist! The boy who would be destroyed as soon as he left his father's side! Because my little brother betrayed me, I hoped that maybe you would understand."

"You know nothing about me," snapped Jack, leaning on one knee.

"You think so?" Nari asked rhetorically, throwing out his arms. "Just look at what we can do together!"

Jack gasped as he realised what the demon meant. The darkness and ice had joined like a wall behind them.

"What goes better together than darkness and cold?" Nari asked rhetorically, looking at Jack's stunned expression. "We can rule this world, you and I. No gods, no demons, no Wayland, and no dragons! Just you and me!"

"And no humans," Jack said meaningfully, turning to his father, who was gasping for breath.

"Jack," said Ullr, trying to get up.

"That useless father," snorted Nari, waving his hand, and the spear in the snow god's body disappeared. "You want to end his suffering?"

Jack looked down at his father, who crawled towards him, conjuring up a tip of ice in one hand.

"Do it," Nari hissed triumphantly. "He lied to you and filled you with expectation. But in the end, he was going to betray you and abandon you!"

"Jack!" a new voice suddenly called out to him.

Jack turned towards the wall of darkness that separated them from the rest of the party. Before the darkness, the silver-white wolf figure appeared from the darkness.

"You're not like him!" shouted Wille, who started walking towards them. "Look into your father's eyes!"

Jack lowered his gaze and looked down at his father, who had managed to crawl to him. Their eyes met, and he could see the tears coming from the snow god's eyes.

"Jack," Ullr whispered. "I love you, and I will never let anything happen to you!"

Jack shivered as the ice tip fell from his hand and shattered on the ground. He sank to his knees and embraced his father, who weakly tried to get up.

"How touching," snapped Nari, raising his hands, and Ullr began to roar in pain.

Wille threw himself forward but was prevented by pointed dark poles rising out of the ground. He tried to bring the wolf cross against the stakes, but the solid form of the darkness seemed more resistant, and it took longer for it to dissolve.

"I created the darkness in his body, and I can speed up the process," Nari hissed angrily, looking down at Jack. "So, you don't want to be my friend? Fine, go your way! But first, give me that ring you have in your pocket!"

Jack took a deep breath and fished out the ring that they had found after the battle in Trollhammer Mountain.

"That's right," said Nari triumphantly. "Give me back my ring, or watch your beloved father turn into a demon!"

Jack looked at his father, who were in agony on the ground, and then glanced at Wille, who was blocked by the darkness from moving forward.

"Give me the ring, and I'll leave you alone. Your friend can pull the darkness out of your father with his cross," said Nari, smiling.

Slowly, Jack extended the ring to the demon, who, in a sweeping motion, grabbed it.

"You've got your ring, now let them go," Jack said pleadingly.

"No," said Nari, laughing. "Did you really believe that? You should have become my friend when you had the chance!"

The demon clenched his fist, and Ullr threw out his arms in a roar of pain.

Then a familiar melody was heard in the air, which was suddenly filled with all the colours of the rainbow as hundreds of fairies flew across the night sky and threw themselves at the demon.

Jack glanced to the side and saw Tulio standing some distance away with his kantele. The energy that flowed from the clear notes made the dark pillars burst, and Wille threw himself forward towards Nari, who formed a cocoon of darkness around him that the fairies tried hard to get through.

As Wille arrived, the darkness teleported Nari away.

"Wille, help!" Jack shouted desperately.

The snow god's eyes had begun to take on a nasty dark hue when Wille and Tulio reached them.

"Help him," Jack pleaded desperately.

Tulio snatched the necklace from Wille's neck and pressed his entire arm into the wound on the snow god's chest.

A sustained roar was heard as both the snow god and the boy screamed out loud.

∞

"Can't you do it faster?"

Tella stood on the ground and watched Ítrek, who was standing on the tree branch to reach the prisoners hanging over the gap. She watched impatiently as he slowly freed the prisoners from the darkness with his mind.

"No," said Ítrek irritably. "Stop rushing me! The smallest margin of error, and that rag will swallow them!"

Tella looked worriedly up at the ledge where the others were. A dark wall had been formed to separate them, and she could hear screaming and crying from both sides of the wall.

"Hold on a little longer," she whispered to herself, and went back to focusing on lifting Ítrek as close to the darkness as she dared.

42. The Gate

Hugo sat bent over Váli while Máni sat beside him, still with the silvery white glow of his hands radiating over the wolf's body.

Váli's breathing was ragged, and his vision began to darken.

"Hang in there," Hugo whispered, putting his face against his fur.

"I've managed to halt the darkness and buy him some time," said Máni. "But he's lost a lot of blood, and I can't do more for him without help from Wille and Tulio!"

A dark wave suddenly washed over them and pushed the moon god away, landing about ten metres away.

"Do you love him so much, boy?" Naris' voice was heard as the demon stepped out of the dark wave and bent down in front of Hugo. "Did you really think you could save him? That you would live happily ever after in Asgard? The other gods wouldn't have tolerated him, laughing at the very idea of two guys together!"

Hugo looked terrified as the demon produced a black dagger in one hand.

"If I remember correctly, we were interrupted last time," Nari hissed, raising his hand with the dagger above Hugo's head.

There was a furious roar as Váli leapt from the ground and pushed Nari to the ground.

"Well, well, well! My dear little brother has some fight left in him," Nari said, standing up and laughing as the black dagger turned into a sword.

Váli dodged the sword and lunged at Nari, who fell backwards, pushing the wolf away as they fell towards the edge of the Grave of Eva.

"Váli!" Hugo shouted as the dark wall behind them gave way, and Wille and Tulio threw themselves forward towards the edge of the chasm.

Nari raised a hand, and yellow flames flared up like a golden wall, effectively shielding him and Váli from the rest of the party.

Váli lunged again at the demon, who dropped his sword, and they both rolled on the ground, dangerously close to the edge of the cliff. Nari got hold of his sword again and gave him a hard blow with the hilt.

"Do you love him, little brother?" Nari asked delightedly as he stood up and raised his sword. "Did you really think I would allow you to be happy?"

Váli let out a furious roar as he lunged forward, knocking Nari to the ground so that the demon's head was dangling over the edge of the cliff, and then he brought his paw down hard on the demon's throat.

"Little brother, I'm sorry! Please don't hurt me!" Nari begged pitifully, looking down into the chasm. "I'll do anything!"

Váli stared into the eyes of the disfigured face – the eyes he had missed. A wave of grief washed through him, and he eased the pressure on Nari's neck.

"Váli!" Hugo's voice sounded behind him.

He turned to see the yellow flames slowly fading, and Hugo lunged towards him.

"Hugo," Váli said, and began to limp. "You came back!"

✧

Hugo sank to the ground and was about to give Váli a hug when the wolf let out a howl. The dark sword pierced Váli's chest, and Nari rose triumphantly from the ground. The demon pulled the sword from the wolf's body, raising it for another strike, as the sky above them exploded and a giant bolt of lightning struck the ground holding up the rock ledge.

The ledge cracked open and Nari lost his footing, and both he and the shelf plunged into the deep ravine. A roar was heard from the demon as he plummeted to the ground far below them.

A silver light lifted both Hugo and Váli into the air, bringing them back to the edge of the mountain, where Máni stood with his arms outstretched.

Hugo glanced to the side, watching Módi lower the axe as Tella and Thrúd tended to the others who had managed to escape the grip of darkness.

The silvery light set them down on the ground as Váli collapsed into Hugo's arms. Within moments, Tulio and Wille were beside them.

"He's lost too much blood," Tulio said, biting his lips. "I can't heal him!"

"What about the darkness?" asked Wille.

"We don't have time," replied Tulio, shaking his head. "The sword blow he received started the process again...it...it's about to take him over, if he doesn't die first!"

"Hugo," Váli said, opening his eyes. "You came back!"

"Of course I came back," said Hugo, unable to hold back his tears. "I couldn't let you die!"

"I'm sorry," he continued, putting one arm around Váli's neck. "If I had gotten here sooner..."

"No," Váli interrupted, gasping. "Maybe it's better this way."

"Don't say that!" Hugo exclaimed, sobbing. "You'll be fine! We're together, and everything will be fine!"

The others had gathered in a circle around them. Siegfried stood leaning on his sword, looking defeated. Tella was holding Tulio, who was crying against her waist. Nyri had sunk down on a rock and turned his face away. Módi was holding Thrúd, who was leaning against him. Magni, who had just landed on the ground behind them, swore loudly and sent a cascade of lightning over the mountain.

Jörgen had stood a little way away with his arms around Jessica, and both looked sadly at the scene in front of them. A little further back, Gustav was sitting on the ground, holding Lovisa, who was sobbing. Gustav himself was ashen-faced, and a streak of tears ran down his cheek. Jack stood wrapped in Ullr's coarse wool coat and leaned sadly against the snow god's waist.

"At least I got to see you one last time," Váli said, giving Hugo a smile.

Hugo's eyes teared up as he met Váli's gaze, which was now almost covered in darkness, before the wolf became lifeless.

"No," Hugo whispered, crying. "Please don't leave me!"

Hugo sank down with his face over Váli's lifeless body, and Wille gently laid his head over his back, while Wille's tears ran down Hugo's jacket.

"I love you," Hugo whispered, his face now filled with tears.

None of the others said anything, the grief had taken hold of them, and not a sound was heard except the crying.

After a while, there was a swishing sound around them, and Hugo looked up in surprise at the sky, which was no longer dark but bathed in the light of the fairies who had joined them. They formed a ring around the party, which was lifted into the air and hovered tens of metres above the ground.

Hugo could see the shock on the faces of the others as the fairies formed a floor under their feet of light in every colour of the rainbow, but they seemed to calm down when a silvery-white glow appeared like a waterfall some distance in front of them.

Suddenly there was a snapping sound as Willie's wolf cross began to be drawn towards the silver light, as did the necklace around Váli's neck. There was a gasp from Tulio as the red diamond also began to float away towards the silver waterfall.

Then the silver waterfall burst into a great aurora, and Hugo could hear everyone gasping for breath as countless animals were seen running in the vast aurora that covered most of the night sky.

After a while, a silver wolf was seen walking through the air and stopping a little ahead of them.

"Silver," Wille said in shock to the wolf, who smiled at them.

"Máni", someone was heard to say behind Hugo, and he saw the moon god floating and smiling in the air behind them.

Then Lovisa pointed to the sides where two women stood on either side of them in the air – a woman with golden yellow hair and a woman with a blue dress.

Váli's body began to float and seemed to be drawn to a point above them. Hugo could see the red diamond, the wolf cross, and the green bead Váli had around his neck spinning in the air above them.

Máni raised his hands, and so did the two goddesses.

Hugo gasped, staring up at Váli's body as the black fur faded away and disappeared. The claws on his paws gave off a strange light, and his hind paws turned into feet. But the biggest change came when the wolf's face contracted to reveal a human face.

There was a flash of light from Váli before his body was lowered back down to the plateau again.

Hugo cautiously leaned towards Váli, who suddenly began to rise.

Váli stood up and examined his hands before smiling and turning to Hugo, who was gasping for breath.

"Hugo," the dark-haired guy said. "It's me!"

Hugo looked scrutinizingly at the guy, who stood naked in front of him. The amber eyes looked back at him in welcome, and he threw himself into Váli's arms.

"It's really you!" Hugo exclaimed, running his hand through Váli's dark bangs.

Máni's silver-white light began to swirl around them in a strong wind, just as the first rays of the sun appeared in the night sky and the aurora borealis reverted to a silver waterfall cascading down around the party.

"But how did this happen?" Hugo asked tearfully, turning to Wille, who shrugged.

"Your love for each other saved him," replied the silver wolf, who had stood opposite them. "Not even darkness can defeat true love!"

"And as for your body, you have indeed proven yourself a true god by your selflessness, your ability to choose love over darkness, and that you were able to make someone love you back despite your wolf form," Máni said smilingly, standing with his arms crossed behind Váli.

"Does that mean I'm free?" Váli asked uncertainly, looking up at his grandfather.

"The darkness that flowed in you two is gone," said the silver wolf, sitting down and looking at Váli and Hugo. "And your grandfather was kind enough to give you your body back too!"

"Thank you," said Hugo, giving the silver wolf a hug.

"Uh…Hugo, I'm not sure he appreciates that," said Wille, as Silver gave him a meaningful look.

"Oh, sorry!" Hugo exclaimed anxiously, letting go of the silver wolf.

"I guess I'll have to get used to that," said Silver with an amused smile.

⁒

"Thanks, Grandpa," Váli said, giving his grandfather a long hug.

"You did most of the work yourself," Máni said, ruffling his hair. "By the way, there are two more people who would like to say a few words to you!"

Váli glanced behind him and saw the two sun goddesses watching him.

"Sunna…Bea…why do you look so strange?" he asked.

Both sun goddesses had begun to fade in outline, and the sun's rays shone through their bodies.

"Don't tell me you're…" Váli started to ask, but stopped himself when Sunna reached out and held out the sun gem.

"We don't have much time," Sunna whispered. "The World Spirit is calling us home!"

"No, please don't leave us!" Váli pleaded, reaching for her outstretched hand.

"We will always be with you," Bea said softly. "And we'll see you again when it's your turn to cross over!"

"What's that?" Váli asked, looking down at the green jewellery in Sunna's hand.

"Don't you recognise the sun gem?" She asked, smiling.

Váli stared in amazement at the sun pearl in the goddess' hand, now shaped like a howling wolf.

"Willes fylgia was kind enough to help us with the last detail, which allows you to form a bond with your own power animal," Bea replied. "It works in a similar way to how Willie's wolf cross does."

Sunna gently placed the necklace in Váli's hand and closed his fingers around it.

"Whenever you want to turn back into a wolf, all you have to do is put the necklace on," she said, before leaning over and giving him a kiss on the forehead.

"Honey, you won't forget, will you?" Bea reminded him, pointing to Gustav, who was standing a bit behind them.

"No, I won't," Sunna replied with a wink before she started to move towards Gustav, who was looking more and more troubled.

"You took my fire without asking permission," she said seriously.

"S...sorry," stammered Gustav, bowing his head slightly.

"Never before has a human been able to carry our fire," Sunna continued, holding out one hand to the trembling boy.

Gustav looked at the Sun Goddess' outstretched hand in amazement and met her gaze before slowly extending his own hand towards hers.

Huge flames embraced Gustav in a circle.

"Take care of my fire," the goddess said before letting go of his hand, and the flames subsided.

Gustav stood trembling as he was bathed in light.

"Are you alright?" Lovisa asked and stood beside him.

"I think so," he replied. "I feel warm."

"You're warm!" Lovisa exclaimed, turning questioningly to the smiling sun goddesses.

"A new god is born," whispered Bea, holding out a blue orb to Gustav. "Give this to our daughter, please."

☙

"Wille," said Silver, who stood next to him.

Wille crouched down and gently stroked his hand through the wolf's fur.

"Thank you," he whispered. "For everything!"

"You're not done with your journey, so don't thank me yet," Silver said, looking up at him.

Wille glanced up and saw a red glow slowly descending towards them. He was amazed to see that the red glow came from his wolf cross.

"The magic of the diamond is now in your cross," Silver said as Wille held out both hands to receive the red cross. "Use it well!"

Silver suddenly took a few steps back and looked meaningfully at the sun goddesses, who nodded in agreement.

The silver fall that surrounded the party washed over the sun goddesses and the silver wolf, and all three disappeared.

"Take care of Sol for us!" Bea's voice was heard before the silver fall faded away, and was replaced by the morning light of the sun.

Hugo wrapped his arms around Váli again in a long hug, and Jessica started clapping her hands, and soon the rest of the friends were standing around, cheering.

"Um…Wille and Váli," Tulio said after a moment, looking from one to the other in amusement. "I don't want to interrupt the celebration, but you know you're not wearing any clothes, right?"

Váli let go of Hugo and stared down at his body in embarrassment before looking at Wille, who had started to blush.

Then both boys burst out laughing, which was accompanied by laughter from the rest of the party.

"Do you want help?" Lovisa asked teasingly, taking the wolf cross from Wille's hand.

"Stop teasing," he replied embarrassedly, trying to cover himself as he looked nervously over his shoulder.

Lovisa gave him a long kiss as she snapped the necklace around his neck, and Wille turned back into a wolf.

"You really need to learn to keep your clothes on, cousin," Jack said, giving him a teasing nudge.

Wille let out a grunt and wrestled the laughing Jack to the ground.

ɕ૭

"Did you have to scare Ítrek away?" Tella whispered, giving Módi a stern look.

"Why are you hanging out with him?" Nyri asked, not feigning her sister's irritation.

"He helped us!" Tella hissed in response. "Without his help, the others would have fallen into the chasm when the demon died, and Hugo wouldn't even be standing here with Váli!"

Quiet!" Magni hissed, coming to stand behind them.

"We'll talk more about that when we get home! Enjoy the happiness instead!"

Tella sighed and turned her gaze towards the centre of the plateau again. They don't know how lucky they are, she thought, watching Hugo try to fasten the necklace around Váli's neck.

☙

"Do you really want to turn back already?" Hugo asked teasingly, fiddling with the clasp of Váli's necklace.

"Come on, Hugo," Váli replied shyly, looking blushingly at the rest of the party standing around them, grinning. "I can change back when we get to Asgard, and I've got clothes to wear."

"I have to tease you a little," Hugo said, giving him a wink as Váli transformed back into the dark-furred wolf again.

"Would you two like the honour of opening the gate to Asgard?" Máni asked, standing next to them.

"How?" Hugo asked in confusion. "The moon has disappeared!"

"Isn't it the moon god you have standing next to you, perhaps?" Máni asked, laughing back and raising his hands.

A silvery white glow once again surrounded the boys, and Váli began to howl while Hugo took out his ocarina.

The fairies, who had formed the plateau on which they stood, began to glow more brightly to the clear notes of their melody, and the plateau was transformed into a bridge while a flash of lightning burst before them, forming a huge gate at the end of the bridge.

A figure appeared in the portal, and Hugo recognised the old man with the long, silver-white beard.

"Lódurr!" Wille exclaimed, and everyone started walking towards the gate.

The old man smiled at them as they reached the gate, through which a huge city loomed in the background.

"Well done, everyone!" Lódurr said, looking out over the party. "I am proud of you!"

"What will happen now?" Jörgen asked, putting one arm around Jessica.

"We've never brought people into Asgard just like that before," replied Lódurr. "We can consider it, but it means you'll have to leave your old lives behind – you can't go back home again once you step through the gate!"

Jörgen and Jessica exchanged a quick glance.

"Dad, this is your dream," Jessica whispered, smiling.

"But what about you?" he asked anxiously. "I can't just leave you!"

Jessica cast a quick glance at Magni, who, despite his serious expression, gave her a wink.

"I'll come with you, of course," she replied, smiling.

Jörgen followed her gaze and smiled wanly when he saw what she was looking at.

"Okay," he said, turning to Lódurr. "We'll come with you."

"We'll have to think about it," Lódurr said, turning to Gustav, whose aura was still glowing.

"And one of you has been given a precious gift, I see," said the old man, smiling. "It will take training for you to learn how to handle it."

Gustav nodded and looked at his hands, while Lódurr turned to Ullr.

"You withdrew from us," he said in a regretful tone. "And you created a new god from dreams that should not exist, why should we welcome you?"

Ullr looked at Jack, who cowered against his embrace, before the snow god turned his eyes pleadingly to Lódurr again.

"He may be made of dreams," Ullr replied. "But he is my son, and I love him with all my heart. If that means we are not welcome, we will go back into exile again."

Lódurr nodded, then turned to Váli, who sat down at Hugo's side.

"And you, Váli," he said. "You may have broken your curse, but that doesn't take away your responsibility for killing your brother and creating the conditions for this whole incident. Why should we welcome you back?"

"I…" Váli began uncertainly but was interrupted by Hugo and Wille stepping forward.

"That's enough!" Hugo shouted. "I'm not going anywhere without Váli! He's proved himself worthy, and if that's not good enough for you, we're staying here!"

"The same goes for Jack," said Wille firmly. "If you're so narrow-minded in your world, we prefer to stay here!"

Hugo noticed that the rest of the party joined in when he said those words. Lovisa sank to her knees beside Wille, and he noticed how Magni put his arm around Jessica.

"Master," Módi said, taking a step forward. "Tell our father that if you don't let all of us in, we won't go either!"

Thrúd nodded in agreement and stood next to her brother.

"The same goes for us," Nyri said firmly, pulling Tella and Tulio close.

"Nyri, what…?" Tella began to ask in surprise.

"Look at them, Tella," Nyri replied. "They're our friends, we can't leave them after all we've been through!"

"I know that!" Tella hissed, wriggling out of Nyri's grasp. "I just didn't think you'd be the one to speak up!"

Lódurr's expression turned into a smile as the old man raised his eyes and looked at Máni, who had been standing silently watching the reactions. The moon god smiled and gave Lódurr a meaningful shrug in response.

"That's the welcome you thought you'd get, isn't it?" Lódurr asked and turned to the rest of the party again. "And now that that's done, I welcome you all to join us!"

The light from the gate suddenly grew brighter, and Hugo could see the outlines of more people appearing behind the veil that separated their worlds.

"You mean it?" Ullr asked, lighting up.

"Did you really think you were not welcome home?" Lódurr asked, giving him a wink and took a step to the side.

Everyone in the party started cheering and walking towards the gate. Hugo watched as several of them hugged before disappearing through the bright light.

"Wille and Hugo, can you wait just a moment?" Lódurr asked, looking kindly towards them.

They stopped abruptly in front of the gate, as did Váli.

"Váli, you can go on," said Lodur, giving the wolf a meaningful gesture. "I think there's someone waiting for you inside. And don't worry, we'll be right there!"

Hugo saw a female figure on the other side of the veil, bending down and flapping her arms.

"Mom," Váli whispered, letting out a shriek of delight before rushing through the door.

"Wille...Hugo..." Lódurr said heavily. "Your mother will be honoured with a ceremony in the coming days. I want you to understand how much she loved you!"

The old man held out a folded sheet of paper, which Hugo took and unfolded.

"She left it to me before the attack," the old man said sadly. "She knew she would not be allowed to come home with you!"

Hugo burst into tears, and Wille carefully read the letter that fell to the ground.

"Wille," Hugo said, wrapping his arms around his brother.

"I know, I know," said Wille, who was also getting teary-eyed.

"We're all going to miss her," said Lódurr sympathetically. "But you're home now, and I promise you'll never be alone here!"

"It's time for you to come home," said Máni, standing behind them.

"Aren't you coming with us, Grandpa?" Wille asked, turning his tearful face towards the moon god.

Máni exchanged a quick glance with Lódurr, who nodded in agreement.

"You're welcome to come with us, Máni," Lódurr said. "I think we need an extra grandpa home."

Máni looked down at Willie's pleading eyes and sighed.

"If you really think it's necessary, I'll come with you," said Máni, smiling.

Hugo looked around as they walked towards the billowing veil. He didn't know what was waiting on the other side, but for the first time since they left the house, he felt happy. He looked at Wille, and they both smiled at each other before walking into the light.

"Know that I think of you wherever you are. One day, our sorrows will end and our hearts will shine bright again!

And who knows? Your journey may not be so hard after all!

Our worlds are separate, but we share the same love – one love, one dream, and one destiny!

Have the wisdom to know that nothing is impossible, the courage to plunge into the unknown, and the strength to never give up!

And the love to overcome the darkness!

Love you!

/ Mom"

Epilogue

Akela whined as the tailless male carried him up the mountain. They had been walking for a long time, and he was hungry. The tailless male seemed to be heading for the top of the mountain, where a strange light was spreading.

"There, there, my friend," said the tailless male as he stopped to give Akela some dried meat. "You'll soon be back with your friends."

Akela chewed the meat slowly before falling asleep in the tailed man's arms.

The tailless male gently tucked him into his jacket and tied it over his shoulder like a sack before they continued up the mountain towards the golden gate above them.

∾

"Correct me if I'm wrong, my brother," said the man, smiling. "So, you were attacked by your own wolf?"

Wayland stood in front of the pedestal with the black flame as the man with the long, silver-white hair approached.

"What are you doing here Hjúki?" Wayland hissed angrily

"Is my big brother so proud that I can't even check on him?" Hjúki asked, looking amused.

"Now you've checked on me," hissed Wayland. "Go back to your preparations!"

"The others are starting to get worried," said Hjúki. "They're wondering if we should postpone the plan?"

"Tell those idiots that the plan is proceeding as planned," hissed Wayland. "And make sure Arawn finds the other part of the sword! We have new allies in Asgard!"

∾

"That didn't go quite as planned, Ítrek," the man said accusingly as they watched the party disappear through the gate. "I thought you said that demon was trustworthy."

"I'm sorry, Master," Ítrek replied, bowing slightly as they both crossed the bridge towards the gate.

"Did you at least get the ring?" the man with the short silver-white beard asked.

Ítrek reached into his pocket and pulled out the gold ring.

"And the demon?" the man asked, accepting the ring.

"As you commanded, Master," Ítrek replied, as they stopped in front of the gate to Asgard.

"Master?" He asked uncertainly. "Was it really wise to take you into the consciousness of the moon god?"

"Are you questioning me?" the man asked irritably.

"N…no, Master," Ítrek replied hesitantly. "Not at all!"

"Good," said the man curtly. "Remember, you can't show yourself openly while we're here!"

ᘒ

"I told you this would happen!"

Hades stood smiling in front of Hela with crossed arms.

"We lost two hundred wolves in the battle, and we're no closer to our goal!" he exclaimed.

Hela grabbed him around the throat.

"I lost two hundred wolves," she hissed. "You're about to lose something else entirely if you keep annoying me!"

"And how are we going to free him now?" asked a woman with snow-white hair who had appeared behind them.

"Don't worry, Skade," Hela said, releasing her grip on Hades. "Just make sure your puppy has the mirror ready when the time comes. We have new allies in Asgard!"

Anders Niclas Lexén was born in 1990 in Horndal, Sweden. His parents were divorced, and his upbringing was marked by alternating living arrangements, new families, and new environments. In his teenage years, he was diagnosed with mild autism, which continued with him into adulthood.

As a teenager, he read a lot of fantasy, primarily by authors like David Eddings, J.K. Rowling, Terry Goodkind, and Philip Pullman. In adulthood, he became interested in various mythologies, especially Norse mythology, and he dreamed of writing his own fantasy stories. Through the book 'The Wolf Cross', he wants to launch his new series 'The Wolf Tale', where he aims to interweave mythologies, local tales, and cultures with each other.

Niclas holds a degree in Swedish law, specialising in Tax law, Real Estate law, and Environmental law. For 16 years, he has worked as a recreational leader and student assistant.